THE CONTRACT

Room 1

EVA HAINING

Copyright

The Contract
©Eva Haining 2024

ALL RIGHTS RESERVED

DEVELOPMENTAL EDITING: **RIA ALEXANDER**
EDITING: **BOOKTIQUE EDITING**

❀ Created with Vellum

Prologue
NADDIE

Fifteen years ago

"I don't want to leave you, Dalton." He cups my face with his strong, warm hands.

"I know, Naddie, but you can't pass up this opportunity. Harvard was the dream. You have a full ride. I won't let you give that up for me."

"The dream was for *us*. We were going to go together. I don't want it without you."

He takes a deep but shaky breath, pinning me with his steely gaze. "You do want it, kitten. It's all you've ever wanted. You have had Harvard pennants on your bedroom wall since kindergarten."

"I could put it off for a year or two. Go to community college with you, and then we can transfer."

"Stop it. My family can't afford the tuition now, and I didn't get the grades I needed. That's my failure, and if you think I'm going to tear down your dream, you don't know me at all."

I'm trying to hold it together, but I crack as tears roll down my cheeks. "I can't do this without you."

"You can, and you will." His lips crash down on mine, rendering me incapable of coherent thought. It's been that way since he first kissed me in the seventh grade.

Dalton and I have known each other our whole lives. We grew up living next door to each other, and as fate would have it, we fell madly in love. The kind of love that alters your perception of the world around you. It leaves a mark on your heart, and when you lose it, you lose a part of your soul.

I drink him in—every detail, including the scent of his cologne and his freshly laundered shirt, the one he knows I love to sleep in. I want to commit him to memory, the way his stubble feels against my skin and his muscular body as it presses tight to mine.

As we kiss, his tongue strokes mine in a decadent dance, slow and sensual, sending every fiber of my being into overdrive. This can't be the end of us. Our love story wasn't supposed to stop here. It wasn't supposed to end at all.

The second he breaks our connection, it's as if my heart has been ripped out of my chest, gasping for its final beat.

"Get in the car, kitten. You have to go now."

"Dalton."

"I won't tell you again. Car. Now." His commanding tone shakes me to the core. Opening the car door, I know we are closing the door on our love story, and the weight of this moment is heavy on my shoulders.

"I love you, Dalton." There's a storm of emotion in the firm set of his jawline as he struggles to keep control. He grabs his Rolling Stones T-shirt, pulls it over his head, and hands it to me, knowing how much I love it.

"I'll always love you, Naddie." The moment the words leave his lips, he turns on his heel and walks across the grass that joins our childhood homes, the *For Sale* sign in his yard like a wrecking ball through the plans we had together—another casualty of his father's bankruptcy.

They say you can't put a price on love, but for Dalton and me, the price is four years of Harvard University tuition. I pull out of the driveway with tears streaming down my cheeks and his T-shirt in my lap.

I can barely breathe as I turn left at the end of our street, embarking on a new chapter of my life, knowing that I'm leaving my heart with the boy next door.

Chapter 1

NADDIE

Present Day

"We could still make this work, baby girl, if you wanted to." His soft, sandalwood scent invades my senses, mixed with leather and sex, the thrumming beat of the music pulsing through me as I shrug on my sweater and grab my purse.

"I'm moving to a different state, Theo. It's impractical, and I don't want to sully what we've had with an open relationship." He's been good to me. A satisfying Dominant, but we're nothing more than good sex, complementary kinks, and friendship.

"Who said anything about an open relationship? I don't share, baby girl."

"And I don't want to remain tethered to Boston. I'm sorry." I reach up, stroking the stubble on his chin. "It's been fun, Sir, but this is where we say goodbye."

I press my lips to his before turning on my heel and leaving the club that's been my oasis here in Boston for the past four years. I found myself within these walls—my voice as a submissive, and I would be lying if I said I wouldn't miss it, but for me, this isn't about love. It never has been.

I make my way through the club, saying my goodbyes to friends, fellow subs, and Doms—the people who have shaped me into the confident submissive I've become since I entered the lifestyle. In truth, it's my friends I'll miss. Sure, I can find another club in New York and a Dom to satisfy my sexual appetite, but friends are more difficult to come by. People who understand and don't judge. Who truly see me for who I am.

I am accepted and respected.

As I say my final goodbyes, Theo strides toward me, tension rolling off him in waves. I brace myself for whatever he has to say, but he simply hands me a sleek black card with an elegant V embossed on one side and nothing on the other.

"What's this?" I say as I turn it over in my hand.

"I'll text you the address. It's the most exclusive club in Manhattan, and it's relatively new. They'll get you settled and introduce you to the right people in our lifestyle."

"Thank you."

"Just don't go spreading it around. It's invitation only."

"But…" He cuts me off as my expression tightens. Surely, he sees the problem.

"I know a guy at the club. Give them my name when you decide to explore. Consider it a going away present. I'm really going to miss you around here, baby girl."

"I'll miss you too." I give him a quick squeeze before making my way to the exit, slipping the card into my pocket as I brace myself for the lonely streets, turning my back on my safe haven.

I shed a few tears as I hail a cab and head for home, where my best friend is waiting to help me pack up my life and embark on a new adventure. Butterflies of excitement swarm my stomach as I take in the familiar skyline one last time, and suddenly, they feel an awful lot like dread.

The last time I said goodbye to a man and left for a new city, I left a piece of my heart behind, hoping to fill the void here in Boston. As many happy memories as I've made in the fifteen years I've lived, studied, and worked here, I never found someone who could piece my shattered heart back together.

At least this time, I'm not a hopeful teenager, unaware that life doesn't give you multiple great loves. I've had mine, and I've made my peace with it. I don't expect to find the new love of my life as I embark on this new chapter. I ponder that on the ride back to my apartment, a tinge of sadness creeping in as I remember. *Him*.

~

"Is this box for the trash, or are you taking it to New York?"

Today is the day I move to Manhattan for an amazing new job at one of the top law firms in the country as their newest and youngest partner.

"What does it say on it?"

My best friend, Jenna, has been helping me pack the important parts of my life into a U-Haul this weekend. "D.R."

I practically snatch the box from her hands. "Keep." My fingers curl around tattered corners. "I'm keeping it."

I haven't opened this box in years, and yet I still think of him often, and every time, my chest constricts at the memory of what we had. Even last night, he came to mind as I left the club. No man has come close over the years, even though I've grown as a woman and in my sexual tastes.

This box finally makes sense to me, but as much as I'd love to sit down with it right now, I take it to my car and set it on the passenger seat, just like I did the day I left my childhood home.

Jenna follows me outside. "What's in the box? Ex-boyfriend paraphernalia? Oh… oh… is it the broody love of your life from high school?"

"Can you stop talking, please?"

"It is! What have you been keeping all these years? I want to see your shrine box."

"It's not a shrine. He was my first boyfriend, and we had all our firsts together. I'm sure plenty of people have keepsakes from their high school sweetheart. It's not a big deal."

"Fine. You're no fun. When I come to visit you in New York, I expect a glass of wine and a look at the contents of that box."

"If it'll make you visit sooner, you've got a deal."

She pulls me into her arms. "This isn't goodbye, bestie. We'll see each other all the time. I promise."

"Are you sure you don't mind overseeing the movers for the rest of my stuff?"

"Yes, I mind. *Because…* I don't want to say goodbye." She squeezes me tight.

"Okay. I better grab the last few boxes before I turn into a snot-fest of tears."

We busy ourselves for another half hour before I really need to hit the road. I want to get there before dark so I can get some of the U-Haul unpacked. With two days until I start my new job, I have to hit the ground running.

After saying my *see you soon*, I hit I-90 and the road to my new life. The cardboard box in the passenger seat weighs heavy on my mind as I put distance between the place I've called home for the past fifteen years and me. The same place that tore me from the arms of the only man I've ever loved. I vividly remember the day I drove to college, the overwhelming emotion as if it were yesterday.

By the time I reach my new apartment, I'm too tired to unload all my crap. I should've let the movers take everything. Thirty-three-year-old me has no patience for this shit.

There's a new bed ready and waiting for me, so I grab the only thing I care about tonight—my cardboard box companion.

As I turn the key to my new apartment, the fact I'm clinging to the same box I was when I moved into my college dorm isn't lost on me. The living room is bare, and the kitchen is immaculate. The high ceilings are stunning, but the walls lack any adornments, and I try to envisage what it'll look like with my pictures and memories hanging in every room.

It looks different than the first time I walked around the rooms. It was a home full of someone else's happy moments.

When I reach my new bedroom, I'm glad to see the bed and set of sheets and pillows I ordered. There's also some sort of hamper with a card on the bed. Setting down the box in my arms, I pick up the card. It's from my new firm.

Welcome to New York.
Mason, Porter & Associates

There's an assortment of fine foods, a bottle of red wine, and two glasses. If there's one thing that'll make you feel lonely, it's a gift meant for two people. I pop the cork and crawl under the comforter with a glass of wine before pulling out my phone and calling Jenna.

"Hey. Missing me already?"

"Yep. I'm drinking, alone, in an empty apartment." I'm definitely feeling sorry for myself at this point.

"It'll feel like home soon enough. I'll visit next month, and we'll make some new, fun, drunken memories."

"Sounds good to me. And by then, I'll have all my furniture and other crap unloaded."

"What have you taken in tonight? The basics?"

"One box. The new bed was here with the covers, and my firm left a hamper with food and wine. The really important stuff. It's a nice bottle of red."

"Let me guess, the mysterious D.R. box?"

"Don't judge me. The last time I moved states, it was to leave him behind. And today really sucked having to leave you. I get one night to wallow. Tomorrow, I'll pull up my big girl, hotshot-lawyer panties and make this place home. Tonight, I just want to drink wine, miss my best friend, and take a trip down memory lane before closing up the box and putting it at the back of my new closet to gather dust for another fifteen years."

"I knew I should've come down there with you. You're not going to drunk dial box guy, are you?"

"Of course not. I don't even have his number."

"Are you friends on Facebook or Instagram? I don't want you cyber-stalking him, either. Drunk sliding into an ex's DMs in not something you want on your dating resume."

"Why do I feel like you're speaking from experience?"

"Because you know me. I'm totally that girl who hits up an ex with a booty call at two in the morning when I've had more tequila than I should. And FYI, the sex was amazing."

"Duly noted. I may have attempted to find him on social media occasionally, but unfortunately, he doesn't seem to have profiles on any platform."

"Well, that's disappointing. No sloppy, drunken sex for you."

"Your eloquence is beyond measure, Jenna."

"Fuck eloquence. It's overrated." I miss her already. Jenna is the yin to my yang. We met at a club in Boston, and we've been best friends ever since. We're complete opposites, but we understand each other.

"On that note, I'm calling it a night."

"Okay. Don't wallow, Nad, you're in Manhattan. You landed the dream job. Enjoy it."

"I love you, Jenna."

"Back at you. I'll see you next month."

"You say that like we're not going to call each other every day. Don't ghost me."

"Go and drink the wine, crazy-pants. We'll talk, text, and Face-Time all the time. You don't get rid of me that easily."

"Okay. Night."

"Night, Nad."

When I hang up the call, the silence is deafening. I pour myself another glass of wine and flip open the lid of my memory box. There it is—the T-shirt he gave me the day I left. I can still picture him in my mind, impossibly handsome, oozing self-confidence. He knew how my body reacted to his and was never afraid to command my pleasure.

I run my fingers over the material, thinking back to when I was a freshman in college. I slept in this shirt every night for years. It comforted me to feel wrapped up in a small piece of him. Boyfriends came and went during my Harvard years, but it wasn't until I graduated that I started exploring my sexual preferences, and it stopped being about wanting someone else to fill the void that he left in my life. My choices became for me alone—what I want, enjoy, and need from a partner.

9

There have been men I've liked, even one I thought I loved, but not enough to change who I am to make him happy. I take off my hoodie and slip the ratty old Rolling Stones T-shirt over my head. The scent of his cologne was lost long ago, but if I close my eyes and quiet my thoughts, I can almost remember his smell.

Delving into the box, I find letters and trinkets of our time together. He didn't like to show his softer side. To everyone else in our high school, he was dark, brooding, and a well-conditioned athlete. He was captain of the soccer team, meaning he could run up and down the soccer field for ninety minutes. Stamina was never an issue for him. His body was lean but muscular, with a beautiful olive tone to his skin that he got from his mom's Italian side of the family.

He really was an Adonis, or at least, that's how I saw him— flawless.

A necklace he gave me on my eighteenth birthday is nestled safely in its box. I used to wear it under my shirt. It wasn't for other people to see but it was of special significance to us. A private agreement. A silver Tiffany padlock on a delicate long chain. His initials were engraved on the back, and although it didn't require a key, the day he gave it to me, there was a small key in the box. He kept it in his wallet and told me that my pleasure was his to control, and his was mine to enjoy.

I couldn't bear to look at it after I left for college, and this is the first time I've set eyes on it in fifteen years. Lifting the delicate chain from its time capsule, I turn it over in my hand, feeling the once-familiar weight. It's tarnished with age, but I run my thumb back and forth over the letters *DR* engraved on it. Looking back, I only wore it for six months before our relationship ended, but it felt like a part of me—a part of him.

As I sift through the rest of the box, I spy the one thing I knew I'd kept. *The Contract.*

At the tender age of sixteen, we wrote a contract, professing our love and desire to be together forever. We'd already been dating for years by that point, but when we decided to take the next step and explore a sexual relationship beyond kissing and heavy petting, we found ourselves talking about it one night as we lay on the grass in his backyard, staring at the stars.

For some reason, it seemed entirely natural for us to set clear boundaries and discuss what we did and didn't want from each other. At the time, it made sense that he and I were more than happy to put our desires out there in black and white and be accountable to each other. Now, as I thumb through the document, I wonder why it took me until I was twenty-nine to realize that I'm a submissive.

It's so clear in the wording of this first contract—a rudimentary declaration between a submissive and her Dom. It gets me thinking —did he find his way into the same lifestyle? Through the lens of a well-trained submissive, I can identify every aspect of his personality that drew me to him and would make for a breathtaking Dominant. He was my first love and the only man who truly satisfied me on every level.

I settle under the covers, laying that once all-consuming contract on the pillow beside me. There's something comforting about this trip down memory lane and being back in his ratty old T-shirt. Tomorrow, I'll set aside my foolish *what-ifs* and return to the business of being an adult.

Chapter 2

DALTON

There's nothing better than a weekend of wall-to-wall sex to set you up for a productive week. I think better when I'm not distracted by my cock. Unfortunately, my life at present doesn't seem to be conducive to anything recreational.

"What do I have on the books today, Audrey?" My assistant rides everywhere with me. She's become my shadow, and she's worth her weight in gold. I wanted her to fly out to Milan with me this week, but she's pregnant enough that I don't want to risk her traveling so far. Unfortunately, that means I'm about to make the biggest deal of my career without my right-hand woman.

"Breakfast with an investor, followed by an eleven o'clock call with your accountant, then a late lunch with your lawyer's office. It's important you keep that appointment. This is your last availability before the Milan deal."

"Do I get to eat dinner without talking shop?"

The way she fidgets with her pen gives me my answer. "I'm afraid not. You asked me to move last week's interview with the journalist from *Forbes* to this week, and tonight was the only time you had free. Shall I push it again?"

"No. Tell me it's at a restaurant where I can get a good steak."

"Of course. I'll text you the details, but the town car will take you everywhere you need to go."

"Thanks, Audrey. They aren't going to waste my time begging about their stupid list again, are they?"

"Of course not. They learned their lesson the year you threatened to sue if they printed your picture and net worth."

"Good. I don't understand why these people *want* to tell the world about their bank accounts. Fame mongers."

"You know you're the odd duck, right? It's rare to find a wealthy man who *doesn't* want to spread the word of their success."

"Quack, quack. I guess I better get going to breakfast, even though I've already eaten. I need to stop having meetings over meals, or my wallet won't be the only thing expanding."

She looks me up and down, devouring me with her eyes. She'd never do or say anything unprofessional, but occasionally, I catch her in moments like this, and it makes me laugh. If only she knew how dark my tastes can be, she'd run a mile. Lucky for her, she won't find out because I never mix business with pleasure. It's my golden rule, and it's served me well. The three F's should never overlap. Financials. Friends. Fucking.

Once I'm updated on the essentials, I go about my day and work long into the night. Meals and deals. That should be my new tagline. I was sorely tempted to break my rule when I sat down to dinner with the journalist from *Forbes*. She was hot, and Friday nights are for fun. Instead, I arrive home alone, quickly shrug on my gray sweatpants, and grab my headphones.

Even after so many years of living alone, there are nights I just can't stand it. People in positions of power will tell you they're spurred onto greatness and success for many different reasons—money, status, *something*. For me, I'm just trying to chase away my demons.

I work hard, play hard, and trust no one. The last person I put my faith in ruined the path I had mapped out for myself. I lost everything and became the business mogul I am now despite his mistakes. If you can't adapt and rise like a phoenix from the ashes, you're just a big pile of dust. I'm sure there's a more elegant way of saying it, but I was eighteen when I made the decision to wipe the dust from my feet and look out for number one. I watched my father being led out of the courtroom in handcuffs, and the next day, I changed my last name. No longer the son of a prisoner, I took my mom's maiden name. Dalton Rutherford burned to the ground, and from his ashes, Dalton Callaghan was born.

~

Saturday night, and there's nowhere else I'd rather hang out. With The Callaghan Group in the midst of a major acquisition, I haven't been to Venom in weeks, with too many late nights and meetings to count. The owner of Europe's biggest mergers and acquisitions business has fallen on hard times and is about to make a deal with me to solve at least some of his problems. They're self-inflicted, far too similar to my father's transgressions, and my accountants aren't too keen on absorbing a company in the midst of scandal, but I know I can use it to my advantage. I won't stand by and watch another family suffer the consequences of a greed-driven patriarch.

Success in the States is one thing, but this acquisition will be a new challenge. The Callaghan Group will become a global name, and I can ensure that the businesses involved don't suffer the same fate my mom and I did.

As I step inside the luxurious bar, the stress of my week fades away.

"Mr. Callaghan, it's so good to see you again. I thought you'd forgotten about us." The bartender at Venom is a shameless flirt, tossing her bleach-blonde hair over her shoulder. She's pretty enough but not my type. I'm not looking for a woman who was only able to drink legally for the first time on her last birthday.

Venom is officially the most exclusive club in Manhattan, but it's underground. If you were to google this place, you wouldn't find anything, and that's the way I want it to stay. I'm a private man, and I wanted a place to hang out that allowed me to keep it that way. Venom has the façade of an office building for anyone walking in off the street. Unless you have a membership and can verify your ID, you'll be turned away, none the wiser.

I take a seat at the bar, loosening my tie and the top button on my shirt after another Saturday spent working. "Whiskey sour, please."

My staff here is thoroughly vetted and made to sign an NDA regarding the club and the wealthy VIPs who value discretion. It's a safe space for those of us who enjoy living life with a low profile.

"I'm just here for a quick drink before I head home for the night."

The bartender rests her elbows on the bar, framing her ample breasts while I try like hell not to stare. "That seems like a waste of a man as handsome and fit as you." She's a shameless flirt.

"I appreciate the compliment." As soon as she pushes my drink across the bar, I take a long swig before scanning the room for any familiar faces.

"Are you looking for someone in particular?" She offers a tight smile.

"Is Flex in tonight?" Her face lights up as if it makes any difference that I'm not looking for a woman.

"He's in his office, but I don't think he's alone."

"Can you call back there and check? I have no desire to walk in there and get an eyeful of Flex's naked ass this evening."

A wry grin creeps at the corners of her lips. "Most women in here would kill for a look."

I can't help but laugh. She's not wrong. "I'm sure, but it doesn't do anything for me."

I wait as she makes a quick call before nodding my way. "He'll be out in a moment." I drop a fifty on the bar and head to a corner table, and thankfully, my best friend is still fully dressed, although the woman trotting behind him seems hell-bent on divesting him of his shirt.

"Sorry to break up the party, but can I steal your date for a few minutes?"

"We're sort of busy right now," she pouts, but Flex is quick to pull her in line.

"Did I say you could speak?"

"No, Sir." She hangs her head until he slips a keycard into her hand.

"Go back to my office and wait for me. I won't be long." He smacks her ass, and she giggles as she scurries off down the hallway.

"The office? Really? Do I need to have it sanitized?"

"One hundred percent, yes. I highly recommend it," he says with a sly chuckle.

"You have no shame."

"Shame is for the weak. Anyway, what's so urgent that I must delay getting my rocks off?"

"I have to go out of town on business for a few days. Can you keep an eye on my mom?" His face sobers at the mention of my mother—his mom, for all intents and purposes.

"Of course. I was planning to go over to your building and see her this week anyway. How's she doing?"

"Not great. The Parkinson's is getting worse by the day, and dementia is taking over the woman who raised me faster than I thought. I have around-the-clock care for her, but all they can really do is keep her comfortable. You know what she's like." I run my fingers through my hair, a tick I've always had when I'm stressed. With work, my mom, and knowing my good-for-nothing father is coming up for parole, it's a miracle I'm not bald.

"She's stubborn. Something her son inherited." His observation isn't untrue.

"It took all my charm to convince her to give up her apartment and then twice as long to get her to agree to have hospice care in the comfort of my building. I should have pushed her to stay in the penthouse with me, but she wouldn't hear of it. She argued that because I own the whole building, she was technically staying in my house."

"Yeah. She called and told me to convince you to… and I quote… drop her off at the local 'home for the infirm' and wash your hands of her."

"Jesus. Is that what she thinks of me?" It makes me physically sick to my stomach at the thought of it.

"No. She was scared of forgetting you… not for herself, but for you. Your mom thinks it's the lesser of two evils. She knew it would break your heart if she didn't recognize you as the dementia progressed."

"It *is* heartbreaking, but I wouldn't have it any other way. She needs me."

"And there's nothing else we can do?"

"I've exhausted all the options money can buy. Unfortunately, it can't buy health when it comes down to brass taxes. Maybe I should take a step back from work. I can spend more time with her. I can convince her to move into the penthouse with me."

"Does she have any quality of life at this point?"

"No, but I like to think she knows I'm there, even when she doesn't know it's me. It's hard to see her when she's awake… the tremors are now full body spasms. And although she's awake, I don't know where she is. Whatever is happening in the room as I stare into her eyes, I don't think she's experiencing the same thing."

"Then take some time to go over your options while you're on this trip. Let me worry about Mom for now. Then, when you get back, we can figure out what to do next. Here…" He pushes his drink across the table. "You look like you need it more than me."

I don't argue. Instead, I down the whiskey sour in one gulp. "Thanks, bro."

"You know I've always got your back. Do you want to come play with us tonight? Lexi is up for anything. Seriously… anything."

"As harrowing as that sounds, I'm going to say a firm no."

"Chicken. Worried you won't measure up?" He leans back in his chair, confidence oozing from every pore.

"Aww, bless your heart. You actually believe that, don't you?"

"I *know* that." He chuckles.

"I don't think I could trust myself with a woman tonight. I'm wound tight as a drum. I don't want to take my stress and anger out on an unsuspecting partner."

"You could throw a rock right now and hit five women who would get on their knees so fast they'd get carpet burn. I'm not saying you anger-bang someone to death, but you'll feel a hell of a lot better."

"Like I said, I don't trust myself right now."

"That's bullshit, Dalton. You're the most trustworthy guy I know. Are you getting off on depriving yourself or something? Is this a new kink? Blue balls? Why wouldn't you sample some of the goods on display?" he says as he gestures to the many women who inhabit the VIP lounge tonight. "Or at least take me up on the offer of joining us. Minimum effort but all of the reward."

"The last thing I need tonight is to see you swinging your schlong."

"You love it. I know you're a kinky fucker. Leave your ethics at the door, man. Live a little. You'll be way more relaxed. If your shoulders get any higher, they'll be earmuffs."

I can always rely on Flex to bring levity to any conversation, even when I'm trying to be serious. "On that note, I'm going to head home. You sure you're okay to watch over Mom?"

"Yes. I've got her."

"And call me…"

"Call you if anything changes. Of course. Now, I have a woman waiting to wrap those pretty lips of hers around my cock. We good?"

"Yeah. Go enjoy yourself."

He slaps me on the shoulder as he stands to leave. "For the love of God, get laid before you leave town. Jesus, it's painful to watch you coiled like a spring."

"I'll take it under advisement."

"Fuck me, bro."

Laughter erupts, and the tension in my shoulders eases if only a little. "I'll never be *that* hard up, Flex. I've told you a thousand times, I'm just not that into you."

He reciprocates with a thunderous roar of laughter. "Fuck you."

"Night, bro."

"Later, brother."

I signal for another drink before I head out, just as one of my good friends walks in. The second she spies me, she makes a beeline to my table.

"The illustrious Mr. Callaghan. You're a sight for sore eyes."

"Hey, Viv. You on the prowl tonight?" She takes a seat, her gaze flitting across the room.

"Maybe," she says with a wicked grin. Viv oozes sex—gorgeous and more confident than any woman I've ever met. "Where have you been lately?"

"Work."

"All work and no play makes Dalton a grumpy boy."

"Flex said something similar. Since when did you and him become so interested in my sex life?"

She stares me down. "Are we wrong?"

"No."

She reaches across the table, resting her hand over mine. "You can talk to me, Dalton. God knows you've been there for me enough."

"Thanks, Viv. I appreciate it. I just have a lot going on right now."

"All the more reason to make time to unwind with friends."

"I promise we'll catch up when I get back from my business trip this week."

"I'll hold you to that."

"I'm counting on it," I say with a wry smile. Standing to leave, I press a kiss to Viv's cheek. "Have a good night. Don't do anything I wouldn't."

"Oh, you just gave me permission to have some real fun tonight!"

"Night, Viv."

"Goodnight, Dalton."

As I wind my way through the bar toward the exit, the cute bartender gives me a not-so-subtle wave, biting on her bottom lip, trying to be sexy. If I cared at all, I'd point out that subtly is a turn-on for me. I don't want the scantily-clad women or the ones who throw themselves at me. The women I sleep with wouldn't be allowed to stroll around in a public setting like this, showing everything that should be for my eyes only. It might be old-fashioned, but I'm a possessive man, and I sure as hell don't share.

The walk home is short, but it gives me time to think over what Flex and Viv said. I do need to find some stress relief with everything that's going on. As soon as I return from closing this next deal, I'll spend some time at the club. Maybe even find myself someone to *destress* with. But for now, it'll have to wait.

~

When I get home, I stop by to see my mom. I don't feel right about leaving her for days, but my lawyers told me in no uncertain terms that we need to close on this as soon as possible. I know I have to go, but it doesn't make it any easier to go when she's so sick.

Stirring as I take her hand in mine, her eyes drift open, her body tensing as she searches my face for some familiarity. I hope beyond hope, only to find fear—of *me*.

"It's okay, Mom, it's just me. Your son."

"*Help! Someone…*" She tries to get out of bed, but her tremors are so bad, and her body is so weak, she couldn't run even with a burst of adrenaline. "*Please, someone, help.*"

The nurse on shift appears at the door, pity in the soft set of her brow as she slowly approaches the bed.

"Candice, you're okay. No one is going to hurt you."

"Get out of my house! I don't know you people. Take anything you want. Money. Jewels. Anything. Just please don't hurt me."

"Mom," I whisper, "You're safe here. I would never harm you. Never."

She only screams louder, forcing the nurse to act. "I need to give her a sedative, Mr. Callaghan. No amount of talking is going to help her right now."

I hang my head as I step back, watching in horror as the nurse administers an injection, knowing my presence was the catalyst.

She continues to fuss and fight—convinced that some *stranger* is trying to attack her, cussing in ways I've never heard come from her mouth—until the drugs kick in, and she passes out. My heart aches, a sadness so profound shrouding me from head to toe. I blink back tears, trying to swallow past the massive lump in my throat.

"You should get some rest, Mr. Callaghan. She won't wake until morning now."

Rubbing a hand over my five-o'clock shadow, I take one last look at my mom, now so still as she sleeps. "Yeah. Let me know how she is in the morning. I'll come by before I head to the airport."

She can see how hard I'm fighting back the emotion threatening to overwhelm me at this moment. "It's not her. Not the mom you know and love. It was the disease talking. I know it's heartbreaking, but I try to hold onto the memory of the woman she was before the dementia took hold."

"You're right... it's heartbreaking." I thank her for everything she does for Mom before turning on my heel and heading for the elevator to the penthouse, repeating the same five words over and over again.

It was the disease talking. It was the disease talking. It was the disease talking.

Chapter 3

NADDIE

"Are you still wearing this ratty T-shirt?" Having Jenna in town is amazing, but she just loves to rifle through my stuff. There are no boundaries when it comes to her and me. "When you told me about it, you promised you'd put it back in the hallowed box I've yet to see."

A possessive, territorial wave courses through me as she holds it up against herself. I quickly snatch it from her hands, cradling it in mine. "It's comfortable."

Her eyes widen. "Girl, what have you been doing since you moved here? Do I need to stage an intervention?"

"Don't give me shit. I know how pathetic it looks. Being here... alone... I wanted some sort of comfort."

"Then I'll give you one of my T-shirts to wear. You can be swaddled up at night in eau de bestie." She pulls her Harry Potter T-shirt over her head and chucks it in my direction.

"It took you all of five minutes to get your tits out. Bravo, Jenna. That may be a new world record." She happily shakes her chest at me.

"Admit it, you missed me."

"I did. But I can see your nipples through your bra." I toss her T-shirt back.

"Do you know how many men would eat their left arm to get a glimpse of my nipples? A lot." One of Jenna's best traits is her confidence. "And while we're on the subject, where are we going tonight?"

"I thought we could do pizza and movie night. I've missed it."

She shrugs into her T-shirt before grabbing me by the shoulders. "We're young and gorgeous, and Manhattan is calling our names."

"I live here."

"And pray tell, Nad, how many times have you painted the town red since you got here *two months* ago?"

"I've been busy," I say, picking at the lint on my sweatpants. "I take the bar exam in a week, I'm still settling in at the firm, and I have to prove myself with their biggest client… in freaking Milan."

"Woe is you. You have to jet set to Italy. Let's play the world's smallest violin for Nadia Sullivan." She rubs her thumb and index finger together, crying fake tears. "Get your ass in a cute dress, some makeup on your face, and a killer pair of heels. We're going out."

"Didn't you just hear me? I have to take the New York bar exam in a week."

"I'm not deaf, but you seem to forget that I'm your stress relief switch. I know you. Let me take a wild guess at your Manhattan experience so far. You've studied into the early hours since you moved here. But, before that, you have takeout delivered to your office because you work so late. The doorman of this building is the only person you've spoken to since you got here. Tell me I'm wrong."

Dammit. She knows me better than anyone, and yet there's a part of myself I keep hidden, even from her. "Fine. A couple of hours."

"Just go and get ready. We leave in ten."

I quickly pull together an outfit—my favorite little black dress I would wear at the club in Boston. Aside from Jenna, the club is what I miss most. I'd found my tribe. No judgment and all the kink I could ever ask for. I hadn't found my forever Dom, but I'd found myself. Maybe I'm a cliché, but I love being a submissive. My day job is high stress and high stakes, and nothing less than my best is always required.

There's something beautiful about handing over the reins to someone I can trust not to push me past my limits. I set the parameters of what I like and don't and what punishments I love or despise. As a submissive, I still have ultimate control with a single word. That's what is so amazing about a safeword.

After I slip into my dress, I grab my favorite Jimmy Choo heels. They've seen better days, but I love them. They were my splurge purchase when I got my first full time job out of college. Some blush, mascara, lip gloss, and I'm ready to go.

"Look at you. Letting your hair down looks good on you." She's way hotter than me, but I appreciate the compliment. "We're going to have some fun tonight."

Linking her arm through mine, we head out into the city that never sleeps, and a weight lifts from my shoulders, if only for a few hours.

"It's my song!" The club is alive, a buzz tangible in the air around us, the beat carrying all my worries away.

Jenna grabs my hand, pulling me into the center of the dance floor, grinding against me as we lose ourselves in the melody. It takes me back to Boston—to my college years—before I knew about BDSM clubs. Jenna and I spent countless weekends partying, which was amazing, but I stopped trying to find a man who could give me what I needed. Clubs like the one we're in now are not the place to find a Dom.

I'm sure I could find a guy who *thinks* he's an alpha male—all bluster and nothing to back it up. The guys who've been trying to get our attention tonight probably believe a little tug on a woman's hair while having sex makes them a bad boy. I have no time or inclination to find out.

The drinks flow as we dance the night away, and Jenna has some hot guy stuck to her face as she gets her freak on. I'd love to go home and crawl into bed, but I would never leave her alone with some random dude in a club.

"I'm going to go grab us some more drinks," I yell at the top of my lungs without success. The booming base drowns out everything else, swallowing my words.

I nudge her shoulder and give the universal signal for drinks. With a quick nod, she returns to sucking the face off—I don't know his name. I doubt she does, either.

Weaving my way through the sea of bodies writhing to the music, it takes a while to make it to the bar, and even then, there's a crowd of people also waiting to order drinks. I scan the length of the bar for an opening I can slink into and speed up this process a little.

There's a handsome guy at the end of the bar, his eyes finding mine as he gestures to the space at his side. He's cute in an obvious way, and that panty-melting smile might work on most women. It's been a few months since I left Boston, and I haven't ventured to the BDSM club that was recommended to me. Maybe flirting with a harmless stranger could be fun.

When I reach where he sits, he rises, signaling for me to take a seat. The second I sit down, he jumps across the bar with a wry grin. "What can I get for you?"

"I don't think it's self-service..." I lift my gaze in question, waiting for a name.

"Eli."

"Well, Eli, it's customary to sit next to a woman when you purposefully catch her eye."

"I take no blame. I've been watching you with your friend for twenty minutes, but you didn't notice me. I'm off break now, so... what can I get for you?" He waits for me to reciprocate.

"Nadia. Two dirty martinis, onions, not olives."

"I like you already." His dark eyes rake over me as he reaches for the optic. When his back is turned, I take a moment to admire his muscular physique.

He returns a few moments later, setting the drinks down on the bar as a long line of patrons start vying for his attention.

"Thanks. How much do I owe you?"

"Your phone number," he says with a wicked grin.

"What time do you get off?"

"I'm closing tonight."

"And how many women's numbers do you have in your pocket?"

"A few, but none that I asked for."

I reach into my purse and pull out a fifty, setting it down on the bar. "This should cover it."

He slides his hand over his heart, every inch the wounded soldier. "Damn, woman."

"It's been a while since you've been rejected. Or has this never happened to you before?" I say, stifling a laugh.

He has the chagrin to look apologetic as he slowly shakes his head, rubbing his hand over the back of his neck. "Don't hate me. You're killing a lifelong streak right now."

I grab a coaster off the bar, sliding it over to him. "Fine, I'll compromise just because you look pathetic right now. Give me *your* number."

I bet he's used this move a thousand times, but he's hot, and I'm new in town and horny.

He scribbles it down as the guy next to me starts shouting his order. "Do I need to die of thirst while you wet your whistle, bro?"

Eli gives a dismissive glare before handing me the coaster, leaning in conspiratorially. "I'm going to spit in his drink." His breath sends a shiver down my spine. "Call me."

Slipping his number in my purse, I grab our drinks, flashing him a smile before facing the sea of people once more, jostling my way back to where I left Jenna.

When I spy her, she's no longer attached to that guy's lips.

"Where did suck-face go?" I inquire as I hand her the martini glass.

"Oh my God, I'll tell you when it's not so loud," she screams.

We dance for a little while longer, enjoying each other's company and our last drink of the night.

By the time we make it outside, my ears are ringing, and my head is spinning. I draw in a deep breath of fresh air—or whatever passes for fresh air in downtown Manhattan. Taxi cabs are lined up, waiting to ferry drunk patrons back to the comfort and quiet of their homes.

The moment our butts are in the back seat, Jenna becomes so animated, her eyes bugging out as she regales me with the story of suck-face. "Holy shit, Nad. The men out here are hot, but fuck me, they're kinky." My ears prick up with that final word.

"What?"

"That guy. We were having a good time, dancing, kissing… he was a good kisser. Then, he slaps my ass hard and leans in, thinking he's so sexy, and says, 'Do you like that, pussy cat? Purr for Daddy.' That was my cue to send him packing. Any guy who calls himself my *Daddy* is getting nowhere near my pussy cat." She fakes puking as the cab driver ducks in and out of traffic.

"You don't like a little spank now and again?" I must be emboldened by the alcohol tonight.

"What? No. I'm not going to let some random dude in a bar go all Christian Grey on my ass."

Laughter comes bursting out my mouth in an attempt to cover my reaction to a *Fifty Shades* scenario. "Right?" It sounds so forced, and Jenna immediately jumps on me.

"Does my straight-laced lawyer friend enjoy a little spank?" She pokes my side, giggling and tipsy.

"I can categorically tell you that I *do not* enjoy a little spank." The trusty lie of omission. A good lawyer can always become creative with their wording. I don't enjoy a little spank. When a Dom spanks me, I want it hard until my cheeks are good and sore and my sex is wet with arousal.

"I could see you enjoying that kind of stuff."

"Why?" I fake offense. I can't explain it, but I'm not ready for her to know that side of me. She might judge me or walk away from our friendship, and right now, I can't lose the one person who grounds me.

"They always say it's the quiet ones you need to watch out for." She's not wrong.

"There's nothing you need to be watching for. If anything, you need to be more concerned with your own bedfellows."

Jenna descends into a fit of giggles. This always happens when she's drunk. "Bedfellows? Oh my God, Nad, you sound like my nana." The corners of my mouth twitch as I try not to blow my cover.

"Does your nana love deepthroating too?" Her giggles give way to a cackle so loud it reverberates off the windows, and I can't help my fit of laughter. She slaps my leg, and her face reddens as she tries to get herself under control.

"Stop! I'm going to pee my panties."

"Same as your nana." I can barely get the words out. "We both take after the matriarch of your family. Who knew!"

It only makes it funnier as she quickly crosses her legs, her face going from hilarious to grim in the blink of an eye. "Seriously. I cannot pee myself in a car at the age of thirty-three."

That catches the attention of the cab driver, who turns to chastise her. "No peeing in my cab. I refuse to let that happen... again."

We erupt into a new wave of hysterics as the cab comes to a grinding halt.

"Out."

There's no saving Jenna at this point. I've been on too many bar hops with her to know when I'm fighting a losing battle. "I'm sorry, sir. I promise she won't pee in your cab. We're only three blocks from my apartment, but these heels are killing me. Please. I'll give you fifty bucks to trust my friend's bladder."

"Fine," he mumbles, pulling back into traffic. "If she pees, I swear to God you'll be cleaning it up."

Thankfully, we make it back to my place without incident, and I hand over the biggest tip I've ever bestowed on a cab driver. Jenna is like a limp noodle as I pull her out onto the sidewalk.

It's only when we reach the elevator that she perks up. "Do you have waffles? We always eat waffles when we're drunk." She slings her arms around my neck, planting a kiss on my cheek.

"Of course. Just because we live in different states doesn't mean I don't have Eggos ready and waiting in my freezer."

"I hate that we live so far apart."

"Me too." The familiar ping of the elevator pulls us out of our pity party. We link arms and stumble out into the hallway. "You should move here."

"You shouldn't have left Boston."

I fumble for my keys before attempting to open the door multiple times. The third time is the charm. As the thud of my purse hitting the hardwood floors echoes through the apartment, I kick off my heels and head straight to the freezer.

"How many do you want?"

"The usual." She's gone from uncontrolled laughter to sleepy in seconds. I really miss having her around.

When I've made a heaped plate of waffles, I grab a few bottles of water and the Advil.

"Here." I thrust the tablets at her. "Take two, and make sure you drink all the water."

"Yes, Mom."

"You'll thank me in the morning. As always."

I pull the blanket off the back of the couch and cuddle up next to Jenna, covering her legs as she tucks into the waffles.

"Want to watch some crappy TV?" She swipes the remote off the coffee table, and suddenly, this place feels like home. We flick through a hundred channels before deciding on reruns of *One Tree Hill*. There's nothing like dated teenage angst to end a night out. We've watched the complete series, start to finish, at least four times since our freshman year of college.

"You promised me you'd show me what else is in that high school boyfriend box when I came to visit. I'm visiting," she says as she rests her head on my shoulder, hogging the blanket as always. It's why I buy them in California King size.

"Maybe tomorrow."

"What is it about that guy? I've never dated a man who made it to the keepsake category." Her words are barely a whisper as her eyes grow heavy. "Why can't you let him go?"

"I don't know." It's easier to lie than speak the truth out loud. A statement of fact that I dare not acknowledge. If the words never pass my lips, maybe I'll start believing it one day.

The boy next door will always hold a piece of my heart that no other man *could* ever, or *has* ever, owned.

As I dump out the contents of my purse, looking for my favorite lip gloss, the coaster with the cute bartender's number on it falls out. I figure, what the hell. Grabbing my phone, I type in his number, saving it for another night—a night when I'm not going to crawl into bed in a ratty old Rolling Stones T-shirt.

My nerves are threatening to get the better of me this morning. Today will make or break my life-changing move to Manhattan. If I don't pass the bar exam, I'll be jobless, hopeless, and within a few months, homeless. It's not like my firm in Boston would take me back at this point. They were pretty pissed I accepted the job here. I was offered more money and the chance to make partner in three years, but something in me felt pulled to accept the job here. I just hope it wasn't the wrong decision.

I need to maintain focus and nail this bar exam. I aced the Massachusetts bar, and I'm more than confident in my role as a lawyer. No one will work harder for their clients, yet my stomach is still doing somersaults this morning.

Jenna brought my lucky Chucks—my favorite pair of Converse that I wore for every exam throughout college, but I can't wear them to sit the bar. It would be inappropriate to walk in there anything less than court-ready. However, I may have rubbed them for luck right before getting out of my car. I stop for a moment, close my eyes, and take a deep breath before striding into the building like a boss.

It's time to take the bull by the horns and own my choices. I want to leave the past where it belongs and move forward as the strong, confident, kickass lawyer I know myself to be.

Chapter 4
DALTON

As we take flight to cross the continent, I look over the contract I've been perfecting with my lawyers for months now and ponder the reason The Callaghan Group exists—spite and bloody-minded determination. I swore the day I sat in court as my dad was sentenced to twenty years in prison that I would become the man my mom deserved—a man who would take care of her without resorting to underhanded deals, scheming, and stealing from the hand that feeds me.

Fraud and embezzling millions of dollars were the legacy of my family name. Those who had been happy to sit at his side, enjoying the spoils of his double-dealing, were nowhere to be found when the Rutherford empire crumbled. My mom and I were left to fend off creditors, bathing in the shame he brought upon us.

We lost everything. *I* lost *everything*—the future I had planned and the life I desperately wanted to live. Success comes at a price, but so does sacrifice. I would do it all over again to ensure my mom would survive my father's sins. She gave everything for me, and I could never—in good conscience—have walked away to serve my happiness when she needed me most.

I used to think we'd weathered the storms those first few years.

Looking back now, I'd give anything for those struggles—the small apartment, countless jobs, and constant worry that the bills would be covered each month. A sick, sad laugh escapes me as I sit surrounded by the ultimate luxuries, and yet they don't matter worth a damn. There are things money can't buy, and if it could, I'd give up every cent I've ever earned, gladly and without hesitation.

When I built The Callaghan Group, I decided at its inception—transparency in all matters. When people hear mergers and acquisitions, they think of suits who have no interest in the businesses they deal with—they'll strip them for parts and sell to the highest bidder.

I'm not that guy. I never have been. My success has come from getting alongside businesses that are struggling or ones looking to expand and become a part of something bigger than themselves. I've built my fortune on one simple philosophy—if I make money, my clients make money. It's an instinct. I know what needs to be done. I can see the big picture and all the moving parts required to make it happen.

I pride myself on the trust I build with everyone I work with. My dad only saw what he stood to gain. It never crossed his mind how his actions would affect his staff, clients, and most importantly, his family. He was out for number one, consequences be damned, but he taught me the kind of man I *didn't* want to be. I give him a lot of credit for that.

The Callaghan Group is a living, breathing entity, made successful by everyone who works for me. From the janitor to the CFO, each role has played an integral part in building the company to where it is today. To the deal I'm about to make.

It's been a long time since I've been excited about work. When I reach this stage of a deal, I'm usually cool as a cucumber, but this feels different. I'm on the cusp of a major breakthrough, and I'm anxious to sign on the dotted line. My portfolio has been somewhat stale the past few years with the same type of acquisitions over and over again—the tried-and-true money earners. This is so much more.

I'm ready to branch out, and this deal will afford me the lion's share of Europe's biggest A&M industry as The Callaghan Group takes ownership of the biggest company on the continent.

With every major acquisition of this nature—commercial property—I like to find a few businesses I think have the potential to be scaled up in a big way. There are a handful of the acquisition premises that house businesses that piqued my interest. Niche markets that wouldn't be on the radar of most A&M companies—medium-sized family companies in the middle of nowhere, but they cater to an elite clientele, and those are the people I want access to.

Initially, none of the owners were interested in even talking with me, but I convinced them to give me a few hours of their time. If they don't like my proposals, they can send me packing. I want these entrepreneurs to think far beyond the day they retire. So many of these medium-sized family-owned businesses don't look beyond the next generation. There is no need for any of them to sell and walk away when the time comes.

With my business plans, each of these owners can retire with the option to consult as much or as little as they want, and they'll earn *a lot* of money for the decades of work they put into the mustard seeds of innovation. I can turn them into an empire while maintaining their culture and ethos, giving them the tools to thrive.

My accountants thought I was crazy when I told them to put together the financial plans for each of the businesses that interest me from this acquisition, but I pay them to crunch the numbers and not give me shit about the companies I choose to spend time cultivating. In my heart, I know these places can be goldmines. My instincts put me on the map—working alongside companies and upscaling them without losing the driving force. Every business I've worked with has something in common—strong family connections. Men and women who strive to give the next generation better than they had. Parents who maintained their integrity while forging a path for their children. My goal is to ensure their grandchildren and great-grandchildren can reap the rewards of hard work and dedication.

My lawyer saw my vision straight away. He always does. He's a legend in New York and across the country. The name Douglas

33

EVA HAINING

Mason strikes fear in the hearts of lawyers everywhere. His unrelenting drive is the reason I hired him. It wasn't particularly easy to find a good lawyer when I started out because another name that rang out in New York was my father's—the fraud, the embezzler, the prisoner—not exactly the foundation for a career that I believe requires trust and honesty.

Douglas and I have always been frank with each other. No bullshit. We're both shrewd businessmen, and when it comes to money, I know he always wants more. If I were him, I'd have retired by now, especially after a heart attack two years ago, but I suspect he'll die surrounded by a pile of contracts, a fistful of dollars in his hand, and a smile on his face.

We spoke briefly about his successor when he was recovering from his heart attack, but he fobbed me off, assuring me there was plenty of life in the old dog yet. I'd be a fool to take his word for it. He's pushing seventy with a bad ticker, and his heir to the throne isn't exactly a chip off the old block.

I've interviewed a few firms who had to sign NDAs before I even set foot in a room with them. The last thing I need is this getting back to Douglas. He'll have my business until his final day, if only because he took a chance on me when no one else would. That unwavering support ends with him. I won't have his son, Robert, taking over out of loyalty to his father. He's a minnow when it comes to law, and I need a barracuda. Douglas knows. I think it's why he hasn't retired before now.

I've asked Douglas to dinner once we arrive in Milan. There are a few things we need to discuss, and as we seal the deal and sign the contracts, I need to look to the future. I think Douglas needs to get real about his longevity at the firm. If I know him, he's been expecting this conversation for a while.

For the remainder of the flight, I busy myself going over the finer details of these contracts one last time before turning my attention to a more personal matter. With the pressure of work and everything going on with my mom, I could use a distraction, so I tap out a quick text to Viv.

34

> **Me:** Can you provide some… stress relief? Saturday night 9pm.

> **Viv:** Oh goody. You're coming out to play.

> **Me:** I love how excited you get about these things.

> **Viv:** You love everything about me.

> **Me:** True. See you Saturday, beautiful.

> **Viv:** You're shameless, Dalton Callaghan. See you then. X

For the first time in months, I breathe easy, not realizing how much I need something to look forward to. My cock twitches at the prospect of losing myself in a beautiful woman for a few hours. Maybe a few days.

"I'll take another whiskey sour when you're ready." The waitress nods with a curt smile as she clears our plates from the table. I insisted that dinner be an adult-only affair. I couldn't be bothered dealing with his simpering son, Robert. Douglas didn't question it, but as he sits across from me, I can tell he's on edge.

"Are you ready to make the biggest deal of your life tomorrow?"

"I'm always ready."

The furrow of his brow tells me he's holding back.

"What's on your mind, Douglas?" He knows exactly why I asked him to dinner tonight.

"You've always been able to read people. A gift you inherited from your father."

"Now, why would you sour my good mood with something like that? He used that 'gift' to fleece people for everything they owned."

"You're right. I do have something to talk to you about. I was going to wait until after we signed the contracts tomorrow, but your desire to have dinner with *just* me makes me think we need to have this conversation now."

"Spit it out."

"One of the team I brought with me is our newest partner." I wasn't expecting him to be so proactive.

"Okay," I say as another round of drinks arrive.

"I want her to take over your account when I retire. I hired her specifically for that purpose." *You've got to be shitting me.*

"Why are you trying to fob me off with some new lawyer right now? I understand that we've discussed your retirement at some point, but this deal isn't the one to test drive your replacement on. I assumed you'd push for one of the existing partners to take over my account."

"I disagree, Dalton. This is the perfect time. If you trusted any other partner with your business, you'd have transitioned the second I had my heart attack. Your reluctance speaks volumes. There's no one else you want overseeing your company's legal affairs, so I found new blood. Someone who has what it takes to do what you need."

The waitress sets down my drink before making herself scarce. "And your son?" I leave the question hanging between us until his steel exterior crumbles.

"Robert is a good son and a decent lawyer, but he doesn't have what it takes. You already know that, or he'd be sitting here with us."

"He's not going to take this lying down."

"He will because as much as I love him, he isn't *entitled* to anything. I employ him because he will put in the work and graft as hard as is needed, but I still see my familial and career legacies as separate entities." He fidgets with the ornate crystal glass, his index finger tracing the rim.

"And you think entrusting it to some person you barely know is a better idea?" If that's what he believes, then he's naïve on multiple fronts.

"Yes. Robert will have the controlling share of the company, but with the caveat that he can choose which *future* clients he wishes.

The contract is cast iron and includes control of my current clients going to a lawyer of my choosing."

"And you believe he'll honor that?"

"He has to. Above all else, my son respects the law more than he's ever respected me."

I lean back in my chair, considering the legend before me. He knows, more than anyone, why my legal dealings are so meticulous and micromanaged and why his judgment matters to me more than anyone else.

"What about the businesses I asked you to contact here?"

"They are open and shut. The deal you're offering is more than generous. They'd be crazy not to sign on the dotted line. I know how important your passion projects are to you, but the deal you should be focusing on is the one we're about to close. Everything else is business for another day. We have time."

"Then, tell me about your prospective replacement." I don't like this one bit.

"She was the top of her class at Harvard. Graduated summa cum laude. I've been watching her career for a while, and I guarantee she'll be an asset to your legal team. Like I said, I hired her specifically for your account."

"I don't know if you're trying to stroke my ego right now, so I won't convince you to stay on a few more years."

He leans back in his chair with an air of confidence I've come to depend on. "Have I ever steered you wrong, Dalton? I promise you'll be in expert hands. Trust me."

"If I must." I signal the bartender for another round.

"If I could wish myself younger and practice law for another fifty years, I would. Unfortunately, my career isn't in medical research."

"That's a shame. You'd be a billionaire," I say with a wry grin.

"I guess I'll have to live vicariously through you."

"It's the same as being a multimillionaire, only with more zeros. You'll sleep just fine on your mattress of millions."

"You're about to become the wealthiest man in the world." I know he's right, but it's the last thing on my mind.

"Money isn't everything." Pressing the heavy glass to my lips, the whiskey slides down my throat, giving a fleeting reprieve from the weight on my shoulders that money can't fix.

"How is your mother?" I find the pity in his eyes jarring. My business and private life don't mix. There's no place for emotional turmoil.

"If I could give up every dollar I've earned and make her better, I would. The Parkinson's is devastating to watch, but now that dementia has taken hold, she doesn't recognize me most days. We've exhausted every treatment and trial available, but there's nothing I can fucking do." Draining the rest of my drink, I shove my glass across the table, the ice as cold as the dread that washes over me.

"You're doing everything you can."

"And it's nothing compared to what she's done for me. When my dad went to prison, our lives were in ruins, and she gave me the strength to man up, step up, and become who I am today. I feel so... useless."

I quickly pull myself together. The first rule of business is to leave your personal life at the door. My mouth starts moving before he can respond with the compassion I see reflected in his gaze.

"I think we're ready. You should go and get some rest, Douglas. We have a massive deal to close tomorrow, and I need you to bring your A-game."

"Of course, Dalton. We'll be ready."

I shake his hand before heading for the penthouse suite, my heart heavy as the reality of my mom's declining health settles like a dead weight in my chest. Tension rolls off me in waves as I slam my keycard against the panel and wait for the doors to close.

It's a small mercy that I'm not forced to share an elevator with anyone right now. Reaching into my pocket, I grab my phone and speed-dial Flex.

"Hey. How's she doing?"

"Why hello, Dalton. I'm fine. Thank you so much for asking." His smartass greeting allays my fears instantly.

"Hey, bro. How are you?"

"I'm good. Sitting with Mom right now. We're playing gin rummy, and she's robbing me blind."

"Can I talk to her?"

"Sure, but she's not coherent today, Dal." My heart sinks.

"I just want to hear her voice." Waiting patiently, I listen as my mom protests, refusing to speak to a 'stranger.' Her words cut me to the quick. If only I could reach through the phone and hold her in my arms right now.

"Hello?" There's a whisper on the other side of the line. "This is Candice Rutherford." She's forgotten that she changed her name back to Callaghan after divorcing my father.

"Hi, Momma. How are you feeling today?"

"Momma? I think you have the wrong person. My son is here with me right now." *Flex.* Her voice dips in and out. "Who are you?"

"It's Dalton, Momma. I'm your son. Flex is my best friend. You've been his momma for years, but you gave birth to me. Dalton Callaghan."

The line goes silent for a few moments before her quiet, unassuming voice becomes a dagger to my heart. "I don't know you." The line goes dead, and a part of me dies with it.

Flex's name comes up on the screen, but I send his call straight to voicemail. I know he's done nothing wrong, but hearing my mom call him her son when she doesn't know who I am stings. He's like a son to her, and I've always loved that—until now.

> Me: I'll call you tomorrow. I have some prep to do for my meeting.

> Flex: She knows you, bro. When you walk in the room, she knows you.

> Me: Sometimes. For now.

> Flex: Good luck tomorrow.

Silence deafens me as I wander through the penthouse suite. Why am I even here? I should be at home, taking care of my mom. Instead, I'm thousands of miles away to make more money. Why? I could live a hundred lives and never spend the wealth I've already accumulated.

I can placate myself with altruistic ideals, but at the end of the day, should anyone else's family legacy matter to me? Or am I just running away from *my* familial problems?

Sleep is the furthest thing from my mind, yet I'm acutely aware that tomorrow marks the biggest deal I'll ever make. Instead of tossing and turning all night, I take my frustration to the gym. It's a poor substitute for my preferred stress-relief, but I don't have a sub right now, and even if I did, I've never had one travel with me. It's too risky.

My choices are my own, but after everything that happened with my father, I swore I would never be in the public eye. It only gives you farther to fall and an audience to watch.

Chapter 5
NADDIE

This week has been such a whirlwind. I didn't think sitting the New York bar exam would fill me with the same level of nerves I felt sitting the Massachusetts bar, but I was so stressed out. Now, I have to put it to the back of my mind for the next two months until I find out if I passed. I can't even contemplate the possibility of failing and the life I've moved here for vanishing before my eyes.

Today, I'm in *Milan*, and I pinched myself this morning to make sure this is real. The firm's most important client is signing contracts on the biggest deal I have ever witnessed, and they thought it pertinent that I be here to familiarize myself as the newest partner. Honestly, I'm a little awestruck. I read the contract in preparation, and it is a thing of true beauty. A lawyer's wet dream.

"You ready?" Mr. Mason holds my gaze as his son flanks him on the right. If looks could kill, Robert's eyes would bore a hole straight through my face. He's not keen on my presence, which I can't fault him for. He's not an idiot, and he sees the path his father is carving for me. If I were him, I'd be pissed too.

"Yes, sir."

"Then let's go." He dips his head in my direction.

Robert gives me a sideways glare. "You should be seen and not heard today. You haven't earned the right to interject. We've been working on this contract for the past eighteen months." Every part of my feminist soul wants to protest, but I find myself nodding like a good little submissive—not something I do outside of the bedroom or a club.

The soft click of the doorhandle sends a thrill coursing through me, tingling down my spine with the expectation of being around a conference room table once more. I've done nothing but study for the bar since I arrived in Manhattan, and I'm itching to get back in the game. That's what law is—a game. If you play it with skill, precision, and one hell of a poker face, the reward is exhilarating. I wouldn't go as far as to say it's better than an orgasm, but it comes close.

Tendrils of warmth weave their way through my veins, a hint of a smile twitching my lips as we step inside.

The bustling room goes silent, but their mouths are still moving. The buzz of the conference room is replaced by a high-pitched tone, whistling in my ears as my heart stammers to a devastating halt.

My world stops turning, and the warmth of moments ago turns to ice in my veins, freezing me to the spot.

It can't be. I must be dreaming.

But it is.

Dalton.

He stands to shake Douglas's hand, and for a split second, I don't think he remembers me.

"Good to see you, Dalton. Let me introduce you to our newest partner, Nadia Sullivan."

The moment his eyes find mine, the wind is knocked out of me, his glacial blue eyes searching my gaze for answers I don't have. Robert thrusts his hand out, but Dalton's attention is fixed on me. "Hello, Mr. Callaghan. I assure you, you won't even know she's here."

"*Impossible.*" His voice is a single malt whiskey. Molten chocolate. A caress I've longed for and dreamed of for so many years.

"Mr. Callaghan?" He changed his name. It takes everything in me not to throw myself into his arms.

"Yes, Ms. Sullivan." The years have been more than kind to the boy I once knew—Dalton *Rutherford*. He offers his hand, but I hesitate, my cheeks flushed in anticipation. I reach forward, dumbstruck, as he clasps his large, strong hand around mine, sending a jolt of electricity straight to my core.

Time ceases to exist, and there's nothing and no one—just us. There's something so familiar in this innocent touch, his thumb caressing the back of my hand, and yet, a man stands before me in the place of my high school sweetheart. The boyish charm of his features has been replaced with the chiseled perfection of a Greek god. Impossibly handsome, his jaw is clenched as he fights to remain professional.

"You can let go of him, Nadia. Mr. Callaghan doesn't have time to hold your hand. Sit over there and take your notepad out," Robert chastises me, breaking the spell and bringing me back to the room. I snatch my hand back, lowering my gaze to the floor, bereft of Dalton's touch.

"She's not a child. If your father thinks she should be in here, then I want her at the table and not kept in the corner. Feel free to give up your seat, Robert." Dalton's voice is lower—a deep, rumbling authority commanding the room.

"I…"

"Then it's settled. Robert, you can sit back there. Ms. Sullivan will learn more from reading the contract."

"It's fine. I'm only here to observe."

"Sit down, Ms. Sullivan." I do as he asks, and I'm eighteen all over again. Dalton could always silence me with one word, my will falling in line with his. Willingly. Eagerly. And without question.

As he sits beside me, the scent of his cologne intoxicates my senses. Resting my hands in my lap, I avoid making eye contact with Robert. I don't have to see his face to feel the anger radiating from him in waves. I'm white-knuckled as realization dawns—I was hired to take over Dalton's account. I uprooted my life for Dalton Rutherford.

"Breathe, Naddie," he whispers under his breath for only me to hear. His hand twitches on the desk, and I know he's fighting the urge to reach for me. I can see the rapid rise and fall of his chest in my peripheral vision. No matter how hard I try, I can't let go of the breath I'm holding. It's not until he brushes his knee against my leg under the table that I exhale, my temperature spiking at his touch.

The representatives for the company Dalton is acquiring today enter the room, saving me from myself. Introductions are made, and we get down to business—Dalton's attention to detail ever present in the way he scrutinizes every page. He's done this countless times before today, I'm sure, but he's still the boy I know at heart, triple-checking everything and signing once.

Douglas pours over every line first before handing them to Dalton, who, in turn, thrusts them in my direction. My lawyer brain takes over the primal desire crackling deep in my core. As I read through the finer points again, I'm filled with pride for the man Dalton has become—a shrewd businessman with a keen eye for potential. I've never seen an acquisition or merger deal as big as this. I knew he'd find his way in the world, but I could never have imagined his stratospheric success.

"What do you think, Ms. Sullivan? Should I sign?" All eyes are on me as heat rises in my cheeks. The way he says my name does something to the submissive in me.

"Yes, but I'm sure you already know that. I'm just an observer."

"You're one of my lawyers now. Your opinion matters."

"Respectfully," Robert interjects, but Dalton shuts him down before he can utter another word.

"In my experience... *Robert*... a sentence that begins with 'respectfully' always ends with disrespect, and you know how I feel about that." Damn, he's hot. His voice is so familiar, and yet the delicious, low rasp that has come with age carries a darkness that envelops me.

"My apologies, Mr. Callaghan," Robert spits, choking on his vitriol. This isn't going to end well for me. What have I done?

"Apology accepted." If it weren't evident before, it is now.

Dalton pulls a pen from the inside pocket of his tailored blue, pinstriped suit jacket and signs his name at every X and initials each page. When he's finished, he pushes it across the desk, and the deal is done just like that. Dalton is now the owner of the biggest A&M company in Europe.

Handshakes are followed by the pop of a cork on the finest bottle of champagne. He hands me a glass, watching me like a hawk as I put it to my mouth. The effervescent bubbles explode on my tongue, and a low growl rumbles in Dalton's chest, his eyes fixed on my lips.

"No drinking on the job, Sullivan. Didn't they teach you that in Boston?" Robert hands me a legal pad with chicken scrawl hand-writing. "Go type these up. I want them before the end of the day." Under any other circumstance, I'd put this little shit in his place, but I don't want to give Douglas any reason to fire me. My entire inter-action with Dalton is a lesson in unprofessional behavior, but I'm powerless to refuse him. So, I do the only thing I have control over.

Taking the legal pad, I turn on my heel and exit the room, putting distance between Dalton and me. My heart thunders in my chest, my pulse drowning out all sounds around me. I'm transported back to high school and the boy I drove away from, except this time, I'm *running* away.

I slam the button for the elevator, desperate to get out of here and away from the ache taking root in the pit of my stomach. Nothing ever happens fast when you're in a hurry. I frantically hit the button repeatedly, overhearing Dalton trying to excuse himself, but thankfully, Douglas is busy talking up 'our' triumph. We're lawyers. Dalton is the one who sought out this acquisition. My eigh-teen-year-old self rears her fiercely protective head. Part of me will aways feel a small sense of ownership for the boy next door.

As the elevator doors engulf me, Dalton appears in the hallway, his eyes finding mine as the safety of the elevator swallows me whole. The furrow of his brow speaks to the same confusion that roils in the pit of my stomach. My pulse is racing, creating an almighty whooshing in my ears, panic taking hold, spreading like wildfire through every cell in my body.

The elevator lunges into motion, spiriting me away to the level of my hotel room. Fifteen floors feel like fifty as I attempt to control my breathing. The last thing I need is to faint in the elevator and be found by my new boss or client.

My head is swimming, threatening to pull me under, but I hold on, scurrying to my room the second the doors open. The walls close in as I sink to the floor, my door the only thing that separates me from falling to pieces. With my head in my hands, the gravity of the moment takes hold, unbidden tears streaming down my face. I don't know if it's shock, terror, or unbridled joy. Perhaps all of the above.

I'm not sure how long I sit, my entire body shaking as I rest my head against the door before there's a knock.

My heart lurches into my throat. "Who is it?"

"Concierge."

I wipe my tear-soaked cheeks and fix my dress as I clamber to my feet. The doorhandle creaks as I steel myself for whatever he has to say. "Is everything okay?"

With a tight smile, he hands me an envelope. "One of the other guests requested that this be delivered to your room."

"What is it? Who is it from?"

"Discretion is part of my job, Ms. Sullivan." He turns on his heel. "Have a good night. Please don't hesitate to call the front desk if you need anything."

"Thank you." Discretion? Either I'm being served my marching orders from the firm or—

Running my fingers over the embossed letters on the back of the envelope, a rush of heat courses through me. I can't breathe.

D.C.

Dalton Callaghan. Even the thought sounds wrong to me. It may have been years since we've been in the same room, but I *know* him. He was once proud of his name and his father. To know it wounded him so deeply that he cut all ties makes me sad.

My hands shake as I slide my finger under the seal and peer

inside. It's a keycard for the penthouse suite, and if that wasn't clear enough, I find a handwritten note. There is a box at the back of my closet back in Manhattan that's filled with love letters in the same elegant script.

Come to me, Naddie.

Nothing more.
Nothing less.
My heart grinds to a halt.
Butterflies take flight in my stomach, their wings fanning the flames of arousal that burst to life. But, as quick as they come, I find myself trying to stamp them out. I can't be in a hotel suite with him. He's probably married and has babies by now. A man like him doesn't stay on the market.

I pace the floor, my hands clammy as I stare at his note, the soft aroma of his cologne on the paper. Closing my eyes for a moment, I'm transported back to the last time he held me in his arms, the same scent of Hugo Boss soothing my soul. Every fiber of my being wants to sprint to the elevator and go to him. Throw myself into his arms—regardless of the life he may now live—and lose myself in him one last time.

It takes a few minutes for me to realize his motives might be far removed from my own. Maybe he wants to fire me as one of his lawyers, or maybe he holds a grudge that I *did* leave him behind. Even though he was adamant that I take my place at Harvard, I'm sure with time, resentment would have taken hold.

Tears prick my eyes before wetting my cheeks as I let the enormity of that thought take hold. *What if he hates me?* It would be the worst outcome imaginable. I'd rather he fire me. I'm a coward, unable to face him tonight. Instead, I retreat to the bathroom, letting my clothes drop to the floor. While I wait for the water to heat, I take a long, hard look at myself in the oversized mirror. The person staring back at me is a strong, confident lawyer, and yet as I examine my face, I'm still the girl I once was. The girl he loved enough to let go.

I can hear the phone ring out on the bedside table, but I make no attempt to reach it in time. Stepping into the shower, I let the water cascade down my face, washing away the tears I can't hold in. The pounding water drowns out the silence that torments me as I fight my decision to ignore his request.

Unsure of how long I've been in here, I turn off the water, only to hear a knock at the door. I quickly shrug into one of the plush, white, fluffy hotel robes and creep into the room.

"Hello?"

The knocking stops.

"Housekeeping."

"I'm fine, thank you. I don't need anything."

There's a moment of silence before my world starts spinning once more.

"Open the door, Naddie." My heart grinds to a halt before slamming to the floor.

"No. You need to leave." Even as I say it, I find myself edging closer.

"Open the door. We need to talk."

"I can't." Every fiber of my being betrays my words, desire pooling deep in my core at the sound of his delicious, raspy voice.

"Do as you're told, Naddie. Don't make me ask again." Oh my God. The submissive in me can't ignore his commanding tone. "Open. The. Door."

I reach for the handle, my hands shaking as I give up the only barrier to my inevitable demise.

The cool, calm, collected businessman from the conference room is gone, and standing in his place, his hands bracing the doorjamb, is a wild-eyed Dalton. The sleeves of his crisp white shirt have been pushed up, revealing the tightly corded muscles of his arms, enchanting tattoos snaking their way around his forearms. The top two buttons of his shirt are undone, and his tie is nowhere in sight. His raven-black hair looks freshly fucked and sexy as hell.

We stand frozen, staring at each other for what seems like an eternity. He has a five o'clock shadow, and I can't help biting my bottom lip at the thought of how it would feel between my thighs.

He devours me with his eyes, the rapid rise and fall of his chest making me wet for him as he grips the doorframe so tight his knuckles are white with the strain. Suddenly, I'm acutely aware of my damp, naked body beneath the robe, and the glint in his eyes tells me he is too.

My pulse is racing, my heart hammering so hard I feel like it's about to burst from my chest.

"Hello, Dalton." My voice trembles as I whisper past the lump in my throat.

Without a word, he steps toward me, invading my space, and I'm helpless to resist. He searches my gaze, asking permission. With a shaky breath, my eyes focus on his beautiful lips, wondering if they still taste the same.

He slides his hands into my hair, holding me in place. "Tell me *'no,'* Naddie." Hesitating just long enough to gauge my reaction, he tilts my face before his lips press softly to mine, *devastatingly tender.* I melt into his long, languorous kiss, but all too soon, he pulls back, leaving me bereft. He walks me back a few steps just enough to kick the door shut behind us and hoists me into his arms, the robe parting as I wrap my legs around his waist.

Chapter 6
DALTON

The road to hell is paved with good intentions. Who am I kidding? My motive for showing up at her hotel room door is far from good. Something inside me snapped when I saw Naddie in that conference room today. All propriety and decorum flew out the window, and every rule I've made about mixing business with pleasure disintegrated with the flush of her cheeks under my gaze.

I've dreamed of her so many times over the years, wishing I could return to that moment fifteen years ago and change the outcome—that she and I could've lived the life we always wanted. It took me a long time to realize I wouldn't have done anything differently. She needed to spread her wings, and I loved her enough to know clipping them would only lead to resentment.

I've imagined bumping into her one day, what I would say, whether or not she would be married with kids, or how she would look after so many years. Not even my wildest dreams came close to how I felt when she walked into that room.

Every nerve ending in my body came to life as if it had been dormant since the day she left, and it's all I can do not to growl with the need to touch her, claim her, and memorize every inch of her skin.

Her lips are softer than I remember, but there's nothing gentle about the way my lips now crash down on hers once more, the second the door slams shut behind us. Suddenly, nothing else matters. The deals. The years. The barriers between us. I cup her ass in my hands and hoist her up into my arms, her legs clamping around my waist.

The warmth of her body seeps through my shirt as I walk us over to the bed. My mind is racing, scrambling to take in every detail, and yet there's something so familiar in the way our tongues twist and tangle in a frenzied fuck.

As I lay her down on the bed, her robe falls open, exposing her naked skin and slick sex. *Holy Mother of God.* I can't stop to undress before pulling her legs to the edge of the bed and dropping to my knees. There's no tenderness in my grip as I splay my hand on her stomach, desperate to feel her pussy on my tongue. Holding her in place, I bury my head between her thighs.

Fucking hell. She tastes even better than I remember as my lips close around her clit, her body bucking beneath my ministrations. My cock is already straining against my pants as her soft mewls of pleasure make music to my ears. Fuck, I've missed her.

She reaches down, her hand fisting in my hair as she writhes against my face. Her arousal is sweet like honey, and she's creaming for me as I slide a finger inside her, keeping time with the relentless pace of my tongue.

Her soft moans become loud groans as I thrust three fingers inside her before pulling out and pinning her legs as wide as they'll go. Just enough to feel the bite and unable to control the onslaught of pleasure as I set a punishing rhythm. I'm ravenous for her, desperate to kiss every last inch of her body and memorize her soft, sun-kissed skin. She was always sexy, but her girlish figure has been replaced with the curves of a siren. I'd gladly be dragged to the bottom of the ocean under her spell if it meant being buried inside her.

I want to take my time, but I'm too greedy for her pleasure. Flicking my tongue against her clit, I can feel her body tensing, readying itself for an explosive release. I'm a man possessed as she falls apart beneath me, screaming as her thighs tremble.

"Dalton. Oh my God. *Dalton!*" My name on her lips is like a red rag to a bull. Primal, feral desire takes hold, and I jump to my feet, her arousal still on my tongue as I kick off my shoes and socks, unbutton my shirt, and loosen my belt, pushing my pants and boxers over my hips, letting them fall to the floor.

Her eyes widen as I stand before her, naked and unashamed by what she does to me. What she always has. My cock is so hard it straddles the line between pleasure and pain, something I know all too well.

"Tell me *'no,'* Naddie." My breath is ragged as I pin her with my gaze, waiting for her to send me away, hoping like hell she doesn't, but instead, her legs part as wide as they can go. She doesn't speak, her eyes telling me everything I need to know. My heart is pounding so hard, every cell in my body is overwhelmed with a clawing *need*.

I crawl between her legs before capturing her breast with my mouth, grazing my teeth over her tightly budded nipple, blush pink and beautiful, just as I remember. Positioning my cock at her slick entrance, I raise myself to meet her lips with mine, nibbling on her bottom lip.

"Tell me *'no,'* Naddie." I wait, suspended on the precipice of an all-consuming need to claim her. She fists my hair, pulling me down just enough to taste herself on my lips.

"My answer will always be *'yes'* when it comes to you." Her voice is a breathy whisper, ethereal as she basks in the afterglow of an orgasm. My lips crash down on hers, claiming what once was mine, as I take her in one hard thrust, seating myself to the hilt.

"Fuck. *Naddie!*" Her pussy tightens around my cock, adjusting to the girth of my rock-hard erection. She swallows my plea with an earth-shattering kiss. I can barely breathe, but I'll gladly take my last breath right here and now if it means being with her.

I concentrate on anything but how amazing she feels. If I don't, I'll shoot my load with a handful of thrusts. As her hands roam my back, she circles her hips, awakening a beast inside me.

Our kiss is hard, desperate, and thirsty for more. Kissing my way to her neck, I flick my tongue over the shell of her ear—her sweet spot when she was eighteen—and it still makes her writhe like a wild animal beneath me.

Her nails sink into my back as I begin to thrust in long, hard strokes. I rear up, grabbing her hands and pinning them above her head. "Don't make me punish you, kitten." I feel her muscles tighten at the term of endearment, and her breath becomes ragged as her eyes find their way to where our bodies meet.

"Dalton." My name dies on her lips as I thrust harder. I know what she wants. Tightening my grip on her wrists, I pull out almost to the tip before slamming into her. Again and again. I'm rewarded as her back arches off the bed, her nipples tightly budded as her breasts bounce with every circle of my hips.

The way she writhes, thrashing against my hand, pinning her down, it's too beautiful for words. The sensation has me thrusting harder and faster, struggling to stay in control. She feels too fucking good, and as she climbs toward the edge of another orgasm, I can't resist, desperate to hear her screaming my name.

"That's it, kitten. Come for me."

As she crashes over the edge, I watch in awe as her body responds to my command.

"Oh my God. Dalton. I... *fuck*. Dalton. Yes... yes... God, *yes!*"

She's breathtaking. I let go, my lips descending on hers as I follow her off the cliff, finding release as she rides out the aftershocks of her own. Her hands fist in my hair, holding me to her as I come so fucking hard it hurts.

I continue a slow, steady stroke, and my cock stays hard, unwilling to relinquish how perfectly we fit together. She rains kisses on my lips, the scruff of my jaw, and my neck with a tenderness I haven't allowed in years. Her kiss-swollen lips are warm against my skin in a gentle caress, and she wraps her arms around me, her hips slowly pulling me under.

"Make love to me, Dalton." Her words are my unraveling. The harsh, fierce fuck of only moments ago gives way to lazy kisses and slow, sultry thrusts. We have sex long into the night, never stopping to question what this all means, and when we finally collapse on the bed, a sheen of sweat covering our naked flesh, Naddie looks at me with those big, beautiful emerald eyes.

I pull her back to my chest, wrapping my arms around her, holding onto this moment as long as I can.

"Dalton…"

"Don't say it, kitten. Not tonight." Selfishly, I don't want to talk about what just happened. Not right now. All I want is to hold her close, drink in her scent mixed with sex, and fall asleep with her in my arms.

"Maybe you should go."

What?

My heart stutters. I'm completely blindsided. Ice spreads through my veins at the thought of leaving her, but I'm not going to beg. If she doesn't want me here, there's nothing more to be said.

Reluctantly, I relinquish my hold on her.

Talk about a walk of shame. She can't even look me in the eye. "Dalton… I…"

"Don't." I zip my fly and leave the rest of my clothes. It shouldn't be this hard to walk out the door, but there's a physical pain in my chest.

She enjoyed a good fuck.

End of story.

Now, it's my turn to avoid eye contact.

"Can we talk tomorrow?"

"I have back-to-back meetings."

"Yeah, I know. I'm going to be sitting in on all of them." Fuck.

Raking my hand through my hair, I fight the urge to put my fist through a wall. "Perfect." Without looking back, I head out the door and into the elevator. How did I go from blissful ecstasy to fucking heartbroken in the space of two minutes?

It's a lonely ride up to my suite as I berate myself for thinking with my cock. I should never have gone to her room. I asked her to come and see me. She didn't. That was the giant neon sign telling me to fuck off.

How am I going to be around her as one of my lawyers? I didn't expect her to come spinning into my life like a fucking tornado, and I have no idea how to do this. I'd like to say I got over her once and can do it again, but it would be a lie. I never got over watching Naddie drive out of my life, taking a piece of my soul with her.

~

"I thought you'd be happier today. You became the wealthiest man on the planet yesterday." Douglas claps me on the back like he always does as if I'm still the foolish young man trying to escape the shadow of my father's misconduct. In truth—for the first time in years—I feel as stupid as I did back then.

"I'm just ready to get back to Manhattan." Today has been exhausting. Being around Naddie physically pains me. If it were anyone else—I don't even finish the thought. I wouldn't be in this predicament if Naddie were some random new hotshot lawyer. She'd be off-limits. Hell, she *is* off-limits.

"It seems a waste to come all this way and not take a few moments to celebrate. We're taking you to dinner tonight. Relax, sit back, and revel in your achievements, Dalton. Your accolades would be impressive no matter the circumstances of your beginnings. The fact that you built an empire from the ashes of your father's disgrace makes your accomplishments that much better."

"I appreciate the praise. I think I just need to decompress." I can't tell him I need to get as far away from his newest hire as possible.

"Exactly. We'll go out, drink some perfectly aged whiskey, and eat a ridiculously priced steak." He's not going to take no for an answer.

"Sure. Give me an hour to make some calls, and I'll meet you in the lobby at eight."

"Good man."

I leave him, patting him on the back for convincing me to celebrate, and the second I reach the elevator, I pull out my phone and call Flex.

"Finally! Hey, brother."

"Hey, Flex."

"Why do you sound like someone just took a shit on your face?" I can always count on him to tell me like it is.

"I'm just tired. How's Mom doing?"

"She's lucid. I'm doing my best to make it a good day for her. I tried calling you, but it kept going straight to voicemail." I pull my phone from my ear, only to see that it's set to Do Not Disturb.

"Fuck." My day just got worse. I'm thrilled that my mom is having a good day, but I'm pissed that I'm not there to enjoy it.

After last night, all I want to do is get back to Manhattan and talk to my mom. She was the one who watched me fall apart when Naddie left. Our lives became a dumpster fire, but it brought us closer than ever as we picked up the pieces and forged a new path for ourselves.

"I'm sorry, bro. I wasn't trying to make you feel bad. I just thought you'd want to know."

"Can you put her on the phone?"

"Sure. Hold on." There's a rustling on the line that lasts an eternity before the sweetest voice I've ever heard makes my eyes well with tears.

"Hi, sweet boy. Where are you, Dally?" Her nickname for me always irked me as a kid. Lately, I've been longing to hear it on her lips.

"Hey, Momma. I'm in Italy right now, but I'm coming home tomorrow."

"Such a jetsetter. Felix explained that you brought me to live next to you."

"I wanted you in my apartment, but you fought me every step of the way." I chuckle.

"You own the building. Technically, I *do* live with you."

"You're feisty as ever. Are you having a nice day with Flex?" Knowing she'll likely be back in the clutches of the dementia by the time I get home sends a pang of agonizing torment straight to my heart.

"Yes, Dally. Don't worry about me."

"No can do. I always worry about you. I shouldn't have come here." *For more reasons than one.*

"Don't you be doing that to yourself, sweetheart. I can see from the love and support around me that you're doing everything possible to help me, and I want you to know how much I appreciate it. Felix told me that my Parkinson's has progressed with dementia. I'm so sorry, Dally, for all the days I don't recognize you and forgetting what an amazing, beautiful son you are." There's a momentary pause, neither of us able to put into words what we have gone through together.

"I'd do anything for you. I love you, Momma."

"I love you too, Dally." My cheeks become wet as emotion trickles over. I don't know *when* or *if* I'll ever hear her speak those words again. "When will you be home?"

"Tomorrow. I'll see you tomorrow night." I wipe the tears from my eyes, berating myself for being such a pussy, and silently praying she'll still know me when I get back.

"Okay, sweetheart. I'll try to hold onto my marbles till then. Bye, Dally." She's always been one to make jokes during difficult moments. She and I both know today is a random gift, and I'm missing it.

Flex comes back on the phone, the silence between us saying more than words could express, and yet I don't hang up. Finally, I force myself to speak.

"Flex…" It's all I can manage.

"I know, brother. I'll take good care of her and fill her in on everything."

"Thank you. Tell her I love her. Until she falls asleep and today becomes a beautiful footnote in an otherwise brutal disease, let her know I care."

"She knows how much you love her."

"I hope so. I'll call you tomorrow."

"Okay, bro. Goodnight."

When I reach my suite, it's cold and lonely as I toss my wallet on the counter. The silence is deafening. I quickly dial Douglas and push our plans back an hour. Dinner and conversation are the last things I want to do, and I need a little extra time to sit and wallow in the silence, emotionally spent.

From talking with Mom.

From making love to Naddie.

After what happened last night, seeing her today was torture.

I can't open myself up to heartbreak when it comes to Naddie. Forcing myself out of her room last night felt as awful as watching her drive off the day she left for college. She's the one woman I never got over.

I shower, shave, and reach for a crisp black shirt, rolling the sleeves up to my elbows, staring *through* the mirror, hollow as I prepare for a night of fake smiles and meaningless conversation. When I'm ready, I grab my wallet, slide it in my back pocket, and head for the elevator.

The second I switched my phone from Do Not Disturb, it's been blowing up with congratulations from various business colleagues, so I shove everything else on the back burner. I can't do anything about the situation with my mom tonight and speaking to Naddie can wait until I return to Manhattan.

As the elevator descends, it grinds to a halt on the fifteenth floor, and my heart sinks. When I got out on this level last night, all I could think about was Naddie. I needed to see her, touch her, and to understand how she came crashing into my world. I didn't even get a chance to find out.

As the doors open, my heart lunges into my chest. Why didn't it cross my mind that Douglas would invite her to dinner? The second our eyes meet, she gasps, and it's all I can do not to swallow it with an unforgiving kiss.

Naddie looks stunning in a black pencil-line dress, hugging her figure and accentuating all the right places. Her luxurious chestnut hair cascades down her back in soft waves, and the scent of her perfume is a cruel tease to my senses. I quickly avert my gaze, moving to stand as far away as I can get in such a small space. The air is thick with tension as the doors close, leaving us in uncomfortable silence. With my eyes fixed on the floor, I attempt to control my racing pulse.

"Can we talk? After dinner, maybe?" Her voice is small and unsure, melting my heart, but I force myself not to meet her stare.

"I can't." Not tonight.

"Oh."

Chapter 7

NADDIE

Dalton looks devastatingly handsome tonight, but the moment he says no, it's like an avalanche, freezing me where I stand, consuming me. I want to explain myself and tell him why I asked him to leave my bed after the best sex of my life.

Being with Dalton again only served to confirm that, to this day, he still owns my body in ways no other man ever has, not even my long-term Dom. Just the memory of his head between my thighs has me weak in the knees.

"Please, Dalton. Can we talk? I can't stand the thought of you hating me."

"Not the time. Not the place," he says as the doors open to the lobby. Douglas and his pain-in-the-ass son are sitting at the bar with the rest of the team, nursing some ridiculously priced scotch that I'm sure will be billed to Dalton.

Dalton waits for me to step out, my heels clacking on the grand marble-floored foyer. He's always a gentleman, even when he's wounded by my actions. With my boss's eyes on us, I struggle to hide the war going on inside me.

If I were alone with him, I'd drop to my knees like a good submissive and ask him to hear me out. I won't beg—or maybe I would—but a man like him would understand the show of respect. There can't be a world where he hasn't grown into a strong Dominant. It emanates from every chiseled, taut muscle in his body. It would be a travesty if he hadn't found his way into the lifestyle.

I hang back a little, watching as Dalton steps toward Douglas with a confident gait, looking mouthwateringly hot. "Douglas," he says as he shakes his proffered hand. "What are we drinking?" He looks at Robert's glass.

"Whiskey neat. Single malt, twenty-five-year Glenlivet."

"That's quite the drink." Dalton nods to the bartender, ordering another round with a drink for himself before turning to me. "What would you like, Ms. Sullivan?"

My name is like velvet on his lips, even though his tone is cold with zero acknowledgment that we've known each other forever. "Prosecco, please."

Douglas pulls up a seat for me while Robert rolls his eyes at my mere existence. My stomach is in knots as I fight to remain composed, my head spinning with everything I want to say but can't.

I feel like everyone is watching me, but that's ridiculous. It's the same nerves that plagued my stomach the night after I lost my virginity to Dalton all those years ago. The school hallways grew smaller in my mind, everyone judging me for the scarlet letter that I was sure had been emblazoned on my forehead.

When my drink arrives, I want to down it like a shot, hoping for some Dutch courage. It takes everything I have to paint a smile on my face and sip the prosecco as Douglas and Robert talk Dalton's ear off. They are congratulating themselves on helping broker this deal. In all honesty, Dalton is the one who deserves to boast, but he sits quietly, tracing his finger around the top of his crystal glass.

I watch, enraptured, as he lifts it to his perfect lips, his tongue darting out as he lets the dark, single malt slide down his throat. My heart skips a beat as his eyes find mine, but I can't hold his gaze, too worried that someone will notice the tension between us.

"Let's get out of here. I made a reservation at a Michelin-star restaurant in the heart of the city." Of course, he did. Robert knows tonight's tab won't be on him, so why not book the most expensive place he could find?

Dalton reaches into his wallet and slips the bartender a generous tip as he tells him to bill the drinks to his suite. The Mason men don't even attempt to protest as they rally the rest of the team. Maybe the rules are different when dealing with a billionaire. My family is well-off, but Dalton is in a league of his own.

We head for the door, everyone taking stock of the handsome man striding confidently across the lobby. You don't need to know him to react. He commands every space he inhabits. There's a black town car waiting when we step out into the crisp night air and an Escalade behind it.

Douglas and Robert clamber into the town car, and I gravitate to the SUV with the others, but Dalton points to the door.

"You're riding with us, Ms. Sullivan."

My breath catches. "That's not necessary."

"Get in the car." It's not a request, and as much of a bratty submissive as I am, I can't walk away from his commanding brogue.

His hand brushes the small of my back as he guides me in, and I can't think when he touches me. I want to run to put space between us, and at the same time, I want him to touch me forever.

Without a word, he slides in at my side, his leg brushing against mine. Heat spreads through my body, my cheeks flushing as I squirm in the seat. There's no escape as the door closes, and the scent of his cologne has me held captive. All I can do is keep my eyes down and hope my boss doesn't notice how uncomfortable I am.

"So, Ms. Sullivan, what brought you to Manhattan?" Why is he talking to me? We didn't even speak last night. It was all sex and carnal, animalistic need.

I clear my throat before forcing myself to look at him. "I studied at Harvard Law and worked in Boston after passing the bar exam. A few months back, Mr. Mason approached me with a job offer I couldn't refuse."

"Douglas tells me you just sat the New York bar exam. How did that go?"

"Well, I think. I won't know for a few weeks."

"I have no doubt she passed with flying colors. I did my research, Dalton. Don't worry. She'll be an asset to your team," Douglas chimes in, taking the spotlight off me, for which I'm grateful.

Robert's cold stare sends a shiver through me. He doesn't want me here, and if I'm honest, I don't want to be here either.

"I'm sure she will."

We ride the rest of the way, exchanging surface-level pleasantries, and I let the men talk while I compose myself. That sounds so antiquated, but I'm in survival mode right now. When we arrive at the restaurant, Dalton steps out of the car before extending his hand to steady me as I try to exit gracefully. If anything, his hand clasped around mine makes me more unsteady on my feet.

"Thank you," I whisper as I smooth my dress. He doesn't reply but ushers me to the entrance, knowing what it's always done to me when his fingertips brush the small of my back.

The restaurant doesn't disappoint. It's stunning, every detail the epitome of opulence. The manager comes to greet Dalton, showing us to the best table in the house.

"I'll have your waiter come and take your order. Can I start you off with some drinks?"

Dalton doesn't hesitate. "Prosecco for the lady, three of your best single malt..." he says, gesturing between himself and the Masons, "... and whatever the others want."

"Very good. I'll be back in a moment."

Dalton pulls out my chair, waiting to sit until I'm seated. Taking the seat across from me, he pins me with his steel-blue gaze.

"Harvard Law? How was that?" He leans back in his chair, crossing his arms over his chest, the tightly corded muscles of his forearms teasing me. My mind floods with the way they looked as they spread my legs, opening me to his ministrations last night. "Ms. Sullivan?"

I must've lost myself for a moment. "Yes?"

"Harvard. How was it?" There is so much more behind his words, but as my boss waits expectantly, I focus on Dalton.

"It was hard. I wasn't prepared for how difficult it would be."

"You expected law school to be easy?" Robert interjects.

Dalton doesn't flinch, his jaw ticking as he keeps his eyes on me. "I didn't ask you, Junior. I was talking to Ms. Sullivan."

I'm relieved when the waiter arrives with drinks and takes our food orders. Anything to divert Dalton's attention from me, but I should know better.

The second we're left to enjoy our drinks, he finds my gaze.

"You were saying… Harvard."

"Law school had its ups and downs. My problems weren't academic. I graduated top of my class, but I learned the hard way that everything comes at a cost. Leaving my life behind was… heartbreaking."

His breath catches, and I know I have to fix this. Douglas and Robert sport the same furrowed brow, clearly perplexed by my candor.

"Heartbreaking? You don't seem the type."

"And what type is that?" I say, with dread in my voice.

"Driven. Your career revolves around being cutthroat."

"Does your job dictate your actions outside a conference room, Mr. Callaghan? That would make you power-hungry, would it not?" Our food arrives before I can say anything else. I've already gone way past unprofessional. After a few awkward moments, Douglas takes over the conversation, leaving me to fidget under Dalton's heated gaze.

"The moment Nadia gets word that she's passed the bar exam, she'll be a point of contact for your account. She's shadowing me right now, and Robert will make sure she knows how you like everything done." I push my food around the plate while they talk business. The next deal. The next contract. "We'll ensure she's versed on your personal contracts. You know the firm has always maintained your privacy."

Personal contracts?

"No." Dalton's voice is ice cold as he drains his drink. "I don't want her taking over those contracts. Robert can deal with those."

"I assure you…"

Dalton doesn't let him finish the sentence. "No. It's not up for discussion." His jaw tightens, anger rolling off him in waves. "I'm sure you're an amazing lawyer, Ms. Sullivan, but some things are too delicate for me to entrust to someone I don't know." His words cut like a knife. He plans to pretend we've never met.

I'm thankful when Robert steps in. "I can definitely do that for you, Mr. Callaghan. Nadia will work with us on your business dealings, and I'll handle your personal contracts."

"Great."

The drinks flow faster as the night wears on. Every few minutes, Dalton runs his hand through his short black curls—a tick he's had since he was a kid. Whenever he got annoyed, he'd mess with his hair until it had that freshly-fucked style I love. *Loved.*

When we're ready to leave the restaurant, I excuse myself and go to the restroom, needing a few moments to regroup. Dalton doesn't want me anywhere near his personal affairs. I was right to send him away last night, but it doesn't make it any easier.

Tears well in my eyes, but I try to blink them back. This is my career. Falling apart over a man I can't have won't help matters.

Staring at myself in the ornate, gilded mirror, I gawp in disbelief. How did I end up here? The promise of a successful career is what I held onto when I left for college. I told myself it would be worth it one day, leaving Dalton behind. Over the years, I had moments when I questioned my decision. I let myself wallow in the 'what-ifs' of our relationship from time to time, but I always forced it to the back of my mind. Now, I'm here with everything I want for my career, and somehow, the universe brought me full circle.

It's a sick joke. If I'd stayed in Boston, I would've made partner in a few years. Instead, I'll be a partner because Douglas wants me to work on Dalton's account as he reaches the end of his career. Everything I sacrificed to be here is a house of cards that could collapse at any moment.

When I've freshened my makeup and composed myself, I take a deep breath before swinging the bathroom door open. I'm met with a wall of heat and a hard chest. "Heartbreaking?" His hands brace me on either side, pinning me against the plush wallpaper that lines the hallway. The scent of his cologne is an assault on my senses, intoxicating me.

"You want to talk now?"

"You're fucking with me. You told me to leave last night, and then you sit there, acting like you don't know me, and say it was heartbreaking back then. We're not those people anymore."

"I know." I can't even look at him, turning my face to the side.

"Why are you here?"

"It's my job."

"Look at me, Naddie."

"I can't." My heart aches in my chest at his proximity.

"Why? Tell me, Naddie. Do you regret last night?"

I should lie. It would be kinder to both of us in the long run, but I *can't* lie when it comes to him. "No. I don't regret it."

Tears spill from my eyes, overcome with emotion. His chest's rapid rise and fall keep time with my own as he leans in, pressing his lips to my cheek in a soft caress. "Don't cry, kitten. I can't bear it."

Without another word, he releases me and turns on his heel, leaving me breathless. As I watch him walk away, it feels like wild horses have trampled my heart. There's so much I want to say, and yet I don't know the words to convey how I still yearn for him after all these years.

Dropping my head against the wall, I fight back further tears. How can I go back out there as if everything is great? Dalton always saw straight through me, and I worry my new boss will sense my reticence.

The car ride back to the hotel pains me with every breath in his proximity, and by the time we enter the lobby, I want to cry. Some of the team head straight for the bar, inviting me to come along, but I'm exhausted. The elevator feels claustrophobic as the rest of us stand in silence. Thankfully, Douglas and Robert have rooms on the level above mine, letting me escape another soul-crushing moment alone with Dalton.

"Goodnight. Thank you for dinner… Mr. Callaghan." He gasps as I step out, unable to look back. If I do, I know I'll see the epitome of a Dom who's not mine to love.

The second I'm behind closed doors in the safety of my room, I fall to pieces, my heart shattered as the gravity of this situation overwhelms me. I sob until there are no tears left to cry, crushed that my new life in Manhattan will be the worst kind of torture.

Could I even have a relationship with Dalton if he weren't my client? I'm a submissive. And as much as he screams Dominant, I have no idea if he is one or if he'd be disgusted by my life choices. That would be a fate worse than death. I let that sink in, pulling me under until I can't catch my breath.

When I manage to stop dry heaving, I fumble for my phone, pulling up Jenna's number.

"Hey, beautiful. You get that it's the crack of ass here, right?" Just when I thought I had nothing left, her voice has me bursting into tears again.

"I made a mistake, Jenna. I can't stay here," I manage between sobs. "I have to come back to Boston."

"Hold up. Slow down, Nad. What's wrong? Are you okay?"

"No. *The T-shirt.* I can't. I have to leave."

"I have no idea what you're talking about. Has someone hurt you?"

"He's here."

"Who? Aren't you still in Milan?"

"Dalton."

"Who's Dalton?"

"My high school sweetheart."

"*What?*" Her tone echoes my disbelief.

"I was brought to New York to take over their biggest client's account. It's him. The one who got away. *My Dalton.*"

"Okay. Take a few deep breaths and tell me everything."

I pour my heart out, starting at the beginning and tell her things I've never told anyone before. I tell her *almost* everything, including what has happened here the past few days. Jenna is always so positive about any situation and doesn't disappoint, comforting me as I sob.

"Why did you ask him to leave? If you had amazing, mindblowing sex, I don't understand what the problem is."

"Most likely, he has a girlfriend or wife to go home to. It took everything I had to leave him when I was eighteen. Jenna, all those feelings just came flooding back, and it scared the crap out of me. I can't do that again."

"But you're not eighteen, Nad. You're an accomplished woman. You live in Manhattan. He lives in Manhattan. What if this is your second chance?"

"It's not. I've already broken the rules of a lawyer/client relationship."

"Okay, so you can't be a couple. You're not going to get in trouble for one night with your high school sweetheart. No one has to know." I feel sick to my stomach as I contemplate what my life looks like from this point on.

"I don't know how I'm supposed to do this, Jenna. He's never going to be just another client. But I can't decline him as a client. They made me partner specifically to take on Dalton's account. If I walk away, my career is over."

My best friend goes silent—not something I'm used to with her. "I have to ask. How did you *not* know it was him?"

"He changed his last name. There are no pictures of him online. He keeps his life very private."

"How? No one has a zero footprint when it comes to social media."

"He probably employs people to keep him out of the spotlight. Only those who run in the same circles know who he is and how powerful that makes him."

"Hold the phone. What is he? Mafia or something?"

"Nothing like that. He's a good man. He is extremely successful and very wealthy."

"Jesus, Nad. If he can evade the media, I'm sure you could see each other under the radar."

"I can't do that. If that ever came out, I'd be disbarred, and what kind of relationship could we have for the long-term? It would never be just sex with him. I don't want hushed corners and stolen moments. With him… I'd want it all."

"Then you need to talk to him, sooner rather than later."

"Ugh. I know you're right, but he doesn't want to talk to me right now. I hurt him last night. I hurt myself. My stomach feels like rats are gnawing on my soon-to-be lifeless carcass."

"I'm so sorry, Nad. I can't imagine what you must be feeling."

"Like my teams lost the Super Bowl, the World Series, and the World Cup all in one day."

"You need to get some rest. Call me when you get back home, and we'll talk some more. We'll figure it out, Nad. I love you."

"I love you too. Thanks for talking me off the ledge."

"That's what friends are for."

"Night, Jenna."

"Night, Nad."

Would Jenna be so quick to encourage a second-chance love story if she knew the truth about my sexual preferences? There's a reason I've never told her because, deep down inside, a part of me has always felt uneasy. Not because being a submissive is wrong in any way. It's not *what* I chose to do, it's *why*. And that's what terrifies me to my core, especially now that Dalton is back in my life. He's the reason I became a submissive. I've been searching for a relationship that could rival what we had all those years ago. He's been the driving force in my life, even in the years we've been apart.

Chapter 8

DALTON

"Please take your seats and make yourself comfortable." My flight attendant is pleasant as ever while everyone files on board.

The past two days have been excruciating—Naddie avoiding me as much as possible, and it may have clouded my vision to the stupidity of the current situation.

I called Douglas last night and insisted on flying the whole team back to New York on my private plane. He didn't hesitate to take me up on the offer or question my 'generosity.' Playing it off as a thank you for all their hard work on the deal was easy. With a guy like him, all you have to do is massage his ego a little, and he'll acquiesce to whatever you want, as long as you're blowing smoke up his ass.

In the cold light of day, I fear it was a bad idea. The cabin seems to shrink as Naddie steps onboard, stealing the air from my lungs as her eyes find mine. What was I thinking?

Being in the same hotel and *not* being with her was the worst form of torture, every cell in my body aching to go to her room once more and fuck her until she couldn't remember her name. I barely slept last night, tossing and turning, wondering how I approach this when we arrive back in New York.

There are twenty seats in the cabin—large leather recliners. The team chatters as they find their seats and settle in for the long flight. Naddie, on the other hand, finds the farthest seat from where I stand making small talk with Robert.

I know I should sit my ass down and let her be, but I'm already making my excuses, leaving Robert to sit next to his father. Striding to the back of the cabin, I watch as Naddie buckles herself in before taking the seat across from her, happy that there's some distance between us and the rest of the team. She's unwittingly giving us the privacy I've been craving for days.

Without a word, I click my belt into place, close my eyes, and take a steadying breath. The air is tense as the flight attendant asks everyone to fasten for takeoff, and we begin taxiing to the runway.

When I open my eyes, I brace myself for Naddie's vitriolic stare, but I'm met with a glassy-eyed, blank gaze. She looks pale.

"Are you okay, Nad… Ms. Sullivan? Are you feeling all right?" I reach out to take her hand in mine, to offer her some reassurance—comfort—whatever she needs.

"I'm not fond of flying. I'll be fine after takeoff." She attempts to pull away, but I hold firm, brushing my thumb over the back of her hand.

"Close your eyes."

She looks to where our skin touches. To where electricity courses through and between us. "Someone could see."

"I don't give a shit. You're not okay. Besides, you made sure to isolate yourself from everyone else, so we're fine."

She grips the armrest with her free hand as we pick up the pace, hurtling toward the sky.

"Take a deep breath, Naddie. You're going to pass out if you keep holding your breath."

Squeezing her eyes shut, she sucks in a lungful of air, blowing it out like she's in labor. Her fingers dig into my hand as the wheels leave the runway, and we soar into the sky.

"Shit," she mutters under her breath. "I hate this part."

"You're safe. I've got you," I whisper for only her to hear. I continue to caress the back of her hand in soothing circles. "I'm here with you, Naddie. Nothing bad is going to happen. I promise."

"Don't make promises you can't keep." The words sting as they leave her flawless lips.

The second the seat belt sign goes off, she quickly unbuckles and makes a beeline for the bathroom.

I fight the urge to check on her for as long as I can, but when she's not back within a few minutes, I'm out of my seat, knocking on the door.

"Are you okay?" Before she can answer, I hear her wretch.

"Go away."

"Open the door." It's a command, not a request.

"Please… I'm begging you… leave me alone. I'm fine. I'll be out in a few minutes."

"Open. The. Door."

"I'm fine. Don't make a scene."

"If you're not out here in five minutes, I'm coming in, locked door or not." I don't care if Douglas and everyone else on this plane has something to say about it. Knowing that she's hurting and having a door between us is more than I can handle.

Forcing myself to sit back down, I hold my breath until I hear the lock's click and the door slides open. Naddie still looks pale when she returns to her seat.

I quickly signal the flight attendant to bring her some crackers and a glass of water.

"Are you okay?" I want to pull her into my lap and wrap my arms around her, but I fight it, seeing the despair in her eyes.

"Does it matter?" she whispers under her breath, her expression defeated.

"Of course it does."

"Why? This can't happen." She motions between us. "Can we just get through this flight without me losing my job?"

I scrub my hand over the scruff of my jaw. "You were just throwing up in the bathroom, and you look white as a sheet. If you don't watch your tone, I'll pull you into my lap, and I don't care who sees it." Color instantly flushes her cheeks, making my cock twitch as she looks anywhere but at me.

"You can't say stuff like that." Oh, *kitten*, let the games begin.

"I can, and I will." I bend forward, putting my lips to her ear. "I gave you the chance to say 'no,' Naddie. I believe you answered by spreading your legs for me, and it was… fucking glorious."

"My boss is just over there," she pants. "Please, I'm begging you."

"I would *never* let you get fired," I say with consternation as I sit back, even though it pains me.

"You're not my boss. Mr. Mason decides my fate."

"Naddie…" She cuts me off, and I swear to God I'm about to put her over my knee.

"If we're going to converse during this flight, can we talk about something else? Tell me about your empire. As one of your lawyers, I need more information than just the paperwork I've read."

"Do you? I'm just like any other client. You read and write my contracts, and everything runs smoothly. No need for personal details." The flight attendant arrives with the items I requested. "Drink. And eat. You need something in your stomach."

"I see you haven't gotten any less bossy over the years." She fights the smile twitching at the corners of her lips.

"You don't know the half of it." And God, I want to show her.

"So, tell me how you got here." She gestures to the luxury surrounding us.

"I became the man of the house at eighteen, as you know. It's a great motivator when the bank forecloses on your entire life. I did what I had to do, and it turns out I'm really good at it."

I watch as her gaze softens, pity in her eyes. "I should've stayed. I'm so sorry."

"Why? Then you would've been punished for my father's mistakes too. I don't need your pity, Naddie. I'm doing pretty well for myself."

"You think leaving you didn't feel like a punishment?" Her admission catches me off guard.

"I would have hated myself for stealing your dream, and you'd have resented me for it. Maybe not right away, but it would always be there."

"You handed me one dream and destroyed another." Her words are a bullet through my heart.

"Naddie…" My hands ball into fists, my jaw tightening as I fight to stay in my seat. It never once crossed my mind that I was depriving her of a dream, so focused on myself and the dream *I* lost that day. In my eyes, Harvard was more important than me. I knew how much she wanted it.

Her eyes flit to where Douglas sits, his eyes closed as the liquor takes effect. "Don't. We've said enough."

"This isn't over."

"It never began." She cuts me to the quick.

"Lie to yourself all you want, Naddie. Your body told me everything I needed to know as it fell apart beneath my touch." Her breath hitches as her eyes find mine. "You should rest. We'll talk when we get back to Manhattan."

"There's nothing to talk about."

"It wasn't a request."

The flight home was torture, watching Naddie sleep as I replayed our conversation repeatedly in my mind. If it were any other woman, I'd take her at her word and walk away, but I *know* her. It wasn't bullshit and bravado when I said her body can't lie. Being inside her felt like coming home for the first time in fifteen years. We fit together as if handcrafted, intended only for one another.

I've made plenty of women scream, but Naddie is different. Her body *purrs* for me, and the memory makes me hard as steel every time I think about it. We got back from Milan a week ago, and it's taken every shred of self-control to give her some space. All of this came out of nowhere. Few things have truly blindsided me in my life —my embezzling father, my mom's diagnosis, and seeing Naddie walk into that conference room.

I'd have been less surprised if lightning struck me where I sat. Every cell in my body reacted to her, and I knew then and there that

I wanted to make her mine. She's always *been* mine. I gave her my heart in the sandbox, and she's held it ever since.

A taste of Naddie wasn't enough for me, yet I know I should walk away. The past fifteen years of missing and longing for her will be for nothing if I continue down this road. It shredded me when she admitted I gave in one hand and took away with the other. At eighteen, I did what I thought was best. I wanted her to have the life she'd been dreaming of—that *we'd* been dreaming of—since elementary school.

Losing the opportunity to go to Harvard with her was worse than anything my dad did. I focused every fiber of my being on creating a life for my mom and me and pushed my feelings for Naddie so deep that I convinced myself I was glorifying the memory of what we were, playing it off as young love.

It wasn't until I laid eyes on her in the conference room that my carefully constructed world came crashing down around me. When we first got back, for a split second, I felt like I was floundering, questioning the path forward for us. It didn't take me long to realize there is only one option. I'm going to make Naddie mine. I refuse to let history repeat itself.

I have a meeting with the team today. I could discuss these matters with Douglas or Robert, but I insisted on everyone's attendance at my offices. I'm not opposed to forced proximity at this point. It seems to be the only way I'll cross paths with Naddie. I reached out a few days ago, but she has yet to respond. I'd be offended if it were anyone else, but she *knows* that being around me will cloud her judgment. We both know it. We've always had that effect on each other.

I watch the hands on my watch tick as I await her arrival.

"Do you have somewhere better to be today, Mr. Callaghan?" Audrey interjects.

"What? When are the lawyers arriving?"

"Nine. The conference room is set up. I had breakfast catered as requested. Everything is ready and waiting." She scrolls her finger on the iPad that details my every waking hour. "Now, about the rest of your day…"

"Cancel it. I told you that yesterday." My words come out more clipped than I intended.

"I already did. I just want to go over the rescheduling."

Tension vibrates through my hands as I fidget with a paperclip, bending and twisting until it snaps.

"Are you okay? You seem… out of sorts."

"I'm fine. I just need a break from all of this. Is there a space in my schedule any time soon? Even a long weekend will do." If I have my way, I'll take a few days, whisk Naddie away somewhere private, and kiss every inch of her body for four days straight, longer if she can spare the time.

"I'll see what I can move around. You're pretty booked for the next few months."

"Thanks, Audrey." She talks me through the imminent changes to my schedule before leaving me to watch the clock again. I cleared the rest of my day with the intention of talking things out with Naddie.

When nine o'clock rolls around, the intercom buzzes. "Everyone is situated and ready for you."

"Thanks, Audrey." As I make my way to the conference room, a persistent churning in my stomach leaves me unsettled and nervous. *I'm fucking nervous.* The last time I felt any kind of nervousness was the day I signed my first million-dollar contract.

I steel myself as I wrap my hand around the sleek metal doorhandle, the familiar click spiking my adrenaline as I step inside, my gaze homing in on her immediately.

The morning sunlight makes her hair shine as it frames her delicate features, her eyes fixed on the legal pad she's scribbling on.

"Good morning, everyone. I hope you've all adjusted back to New York time after last week."

In unison, they kiss my ass. "Good morning, Mr. Callaghan." All except Naddie. She can't even look at me. I bristle at her reluctance, taking my seat at the head of the table. She looks fucking stunning today, a figure-hugging navy dress accentuating the delectable curve of her breasts. Jesus, if I don't stop staring, I'm going to be hard as a rock. She's every inch the powerhouse lawyer I now know her to be.

I had Audrey pull up everything she could find on our newest team member's career—all in the name of being a shrewd business-man. I need to know who's going to be working for me. Total bull-shit, but reading her achievements and reputation in Boston had me full-to-bursting with pride. Without knowing who she is, I would hire her on the spot with her accolades. I have to hand it to Douglas —he did his homework.

"Audrey has prepared a packet for each of you with prospective projects I want to look into over the next few months. If you'll turn to page twenty, there's a list of companies. I need everything you can put together on them."

We spend the next three hours poring over every page, discussing who will take on each project, everyone chiming in at points. But not Naddie, and it pisses me off. She's a shadow of the fierce lawyer I read about.

"And what of you, Ms. Sullivan? You're the newest addition to the team. Is there nothing that grabs your attention?" I'm a dick for saying it and letting every drop of innuendo hang between us. All eyes are on her.

"On the contrary. I am simply letting my esteemed colleagues work to their strengths. They know your business much better than I do. I am happy to work on any of these projects. You have a very diverse portfolio, Mr. Callaghan." My cock twitches at the way she addresses me. It's hot as fuck.

"Wise decision." I turn my attention to Douglas. "If you can spare her, I want to give Ms. Sullivan a tour of my little empire when we're done here. She needs to acquaint herself with the way I run things and what I expect as she becomes more involved in my affairs."

"Of course. That's a great idea, Dalton."

"Thank you, Mr. Callaghan. Only if you have the time… I'm sure you're busy." Her eyes find mine, all fire and brimstone. God, she's beautiful.

"Not at all. It's important that you know my business dealings… inside and out."

She chews on her bottom lip, and all I want to do is dismiss everyone else and take her here on the conference table.

It's a testament to my control that we make it to the end of the meeting, and as everyone files out of the room, I shake Douglas's hand and promise to stop by for a drink sometime soon.

When there's no one left but us, Naddie shuffles the papers in front of her, taking her time to file them away in her briefcase, keeping as much distance between us as possible. I close the door before stalking toward her, perching on the edge of the conference table at her side.

"Hello, Naddie."

"Hello, Mr. Callaghan." She refuses to meet my gaze.

"You know, if you're trying to put me off, calling me that is the wrong way to go. It's most definitely a turn-on." Her eyes snap to mine, and my shallow breaths betray my cool, calm exterior.

"Shall we begin the tour?"

"Not before you tell me why you neglected to respond to me this week."

"I can't do this with you."

"Why?"

"Because it's too hard." Her eyes swim with a deep sadness that leaves me desperate to reach out and touch her. Soothe her.

"It doesn't have to be. All I wanted was a conversation."

"And you and I know that conversation would've ended in your bed... or mine."

"Not necessarily. We could have sex anywhere, Naddie. I don't need a bed to have you screaming my name." She shifts in her chair, squirming at the thought of it.

"This is exactly why I didn't come to speak with you."

"Because you're afraid I'll splay you on this table, peel off that... glorious dress... and bury my head between your legs?"

"Yes." Her voice is nothing more than a whisper as she looks up at me through hooded lashes.

"Would that be so bad?"

"No. It would be earth-shattering. And I'd want to do it again and again." Her eyes flit to the growing erection straining against my thigh.

"You're all I've thought about since we got back. What it felt like to be inside you, kissing you, and remembering what you sounded like as you came on my tongue. I want you, Naddie. More than my next fucking breath." My admission hangs between us, the silence deafening as I await her reply.

She takes a deep, shuddering breath as she looks me dead in the eye. "I got over you, Dalton. What happened in Milan was lovely."

"*Lovely?*"

"But it was chemistry from another lifetime. We went our separate ways. You have your life, and I have mine. You must have a wife or girlfriend. A man as successful as you."

Anger has me clenching the table's edge until my knuckles turn white. "That's what you think of me? That I'd fuck you if I had a woman waiting at home?"

"No. I don't know. We were kids the last time we saw each other."

"I didn't have a fucking lobotomy in that time, Naddie. I would *never* cheat. Should I assume you have a boyfriend here in Manhattan? Or a husband?" *Please say no.* I couldn't bear any other answer.

"No. I don't have a significant other, but that doesn't mean you and I are going to pick up where we left off. I don't feel that way." She breaks my gaze, her eyes cast to the floor.

I reach down, lifting her chin to face me. "I don't believe you."

Her breathing is ragged as I lean in, my lips an inch from hers. "Look me in the eye and tell me you don't feel this." My heart is hammering in my chest, my pulse racing at the scent of her perfume and the way she licks her lips, a whisker away from my own.

"We're not right for each other. I'm a different person now. I want things you can't give me." Her words hold no meaning. I could always tell when she was lying. She makes no move to put any distance between us, her eyes falling to my mouth.

"Say it like you mean it… *kitten.*" Her lips press to mine in a fierce kiss, her tongue darting out to meet mine. I fist my hands in her hair, holding her in place as I reciprocate, ravaging her mouth, fireworks exploding my senses as desire spreads through me.

When she pulls back, pushing her chair out, I'm left bereft. "I'm sorry. I shouldn't have done that," she says, grabbing her briefcase.

"Don't apologize. And don't tell me you don't feel anything. Talk to me, Naddie."

"That was a goodbye kiss. Our relationship needs to be professional from here on out."

"One hell of a goodbye kiss. I'm intrigued to know how you'd kiss me if you craved my touch."

"Please, don't contact me unless it's work-related."

"You kissed *me* just now."

"I have to go. I'm so sorry." She rushes for the door.

"Stop. Do *not* walk out on me, Nadia." She stills at my command. *Fuck.* She's such a good girl—the things I could do to her. "Talk to me, Naddie. I don't understand. You being my lawyer doesn't mean we can't be together."

"That's exactly what it means. If you ever loved me, please don't do this." I can see how pained she looks, but I can't hold back.

"*Do what?* Want you? Fucking *love* you?"

"Yes."

And just like that, all the fight in me dies.

She doesn't move, still frozen to the spot where I told her to stop. We stand in silence for long minutes until her words cut me to the quick. "May I leave, Mr. Callaghan?"

"You are free to go, Naddie. I won't force you to want me, and I can't make you love me."

Without another word, she makes her way to the door, glancing back for a second. Long enough for me to see the tears welling in her eyes as she disappears out the door.

Chapter 9

NADDIE

After weeks of tense meetings and no further conversation between Dalton and me, it's clear he's choosing to respect my wishes. I know it's for the best, but I crave him every second we share the same airspace. And every moment we're apart.

I've been going over it in my head since day I told him I don't feel anything for him now. Did he see right through the lie? I intended to be convincing, but a part of me needs him to know I didn't mean it—the selfish side of me.

I thought of coming clean after our last meeting two days ago, but I couldn't risk telling him the truth about me and what I need in a relationship. The fact I could lose everything I've worked for if I pursue him is only part of the reason I pushed him away. All of my fears about telling anyone I'm a submissive only magnify when it comes to Dalton. Yes, he'd be a perfect Dom, but what if he never indulged in that side of his personality? It would kill me to see him look at me differently, and I'm not sure I would survive it.

I've spent the past two weeks coming home from work and crawling under the covers in his T-shirt, stewing over every word spoken between us. But tonight, I'm forcing myself to live with my decision. I told him to leave me alone, and he has.

So, I made myself get dressed up tonight and took a cab to this address, but I think I'm in the wrong place. The light marble floors and bright modern décor don't scream BDSM club.

Electricity courses through my veins as I reach for the business card in my pocket and hand it over to the intimidating guard in the lobby. Not the good kind of nerves.

"I'm not sure if I'm in the right place," I say as he inspects me.

"What's your name?"

"Nadia."

He looks me over, his ruggedly handsome face marred by the tight-knit of his brow. "Are you on the guest list?"

"No. A friend from a club in Boston gave me this card when I moved here and told me to come." Nerves take hold like I'm being interrogated by the police.

"And the name of that friend?"

"I must be at the wrong address. I'm sorry." I feel like a fool, clearly in the lobby of an office building, dressed up with nowhere to go on a Friday night, and my mind on a man I can't have.

As I turn to leave, his voice is low. "You came for the club. You're in the right place. I just need to confirm who referred you."

My pulse quickens as I whip my head round to face him. "Theo Randall." The man who taught me to be a submissive.

He nods in confirmation. "Mr. Randall. Lead with that the next time. He's a regular."

"He is?"

"All I need now is to check your ID, and you can make your way inside."

"I'm well over twenty-one."

He gives a breathy chuckle. "All patrons have their ID scanned. It's an invitation-only club, Miss…"

"Sullivan. Nadia Sullivan." I reach into my purse to retrieve my driver's license, my interest piqued at what this club is like. I've never had to answer questions or provide references to go to a BDSM club before.

After noting a few details, he directs me down the hallway and up to the fourth floor. "Welcome to Venom. Enjoy your evening."

Following his instructions, I bid him goodnight and head for the elevator, grabbing my phone as the doors close behind me.

My heart is racing as I tap out a message to Theo.

> Me: I'm at Venom. Should I be worried? I just had the Spanish Inquisition to be allowed in.

He's quick to reply.

> Theo: Oh, you're in for a treat. Don't do anything I wouldn't, baby girl. ;0)

> Me: I can get in all kinds of trouble.

> Theo: Wish I could have been there to ease you in...

My chest tightens at the memory of his hands on me before something else takes over. *Guilt.* I push the feeling down as the doors open into another lobby, this one in dark, sumptuous colors.

Taking a deep breath, I force myself forward in an attempt to quash the ache in my chest. It's all I can do. I can't live in the past. That's what I'm telling myself as a stunning woman approaches me, her long, dark hair cascading over her shoulders.

"Welcome to Venom. Are you meeting someone in the bar or a private room?"

"Just me. If you could tell me where the bar is, that would be great." She looks me up and down, a sultry grin on her face.

"Follow me." I fall into step behind her as she opens oversized double doors into the most luxurious bar I've ever seen.

The music isn't too loud, and the ambience is opulent but inviting as people mingle at the bar, others sitting in ornate booths. Chandeliers hang from the high ceilings, stunning in their elegance.

"Wow," is all I can muster as she leads me to the bar.

"First time?"

"Yeah, I just moved here from Boston."

"Who recommended you?" Her tone is pleasant, and her voice is silky smooth.

"Theo Randall."

"I know him well." She reads my expression before I get the chance to school my features. "Not *that* well. I'm a Domme. We've been good friends for a long time."

"I didn't mean to pry."

"You didn't. If you're going to become a regular, you'll soon realize that I don't say or do anything I don't want to. I'm Genevieve." She reaches out her hand in introduction.

"I'm Nadia. Nice to meet you, Genevieve."

"Pick your poison," she says as we reach the imposing ebony-polished bar.

"Dirty martini. Onions, not olives."

The bartender greets her, his eyes fixated on her lips as she orders our drinks. She's every inch the Domme—beautiful, commanding, and aware of the effect she has on those around her. When she dismisses the bartender, she turns her attention to me.

"Do you mind if I join you for a little while?"

"I would love that. I wasn't particularly excited at the prospect of sitting alone."

"Trust me…" she purrs with a wicked grin, "… you won't be alone in here for long. You're stunning."

When the bartender returns with our drinks, I reach for my wallet, but before I can even offer to pay, my new friend tells him to put it on her tab.

"You don't have to do that."

"You're a brat, aren't you?" Her lips twitch as she levels me with a knowing look.

"How…"

"I've told you once that I don't do anything unless I want to."

"I…"

"It's cute. Do you have a Dom?"

"No. Theo knew I was moving, and suggested I come to dip my toe in the scene here. I said goodbye to my Dom when I decided to take a job here in New York."

"Was it love?"

That's a question. With my previous Dom? No. With Dalton—I push past the lump in my throat. "No."

"Good. I have a few Doms in mind to introduce you to." The last kiss I shared with Dalton floods my mind. I don't think I can do this. Lifting her glass, she gestures to make a toast. "Welcome to Manhattan, Nadia. Here's to new friends."

"Thank you." I take a sip, my eyes scanning our surroundings. It's truly beautiful in here. I can see why Theo sent me.

"So, Nadia, tell me about yourself. What brought you to New York?"

I'm not usually one to tell strangers any details about myself, but the conversation flows so easily with her, so I explain what I do and how I came to be here tonight.

When our second drink appears on the bar with nothing more than a nod from Genevieve, I shrug off my coat, content to stay a while.

"Come, let me introduce you to some people." I have my hands full, and she quickly grabs my coat and purse. "I'll have them check your stuff. No need to be walking around with it."

"Are you sure?"

"Of course. They'll bring it back when you're ready to leave."

"Okay. Thank you."

"You're very polite for a brat." She smirks.

"Only with my friends. My Dom... well, it's always fun to poke the bear." I give her a wink, enjoying that she knows exactly what I mean.

I've missed having friends in the lifestyle to talk and joke around with. She links her arm with mine, pulling me toward a table of ridiculously handsome men deep in conversation.

As we approach, one of them catches my eye, a panty-melting smile spreading across his face.

"Evening, Genevieve," he says, standing from the table.

"Evening, Flex. I'd like you to meet my new friend, Nadia. She just moved here, and I thought I'd introduce her to some of the regulars."

He holds out his hand, "Nice to meet you, Nadia. Please sit down. Let me introduce the rabble."

Another gentleman at the table pulls up chairs for Genevieve and me.

"We'll start with the most important. I'm Felix, but my friends call me Flex. Going clockwise, we've got Pierce, our resident surgeon, Mateo, Ford, and this youngster is Ryder."

They each welcome me, shaking my hand as I take a seat. I'm not a huge fan of everyone's eyes on me, so I'm thankful when Genevieve interjects, steering them elsewhere.

Other patrons come and go, as do the gentlemen at the table. They seem like a laidback bunch, some more than others. Doms are always so comfortable in their own skin, oozing confidence. They don't seek anyone's approval, and I find it sexy as hell.

"Can I take a guess?" I love that they instantly know what I mean.

"Go for it."

I go in the order they were introduced, "Dom, Dom... sub... voyeur," and then I turn my attention to Flex, his shit-eating grin telling me I was right. "You are a Dom, for sure."

"Five for five. She's got your number, boys." Genevieve laughs.

"Impressive."

"Thank you. Reading people is part of my job."

"What do you do?"

"I'm a lawyer."

Flex bites down on his fist, his eyes pinned on me. "Jesus, woman. That's hot. You're a sub for sure."

"What makes you say that?" I drain the rest of my drink.

"Ballbuster by day. It makes sense that you'd want to leave that at the door when you come somewhere like this."

"I've *never* been somewhere like this. This place is..."

"Palatial. Sinfully decadent. Fucking amazing," Mateo interjects.

"All of the above."

"Can I get you ladies another drink?" Flex offers.

"Sure."

"Why don't you come with me, Nadia? I can give you a tour of the immediate surroundings."

"Great." As I stand to follow, Genevieve throws a sly grin my way as she starts chatting with Ford.

We make our way to the bar, and I fall in step at Flex's side. He's easily six foot four. I'm in four-inch heels, and he's still more than half a foot taller than me. "So, Flex, what do you do?"

"I own a security firm. I'm the head of security for the club."

"Oh, wow. So you could put me in a chokehold right now without even flinching?"

"Are we talking about my job or your sexual preferences?" There's endless mischief in his eyes as he lifts a drink to his lips.

"You think you're hardcore enough for me?" I jest.

His eyes find mine, a mischievous grin tugging at the corners of his mouth. "I do like it *hard*."

"I bet you do. So, about that tour…" He's easy to flirt with, but an uneasiness settles in my chest.

"I'll save the best till last… my private room."

"Presumptuous of you. Why would I trust a veritable stranger in a private room?"

"We won't be strangers by the end of the night, Nadia."

"Call me…"

"Naddie." My name is a bucket of ice down my spine, his thunderous growl familiar as I turn to see him. *Dalton.*

He grabs my hand, pulling me to his side.

"Hey, Dal. I wasn't expecting you here tonight." They know each other?

"Neither was I. Excuse us, Flex. Nadia and I need to talk."

"We're kind of in the middle of something here, bro."

Dalton levels him with a stare so cold it could sink the Titanic. "Whatever you *thought* was happening, it's not. She's mine, Flex. Back the fuck off."

"What the…"

"I'll explain later."

He doesn't give me a chance to speak, his grip so tight my hand starts to tingle, almost numb, as he strides across the bar with me click-clacking behind him, trying to keep up down a dimly lit hallway before slamming a keycard against a door and pulling me inside.

My heart is pounding so hard it might break through my ribcage and thud onto the hardwood floor.

"*What the hell, Dalton?*" As the door locks slide into place, I pull my hand from his grasp.

He rounds on me, his eyes blazing, in a stunning, tailored, black suit. His tie is tugged down, and the top button of his crisp white shirt is open. His hair looks freshly fucked, like he's been wringing his hands through it—or someone else has. The thought makes me sick to my stomach.

"I reached out. I've tried to give you some space... some time to wrap your head around you and me..."

"There is no you and me," I say with zero conviction.

"Then why the fuck are you here?"

"What?"

"How did you find this place? All you had to do was answer one of my messages. Come to my fucking house. Why here?"

"I have no idea what you're talking about. I came here tonight to... I don't know... make some friends. Someone back home in Boston suggested it. *That's* why I'm here, and I don't see what that has to do with you."

He stalks toward me, stopping an inch from my face. "This is *my* club, Naddie."

Realization dawns. He *is* a Dom. My stomach lurches up into my throat. "I had no idea."

Dalton backs me against the wall, his arms hemming me in on either side, his eyes like the bluest roiling seas as his gaze flits between my lips and my frozen stare.

"So, you weren't looking for me. You were looking for a different Dom to fuck."

"I didn't know you were a Dominant. I've been trying to stay away. I... you know we can't be together, Dalton."

He pushes himself off the wall, tugging his jacket and tie off before rolling up the sleeves of his white shirt. God, he's beautiful as he begins to pace, raking his hands through his hair.

"We haven't even tried to find a solution. I've been going out of my fucking mind, and you've already moved on. Milan meant something to me." He can't even look at me. "And here you are, looking for a man to do all kinds of depraved things to you."

"*It's not depraved!*"

"I fucking know that! But the thought of another man touching you…" Tension rolls off him in waves, his jaw tight as he awaits my answer.

"What? What does it do to you? The thought of me being another man's su…"

"Don't say it. I can't hear it right now. I'm the fucking idiot who thought you came here tonight for me. *For us.* Instead, I find you heading to a private room with my best friend of all people. This is *not* how I pictured this moment with you." My resolve cracks.

Tears well in my eyes. "Flex? He was just being friendly, showing me around. I came here alone, Dalton. I had no intention of bedding someone tonight."

"You've made it pretty clear it's none of my fucking business. It's been weeks since Milan. Not a phone call or a text. Not even a fucking business email. Every time I've tried to talk to you, you run away. I should've gotten the message by now. I was just a trip down memory lane for you." Now, I'm pissed.

"Do you think this is easy for me?"

"Yeah," he says with anger radiating off him, so hot I fear I'm going to get burned. He turns to face me, closing the distance between us.

"Well, it's not! I gave up an amazing career in Boston to move here. Seeing you and being with you again… it's taken every ounce of strength I have not to come to you these past few weeks. I've fought myself on a daily basis."

"Why?"

"Because my *career* is over if I cross the line with you again. I could lose everything." Tears spill from my eyes as he closes me in again, his tattooed forearms at either side of my head, his hands practically digging into the wall.

"Or you could gain… everything we ever wanted." I can feel his breath on my lips, the rise and fall of my chest heaving against his.

"I… can't."

"I'll find a way, Naddie. I'm not a dumb kid anymore. Walking away isn't an option. I barely survived the first time."

"Dalton." His name is a plea on my lips for what, I'm not sure.

He caresses his thumb down my cheek, so light I can barely feel it—a whisper on my skin. His voice is low, rumbling as he presses his lips to my ear. "You're a *submissive*."

"Yes," is all I can muster, my voice unrecognizable, dripping with the need to kiss him.

"What's your safeword, kitten?" My insides tighten at the pet name he used when we were young and in love.

"Blue," I whisper, letting my head fall back against the wall, closing my eyes to stop myself from devouring him.

"Say it again, and I'll walk away." He runs his thumb over my bottom lip. My pulse is drowning everything else out, pumping so hard in my ears.

"Dalton… it's not that I don't want this."

"What do you want, kitten?"

"Does it matter? I can't have it." I slip out from beneath his arms, heading for the door. My heart can't take any more of this.

"So that's it? You just give up?"

"It's not fair. You have nothing to lose here, Dalton. My career is on the line."

"You think I have nothing to lose?" He bellows, sending a shiver through me. "You want to know what's unfair, Naddie… sending you away fifteen years ago, losing the only thing that mattered to me in this life. Nothing to lose… are you fucking kidding me? I have more money than I could ever spend and *nothing* I want. You want to talk about unfair… how about you showing back up in my life and making me fucking *love you*, only to have you walk away… again. Into the arms of another Dom at my own goddamn club."

My heart shatters in my chest.

"You don't think I feel the same way? I never stopped loving you, Dalton, but what good will it do me to admit that? It doesn't change anything."

"It changes everything."

"*No, it doesn't!*"

"Say it anyway."

"Why?"

"Say. It."

"*I love you, Dalton. I always have. There, I said it. What the hell does it matter?*" My breath is ragged as I scream the words at him, angry that it hurts so bad it's a physical pain in my chest.

Without a word, he barrels into me, grabbing my face in his large, warm hands as his lips crash down on mine, every fiber of my being sparking to life.

In this moment, nothing else matters. I've fought it these past few weeks, but I can't fight this—the way his mouth feels on mine, our tongues twisting and tangling with greedy desire.

I reach for his shirt, ripping it open in my need to touch him.

Hitching my dress up, Dalton grabs my ass, hoisting me up into his arms, coaxing me to wrap my legs around his waist, every kiss hungrier than the last. My back slams against the wall as I slip my hands between us, grappling with his belt and pants until his erection springs free, hard and heavy in my hand.

"There's a condom in my left pocket."

"No, you don't need it. I want to feel you. I'm on the pill."

"*Naddie.*" With me tight against the wall, Dalton's harsh kiss doesn't falter as he shoves my lace panties to the side before positioning himself at my entrance and slamming into me with one hard, soul-destroying thrust of his hips.

"Jesus," he roars. "You feel so fucking good."

I fist my hands in his hair, pulling his mouth to mine, craving more as I take every hard inch of him, swallowing his groan of pleasure as he seats himself to the hilt.

The boy I once knew is gone, replaced by this beast of a man, his broad shoulders flexing as I rake my nails down his back, holding him closer as he begins to move. With every powerful thrust of his hips, he pushes us closer to the oblivion I know will decimate me—a pleasure that will ruin me for any other Dom.

"You're mine, Naddie," he growls, returning to devour my mouth, his tongue fucking me in perfect time with his cock.

I can't get enough—the feel of him claiming me, shattering any coherent thought as I give myself over to him completely.

"Dalton… oh God…"

He slams into me over and over again, my body tightening—a coiled spring, ready to be released.

"That's it, kitten. Let me hear you scream my name." He hammers into me relentlessly as he quickens his pace, forcing me to the brink.

"Yes… *Dalton*… Dalton… I…" He consumes me with a ferocious kiss, his hands everywhere at once as he presses me against the wall with effortless ease.

When I can't hold back any longer, I fist my hands in his hair, tugging his lips from mine. "Dalton, I'm so close."

"Not yet. Your orgasm is mine, kitten."

"I…"

He fucks me into submission, every nerve ending in my body poised and ready, my release coursing through me like a tsunami, threatening to overwhelm me as it fights to take over.

His strokes become harder and faster, his cock pulsing inside me as he climbs to the edge of the cliff, chasing his own release.

"*Now, Naddie!* Come for me now," he groans as he grips my ass, taking me so hard I can barely breathe as I detonate around him, clawing at his back as wave after wave of ecstasy rips through me. Through him. As we find our release together. "Fuck, Naddie… yes… Naddie."

We're both struggling to take a breath as we ride the aftershocks together, Dalton's thrusts slowing down, still torturously delicious as his cock remains hard inside me. Leaning his forehead against the wall, his chest's rapid rise and fall are in time with my own.

"I've imagined you in this room so many times." My core tightens at his words. I'd forgotten we we're in his club. The one I came to in a pathetic attempt to get over him.

He continues to move inside me with lazy strokes, peppering kisses down my neck before his lips find mine in a slow, sensual fuck. I drink him in, never wanting this moment to end. In this room, there is only us and how our bodies fit so perfectly.

We find release together in each other's arms once more. However, this time, it's not a frenzy but a gentle entangling of heart and soul. Only in the silent aftermath does my entire body ache, not from exertion but the reality of our situation.

A heaviness descends as Dalton pulls out of me, and I'm left bereft as he gently sets me down, gripping my waist until he's sure I'm steady. Lifting his hand to my face, he brushes an errant tendril of hair off my sweat-sheened cheek, his eyes fixed on mine. "You're so fucking beautiful, kitten."

I right my panties before pulling my dress back into place. What did we just do? Nothing's different, and yet, everything has changed.

"Dalton, we shouldn't…" My voice is a strangled whisper, my throat hoarse from screaming his name.

His carefree smile is replaced by a cold, hard line. "If you're about to say this was a mistake or list all the reasons you think this can't happen…" he gestures between us before zipping his fly, "… I'm not interested."

"I would never call us a mistake."

"But you also wouldn't call us something worth fighting for."

"As much as I want you, I'm your lawyer."

"Did we just experience the same thing? It was fucking transcendent, Naddie. Why are you so afraid?"

"I could be disbarred."

"Understood." He turns on his heel, reaching for his ruined shirt, slipping it over the stunning planes of his back, his voice void of emotion. "Be in my office at eight on Monday morning."

"This was… amazing, but…" I hate myself in this moment. My heart is screaming at me to shut the hell up and fall into his arms, but my head is waging war as he shrugs his suit jacket on without looking at me.

"Amazing… *but*. Everything a man wants to hear after fucking your brains out. Be sure to rate me on *Yelp!*" He strides to the door, running a hand through his sex-mussed hair, chancing a glance back at me as he swings it open. "Eight o'clock, Monday. My office. Don't be late." There's so much emotion swirling in his eyes like a cyclone, reflecting how I feel, but when I scramble to say anything to stop him from walking out, there are no words.

"I'll have my driver take you home. He'll be waiting out front whenever you're ready."

"Dalton…"

"And kitten…" he says with cool confidence, "… the next time we're in this room together, you *will* address me as *Master Callaghan*."

My heart beats so rapidly that I reach for the nearest surface to steady myself, completely lost for words.

Master?

Chapter 10
DALTON

The past twenty-four hours have been the longest of my life. Walking out on Naddie at the club took every drop of self-control I had. As I stepped out into the open night air, I could still smell her arousal on my skin, sweet and sexy.

I drowned myself in research the moment I got home, failing to go to bed, searching the legal ramifications of a relationship between us, what it could do to Naddie's career, and how I can make this right. I've never been one to give up on a challenge, and after exploring every avenue, I believe there's a way to make it work.

I can't lose her again. A better man might leave her alone and let her find love with a man who deserves her, one who wouldn't jeopardize everything to have her, but every fiber of my being knows she's mine. We were always meant for each other.

The easiest route would be to marry Naddie. It circumvents the issues that arise if we start dating. I'd do it tomorrow if I could, but I wouldn't want that for her—to always wonder if I proposed this as a problem-solving exercise.

I need to distract myself. After telling her to be in my office on Monday, I have to wait it out, and I know exactly who to call when I need some mindless entertainment. Grabbing my phone, I hit speed dial.

"You home?" I can't stand the silence of my bedroom tonight.

"I'm at the club. You ready to tell me what the fuck that stunt you pulled last night was all about?"

"It's fine. Go and get your rocks off, bro. I don't want to mess up your plans. Maybe we can grab a drink tomorrow night?"

"Do you want to meet at Venom? I can have them get your room ready and find you a friend for the evening." Venom. Until last night, the club would've been my first go-to when I'm stressed. It's the only business decision I've ever broken my own rules for. *Never work with friends.*

It became a joint venture with Flex as head of security and our friend—and the owner of the hottest non-sex clubs in Manhattan— Carter de Rossi. He was the perfect choice for a business partner. He's not a Dom or a sub, but he doesn't need to be in the lifestyle to make Venom a success. He is the master of opulence and discretion when it comes to exclusive clubs, bars, and VIP lounges all over the country.

I could take a sub into his nightclub, Viper, slip into a 'private party room' and indulge in my darkest desires, knowing that my privacy would be respected at all costs. It would still feel like hiding, though.

I wanted somewhere with maximum security, anonymity for guests, and custom rooms to suit a patron's specific needs and particular kinks. We created an opulent, high-end place for people to explore their sexuality without judgment or fear of exposure. There's one area that has the feel of a VIP lounge, with a stocked bar and discreet staff. However, it's not necessary to go through the bar area to reach the private rooms for those who want to remain fully incognito. Each private room is stocked with everything a Dom could want, and we have private rooms available for long-term lease and exclusive use. The rest can be booked for the evening.

If having people watch is your kink, we have a room for that. If you want to fuck ten strangers at once, there's a room for it. My main requirement was that I don't want *my* subs seeing other men with their cock out as we navigate the club, and *no man* will ever set eyes on a woman who belongs to me.

"I'm not really in the headspace for it."

"What's going on with you, Dal? I have no fucking idea what happened last night."

"There's just a lot going on. I'll text you tomorrow with a time for drinks. I've taken enough of your time."

"I deserve an explanation."

"I know. Tomorrow."

I end the call and toss my phone on the nightstand before changing into some gray sweats and a plain white T-shirt. I'll have to make do with a whiskey sour and silence. Not bothering to switch on the lights, I navigate my apartment by moonlight as it kisses the stark loneliness of my surroundings.

Flex isn't wrong. I definitely need a release, but until Naddie agrees to give me a chance, I'm stuck with aching balls. The tension in my body of late is oppressive. A momentary angry fuck with Naddie didn't come close to sating me. I want to worship her body for hours. Tease her to the edge of madness and watch her orgasm over and over again. If I don't loosen the release valve again soon, I'm going to explode.

An hour later, as the last of my drink glides down the back of my throat with a burst of heat, I'm startled by the click of the doorhandle. Flex lets himself in with a bottle of Glenlivet in hand.

"What are you doing here?" My eyes squint as he flicks on the lights.

"I called bullshit on waiting until tomorrow. You're sitting in the dark, drinking alone, dressed like a bum. It seems I was right." He makes himself at home, grabbing a glass before sitting next to me at the expansive kitchen island, filling our glasses before taking a long swig.

"It's fucked up. All of it."

His brow is tightly-knit as he considers me for a few moments. "Start at the beginning."

"I was five at the time."

"Jesus, I don't think I brought enough alcohol if we're going back that far."

"Probably not." I press the glass to my lips, downing my drink in one gulp.

"What the fuck happened?"

"Do you remember when I told you about my first unofficial sub?"

The corners of his lips turn up with a knowing grin. "The hot girl next door. Yeah. I'm jealous. I wish I'd tapped into my inner Dom with my prom date. She was up for anything."

"She's my new lawyer."

"Who's your new lawyer?" he says as he refills my glass.

"The only woman I've ever truly loved. I went to Milan, sat down in the conference room to sign the biggest deal of my career, and in she walked, looking so fucking... perfect."

"*Oh shit.*" Oh shit, is right. Over the years, I've given him snippets of information when we've had a few too many drinks, so he knows this is a problem for me.

"Did she know?"

"No. We were both dumbstruck and awkward as fuck. Mason started talking about her working on my account, including my personal contracts."

"Fuck. Your subs? What happened?" I tell him everything that happened in Milan. Her hotel room. Our dinner. The past few weeks of pretending we can be strictly professional.

"Holy shit. Why am I only hearing about this now?"

"Because I walked in to see you giving her a tour of the club yesterday and looking pretty intent on trying to fuck her." His eyes go wild, everything about last night falling into place.

"Shut the fuck up! Nadia?" He slings back the rest of his drink, shock evident in his voice. "The hot new submissive is your girl next door?"

"Call her hot again, and I'll knock you out."

He throws his hands up. "Oh, you've got it bad. You are so screwed."

"Tell me something I don't know. It's bad enough that she can't date a client, but she's a fucking submissive. The woman of my dreams, who brought that side of me to life, is a sub. How can I walk away?"

His palm connects with my shoulder in an almighty slap. "That's fucking perfect. Why the hell would you walk away? It's your dream scenario."

"This isn't a good thing, Flex. The firm hired her and made her partner with the sole purpose of taking over my account when Douglas retires."

"So?"

"You're a smart guy, but sometimes you can be really dense. It's not just frowned upon here in New York. If she got reported for seeing me, she could be disbarred. Her career would be over."

"Did you guys talk about it?"

"Not exactly. We had fucking amazing sex."

"Last night?" he says with a sly grin. "The anger bang. Nice."

"Seriously, you don't need to say shit like that about her. I told her to come by my office on Monday morning, and I need to convince her I'll find a way round it."

"Okay, so what are the options?" He pours us another drink, which I happily down like a shot.

"Easiest loophole is to marry her."

"Jesus. Slow down there with the thermonuclear option. You can't marry a woman just so you're free to date her."

"I know."

"Good. I was going to have to get you committed if you thought that was a solution. What are the other options?"

"Buy her a firm of her own."

"You need to work on your troubleshooting. If her career is as important as she says it is, she'll hate you for meddling like that. She *earned* partner. There has to be a way that avoids purchasing a law firm or marriage."

"There is. I just haven't figured it out yet."

"Then, there's only one question you need to answer honestly."

"And what's that?"

"Are you *sure* you're still in love with her? Or could it be the *idea* of her? Your first love, teenage angst, and all that fun stuff."

"It's ridiculous, right? I haven't seen her since we were teenagers. It's been fifteen years." My heart hammers in my chest as I reach for the whiskey bottle. I can say it's stupid and foolish, but I already know the truth.

"Answer the question. Whether it's ridiculous or not has no bearing on the answer."

"Don't push me, Flex." I press the bottle to my lips before dropping my head back and letting the warm liquid wash away the three little words I want to roar from the rooftop.

"You called me. I'm not going to placate you with bullshit and make you feel better. If this is about scratching an itch and seeing what it's like to have this woman as a sub, then it's not worth the risk. If you're going to risk it anyway, then write a contract and keep it on the down-low."

Shoving myself away from the kitchen island, the barstool goes crashing to the floor as I try to escape. I wring my hands through my hair as I stride into the darkness of my living room, but Flex is hot on my heels.

"Just fucking say it. You'll feel better. It's written all over your face."

"It won't do me any good."

"Stop being a pussy. Fucking admit it!" He gets in my face, squaring his shoulders as he pushes me to my limit.

"She point blank asked me to leave her alone a few weeks ago."

"Then she let you fuck her in your sex club. Do you really believe she doesn't feel the same way?"

"No."

"Then admit it. It's only us here, bro. Let it out."

"*I love her!*" A rush of relief floods my entire body, washing over me with disturbing clarity. "I've always loved her. Everything I've done... everything I've achieved... was to become a man worthy of her. *I. Fucking. Love. Her.*"

He grabs the back of my neck and pulls me into his arms. "Then do whatever is necessary to make her yours. You're Dalton

Callaghan." His words hit me like a tsunami. He's right. I've loved Naddie from the day we met. I won't let her walk away again.

A contract.

Why didn't I think of that earlier? We can write a contract that creates a timeline. Until she passes the bar, *she's mine.* Technically, she's not breaking any rules in this state until she's officially a qualified New York lawyer. I can figure out the next steps from there. I'm Dalton Callaghan—I can make this work.

"Feel free to share what's going on behind the maniacal grin on your face right now."

"You're a fucking genius, Flex."

"Of course I am. Why?"

"A contract. What's the way to a lawyer/submissive's heart? *A fucking contract.*"

"I am amazing. But considering you just admitted that you're a chick flick away from professing your undying love for this woman, isn't it just a temporary solution?"

"All I need is a little time. I'll make it happen. You were right. I need to do whatever it takes to make her mine. I'm not making the same mistake twice." I flip on the lights and stalk to my office in search of paper and a pen. Flex follows, pouring another drink as I take a seat and get to work.

"What are we doing right now?"

"Writing a contract."

"Bro, you're drunk and have a standard contract for subs. Can't this wait until you're sober?"

"My head is clear for the first time in weeks. And Naddie isn't just a standard contract kind of girl."

Flex slumps down onto the couch on the other side of the room. "You're a lucky son of a bitch."

"You make your own luck in this world, Flex. When you get handed a shitshow of a situation, you make lemonade."

"You're definitely too drunk to be writing anything right now." He chuckles.

"Fuck it. She needs to know I'm serious about this."

"Genevieve is going to flip her lid when she finds out."

I stop writing. "Viv can't know about this. Yes, everyone at the club will find out we're together, but I don't want them knowing our back story. Not right now. Not until I figure out a long-term solution. Promise me."

"Fair enough, but eventually, if she finds out I kept it from her, she'll come at me with that whip of hers."

"You'd love every second," I say with a wry grin.

"I love a sturdy whip when *I'm* the one doing the whipping."

"Don't tell me you and her have never hooked up." I continue to write the terms before moving to my cabinet and grabbing a standard contract to add to my one handwritten page. It gets me thinking. What are her hard limits? What kind of sub is she? Will her kinks align with mine?

As I mull it over, I realize that none of the rules I've had until now apply. Whatever she wants, I'll gladly oblige. I suppose that's not strictly true. I won't share her. *Ever.* That's nonnegotiable.

Shit. The more I think about it, the soberer I become, and the more I become concerned about what Naddie might need from me. If she wants to fuck in front of other people, there is no way I will allow it. She's mine, and I won't have anyone else watch her come.

"Why do you look like a lost puppy? You were all gritty determination like three seconds ago." He grabs his empty glass, pouring a generous measure of whiskey before bringing it to me. "You need this more than I do."

I don't hesitate, needing another burst of Dutch courage. "What the fuck am I going to do if her kinks involve having others watching or participating?"

"Fuck…" Flex knows me better than anyone. I enforce my hard limits with subs that are nothing more than a satisfying partner to pass the time. With Naddie, I can't even finish that thought. "One thing at a time. Write the contract with your terms, and then see if she's even going to entertain the idea. If she does, then you have to know what she needs. It wouldn't be fair to her if you know you can't do something she wants."

I sit back in my chair, hating that he's right.

"If she needs either of those things, I need to figure out how to be okay with it. The alternative is…"

"Be real, Dalton. You lost your shit when you saw me *talking* to her last night."

"I know her. I really don't think she'd want company."

"Okay, then stop worrying. Until she tells you what she likes, it's all speculation."

"Why does this have to be so complicated?" I leave my hard limits blank on the standard contract. In the end, I know I'll do anything to make Naddie mine, even if it breaks me.

"Because *life* is complicated."

"Yours isn't. You fuck who you want when you want and as many as you want." A fleeting expression drifts across his features—something I've never seen before.

"Trust me, Dal, I have my own complications."

"Everything okay?"

He immediately plasters his usual easy-going smile on his face. "This is your shitshow. We can deal with mine another time. Finish the damn contract. I came here to drink, and I have some ideas for the club that I want to run past you while you're good and liquored up."

"I'm definitely going to need more whiskey. Everything running smoothly over there right now? I've been so caught up with the European deal, I haven't checked in for a while."

"Carter and I have got it under control. This is what I wanted to talk to you about."

I finish the last of my contract for Naddie and set it aside, happy for a distraction.

"You're giving off that it's-going-to-cost-a-lot-of-money vibe." We head back to the kitchen for some food to go with the whiskey. I can tell it's going to be a long night.

"You know me so well. I want to start developing the floor above the club. To expand what we offer. Some of the communal kink rooms we offer are too small. We need to think bigger. There's a demand for it."

"Yeah? How's membership?"

"We're turning people away because we don't have enough private rooms. Carter and I have been working on some plans for the space. We're going to be wall-to-wall kink and raking in the cash."

"Aren't we already *wall-to-wall* kink?"

"We've only scraped the surface, Dal. I have ideas for kink that would make you blush."

"Bullshit," I say with a wicked grin. I could design a completely new room for Naddie and me. Fuck, I could have Flex design an entire floor. I own the whole building.

"Pull up a chair. I'm about to blow your fucking mind."

He doesn't disappoint. By the end of the night, I'm drunk as hell and giving him carte blanche to turn our club into a goddamn empire. As I sit back and contemplate the possibilities, it only serves to strengthen my resolve when it comes to Naddie. I'm going to make her my submissive. I may not have been her first Dominant, but I'm sure as hell going to be her last.

Chapter 11
NADDIE

I've been both dreading and anticipating this morning since the moment Dalton left me sated and saddle sore at the club. The words he spoke as he walked out the door have plagued my dreams the past two nights. *The next time we're in this room together, you* will *address me as Master Callaghan.* The next time. A threat and a promise of a pleasure I won't have the strength to say no to.

My mind has been all over the place. The lawyer in me had to reread every scrap of information I had on The Callaghan Group. The other part of me, who wants to feel Dalton's hard cock inside me again, had me sliding my hand between my legs more times than I can count—the memory of his body hammering into me, making me quake.

It took me an hour to pick out an outfit to wear to his office today, and as I stand outside the building, I still question my choice.

I took a detour via my own office this morning, hoping to go unnoticed, but Douglas called me in to inform me that Mr. Callaghan has requested my presence for the next few weeks. He wants to personally get me up to speed on the various contracts I'll be working on with him.

I had to school my face, rolling my eyes internally. I should have known Dalton would find a way to have us work closely together. He's always been sneaky but with the best intentions in the world. He could be speeding down the highway at 120 miles per hour, get pulled over by the meanest son of a bitch on the force, and have him laughing by the end of the conversation. Then, he'd drive off with no ticket and a wicked grin. It's sexy as hell, but I'm now realizing as I stand in the foyer of The Callaghan Group building, that all his charm will be focused on me today. I can't even imagine what the coming weeks will bring, but whatever happens, I know he'll bring me to my knees and have me begging for more if I don't make it clear that my career comes first.

"Here is your ID badge and the keys to your office. Take the elevator on the left up to the eighty-first floor."

"My office?"

"Yes, ma'am. Mr. Callaghan handed them to me himself this morning. He was very clear."

"Can you tell me where I can find Mr. Callaghan?"

"He'll be waiting to greet you on the eighty-first floor. He asked that I alert him when you arrived." Of course, he did.

My stomach drops as the elevator rises, nerves taking flight as this metal cage takes me into the clouds. It stops at too many floors to count, adding to the anticipation of seeing Dalton. When it reaches the eighty-first floor, my breath hitches as the doors open, and I catch a glimpse of him. He's downright gorgeous in a three-piece suit.

I wait for everyone else to file out of the elevator, steeling myself for the day ahead.

"Good morning, Ms. Sullivan. Welcome to The Callaghan Group." Dalton's sly grin does things to my insides, a warm glow spreading from head to toe.

"Mr. Callaghan." I fall in step at his side. "I was handed keys to my office. There must be some mistake. I don't work here." His knuckles brush mine for a second, but it lights a fire deep in my core.

"I spoke with Douglas this morning. We both agreed that it would be prudent for you to take this time as you wait for your bar results to get to know my business and the intricacies that go along with representing it."

"He told me. Wow. You've basically kidnapped me."

"I don't see any restraints on you, Ms. Sullivan… *yet.*"

The way he strides confidently through this palatial office space, all eyes on him, is pretty damn hot. I, on the other hand, want to disappear, worried that it's written all over my face—we had sex two days ago.

"Take a breath, kitten," he whispers for only me to hear.

Nerves swarm my entire body as he opens the door to a stunning corner office, his name on a sophisticated metal plaque. Resting his hand on the base of my spine, he ushers me inside.

"Welcome to The Callaghan Group. This is my office. You can take a seat at the desk." I do as he asks, smoothing my skirt as I sit across from his oversized, wingback leather chair. When he takes a seat across from me, he pins me with his burning gaze. Steepling his fingers under his chin, he becomes all business.

"Why am I here, Dalton?"

"I told you. You need to learn the ropes."

I take a breath, letting myself calm down before I speak, but he beats me to it.

"I have a proposal for you. You made it clear the other night that we can't happen unless your career is safe. It's not enough that I ask you to trust I'll find a way. We've been estranged for many years now. So, I wrote us a contract."

"What?" My pulse begins to race.

"You will be my twenty-four-seven submissive until the day you get your bar results. If, by that time, we haven't found a way to be together long-term, the contract will terminate, and you are free to go about your life without any further input from me."

He slides a few sheets of paper across the desk—a contract. I'm transported back to the day he and I sat in my bedroom all those years ago, writing promises we had for each other, signing our names together. Back then, we said *forever*. I know I can't let myself hope for that this time around, but am I willing to put myself through this and ensure that my heart will be broken when this contract expires?

I flick through the pages of a standard Dom/sub contract, with spaces left for my soft and hard limits. It's not those paragraphs that concern me. I'd let him do anything to me. I have no hard limits when it comes to Dalton.

It's the final page—handwritten—that makes my heart beat wildly in my chest.

I, Dalton Callaghan, propose a Dominant/submissive relationship with Nadia Sullivan. This will be a twenty-four-seven arrangement and not limited to the bedroom or Club Venom. I will take care of all emotional, physical, and relationship needs. I will adhere to all hard limits and take all preferences and kinks into consideration.

Regarding the career of the above-mentioned submissive, I agree to terminate my relationship as Dominant to Nadia Sullivan upon receipt of her New York bar results if a suitable solution to the lawyer/client relationship cannot be found and agreed upon by both parties by that time.

"Shall we discuss your preferences and limits now?"

"No."

He shifts in his chair, rubbing his palm over the scruff on his chin. "Do you need time to consider my offer?"

I read it over once more, the silence growing.

"Say something, Naddie." The tight-knit of his brows betrays the cool tone of his request.

"I don't need time." My hands are trembling as I set the contract down on the desk.

Raking his hands through his hair, he fixes me with his gaze, entreating me to give him an answer. "Naddie…"

"Do you have a pen I could borrow?" Without a word, he hands me a stunning Mont Blanc fountain pen, the weight speaking to the gravity of this decision. "And some paper."

Pulling a Callaghan Group letterhead from his drawer, he pushes it across the desk, his breathing shallow with anticipation.

I score through the limits portion of the contract and quickly fill in some of my preferences. Then, I get to writing my own contract —everything I need from Dalton in the coming weeks. The very thought makes me write faster, desperate to sell my submissive soul for however many days of heaven that will need to last me a lifetime.

> I, Nadia Sullivan, agree to be a twenty-four-seven submissive to Dalton Callaghan from the date of signing until receipt of my New York bar results. As his submissive, I will submit in whatever way he sees fit. There are no hard limits when it comes to my submissive relationship with Dalton Callaghan.
>
> I, as the submissive, will trust and respect Dalton Callaghan as my Dominant until the contract expires. Until then, I belong to Master Callaghan.

Any thought of stopping this inevitable twist of fate disappears as I hand him my promise of submission, and I'm rewarded with his sharp intake of breath before a stunning, heartfelt smile spreads across his stupidly handsome face.

"Are you sure you want to do this? To be mine?"

I swallow past the lump in my throat, apprehension coursing through my veins. "Yes."

He presses the intercom on his desk. "Audrey, can you please come in here and bring your notary stamp?"

His wicked grin is ten steps past mouthwatering. "Your secretary is going to see this contract? Are you crazy?"

"Don't worry, kitten. Do you trust me?" It would be a flippant comment from anyone else, but with Dalton, he means what he says. I take a second to consider his question, even though I know the answer.

"I trust you, Dalton. Don't break my heart twice," I entreat him, my heart galloping like a wild mustang. I'm trusting him with my life. My career. My heart and soul. This could mean so much more than a few weeks of pleasure.

"I won't."

There's a knock on the door as a flutter of apprehension mars his exquisite features.

"Come in."

A catwalk-gorgeous brunette struts in with legs for days. She's got a tiny baby bump, and yet she's still breathtakingly beautiful. This is his secretary?

"Good morning, Mr. Callaghan. What are we notarizing this morning? I wasn't aware we had any contracts on the schedule."

"Personal contract."

Her gaze flits to me, a warm smile on her face. "Very good."

Moving to my side of the desk, he wastes no time signing his name on the dotted line before handing it to me. His proximity only serves to heighten my nerves, my pulse roaring at the sight of his signature. I stand, my foot tapping the floor as I scan it one last time.

"You can still walk away, Nadia." I hate when he uses my given name. There's something so cold and detached about it. If he believes I could walk away now, he's kidding himself. I grab the pen, his fingers grazing mine as I clutch it tight and sign my name.

"Don't call me that."

Seeing it in black and white, a thrill courses through every fiber of my being. *I'm his,* at least for now.

My breath catches as he moves his hand to rest on the small of my back. Every touch is electric with him.

"Do your thing, Audrey." I dare not say a word as she looks

them over and notarizes them, holding my breath until she hands them to Dalton.

"Is there anything else I can do for you?"

"Can you clear my morning? I want to get Ms. Sullivan situated in her office."

"Of course. Should I go ahead and set up a laptop and access to current contracts?"

"Always three steps ahead, Audrey. That would be perfect. Thank you."

She turns her attention to me, but there's not even a hint of judgment, and I'm not sure if it's good or bad. Has she done this for every other submissive that Dalton has contracted? Or is she just masking it well? Women who aren't in the lifestyle don't tend to be understanding.

Maybe she's a submissive? Has she been Dalton's submissive? The thought makes me want to dry heave.

"If you need anything, Ms. Sullivan, don't hesitate to ask. Just call extension 315."

"Thank you."

She takes her leave, and Dalton wastes no time turning me to face him, his strong, muscled arms on either side of me, forcing me to sit on the table's edge. A lightning bolt of desire jolts straight to my core, the scent of his cologne intoxicating my senses.

"You're mine now, kitten." His lips brush mine with such tender control it makes me moan.

"I'm yours, Master Callaghan." Just saying the words feels different, and the flare of his hungry gaze tells me he feels it too.

"Fuck, that sounds so damn good on your pretty little lips." Heat pools at the apex of my thighs as Dalton's hands wander up beneath my skirt, making me gasp as his fingertips caress my sex through the thin lace of my panties.

Letting my head fall back, I close my eyes. "Oh God."

"He's got nothing to do with it. Your mine. You'll be moaning my name from now on."

"Someone could walk in. Does your door lock?"

His lips caress my neck as he shifts my panties to the side, his flesh touching mine, sending a shiver down my spine. "It's not your place to worry about that. I'm your Dom now," he says as he runs his thumb over my clit. "You signed the contract, Naddie. If I want the door wide open as I pleasure you, that's what will happen. Understood?"

"Yes, Master." My voice is a breathy whisper as I contemplate such a scenario.

"Stop overthinking it. Give yourself over to me and revel in how freeing it can be."

He leans in, pressing his lips to mine in a ghost of a kiss. "Let go."

I close my eyes, taking a deep breath, letting his words move through me. He would never do anything to hurt me. I'm his submissive now. I'm *Dalton's* submissive. A wave of contentment washes over me, my nerves dissipating as I lean into the comfort of our contract.

"Yes, Master Callaghan."

"Good girl. Now, take your clothes off, kitten."

"What? I can't. Not here."

He gently cups my chin, forcing me to meet his gaze. He's every inch the Dom and my arousal spikes. "Such a brat. It's time to fix that. Besides, I know you want to. You're wet for me. I want a perfect view of your slick little pussy."

There's an ache growing between my thighs. "Master…"

He hooks his fingers under my panties. "Lift." I do as he asks, watching in a haze of desire as he slides them down my legs, exposing the evidence of my arousal. "Take. Off. Your. Clothes. Don't make me ask again."

He removes his hand from where I need him most, striding to the door, hesitating with his hand on the lock.

I'm shaking as I stand from the desk, slowly unbuttoning my blouse. In all my years as a submissive, I've never been a sub outside of a club. This is dangerous, yet every cell in my body is screaming for release.

"Let me see those rosebud nipples, kitten." I let my blouse drop to the floor before unclasping my bra and letting it follow. The cool breeze of the air-conditioning kisses my skin, my nipples tightly budding under Dalton's gaze.

"What next, Master?" I can't believe I'm doing this.

"You can keep the heels on. I forgot how fucking hot you look in them. Lose the skirt."

My pulse is racing as I unzip my pencil skirt, letting it fall to my feet.

On the eighty-first floor, Manhattan is on display through this corner office with floor-to-ceiling windows on two sides, laid bare for all to see as I am in this moment.

For the first time in years, I'm shy, casting my gaze to the floor, my pussy so wet I can feel it against my thighs. I've never been more turned on than I am now.

"Good girl." I'm rewarded by the soft click of the lock as it drops into place. "You are so fucking beautiful, Naddie. The lock is a reward for doing as you're told, but I won't always be so gracious. If you question me next time, I will have no hesitation in keeping the door unlocked. Look at me."

As my eyes find his, he walks toward me, a growing erection straining against his suit pants. God, he's handsome. And he's mine. Circling me, so close yet so far, I ache for his touch.

"Rule number one. When I ask you to assume the position, I expect you to drop to your knees, legs spread wide, and your hands behind your back. I'll let you know if I want you clothed or naked, depending on our location."

"Yes, Master." I watch as his cock twitches, and it fills me with joy.

"You can take the position."

As I lower myself, I sink to my knees and spread my legs, clasping my hands behind my back, my eyes cast to the floor.

"You can look at me." I do as I'm told, my sex pulsing with need, so overwhelming I struggle not to press my thighs together in an attempt to relieve the ache.

"Am I doing it to your liking, Master Callaghan?"

"Yes, kitten. You look… breathtaking." A thrill courses through me at his praise.

"Thank you, Master."

Cupping my face with his hands, he leans down to kiss me, his tongue licking the seam of my lips, begging for entrance, which I freely give. It takes everything I have not to reach up and fist my hands in his hair, but I want to be good for him. I want to please him.

His hand begins to wander, his firm grip palming my breast before traveling down to where I need him most. When his hand slides between my legs, he lets out a feral growl. "You're so fucking wet for me. You love being on display, don't you, kitten?"

"Yes, Master." The rapid rise and fall of my chest have me struggling to breathe.

Leaving me bereft, he lifts his thumb to my lips, smearing the evidence of my arousal before kissing me with a ferocity that makes me forget my name. "You taste divine, don't you agree?"

"Yes, Master, but I'd rather taste *you* on my lips." His eyes flare as he adjusts himself.

"As much as I want to fuck that pretty little mouth of yours, I won't reward you for being a brat. If I ask you to tell me how you want your pleasure, then you can request this," he says, grabbing his crotch. "Today, I think you need to learn the art of anticipation."

"As you wish, Master Callaghan." If he keeps talking to me like this, I might come without provocation. The low rumble of his voice is enough to send me over the edge.

"I have some work to do, but before I get to that, I want you to sit on the edge of my desk." He takes my hand, steadying me as I get to my feet.

"What side would you like me on, Master?"

"My side of the desk." I perch on the edge, the cold wood sending a shiver down my spine. Bracing my hands on either side of me, Dalton slips his hands between my thighs, pushes my legs apart, and opens me to his gaze.

He drops to his knees, pulling me to his lips as he darts his tongue out to taste me, lapping at my folds, a slow hum reverberating through me, pleasure spreading down my legs, making me shake. "Fuck me, kitten. You taste is so damn sweet. I could feast for hours and never tire of you."

The scruff of his jaw is a stark juxtaposition to the softness of his lips, tantalizing my senses. I grind my hips, only to have Dalton pull away, leaving me wanting. "Please, don't stop."

"Do you need me, kitten?"

"Yes, Master."

"Who do you belong to?" He leans in, pressing soft kisses to my pussy like he would my lips. "Tell me who you belong to."

"You. I belong to you, Master Callaghan."

"That's right. You're *mine* now. Mine to pleasure and mine to command."

"Yes... yes." His kisses drive me to the edge of madness, over and over again, until I want to scream his name and beg for release. At this moment, I don't care where we are or how I should behave as a lawyer. All I want is Dalton. Nothing else matters as I teeter on the brink of orgasm, knowing I'm his submissive.

When I can't hold my moans of pleasure any longer, and I'm ready to detonate, Dalton pulls back, wiping the evidence of my arousal from his lips, an impressive erection straining so hard in his pants.

"Time to get to work. We can pick up where we left off tonight."

"What?" It comes out harsher than I intended, but I'm so turned on that I feel like I'm going to lose my mind if I can't find release.

"You can get dressed. We have work to do, and if you're a good girl, I'll give you everything you crave this evening."

"Dalton..."

"Oh, kitten, this is exactly why you're not riding the aftershocks of an orgasm right now. You questioned me when I told you to remove your clothes. You're questioning me now, and you know how you're supposed to address me."

I quickly grab my clothes, putting them on in silence, unwilling to give him the satisfaction of looking in his direction. It's one thing to have delayed pleasure in a club during a scene, but this is torture.

"Sorry, Master Callaghan," I practically spit the words at him. This isn't how I imagined my first moments as his submissive.

In a few short steps, he's on me, clasping my chin with his strong, warm hand, forcing my gaze. "I suggest you say that again without the sarcasm, or there will be no release for you today."

"I'm perfectly happy to finish the job myself."

"That's not going to happen, kitten," he says with a wry grin. "You won't touch what's mine unless I tell you to do so."

"Are you serious?"

"As a heart attack. Your pussy is mine, Naddie. I'm the only one who's going to make you come."

"So you brought me to your office to tease me?"

"No. I brought you here to work. The teasing is just a perk." He reaches into his pocket and hands me a keycard. It's matte black with a sleek, glossy V embossed on the front, with Number '1' in gold on the back.

"What's this for?"

"I want you at the club tonight at seven o'clock. You should know your way around after the other night." A thrill courses through me.

"I'll be there, Master Callaghan." His face lights up, his gorgeous blue eyes sparkling as he cups my face in his hands, pressing his lips to mine.

"Good girl. Now…" he says, "… let me show you to your office. We have work to do." I'm loathe to leave his office, my sex still aching for relief.

"What should I call you when we're at work?" As much as I would love to call him Master, it's not exactly practical if I want to keep my job. "Mr. Callaghan?"

The furrow of his brow is endearing. He feels the same way. It's written all over his handsome face.

"No. Call me Dalton when you're here. But if I close the door and ask you to take the position, you call me Master." God, I don't know how I'm supposed to get any work done when he's close. Knowing he's my Dom makes my pulse race and my nerve endings alight with anticipation of the next caress or stolen kiss.

"Yes, Master."

Chapter 12
DALTON

Today was torture and sheer elation wrapped in one. Anticipation was heavy every second since Naddie signed our contract making her mine. I've longed for this from the moment she walked back into my life. Seeing her naked and in the position in my office was the sexiest thing I've ever seen. It took every ounce of self-discipline as a Dom not to fuck her right there and then.

The rest of the day went by in slow motion, my mind wandering to thoughts of her as I navigated my afternoon. I wasn't lying when I told her she needs to immerse herself in The Callaghan Group for her current role as part of my legal team and for the future. *Our future*. I'm also a selfish man, and I want her close—the desire to have her as my twenty-four-seven submissive so primal I can't concentrate on anything else.

Music reverberates in my chest as the doors of Venom open, and a wave of desire washes over me, knowing that Naddie will be here soon. I arrived two hours early to check everything is perfect in my private room. I called Carter this morning and asked him to have the furniture changed out—a new bed and chest of drawers with every play item I want to use on Naddie. As always, he knocked it out of the park. The room looks nothing like it did the last time I was here. I wanted a clean slate for her—for both of us.

I'm giddy like a kid on Christmas morning, desperate to have *my submissive—my kitten*—in here with me. With everything set, I make my way to the bar, taking a seat next to Flex. I told Naddie to be at the club at seven so I have time to kill.

The bartender sets my usual down in front of me, and Flex clinks his glass against mine before taking a sip of whiskey. "In a better mood today, I see. I'm assuming the contract went according to plan this morning by the shit-eating grin on your face."

"Oh, it was... delectable." The scent of luxury hangs in the air —all hardwood, leather, and the best liquor you'll find in Manhattan. Remembering the way Naddie looked this morning—naked in my office—I can't wait to see her in my private room in the same position.

"So, do I get to chat some more with your high school sweetheart tonight without fearing a punch to the face?"

"No. The plans I have for her tonight don't include anyone else. Or talking. Or clothes."

"Bro..." he claps me on the back, "... balls deep in vintage pussy. I can't blame you."

"Mention her pussy again, and the only room you'll be frequenting this evening will be the emergency room."

He rolls his eyes, and I'm sorely tempted to connect my fist with his face. "Is this what I have to look forward to now? You with zero sense of humor when it comes to sex." I know I've been happy to share details in the past, but it's different with Naddie. She's unlike any sub I've had in the past. I didn't share details in the locker room in high school, and I won't be sharing them now.

"Yeah. She's not the kind of woman you talk about over drinks."

His face sobers as he grips my shoulder. "I know this woman means something to you, but I don't want you to do anything stupid and find yourself in a bad situation. Promise me that you'll stick to the terms of your contract with her?"

"The contract will be moot before it expires."

"I hope so. I'm not trying to be a dick. I just want you to be careful."

"I will be. Once you get to know her, you'll understand."

We order another round, and as the clock hits six fifteen, I spy Viv ushering Naddie to my room. She looks fucking stunning in a tight burgundy dress and killer heels.

"Jesus Christ." Flex mirrors my sentiment at the sight of her but thinks better of continuing down that road as I dagger him with my stare.

My hands ball into fists. "She's mine."

He throws his head back and laughs. "I know you're possessive, but this is next-level shit. I value my dick being attached to my body. I'm well aware that she's yours in writing. Good luck explaining to the rest of them that they're not even allowed to look at her. She made quite the impression on everyone the other day."

Her eyes find mine across the room, and I'm as hard as a rock instantly.

I acknowledge her with a nod, her instructions clear from the note I sent to her apartment this afternoon. With a shy smile, Naddie follows Viv toward the private rooms, and my adrenaline spikes.

"I've never seen you look at a sub that way before. You are so royally fucked."

"No shit, Sherlock. I know she could make me the happiest man alive or rip my beating heart from my chest."

"Rather you than me, bro. I never want a woman to have that kind of power over me."

"I've told myself the same bullshit lie for the past fifteen years, Flex. It took exactly one second for that to change."

"Then, what are you waiting for?"

I drain the last of my whiskey sour, fighting the urge to follow Naddie like the lovesick puppy I am. "She needs a little time to follow my instructions. It's all about the anticipation, Flex. By the time I go in there, she'll be... ready." If it were anyone else, I'd be calling it like it is. She'll be wet and ready for me to dominate every last inch of her body. Just thinking about how wet she was in my office this morning has me straining against my pants.

"It's crazy to me that the girl you lost your virginity to is a submissive. Another feather in the cap of the luckiest son of a bitch I know."

"Honestly, I don't think it's sunk in yet... not the fact that she's a sub. The moment I became a Dom, it was clear to me, looking back, that she was my first sub. We didn't have the knowledge to name it, but hindsight brings clarity."

"I saw the girl I lost my virginity to at my ten-year high school reunion, and I can honestly say I wouldn't touch her with a fifty-foot pole. Time wasn't kind to her or the once-prom-king jock she married after he knocked her up at eighteen. To say they peaked in high school would be a kindness."

I can't help but laugh. "She'd probably enjoy your kink these days, reading all the mommy porn she can get her hands on."

"Bro, she looks like someone has already been giving her a good paddle... to the face. She did not age well at all."

"That's brutal."

"I speak the truth."

"Where's your latest sub? Is she enjoying your predilection to mix pleasure and pain?"

"I ended it a few days ago. The woman is a pain in the ass. She'll comply in a scene, but outside, she wants a boyfriend to snuggle with. I don't have time for that shit."

"And on that note, I'm going to go and acquaint my new sub with the rules of engagement."

"Rub it in my face, why don't you."

"I speak the truth." He smirks as I use his own words from only moments ago.

"Later, bro. I want details."

"Not going to happen, Flex. This one is private." I stand and drop a fifty on the bar before heading toward my room.

"Buzzkill," he exclaims, chuckling as he orders another drink at the bar.

~

The room is dimly lit, warm, and inviting as I close the door behind me, but I'm not prepared for the sight of Naddie kneeling by the bed, her legs perfectly spread, hands behind her back, and her eyes cast to the floor. Fucking hell. She's perfect.

"Good evening, Naddie." I take my time walking toward her, removing my cufflinks and setting them down on the ornate play chest for safekeeping.

"Good evening, Master Callaghan."

"How would you like me to address you in this room?"

"Kitten, if it pleases you, Master Callaghan." She practically moans, sending a lightning bolt of desire straight to my core.

"Master will suffice."

"Yes, Master."

When I'm close enough to touch, I reach down, wrapping her long, silky hair around my fist before tugging her head back, forcing her to meet my gaze. "You look beautiful tonight, kitten."

"Thank you, Master." Her lips are so inviting it takes every ounce of control not to unbutton my pants and fill her mouth with my growing erection.

I lean down, pressing a chaste kiss to her blush-pink lips before stepping back to admire her.

"Goddamn, kitten, you look stunning, ready and waiting for me. Tell me, do you like the room? I had it redecorated for you."

She is breathtaking, kneeling by the bed, her thighs spread wide, her pussy on display for my eyes only.

"It's beautiful. Thank you, Master."

"You look magnificent tonight." She casts her gaze to the floor. "You may look at me, kitten."

I walk to the foot of the bed, the warm lighting giving me just enough light to enjoy every inch of Naddie as she kneels at my feet. She meets my gaze, her emerald-green eyes piercing my soul.

She watches intently as I systematically roll my sleeves up and then slowly unbutton my shirt, delighting in the way her breath hitches as she licks her lips.

"Do you need to squeeze your thighs together, kitten? You seem aroused by such a small thing as my bare chest."

"Yes, Master. I'm already wet at the thought of you." With Naddie, I struggle to make her wait for release. It's the essence of who I am as a Dom. I thrive on foreplay, and I've never had an issue making a sub suffer before. Anticipation is what does it for me. Perhaps a little pain to heighten the senses, but nothing like Flex is into.

When it comes to Naddie, all bets are off. I want her more than my next breath, and the way she's looking at me as I unbuckle my belt and unzip my fly has me desperate to watch her come.

"I think you've seen enough, kitten. If you keep looking at me with those fuck-me eyes, I'm going to lose it and fuck you till you can't walk."

"Would that be so terrible... Master?" she says as she casts her eyes to my feet.

"Only a brat would question me." I casually walk over to the heavy ebony drawers that house some of the toys I plan to use on Naddie tonight. First things first—a blindfold. Blush pink satin to match the hue of her cheeks when she succumbs to orgasm. I made sure she won't be able to see anything through the delicate material. I want her at my mercy, heightening her other senses as I caress, lick, and tease every inch of her naked flesh.

Kneeling at her back, I let my fingertips brush her skin, sending shock waves through every cell in my body. She's electric, creating her own gravitational field, and I'm helpless in her orbit.

I pepper featherlight kisses up her neck as I tie the blindfold tight, plunging her into darkness.

"What do you want, kitten?" I whisper in her ear, delighting in the shiver that runs down her spine.

"You, Master Callaghan." Fuck. I could come right now just at the sultry tone of her voice as she caresses my name.

"Do you trust me?"

"Yes, Master," she says in a breathless whisper.

I stand and move in front of her, taking her hands in mine and lifting her to a standing position. "Did you take a good look around the room while you were waiting, kitten?"

"No, Master. I kept my gaze on the floor as you requested." I'm happy to hear that. The less she knows, the better she'll feel by the time I'm done with her. I slowly guide her to the far side of the room, where a St. Andrew's cross adorns the wall like a piece of art. It's beautiful in its simplicity, but Naddie is going to look *exquisite* chained to it.

"And did you follow the rest of my instructions?"

"Yes, Master. I came straight to the room, stripped off my clothes, and folded them on the chair, just the way you wanted."

"Such a good girl. The thought of you in here, alone, naked, does things to me." With my pants hanging open and my cock straining to escape my boxers, I let her feel the effect she has on me. Naddie's breath catches as she wraps her delicate fingers around the head of my cock.

"Mm…"

"All in good time, kitten, but first we play." I ache for her touch as I remove her hand from my erection and position it against the cross before sliding the restraints around her wrist. She doesn't disappoint. With a sharp intake of breath, she clenches her thighs together to ease her growing arousal.

Tracing a line from the rapid pulse in her wrist, I work my way down her arm and across her chest, watching in awe as her pretty, blush-pink nipples pebble under my ministrations.

"You are… so fucking beautiful, kitten." Lowering my lips to follow the trail of my fingers, I capture one nipple with the warmth of my mouth, flicking my tongue over her tightly budded flesh before moving to the other side. Her soft mewls of pleasure go straight to my cock as she arches against my lips, hungry for more.

Grabbing her other arm, I secure her wrist with the restraint, making sure she can't move.

"I'm going to kiss every last inch of your body tonight. Think you can handle it?"

"Yes, Master." Her voice trembles as I slide my hand down her stomach and between her legs, cupping her pussy, slick against my palm.

"Oh, kitten, you're more than ready for me. How long have you been wet?" I lift my thumb to her mouth, wetting her bottom lip with her arousal.

"Since I got into position for you, Master Callaghan. The moment I spread my legs in anticipation of your arrival. Thinking about you claiming me as yours made me ache for your touch."

Dropping to my knees, I slide my hand down her left leg, coaxing her to adjust her balance as I pin her to the cross, kissing my way to the apex of her thighs. She tastes so fucking good. I'll never get enough of her.

"Spread your legs, kitten. As wide as they'll go." She does as I ask without hesitation, her stance so vulnerable as I fix the restraints to her ankles. She is completely at my mercy, unable to quell the mounting ache between her legs.

I stand to admire my handiwork, seeing her naked and splayed wide for my eyes only. She's a work of art, a masterpiece—her soft curves in glorious technicolor, a juxtaposition of the hard, ebony cross and cold metal restraints.

"Safeword."

"Blue."

"Any time you feel uncomfortable or you've reached your limit, you say your safeword."

"Understood, Master Callaghan." The words drip from her pouty pink lips like warm honey, coating me in desire.

"Good girl. I must say, you look breathtaking, kitten, your pretty little pussy ripe for the taking. And the way you taste... divine."

The rapid rise and fall of her chest make me harder still. There's nowhere for her to go or a way to shield herself from my gaze. It's a heady feeling, knowing how much she trusts me as her Dominant.

I set out a few different toys on the bed for later, but the hard leather handle of a flogger sits comfortably in my hand, the soft tails swaying as I make my way back over to Naddie. I start at her ankle, slowly working my way up her leg, her naked flesh trembling beneath the soft leather as it caresses her skin.

"Who do you belong to, kitten?" I say with a deep, primitive rumble.

"I belong to you…" she chokes out as the leather reaches the apex of her thighs, "Master Callaghan."

"That's right. You're mine." With a flick of my wrist, the flogger slaps her pussy, eliciting a moan of pleasure from her lips.

"*Yes.*"

"Do you like that, kitten?"

"Yes, Master. It feels so good." Jesus, I'm so turned on my cock hurts.

I flick my wrist once more before trailing the flogger up her torso. "Tell me, kitten, do you want it softer… or harder?" I do love straddling the line between pleasure and pain in the name of an explosive orgasm.

"Harder, Master." *Fuck me.*

Her nipples tightly bud as I trace her curves with the supple leather flogger, intoxicated by the way her body responds.

One short lash. "I'm going to do ten lashes. Count for me, kitten."

"One, Master."

"Good girl." I move to the other breast, and with a short, swift movement, she's gasping, biting down on her bottom lip.

"Two, Master."

Again and again, I flog her, moving between her breasts and her delicious pussy.

"Ten… Master Callaghan." Her voice is hoarse as she screams my name, begging for more. "Yes… oh God… yes, Master."

A soft sheen of sweat coats her skin, and the black leather tails are slick with her arousal, too inviting to ignore. I drop to my knees, pressing light, open-mouthed kisses between her thighs, teasing myself with the taste of her.

"Do you have any idea how sexy you are when you submit? You're truly exquisite." When she doesn't answer, I drag my tongue across her clit, pushing her a little closer to the edge before leaving her wanting more.

"Did you forget your manners, kitten? When your Dom compliments you, what should you say?"

"Thank you, Master."

"That's better," I say as I flog her breasts and bury my head between her thighs.

"Oh fuck! I'm close." Another flick of my wrist, and she's crying out.

"No swearing when my mouth's on you. I won't tolerate such bratty behavior. Understood?" I reluctantly remove my lips and replace the warm lash of my tongue with the leather tails.

"Yes, Master. I understand. Please... don't stop."

"Oh, kitten. I haven't even started yet. You won't come until I say so." I capture her pussy with my mouth, darting my tongue in her entrance, my eyes fixed on her as her entire body shudders against the restraints.

"Yes, Master." When I know she's on the brink, I get to my feet and capture her lips, letting her taste herself on my tongue.

"How do you taste?"

She hesitates, licking her lips and driving me wild. "I taste sweet, Master. I hope I'm to your liking."

Sliding my hands up her arms and into her hair, I kiss her with everything I have, ravenous for more. "You were made for me, kitten. I could eat you every day for the rest of my life and never tire of how... fucking... good your pussy tastes." I press my body to hers, letting her know exactly what she does to me as my cock strains against the fabric of my boxers, now soaked with her arousal. My pulse is racing as I fight the urge to take her hard and fast. I want to fuck her in this room, in my apartment, on every surface, in every way possible. *She's mine.*

As our tongues twist and tangle in a frenzied fuck, I grind against her, loving how she moans with pleasure. There's a bite of frustration as she fights the restraints, unable to control the onslaught of desire coursing through every nerve ending in her body, flushing her skin with every lick and nip of her lips.

She's so close I can almost taste it, and I force myself to pull back, leaving her bereft, if only for a few seconds. I grab a toy and some lube off the bed. The sleek sliver bulb is cold in my hand with a jeweled tip.

Ghosting a kiss on her neck, I alert her to my proximity as I squeeze a generous amount of lube on my fingers and position them on her ass, rubbing in soft circles.

"Do you enjoy feeling full here, kitten?" I whisper, pressing my fingertips in just a touch before sliding out.

"Yes, Master," she pants.

"You like being a dirty little brat, don't you, kitten?"

Her sharp intake of breath has me thrusting two fingers inside her. "Yes, Master Callaghan." *Fuck.* She's so fucking tight, but she takes me with a seductive moan. This was one of the kinks she put in her contract, and to put it mildly, I was fucking ecstatic.

"I can tell. Your ass is greedy for more." I insert a third finger, loving how her muscles cling to me.

"Yes… Master."

"Let me hear you ask for it." I leave her wanting more as I coat the butt plug in lube, my cock twitching at just how fucking full she'll feel with it in her ass and my erection filling her pussy until she can't take any more.

"Please, Master, I need more. I *need* to come."

I caress her voluptuous ass as I slip the cool metal between her cheeks. "What do you need? Where do you want me?"

"Everywhere. My mouth, my ass, my *cunt*." Jesus Christ. Her filthy mouth is in need of a good fucking, but she's hardly in the appropriate position right now.

I lean down, grasping her nipple with my teeth, applying just enough pressure to make her squirm. "You have a dirty mouth, kitten. I should deny you for calling *my* pussy a cunt."

"I'm sorry, Master. Please…"

"Should I make you come?"

"Yes…"

"Maybe I'll make you come, over and over again, until you can't take it anymore. Then, and only then, will I fuck you. Maybe then you'll remember to address me properly at *all* times."

I drop to my knees, ravenous for the taste of her, my tongue circling her clit as I insert the butt plug into her ass, reveling in the way her body strains against the cross.

"Master."

I devour her with my mouth as she cremes on my tongue. Her body tightens, fighting the need to come. "Tell me how much you want it, kitten."

"More... than my... next... breath... Master."

I graze my teeth over her tender clit, pushing her higher and higher until I know she can't hold out much longer.

With a long, languorous lick from her entrance to her clit, my cock aches to be inside her. "Come for me, kitten. Let me hear you." The second the words leave my lips, she detonates on my tongue, screaming my name as release takes over her entire body.

"Yes... *yes*... Master Callaghan!"

Chapter 13

NADDIE

My muscles tremble as I give myself over completely, trusting that the restraints will keep me upright as I collapse under the gravity of the orgasm ripping through my body. Dalton continues to kiss and suck my pussy, letting me ride the aftershocks pulsing through me until my head drops forward, my breath ragged, and my skin glistening with sweat.

"I could eat you for hours. You're so fucking beautiful when you come."

"I... can't." I'm not sure I can take another orgasm so powerful.

"If you want me to stop, you need only utter your safeword. If not, then I'll take what's mine, kitten."

A shiver runs down my spine, knowing I won't tell him to stop. I'm lost in the darkness, desperate to see his face and watch as he pleasures me, kneeling between my legs spread so wide it hurts. No matter how intense his touch is, I can't control it. I'm unable to tense my legs and squeeze my thighs together to lessen the desire unfurling deep inside me.

The pain is so good. I want more, even though it feels like my body can't take it.

Dalton peppers soft, silky, open-mouthed kisses at the apex of my thighs, my pulse still racing from the earth-shattering climax only moments ago.

He kisses me with the same tenderness he kisses my mouth, reverence in every brush of his lips on my most sensitive skin.

"You're mine, Naddie."

When he uses my name in this room, it affects me in ways I can't explain, as if it were a litany of worship enchanting and filled with such love only meant for me.

He continues to kiss me, flicking his tongue over my clit. "Your pleasure is mine."

"*Yes...*" I groan, desperate to see his wicked mouth on me.

His lips are gone, leaving me stranded between ecstasy and aching.

"Yes, who?"

"Yes, Master Callaghan."

"We have some training to do." His voice sounds distant, followed by something—ice—clinking into a glass.

I wait patiently for his return, my legs still twitching from orgasm, and yet desire unfurls deep in my core. I'm greedy for more of him—all of him.

There is something so freeing about submission. I've missed it so much since I left Boston, but it was never this good. Although I crave release, my soul is at ease, sated, and content in the knowledge that I belong to Dalton.

As I listen for where he is in the room, I relish being brazenly displayed for him, my pussy so wet and greedy for his cock. My clit is pulsing from the lash of the flogger, poised on the brink of release and ready to detonate again.

"Tell me, kitten, how does that pretty little ass of yours feel?"

"Full, Master. Wickedly full."

"Oh, you're not even close to full yet. Do you want me to fill you?"

"Yes, please, Master."

"You're such a good girl. Asking so nicely for my cock." A thrill courses through me as his voice gets closer. "Not feeling like such a brat now?" My body quivers as his lips graze my neck.

"No, Master. I want to be a good girl for you."

A low growl escapes him as his lips find mine, and his hand slides down my stomach, between my legs. "Did you enjoy being a good girl in my office today? Naked. Vulnerable. Naughty." He thrusts a finger inside me, and I can hardly stand it. I want more. I *need* him.

"Yes. More than I want to admit."

"And why is that? Are you ashamed?" He pulls back before thrusting two fingers inside me.

"Only of how much I want you."

He leaves me craving more before rubbing his thumb over my bottom lip. His kiss is slow and measured but deeper than the ocean. I can feel his breath against my ear. "*Never...* be ashamed of what you want and how you want it, kitten. Do you have any idea how fucking resplendent your naked submission is?"

"Please, tell me, Master," I entreat him as his fingers continue to tease me, circling my clit before plunging back inside me.

He caresses my neck with his lips, moving lower until the warmth of his mouth surrounds my nipple. "I've never seen anything so beautiful in my life." He flicks his tongue over the tip as it pebbles for him, my breasts becoming heavy with need. "The sight of you on your knees. This perfect pussy is wet and ready for me. God, kitten, it was more than I ever could've dreamed of in my wildest fantasy."

I can't help the moan that escapes me, sensation taking over.

"Do you want to see how stunning you look tonight, kitten? Do you want to watch as I fuck you?"

"Yes, Master Callaghan."

Dalton ghosts featherlight kisses over my cheeks as he reaches behind my head, undoing the blindfold and letting it drop to the floor as he presses his lips to my eyelids, and every muscle in my body sings with anticipation.

"Look at how well you submit for me," he whispers in my ear as he steps aside, the mirrors on the opposite wall coming into view. My pulse quickens at the sight of myself shackled to the St.

Andrew's cross, my breathing shallow with the rapid rise and fall of my chest.

I can feel Dalton's eyes on me as I take in every detail—the tightness of my blush-pink nipples, my pussy so ready to be fucked.

"Aren't you beautiful, kitten?" He reaches between my legs, his fingers teasing my clit, slick with my arousal.

"Yes, Master." His touch sends fire licking through my veins, my body climbing toward release.

Stepping back, he leaves me wanting more, but I watch in awe as he slips his shirt over his shoulders, striding to the chair he had me lay my folded clothes on. I can't take my eyes off him as he puts on a show. With his back to me, his broad shoulders and muscular frame taunt me as I wait impatiently for him to return. The growing ache between my thighs is almost unbearable as he turns to face me, a wicked grin complimenting the dark desire in his gaze as he pushes his suit pants and boxers to the floor. His impressive erection springs free, and I let out a whimper. I'm so greedy for him.

He takes his time, folding his pants and setting them on the chair before striding toward me, gloriously naked and every hard inch the Dom I crave. He stops two feet in front of me, fisting the base of his cock. "Is this what you want, kitten?" He bites down on his bottom lip as he relieves the ache I know he must be feeling at this moment.

"More than anything, Master."

He drops to his knees at my feet, and I'm so close to climax it hurts. He presses open-mouthed kisses at the apex of my thighs before blazing a trail down my left leg, his fingers undoing the restraint on my ankle, massaging it as he retraces his steps up my leg and across my pussy before doing the same thing down my right leg, making short work of the restraints.

Running his hands up the back of my legs, he applies slight pressure to the butt plug he inserted, sending a jolt through me.

"You're mine," he growls, and he's on his feet in one fluid motion, hoisting me into his arms, coaxing me to wrap my legs around his waist. My arms are still in restraints, leaving me unable to touch him. "Say it."

"I'm yours, Master Callaghan. I'm yours." Without another

word, his lips crash down on mine, swallowing my cry as he thrusts into me, filling me with every hard inch of his cock.

"*Fucking hell*," he roars as he claims me, the combination of his cock and the butt plug creating a fullness so unbelievable I almost come as he seats himself to the hilt. "You're so tight, kitten… and so fucking wet for me."

I delight in every move he makes, my hips free to meet his, circling and grinding as he buries his head against my neck, kissing, nibbling, and driving me wild as his tongue darts out on the spot he knows will make me buck and writhe on his cock.

With one hand braced on the cross, his other snakes around my waist as he pushes us higher, setting a punishing rhythm as he rocks into me over and over again.

"That's it, kitten. Take all of me." The sensation of his cock is overwhelming, every stroke sparking a wickedly delicious grind against the hard steel that fills my ass."

"Yes… oh God… yes… *yes! Master.*" When I'm on the brink, it's painful to hold back, having been pushed to the edge so many times tonight. My heart is beating wildly in my chest as I fight the urge to let go.

Dalton sets a vigorous pace, both hands now bracing the cross, my legs locked tight around him as he hammers into me, fucking me so hard I can't breathe, think, or do anything other than *feel*. His cock starts to pulse as he chases his release.

"Come with me, kitten. Let me hear you scream." His words are my undoing, my pussy tightening as we throw ourselves off the cliff, headlong into the ecstasy of orgasm.

"*Yes, Master!* Yes… yes… oh God… yes." I spiral out of control as he comes hard, every hot spurt of cum emptying inside me as I unleash my climax, screaming myself hoarse as I let go, our breaths heavy as we ride the aftershocks together. Dalton whispers sweet nothings as his lips find mine, and our souls entwine, curling around each other with the ease of familiar lovers. I bury my head into his neck, my heart laid bare as tears spill from my eyes.

"Shit. Did I hurt you?" He searches my gaze for answers, his brow furrowed.

"No. You didn't hurt me, Master."

"You're crying." He looks pained as he wipes my tears with his thumbs.

"I'm just... I can't believe I'm here... with you."

Dalton loosens the wrist restraints, my body spent as I slump against him. He bundles me into his arms, wrapping me in his warm, strong embrace. "It's real. This is the way it's supposed to be." A soft sheen of sweat covers our bodies, and Dalton brushes a tendril of hair off my face. "You and me."

"Are you sure?" The dam walls break, all my trepidation comes flooding out, and I'm desperate to know I pleased him. "Am I enough for you as a sub? Did I do well?"

"Yes, kitten. You did so well tonight. I'm so proud of what a good girl you are."

His words are like a cocoon, transforming me into the beautiful butterfly I've always wanted to be. In his arms, I'm safe. In his arms, I can truly be myself.

"Thank you, Master."

He walks us to the bed, pulling back the luxurious covers and nestling us underneath. He looks effortlessly sexy as he props his arm behind his head.

Tracing lazy lines on my shoulder, Dalton drinks me in. "Are you okay?"

"I've never been better." As I speak the words, I know them to be true.

"You..." he lifts my chin with such tenderness, imploring me to meet his gaze, "Naddie..." There's so much to say, and in this moment, no need to voice it. I lean in, letting my mouth brush his kiss-swollen lips.

"I know."

I nuzzle against the crook of his arm, my body weary and sated. We lie in comfortable silence for a while, wrapped in each other's arms, and I've never felt so content.

"Do you want to stay here a bit longer? Or do you want to sleep at my place?"

"I should probably go home."

He catches hold of my chin, coaxing me to meet his ice-blue gaze, a playful grin on his impossibly handsome face. "That's not an option. You're my submissive. You sleep with me. If you want to sleep in your own bed, I'm staying at your apartment."

"I've never been a twenty-four-seven submissive before." My cheeks flush at the admission, as if it makes me some kind of virgin, embarrassed by my lack of experience.

He gently presses his lips to mine. "Good. Another first for us to share. The first of many."

My heart skips a beat. "Is it a first for you?"

"Yes." If joy were wings, I'd be Icarus, flying too close to the sun.

"Really?"

"Is it so hard to believe that I've never found someone I wanted to be with in this way? You ruined me at eighteen. The bar was set too high." There's a sadness in his eyes. It's fleeting and quickly replaced with a warm smile and a whisper of a kiss.

"You're so successful and sure of yourself. I assumed you would have whoever you want, whenever you want."

"You're not exactly a slouch. A successful lawyer, making partner at a young age. Douglas headhunted you. Why haven't you found a forever Dom?" It pains him to even say the words, his voice thick with apprehension.

"Because it wasn't you."

With a deep rumble, Dalton captures my lips with his. "You're sleeping in my bed tonight, kitten. And every night from now on."

"Yes, Master Callaghan." The war that's been waging inside me since the day Dalton walked back into my life dissipates as I relinquish control.

"Good girl." His cock hardens against my hip before he rolls me onto my back, kissing me with the tenderness of my high school sweetheart before slowly easing inside me, owning every fiber of my being as the Dom he has become.

We make love long into the night, and Dalton takes such tender care of me afterward it makes my heart swell so much I find myself crying once more. Eventually, Dalton leads me through the silent club, taking me back to his penthouse. Falling asleep in his arms is more intimate than anything we've done tonight, and it's the one act I know is addictive. I could spend my whole life here, in his bed, his body cradling mine as we drift off, carried on the wings of a dream into a deep, sated sleep.

~

The past few weeks have been exhausting. I'm working my ass off during the day, learning all the ins and outs of The Callaghan Group, and in the evenings, Dalton is working me hard, teasing every ounce of pleasure from my body. My muscles ache in the most enjoyable ways, but I'm starting to feel the effects of operating on little sleep. It doesn't matter how many times we have sex, I crave more of him. Adjusting to being a twenty-four-seven sub is proving more difficult.

Dalton was right when he pegged me as a brat. I'm an independent woman, and though I want to trust him in all aspects of our relationship, I've never had to submit outside the bedroom. Although he says I'm his first fulltime submissive, he has taken to the role like a pro.

After the day we signed our contracts and Dalton had me strip naked in his office, we've remained professional during our long workdays, but our chemistry is palpable, always there, threatening to boil over.

When I'm ready to leave for the night, I see Dalton deep in conversation as I walk past his office. As if he can sense my eyes on his, he finds my gaze, tracking my every move as I keep walking. I can go back to my apartment for a couple of hours, although I wouldn't call it home. I haven't been in Manhattan long enough to put down roots, and since becoming a twenty-four-seven sub, I've barely set foot in my apartment. It's a glorified walk-in closet.

The elevator doors slide open just as my phone vibrates in my pocket.

> Dalton: Where are you going?

> Me: Home. You're busy. I'll just go back to my apartment tonight. I'm exhausted.

> Dalton: Okay. I'll see you tomorrow.

As the doors close and the elevator descends at a rapid speed, my stomach drops. I expected him to have something to say about my text, and the brat in me is ill at ease. This is the first time we'll spend the night apart.

> Me: Okay.

As I step out into the lobby and head for the street, Dalton's driver is ready and waiting as the warm evening breeze blows through my hair.

"Good evening, Ms. Sullivan."

"Hi. Dalton is still working."

"I know. He just text and told me to take you to your apartment."

"That won't be necessary. I can make my way back."

"I'm sure you can, but if it's not too much to ask, just let me drive you. I enjoy the path of least resistance. Anything for an easy life. That's what my wife says. If I have to tell him I left you to walk home, just between you and me, he'll chew me out."

That sounds about right. "Well, I wouldn't want you to get chewed out on my account. Thank you, Ryan."

It's a short journey to my apartment, and in the end, I'm grateful for the ride home. I almost fell asleep in the back seat. The second I get inside, I kick off my shoes, drop my bag on the counter-top, and head for the shower.

Peeling off my clothes, I let them fall to the floor before stepping into my steam-filled shower, the water beating down on my tired muscles. I brace my hands on the marble tile, holding myself up as a rainfall of droplets cascade down my body.

When my fingers begin to prune, I wrap myself in a plush, fluffy white towel, my hair dripping on the cool tile beneath my feet. It's nice to be around my things, but I'm acutely aware of the silence. Here, alone in my apartment, I'm not a submissive. For the first time in weeks, I'm just—me—and it leaves a bad taste in my mouth.

My eyes sting with exhaustion, but even when I crawl into bed, snuggling under the comforter, I can't sleep. Watching a show or two doesn't help, and my body is restless without Dalton. I've already become accustomed to the warmth of his body against mine, his arms around me as I fall asleep. It's only been a few weeks, and yet I feel like part of me is missing.

When the clock hits eleven, and I haven't heard from Dalton, I give in, grabbing my wallet and keys. The need to be where he is is so overwhelming I can barely breathe. The moment I exit my building, I hail a cab and head to Dalton's building.

My pulse is racing the closer I get, whooshing in my ears as I enter the lobby, accosting the concierge. "I'm here to see Dalton Callaghan. Can you call him, please?"

"No need, Ms. Sullivan." He reaches under the desk and hands me a manila envelope. "Mr. Callaghan asked that I have a key to the penthouse made for you yesterday. There's one for the elevator to the penthouse and one for the main door."

I rip open the envelope, snatching the keys out like Gollum from *Lord of the Rings*. It's pathetic, but it seems I have no shame as I run to the elevator. I tell myself it's just the sleep deprivation. I need to get some rest, and if his bed is the only place that can happen, then so be it.

As I turn the key in the lock, the clang of metal-on-metal rings out. When I push the heavy hardwood doors open, the apartment is cloaked in darkness.

"Dalton? It's Naddie. Are you here?" An uneasiness sweeps through me like a ghost from my past. "Dalton?"

Maybe he's working late, or he's already asleep. I kick off my shoes and pad down the hallway toward his bedroom as quietly as possible. My heart is pounding so hard it fills the apartment, surrounding me as I crack open the door to his room and find an empty bed.

I go in search of him, hoping he's in his office, an irrational fear settling in my chest.

"Dalton?" He's nowhere to be found.

I'm not this girl—the one who worries that the guy she's seeing is up to something behind her back. Why am I questioning the one man I *know* only has my best interests at heart? It's pathetic.

I don't want to leave because I'd rather he knows I came over when he gets back. If he's still not here in the morning, I'll deal with it then. Returning to the living room, I curl up in the corner of his plush, oversized sectional couch and make myself as small as possible, resting my head against the soft fabric, closing my eyes as emotional and physical exhaustion finally take over, pulling me into a deep, dreamless sleep.

Chapter 14
DALTON

Work was grueling today. All I wanted was to leave with Naddie when I saw her walking past my office, but I've been pushing meetings left, right, and center so I could leave at the same time as Naddie this past week. I can't get enough of her, but I still have a company to run.

I didn't want her to go back to her place alone, but by the time I finished it was late, and I started working on what I need to say to Douglas. I want it resolved sooner rather than later. Naddie has to be mine, for good.

Figuring I would take the opportunity to visit Mom for a while, I went straight to her apartment after work. I've spent less time with her since Naddie became my sub, and I need to do better. Tonight, we've discussed everything from politics to movies and the story of how she met my father on a loop. That one stings, but she remembers so much of her life with him and what we both thought was a perfect time for our family. She tells me all about her child, Dalton, and how her ten-year-old son aspires to be like his daddy.

I'm enough of a man to admit I fight back the lump in my throat when I watch the woman who raised me disappear before my eyes. I indulge anything she wants to talk about, committing as much to memory as I can. Sadly, I know there will come a time when we won't be able to have these conversations anymore, and I dread the day. I pour billions of dollars into research for dementia and Parkinson's disease, knowing it won't help my mother. For her, the breakthroughs will come too late, but maybe it will save someone else from suffering the same fate in the future.

"You look a little like my boy. I imagine he'll grow up to be a strapping man like yourself. Handsome and kind." Her smile is as radiant as ever.

"My mom always told me I was a handsome devil," I say with a conspiratorial wink.

"And does she also tell you that you should be out enjoying yourself and falling in love instead of listening to an old lady harp on about all sorts of nonsense?"

"Once or twice, but I so enjoy our chats, Candice. And you're not old." It's the truth. She's far too young for this to be her life, and I hate it for her. "You've lived such an interesting life." I reach for her hand.

"Me? I'm just a housewife. My husband is the one who's interesting. I think you'd like him. I'm surprised you haven't met him yet. Is he home from work?" It breaks my heart anew each day, placating her longing to see her one true love. Since Naddie walked back into my life, I have a new understanding of how fucking awful it must be for her to ache for him.

"I think he has a late business meeting tonight. If it's okay, I'm going to keep you company."

"Are you sure you don't have anywhere better to be?"

"There's nowhere else I'd rather be." This is the one thing I can promise her.

"Do you know where my son is? He's only ten."

"He's safe and sound, don't worry. He just wants you to get some rest."

"That sounds like him. He's such a sweetheart." The wistful look in her eyes has me fighting back tears.

"I'm sure it's because you're such a sweet momma, Candice."

"I hope so. All I ever wanted was to be a mom. Dalton is my

little miracle. The doctors said I would never have children of my own, but God blessed me beyond measure. There has never been a child more loved, cherished, and wanted than my Dally."

I had no idea. This wasn't something my mom ever shared with me. It should make me happy that I was wanted so badly, but everything inside me goes numb. How did we get here? My dad rotting in prison. My mom wasting away before my eyes.

We move onto other more trivial topics, and I stay by her side until she drifts off. In slumber, my mom is freed of the body that's failing her and the mind that can't quite grip everything she holds dear. She is peaceful, and the woman I know and love peeks through the darkness, reminding me of everything that's slipping through my fingers.

The door to my apartment was locked when I left. Adrenaline spikes as I creep inside, even though I logically know that someone would need to be a burglar savant to get past my security detail. Nothing looks out of place, but there's a faint hint of vanilla in the air, and a wry grin spreads across my face. I'd know her scent anywhere.

I switch on a lamp, careful not to wake Naddie if she's sleeping. It's one in the morning, and I wasn't expecting to see her tonight. When I spot her curled up in a little ball on the couch, my heart swells. After the night I've had, the sight of her is a soothing balm to my soul.

Loosening my tie and the top button of my shirt as I stalk toward her, I lean down, drinking her in—vanilla. She smells like home. Not the chaotic and often times lonely house I knew after Naddie left for college all those years ago. She's the home I've craved—a glimmer of calm in the storm.

Gently, I scoop her into my arms. She always was a heavy sleeper. She doesn't stir as I carry her to the bedroom and lay her down, pulling the comforter over her small frame. I quickly shower before crawling in beside her, draping my arm over her waist as her rhythmic breaths quiet my mind.

I'm not sure why she came here tonight, but it's as if she knew I needed her. I live to protect those I love, and I don't hold up too well when I feel completely helpless—it's why I let her leave tonight without resistance. I don't want to taint our contract with my problems. I'll figure out how to make Naddie mine for good, but some things transcend even her.

She stirs in my arms, her body reacting to mine in slumber, resting her head on my chest. I smooth her mussed hair off her face before pressing my lips to her forehead.

"I love you, Naddie. I always have." Her arm snakes around my waist as she slings one leg over mine. She was a bed-hogger in high school. Some things never change, and I need that in my life right now.

Placing my hand over hers, I let the day's tension leave me, hoping tomorrow will be a better day.

~

"Morning, kitten," I say as she pads down the hallway to where I'm sipping my first coffee of the day.

Rubbing her eyes, she yawns, her hair going in a million different directions. She's the cutest creature I've ever seen. "Hey." Her voice is husky in the morning, making my cock twitch.

"Come and sit down, and I'll grab you the biggest mug I can find." As she crawls into the chair, her knees to her chest, I can see there's something on her mind.

"Thanks. I'll need to be quick. I didn't bring clothes for work."

As promised, I pour her a massive mug of coffee, and I watch her smile fade as she takes it from my hand.

"I thought you wanted to spend the night at your place."

She scrunches her face, squirming in her seat.

"I couldn't sleep. Apparently, I'm *that* girl. And you weren't here anyway." That last sentence is dripping with disdain.

"Careful, kitten. You sound like a brat. If you'd called me, I would've been here to greet you. You were the one who wanted a night away from me."

"I know what I said, but I couldn't sleep without you. Trust me, I hate myself for it."

"Why? There is nothing wrong with wanting to be here with me." As I take my seat, I gesture for her. "Come here."

"No."

"No?" It's too early for this.

"I don't want to."

"Did I ask if you want to? Come here, kitten. It's not a request."

Her expression is surly as she sets her mug down and reluctantly stands, walking to my side, refusing to meet my gaze.

Pulling her into my lap, I wrap my arms around her. "I love that you couldn't sleep without me. Coming home to find you here was the highlight of my day." She bristles at my touch, her body tensing without a hint of warmth toward me.

"Where were you?" I am mentally and emotionally wrung out after last night. This isn't the time to sit down and explain my mom's rapidly declining health with Naddie. Besides, she's being a brat.

"I think you're forgetting who you're talking to. Have the decency to address me properly and meet my gaze when you talk to me."

"I'm sorry... Master." She practically spits it at me.

"Say it like you mean it, kitten."

"Where *were* you... Master?" My blood boils that she doesn't trust me.

"I want you in the position *now*."

"What?" She jumps off my lap, her hands on her hips in consternation.

"If you don't trust me, then what are we doing here? You signed the contract. I don't have to explain myself to you, not like this. Approach me when you've adjusted your attitude, and I'll tell you anything you want to know. Now, either get in the position or go. I'm not kidding around, Naddie. You trust me or you don't. There's no in-between."

My brain is screaming, begging her to stay, but after last night, I have no patience for bratty behavior. I have shit going on, and I'm running on very little sleep.

Naddie turns on her heel and heads for the door. Is she serious right now? We've waited this long to be together, and we're falling at the first hurdle. I can't go after her. As her Dom, I can't chase her down and beg her to stay.

As the door closes behind her, I grab the mug of coffee and launch it against the wall. I'm fucking up, trying to be everything to everyone and falling woefully short. Reaching for my phone, I tap out a quick message.

> Me: I need to speak with you this week. Do you have time tomorrow?

> Douglas: Is everything okay? What time do you want me to come by?

> Me: 11 am. Everything's fine. Thanks.

> Douglas: I'll see you then.

It's now or never. Even though I'm pissed at Naddie, our spat this morning just speaks to a bigger issue. We can't build on a foundation of existing in the shadows. I need Naddie to trust that I'm going to care for her, consider her, and satisfy *all* her needs. That starts with making good on our contract.

I take my time getting ready for work, needing a little time to myself. Standing under the burning hot showerhead is as close to therapy as I'm going to get. I let it all wash away—the stress, the heartache, and my annoyance from this morning. I can see why Naddie was upset, even if I hoped she'd know to trust me. I would never do anything to hurt her.

By the time I reach the office, I've decided that I'm going to tell her what's going on in my life, but not today. First things first, we need to deal with Douglas. Before getting down to business for the day, I head straight for Naddie's office on the opposite side of the floor.

She doesn't so much as lift her gaze when I close the door

behind me, sliding the lock into place. Fuck, she's sexy as hell when she's mad.

"We're meeting with Douglas tomorrow at eleven o'clock. Be sure to clear your schedule."

"What contract are we discussing?" she says with indifference.

"Ours."

Her eyes snap to mine. "What?"

"You didn't trust me this morning, Naddie. The only way forward for us is honesty in all things. I can meet with Douglas alone if you wish, but I thought you deserved the respect of being included. It is your career on the line, after all. The choice is yours."

"What are we going to tell him?" There's my kitten, her stern expression softening.

"The truth. Then, I want you to let me deal with it as I see fit. You might not like it."

"What do you mean?"

"I might need to pay him off."

"No." She's up and standing toe-to-toe with me in seconds. "You're not paying for me to have a job."

"I didn't pay for you to be hired, but guys like him respond to dollar signs when it comes to keeping things quiet."

"Maybe he'll be okay with it." There's no conviction in her voice, and as much as I'd love to reassure her, I'm already prepared to do what's necessary.

"There are a few other options." I keep my hands in my pockets, forcing myself not to touch her. There's still the matter of this morning to deal with.

"Tell me."

"Forgetting your manners this morning?"

"*Please.*"

"We could get married." My pulse quickens as I speak the words out loud. For me, this is a done deal. Naddie and I *will* get married eventually, sooner rather than later if I have any say in the matter. I'm met with a wall of silence. "Or... I could buy the firm. I could buy a different firm if you want."

"Money or marriage? That's your solution?" She starts pacing the room. "Buy my career or me."

"Hold the fuck up. I would *never* try to buy you. If that's how you'd view us getting married, then maybe we're wasting our time here. I get that this isn't ideal."

"*Not ideal…*"

"Don't interrupt me when I'm speaking… kitten. Sit down and listen to me." If looks could kill, I'd already be dead, but after she takes a moment to calm her breathing, she does as she's told.

"I'm listening."

"I will explain everything to Douglas in hopes that he simply agrees to a contract absolving the firm of any consequences that could come from our relationship, with no money involved. However, I know him to be a fierce businessman, and I doubt he'll pass up the opportunity to pad his retirement fund. I'm just giving you fair warning that I'm going to do whatever it takes to ensure your safety, whether you like it or not. You're mine now, Naddie, and I won't apologize for the lengths I'll go to keep it that way. Take the day to think it over, and let me know if you want to sit in on the meeting."

Naddie left the office without so much as a goodbye tonight, so when I'm done for the day, I head to her apartment. I'm not going into this meeting tomorrow without talking to her. I know she's scared, but I need her to know she's safe with me.

There's no answer at her apartment. Either she's avoiding me, or she's not home. Pulling out my phone, I dial her number, but she doesn't pick up. The thought of her being out at this time of night —alone—is a slap in the face of reality. Maybe she's realizing this— us—isn't worth it to her.

> Me: You're not home. Call me when you get in.

I wait for the annoying dots to appear, but they don't come. She could be anywhere.

When I get back to my building, I go straight to my mom's, wanting to check in on her. Thankfully, she's resting peacefully. With her sound asleep, safe from the perils of her mind—if only for a few hours—I drag my ass up to my apartment. This morning feels like days ago, and as I turn the lock, I check my phone one last time to see if Naddie is home. I won't sleep, no matter how tired I am. Not until I know she's okay.

Dropping my keys on the counter, I kick off my shoes and grab a bottle of water from the refrigerator. It's only been a few weeks, and yet this place already feels empty without Naddie. She can be mad as hell or bratty as can be, but I want her here with me.

When I reach my bedroom, I flip on the lights, and the breath is knocked out of my chest by the sight before me. Naddie is in the position at the foot of my bed, her legs spread wide with only a scrap of lace covering her pussy. Her breasts are on display, her nipples pebbling under my gaze. She has her hands clasped behind her back and her eyes to the floor.

I wait for her to speak, but she awaits my permission.

"Why are you here, Naddie?" She shivers at the use of her name.

"I came to apologize, Master Callaghan. I was out of line this morning. I shouldn't have left."

"No, you shouldn't have."

"May I look at you, Master?"

"Why?" My pulse is racing and my cock is as hard as a fucking rock. Seeing her like this is a test of my fortitude as a Dom.

"Because I would like you to see the genuine remorse in my eyes." God, she kills me.

"You may look at me."

As her eyes find mine, it's like being slammed by a Mack truck at ninety miles per hour. Everything I've ever wanted is at my feet.

"Master, I'm so sorry for leaving. I should have trusted you."

"Yes, you should. Have I ever given you a reason not to?"

"No, Master."

"Then why did you leave instead of giving me the benefit of the doubt?" It takes every ounce of self-control not to drop to my knees and ravish her.

"Because I'm scared."

"Of me?" Fuck. Please say no. I can't take another blow right now.

"No. Yes. I'm scared of how much I want you. I never got over you, Dalton," she says my name with such trepidation, and yet she knows it's the right way to address me at this moment.

"I accept your apology. I understand how you feel because I'm scared too. You're... we're... us. You have to trust me. If I don't tell you something, it's because I've deemed it to be in your best interests. I would never be unfaithful to you, Naddie. Tell me you know that."

"I trust you, Master. And I will trust whatever action you see fit tomorrow." My heart swells in my chest, threatening to burst with love for this woman. I know how hard this is for her to relinquish control.

"Thank you, kitten. I'm so proud of you for coming here tonight. I know it can't have been easy." Naddie isn't one to offer an apology lightly. "I am sorry you were worried about me, but in the future, you sleep here. It's not up for discussion. Understood?"

"Yes, Master Callaghan." I will never tire of this moment, having Naddie call me Master, her legs spread wide as she eagerly awaits instruction. I want nothing more than to make her come all night, but there's a fine line as a Dom who often uses pleasure to discipline.

I let her watch as I unbutton my shirt, her eyes wide as saucers, her greedy gaze settling on my happy trail. Taking a step toward her, I'm so hard it's painful.

"Loosen my belt, kitten." She doesn't hesitate, making short work of the buckle, biting down on her bottom lip as her fingers brush my waistband. "Now unzip my fly and release my cock."

The second her hand reaches inside my boxers, wrapping her fist around my erection, I can barely contain a growl. Jesus, her hands feel good on my aching cock, but I let her sit back, anticipating my next instruction. Wrapping my palm around the base of my cock, I watch the rapid rise and fall of her chest with satisfaction.

"I'm not sure if I should reward you with this," I say as I pump my fist. Naddie's hungry gaze looks set to devour me whole.

"I don't deserve to be rewarded, Master. I will do as you see fit." Right answer.

"Your punishment will be the ache between your thighs as you pleasure me. It'll remind you what you'll be denied when you act like a brat."

"Yes, Master." I can tell she's already suffering. The position is designed to cause maximum discomfort and desire at the same time. One flick of my tongue right now, and she'd fall to pieces. She has no way to alleviate the growing, heavy throb of her pussy.

"Now, put that pretty little mouth to good use. I want to see those lips wrapped around my cock."

"May I use my hands also?"

"No. I'll guide you. Hands clasped behind your back, kitten." She does as she's told without question. Reaching down, I clasp her chin and position myself against those luscious lips. "Open your mouth for me."

The wet warmth of her mouth is so fucking good that I actively distract myself so as not to shoot my load in three strokes. Setting a slow, steady rhythm, allowing her to get used to the girth of my cock, I can't get over how goddamn beautiful she is on her knees, greedily lapping at my cock, her soft tongue working the hard length of my shaft. Every murmur of desire sends a vibration through me, making it all the sweeter as I watch in awe of the woman before me.

I'm terrified that I'll wake up from a dream, Naddie will be gone, and all of this is a figment of my imagination.

Fisting my hands in her hair, I thrust deeper until I hit the back of her throat, and she takes every hard inch, her hands interlaced behind her back as she gives herself over to me.

"You're so fucking beautiful, kitten. Your mouth was made for me."

A moan escapes her, and I tighten my grip, steadying myself as I slide in and out of her lips, mesmerized by the sight of her perfect pout sucking my cock. As I continue to fuck her mouth, I wrap her long, chestnut locks around my wrist, picking up the pace, watching as her breasts bounce with every thrust.

When the beginnings of release spark to life, I pull out, knowing she wants this as much as I do at this moment.

"Slide your hand between your legs and tell me how wet you are for me." With her eyes fixed on me, she does as she's told, and I could detonate without another touch. God, she's breathtaking.

"I'm soaking wet for you, Master."

"Taste yourself." She slips her fingers into her mouth, moaning as she tastes her arousal. "Do you taste good?"

"Yes, Master." Fucking hell.

I lean down, tugging her panties to the side, drenched with desire. "Oh, you love sucking my cock, don't you, kitten?"

"Yes, Master Callaghan." Her voice is a breathy whisper as I thrust two fingers inside her before leaving her bereft as I lift them to my lips, darting my tongue out to taste her for myself.

"You taste so fucking good. Wrap those lips around me, kitten. I want you to swallow every drop like a good girl."

This time, I don't set the rhythm, letting her mouth do the work as she takes as much of me as she can, her tongue swirling around the crest of my cock, pumping harder and faster until I can't hold back any longer.

Every muscle in my body tightens as release takes hold, pulsing down my cock until warm cum spills into her mouth. She swallows every last drop, her moans of pleasure making me come harder than ever before. Wave after wave of pleasure courses through me as I throw my head back and sing her praises.

"Fuck, *yes*… that's it, kitten. You're so fucking good."

Chapter 15
NADDIE

Dalton's cock is still hard as he pulls out of my mouth, the ache between my thighs painful as I remain in the position, unable to quell the desire pulsing through my core.

"You did well, kitten. Tell me, how badly do you crave release right now?" He runs his hands through his raven-black hair, only serving to make me want him more with his sex-mussed style.

"It's painful, Master. You felt how wet I am for you."

"Yes, I did. Will you remember this feeling?"

"I will, Master."

"That's how my heart aches when you don't trust me as your Dom."

"I'm sorry, Master."

"You're forgiven, but as much as I want to let you ride my face right now, I can't."

"I know, Master." I drop my gaze to the floor, my shame too much to bear. "I will learn to be a good submissive. *Your* twenty-four-seven submissive."

"That's right, kitten, you're mine." He holds his hand out to help me up before cupping my face with such tenderness I melt. "Come with me."

I follow him as he leads me into the bathroom, lifts me onto the countertop, and starts the shower. There's a comfortable silence between us as he divests me of my panties before taking off the rest of his clothes. When the water is hot enough, he guides me inside the oversized, opulent shower, letting the weighty glass door swing shut as he captures my lips in a sultry kiss.

The frenzy of moments ago is gone, and in its place is a soul-deep, earth-shattering kiss.

The kind of kiss that makes you want forever.

Encircled by steam, under the heavy pounding water, Dalton and I lose ourselves in each other, every brush of his lips on mine, a litany of worship.

When he finally relinquishes my mouth, I'm left wanting more. He pumps shower gel into his hands before washing every inch of my body, so tender and loving, without the need for more. Right here, at this moment, I feel loved and cherished in a way I haven't since I left for college all those years ago.

He *sees* me, and he *wants* me.

When he's made sure I've been lathered and rinsed, he shuts off the water and grabs a fluffy white towel from the rail just outside the shower, wrapping me up before directing me out into the bedroom. The lights are low, and the bag I brought with me sits in the corner.

"Did you bring anything to wear to bed?"

"Yes, Master." A thrill runs through me, eager for his approval.

"Then get ready. I know I've had you running on a few hours of sleep. That needs to change."

I drop the towel, letting it puddle at my feet. He doesn't say a word as I calmly walk over to my bag, bending down to unzip the leather tote.

"Fuck me, kitten. You should be illegal. You look so fucking good."

My hands tremble as I shrug into my pajamas—his Rolling Stones T-shirt. Turning to face him, I'm rewarded with a stare so fierce it could set the whole room on fire.

"Thank you, Master." His eyes rake the length of me, his cock standing at attention beneath the towel wrapped around his waist.

"*Oh, kitten,*" he purrs. "I can't believe you kept it all these years." Closing the distance between us with a few short steps, his hands fist in my hair before his lips capture mine in a desperate kiss. As his hands begin to roam, desire is heavy at my core, the unsatisfied ache from earlier returning with a vengeance.

I savor every flick of his tongue and his groans of pleasure as my body brushes against his cock. When I'm sure this kiss will end with a screaming orgasm, he pulls back, a petulant moan escaping me.

"Get under the covers, kitten."

If there were ever a time for puppy dog eyes, it's now, but he remains unaffected. "Yes... Master."

"There's that bratty tone again. What am I going to do with you?"

"Fuck me? Hard. I promise I won't take any pleasure in it," I say with a sickly-sweet smile.

"Nice try. Under the covers. Now."

I do as I'm told, sure to let him know I am *not* happy about it.

"If you'd rather sulk alone, I can sleep in one of the guest rooms."

"That's not funny."

"It wasn't supposed to be." His tone is every inch the Dom I need him to be.

"I want to sleep next to you... Master." He drops the towel and slips in beside me, opening his arm for me to cuddle into the crook of his chest, where I gladly snuggle close, drinking in the scent of his skin as I listen to the rapid beat of his heart. It's torture to have the hard planes of his naked flesh against me. I want so badly to have him claim me with his cock, marking me as his.

"You sleep here now. I meant what I said earlier." He trails his finger softly down my arm, a stark juxtaposition to his commanding tone.

"I know. Can I ask you a question first, Master?" His body tenses at my words, making me more nervous about what I'm going to say next, but it's the elephant in the room.

"Go ahead."

"If you move my stuff here, what happens at the end of our contract?"

"We sign the next contract, and you continue to sleep right here in my arms."

"But…"

"I've got it under control. Stop worrying about tomorrow, Naddie. Be here with me today. You may have given your body over to me, but I need you to give your trust. Everything is going to work out the way it's supposed to."

"Yes, Master. Thank you for letting me ask."

"You're welcome. Now, go to sleep."

"Goodnight, Dalton."

"Goodnight, Naddie." He presses his lips to the top of my head before shutting off the lights.

As I lay in Dalton's bed, my head on his chest, staring up at the ceiling, a cold dread takes root, wondering what tomorrow will bring—the end of my career or everything I've ever wanted? I can't shut off my brain, and after ten minutes of silence, Dalton flips his bedside lamp on.

"Even when you're quiet, you are loud, my little brat. What's on your mind?" Dalton's voice is smooth like silk, warm and inviting as he gently runs his fingers through my hair.

"I don't want to lose this."

"You won't. It'll all work out, Naddie."

"And if it doesn't? I might not have a job tomorrow. Or a career."

He heaves a long, measured breath before he speaks. "You can still walk away, Naddie. I won't hold you to the contract's timeframe. If you don't want to risk it, I understand." There's no malice in his voice, only love and tenderness, and it makes my heart ache.

"You'd let me go?"

His fingers are still in my hair, and his whole body tenses. "If that's what you want. I won't hold you against your will or force you to pick between me and a career you've worked so hard for. It's no secret that I'll do whatever it takes… but only if you want to fight for us too. If not, then you have to walk away now."

"It would be easier if I walk away."

"Do you really believe that?"

"No."

With an audible sigh of relief, he starts caressing my hair once more. "Then, tell me what you need, Naddie."

"I *need* you." I tilt my head to meet his gaze. "I desperately want it all. Is that selfish of me?"

"Not at all. I'm the selfish one, Naddie. I couldn't stay away from you. I tried. A better man would have."

"I love you, Dalton. The boy you were. The man you are. The Dom I need."

We lie in companionable silence for a while, lazily touching each other in tender, loving caresses.

"When did you become a Dom?" I want to know his story and how we came to find ourselves and become the people who seem so perfect for each other, even after fifteen years. My words are tentative, almost fearful of the answer.

"I told you to go to sleep."

"Please, Master. I want to know."

He shakes his head in resignation. "About a year after you left for college. Looking back, it was obvious. You and me." My heart sinks. All this time, he's had other submissives kneeling at his feet when it should have been me.

"I was your first sub."

"And I was your first Dom." He runs his thumb down my cheek, such longing in his words.

"Yes." I take a moment to compose myself, tears welling in my eyes for the life that could have been. "Have there been many... subs?"

"Do you really want to have this conversation, kitten? It seems unnecessarily cruel. Fifteen years is a long time."

"I just... even if it hurts... I need to know about your life. In the end, it brought us to this moment."

His gaze softens, understanding clear as he resigns himself to the details he's about to share. "Yes, there have been many subs." A burning sensation spreads throughout my body. It hurts more than I thought it would.

"I shouldn't be surprised. Look at you. You're the whole package."

"It's not what you think, Naddie. I'm not some manwhore who fucked anything that moved."

"You don't have to justify anything to me, Dalton. I asked, and you answered." I fight past the lump in my throat.

"And if life were that simple, it would be a hell of a lot easier. As I told you, I've never had a twenty-four-seven submissive before, but I've always been monogamous within any arrangements. I never even brought a sub back to this apartment."

"Really?"

"Naddie, I never loved any of them. I wanted to. My life has felt so lonely at times, and don't get me wrong, I cared for each of them and provided what I could offer as a Dom, but… I was never *in* love with anyone. You ruined me at eighteen. No one ever came close to how I felt and still feel about you, kitten."

"I just hate that we lost so much time together."

"But we're here, in this bed, together. We can't change the past, but we can be here, in the present, and be thankful for every minute."

I kiss his taut pec muscles before settling back down, trying to digest what he's told me.

"I'm not sure I even want to know," he begins. "How long have you been a submissive?"

"Four years." He rubs a hand over his heart as if trying to alleviate a physical pain.

"Yeah, I didn't want to know."

"I'm sorry." I understand his reaction. The thought of him with any other submissive makes me what to hunt them down and claw their eyes out.

"Don't apologize, kitten. You have nothing to be sorry about. I asked. You told me."

"Okay."

"Did you love any of your Doms?"

"If it pains you, why do you want the details?"

"Why did you?"

"Fair enough. I had love for the man who trained me, but I wasn't *in* love with him."

"Was he in love with you?" I think of my final interaction with Theo.

"Maybe. If he was, he never said it. He did offer a long-distance relationship before I moved, but I declined."

"What about the others?"

"There were no others."

His body stiffens beneath me. "You've *only had one* Dominant?"

I push myself up into a sitting position. "Yes."

He puts his arm over his eyes, shielding the pain I hear echoed in his voice. Dalton's hands ball into fists. "I hate that another Dom got four years with you."

"I was never his, Dalton. We had a contract. We slept together."

"He was your first."

"*You* were my first, Dalton. I have never belonged to anyone but you. Please..." I reach for his arm, coaxing him to look at me. "Don't hate me. I was trying to find my place in the world without you." My heart aches, my pulse thundering in my ears.

He sits up, cupping my face with his warm, callused hands. "I could never hate you, kitten. I just... I'm jealous. I know I have no right to be, but when it comes to you, all rationality goes out the window."

"And you think I don't feel jealous of the subs you've had in the past fourteen years? You're mine, Dalton. *My Dominant.*"

His lips crash down on mine. "Say it again."

"You're my Dominant. Mine, Master Callaghan."

"I wish I could say you won't be getting any sleep tonight because that is the sexiest thing I've ever heard."

"Do with me as you please, Master." His voracious kiss swallows my words as he pulls me back down onto the bed.

Grabbing the hem of his ratty old T-shirt, he pulls it over my head, tossing it to the floor. "I'm afraid not, kitten."

Dalton leaves me craving him with every fiber of my being as he pulls my back to his chest.

"Goodnight," he whispers at the shell of my ear, his erection hard against my ass. He's really going to leave us both frustrated.

"Master, ple…"

"Goodnight, kitten."

As I fall asleep in his arms, my fear of what will happen tomorrow seems insignificant, if only for tonight, because at this moment, there's only us, and nothing else matters.

"How can you be a lawyer without a poker face?" Dalton thinks he's cute this morning as I pace his office, waiting for Douglas to arrive. My stomach has been in knots since I left Dalton's apartment this morning. He chastised me for not moving some clothes to his place already, but I've been reluctant until we know what's going to happen.

My hands are clammy as I play out the possible outcomes of this meeting. I could be jobless in a few hours. I could have to leave and return to Boston to practice law. The thought of leaving Dalton makes me lightheaded.

"This isn't funny."

He moves to where I am, pulling me into his arms. "I know that. What you're doing to give us a shot at forever is… amazing. I don't take it lightly. Come and sit down. You look white as a ghost."

Wrapping my arms around him, I inhale the comforting scent of his cologne. "Forever?"

"I know you meant that as a statement rather than a question, kitten." He presses a kiss to the top of my head. "Now, do as you're told and sit down."

He leads me to one of the chairs on the opposite side of his desk before kneeling at my feet, taking my hands in his.

"It's all going to be okay. I won't let anything bad happen. Do you trust me, Naddie?" His gentle gaze is filled with so much love it makes my heart melt.

"Yes, Master Callaghan."

"That's my girl," he says, pressing his lips to the back of my hand. I can't take my eyes off him as he stands and moves to his throne on the other side of the desk.

"Would it be better if I explain everything?"

"No." He leaves no room for discussion. "Let me, Naddie. As your Dom, I have to do this. Please understand. Maybe I shouldn't ask that of you. I know it's your career we're talking about."

"I understand. I've always been so self-assured when it comes to work. It feels unnatural to me. Being a twenty-four-seven sub is an adjustment."

"I know, and you're doing so well." My nerves lessen at the acknowledgment, letting his praise wash over me.

"I love you."

"I love you too."

The buzz of the intercom interrupts our tender moment. Audrey's voice is tight as she announces the arrival. "Mr. Callaghan, if you are ready, Mr. Mason and... Mr. Mason have arrived."

My gaze shoots to Dalton. "Robert is here too?"

"He wasn't invited. I'll get rid of him. Wait here." A wave of nausea takes hold as he strides to the door.

I take a few deep breaths in through my nose and out through my mouth, steeling myself for whatever comes next. I'm an awesome lawyer. Loving Dalton isn't a defining moment in my career. We'll deal with it and move forward.

I'm an amazing lawyer. And I'm hopelessly in love with my Master.

When Dalton returns, Douglas follows close behind, surprise evident in the deep set of his brow, his eyes on me. "Good morning, Nadia. I wasn't expecting to see you today."

He looks to Dalton as he takes a seat.

"Is everything okay?"

"Yes. Nadia has been working hard to learn everything about The Callaghan Group. You made a great choice when you hired her, Douglas."

He looks between us, clearly concerned as to why his son was asked not to join our meeting. "Then, why am I here?"

161

I clasp my hands in my lap, my gaze fixed on Dalton as I fight the urge to start pleading my case to my boss.

"Douglas, you and I have known each other for a long time. I trust you with all my business dealings."

"I would hope so. It's been what... twelve years?"

"Yes. You know I'm a man of integrity."

"Of course."

"So, I'm trusting you with what I'm about to tell you as my lawyer. It doesn't leave this room."

"As always."

"I knew Nadia before she came to work at Mason, Porter & Associates."

"Why is this the first I'm hearing of it?" Douglas asks, his eyes on me.

"I asked her not to disclose our relationship until I saw fit. Nadia and I grew up together but hadn't seen each other in fifteen years. We were both rather surprised when we ended up in the same conference room in Milan."

"Am I to believe you had no knowledge before I offered you the job?" I can see Dalton growing irate that Douglas keeps directing his questions to me, but I completely understand.

"You're well aware that I changed my name to get out from underneath my father's sullied reputation." Dalton commands his attention. "And you've been party to every contract written with the explicit purpose of keeping me out of the limelight. She didn't know."

"I'm assuming there's more." His disapproving tone does nothing to allay my fears.

"Nadia and I are in a relationship. My understanding is that this could be cause for concern, but considering our prior knowledge of each other, I believe it shouldn't be an issue for you, Douglas." He chooses his words carefully. "You and I have a long history, so you know I wouldn't enter into this lightly." He pins Douglas with his stare.

"If it weren't cause for concern, I wouldn't be sitting here right now. I know you understand that this is a major conflict of interest, not to mention a potential concern for the firm. A current relationship prior to Ms. Sullivan joining your team would be less of an issue for the Bar Association. Being childhood friends who had no contact until her being hired with the specific intention to take over your account is something else entirely."

"I don't see why. My father's downfall ended our relationship, and now I'm righting the situation."

"Nadia, this could mean your career in New York. You've got such promise. Is it worth it to run the risk?" I'm about to answer when Dalton interjects.

"With all due respect, Douglas, I'm the one speaking to you right now, and I expect you to direct your answers to me." His shoulders tense as he fights the urge to physically enforce his place as my Dom. I can feel the distance across the desk eating at him.

"And with all due respect... Dalton... your personal contracts hold no sway within *my* firm. Nadia is my employee, and I won't jeopardize my credibility for not only an inappropriate relationship between one of my lawyers and clients but a relationship that would not be viewed favorably if it came to light."

All of my worst fears are confirmed. Being Dalton's girlfriend is bad enough. Being his submissive is career suicide.

"Be careful of what you say next, Mr. Mason. I'm your biggest client, and I have sway with most of your client base. How dare you judge us for the way we choose to conduct a consensual relationship. You've never had a problem profiting from my personal contracts in the past."

"What you do in your own time is none of my business, but if it involves my employee, that changes things."

"Are you duty-bound to report this to the Bar Association?"

"Ethically, yes."

Dalton meets my gaze, silently reassuring me before he continues.

"Douglas, I didn't ask you here to seek your approval for a momentary dalliance. I am proposing a contract between myself, Ms. Sullivan, and the firm, absolving you of any conflict of interest.

I've already done the research, and this will be a nonissue when Nadia and I are married."

My heart stutters to a halt. *Marriage.*

"You've been together a month at best."

"That's not your concern. I'm not wistfully hopeful for the future, I'm stating fact. I'm going to marry Naddie, so the only thing I need from you is an agreement in the interim."

Douglas is aghast, as am I at this moment, and yet, as my eyes find Dalton's, a massive grin spreads across my face.

When I turn to Douglas, I feel more self-assured than ever. "I'm sorry I didn't tell you sooner, Mr. Mason, but Dalton is correct. This isn't a fling. I would never risk my career for something so transient. I am still as committed to the firm as I was the day I accepted the position as partner."

"If I am to believe you and continue with your appointment as partner..."

If.

Cold reality hits me like a slap in the face.

"I should be compensated for my cooperation."

Dalton saw this coming. He tried to warn me that a man like Douglas responds to dollar signs. If I'm to keep my career, I have to let Dalton bribe him, or I need to find another firm to work for.

Who is going to want to hire me when I seem like a firm hopper? Even if Dalton pays Douglas to stay quiet, I'll always know my position is paid in hush money. I don't want that. I've worked too goddamn hard to earn every accolade. I love Dalton with all my heart, as a man and as a Dom, but I won't submit my career to anyone.

I suddenly have the clarity of what I want and the terms on which I'm willing to get it, and peace washes over me.

"I appreciate you taking the time to meet with us today, Mr. Mason. I can't in good conscience allow Dalton to purchase my continued employment. Please consider this my verbal resignation. I will tender my written resignation by the end of the day."

Then, I turn my attention to Dalton.

"May I be excused, Master Callaghan?"

Chapter 16
DALTON

My heart grinds to a halt as the words leave her lips. This was not in my plan for today. I'm simultaneously angry as hell and proud as can be. I told Naddie to let me handle Douglas. I could see that she was holding out hope for a discreet understanding from the old man. In an ideal world, that would've been the perfect scenario, but he didn't get his reputation as a shark by playing nice.

Nadia is the picture of serenity right now—calm in the eye of the storm. She has just upended her whole life for me, and yet here she sits across from me, her hands clasped behind her back in a show of respect, addressing me as her Master. *She's my submissive, and it's as painful as it is beautiful.*

"Yes, you may leave. I will speak with you later. I still have a few things to discuss with Douglas."

"Thank you, Master." She turns on her heel and heads for the door with the confident strut of the woman I've always known she would be.

The second the door clicks shut behind her, I pin the old man with a murderous stare.

"I'm sad to say you didn't disappoint, Douglas."

"Come now, Dalton. We're both businessmen here. I brought

her here in good faith, but I can't in good conscience let her take over my clients when she doesn't have the instinct for self-preservation. She would willingly flush her career down the toilet for a good lay."

"Insult her one more time, and I'll have security escort you from the building, and you can consider our business relationship terminated."

"No need to get so hot-headed about it all. Young love. I thought you were smarter than that. You're thinking with your dick, and it's affecting my retirement plan. Nadia was supposed to be my seamless transition. How am I to retire now?"

"Well, she just resigned, so your retirement is fucked either way. All you had to do was agree to a declaration of our relationship to shield her and the firm from any repercussions."

"I didn't say no."

"You know what a great lawyer she is. You headhunted her for this position. Do you really think she would be okay with her job security hinging on your 'compensation?' "

The old man leans back in the chair, steepling his fingers with a snide grin. "I didn't…"

"Watch what you say next," I practically growl at him.

"If Ms. Sullivan wants to be a lawyer in New York, you need my cooperation. I know you're not foolish enough to set up this meeting without having a plan B, C, and D. So, let's hear your offer."

I am going to rip his legacy to shreds. Not today. That would be too easy. I'll wait until he least expects it, and then I'll ruin him for the way he treated Naddie.

"You sign an NDA regarding my relationship with Ms. Sullivan. She continues her path as a partner without interference from you, and in exchange, when you're ready to retire, I'll buy out your share of the company for twenty percent above market value."

"She just resigned, or did you miss her little speech?"

"You don't speak another word about her today. Understood?"

"What of Robert? He may not be the heir I wanted for the firm, but it's still his legacy."

"He's not my concern. You need to decide if you want his inheritance to be the business itself or the increased monetary value I'm offering in exchange for your silence. You do not speak a word of this to him. If you do, there will be consequences."

"And my other options?"

"They are no longer on the table." I lean back in my chair with the easy confidence of the businessman I've become over the years. "You really should have been nicer to Nadia. You can either sign the NDA and enjoy having such a talented lawyer work for you, retire, and sell to me. *Or*, you can sign the NDA to ensure I don't *fucking destroy* your precious firm. Either way, get the hell out of my sight." The old man bristles at my words.

"I want assurances that your account will remain with the firm."

"Then I suggest you put together a proposal that works for The Callaghan Group because believe me when I say this… I'm leaning toward tearing your firm to shreds."

"You've always been such a level-headed businessman, Dalton. Is this the hill you're willing to die on?"

"We're done talking. This conversation goes no further than you and me. If it does, you'll be violating lawyer/client privilege, and you can imagine the lengths I'd go to… to right such a grievous wrong. Now, get out of my office. I'll have an NDA drawn up and sent to your office."

"Dalton…"

"Meeting's over, Douglas. You can go." My calm exterior betrays the beast inside me that wants to unleash hell on him for talking down to Naddie.

As he stands to leave, I enforce my final stipulation. "If you breathe so much as a word to Robert, you can kiss any kind of 'compensation' from me goodbye. Understood?"

"Loud and clear."

Pacing my office for the past hour has done nothing to calm the anger coursing through my veins. At Douglas. *At Naddie.* I had hoped he wouldn't be the asshole I've paid him to be on my behalf for over a decade, but I knew it was a long shot.

Naddie, on the other hand, blindsided me in that meeting. She pushed me away in the beginning because she wanted to preserve her career. I conceived of ten different outcomes for my conversation with Douglas today, and none of them involved her quitting her job and calling me Master in front of him.

Don't get me wrong—that may have been the single hottest moment of my life. Liberating in a way I've never experienced as a Dom. Even with an agreement to have Naddie as my twenty-four-seven sub, it's behind closed doors. There's an illusion of being out in the open when she's locked safely in my office, and we can do as we want, but today was different. Without a sexual component to muddy the waters, Naddie was submissive to me in the most innocent and respectful ways possible. God, it made my heart ache with love for her. She's everything I want, and *that* scares the shit out of me.

She just quit her job for me. Her career.

I knew having her sit in on the meeting was a bad idea, even though it was the right thing to do. When we were kids, she would be the sweetest, most levelheaded person until you crossed her or someone she loved. Then, she would snap, and all hell would break loose. I was hoping she'd left that particular trait behind, but it seems she's still the same spitfire I fell in love with.

Fuck!

I should be the happiest man in the world right now. There are no barriers between Naddie and me building a life together, and yet I'm overwhelmed by guilt. Shame even.

There's a soft knock at the door to my office.

"Come in." It's Audrey.

"Would you like me to clear your meetings for the rest of the day?" She rubs her hand over her growing pregnancy bump, already such a maternal presence in the room.

"Yeah. That would be great. Thanks. I have some stuff to take care of," I say as I grab my suit jacket, wallet, and keys.

"Consider it done. Is everything okay? Mr. Mason stormed out earlier, and Ms. Sullivan didn't seem fine when she came out." A pang of guilt tugs at my insides. I should never have pushed her.

"Did she leave?" I feel a sudden panic at the thought.

"As far as I know, she's still in her office."

"Thanks, Audrey."

I force myself not to break out in a run as I make my way across the offices to where Naddie is probably freaking out. The moment I fling open her office door, the wind is knocked out of me at the sight of her.

"What the hell were you thinking?" I had planned to keep my cool, but I'm just so fucking mad as I watch her packing up her office.

She stops dead in her tracks, her eyes dark with fury. "How dare you!" She storms toward me. "What the hell was I thinking? What the hell were *you* thinking? You thought I would be okay with Douglas fucking us over? Paying him to *let* me work my ass off for him? I'm a freaking superstar lawyer, Dalton Callaghan."

"I know that." She cuts me off, poking me in the chest with her tiny finger.

"I refuse to submit to a man like him. I've worked too damn hard and lost too much to let him own me."

"Naddie…"

"Just shut up for a minute."

"Watch your tone."

"No." Oh, kitten. You're going to pay for that later. *"You* are going to listen to me right now. *What the hell was I thinking?* I was thinking that I choose you, and I made the wrong decision fifteen years ago when I left you behind. It wasn't some rash moment of lunacy! For the first time in forever, I had absolute clarity. It's *you*. It's always been you, and it's always going to *be* you, Dalton. You want the truth? I belong to you, Master Callaghan. I'll figure out the career stuff. I can rebuild and come back stronger, but I can't survive losing you again. Do you understand that? I *won't* lose you again."

I slide my hands into her hair, leaning in to capture her lips with mine, savoring every second as love and desire unfurl in a deliciously slow dance of our tongues, every caress and stroke a song for the ages.

"I love you, kitten," I whisper between kisses. "So much it hurts." It's the truth. I don't remember the last time I felt cherished and cared for. I've been on my own, trying to outrun my father's shadow and hide from my mom's for so long now I didn't even realize how alone I've been.

"Then, let me love you, Master."

I don't know how long we stand, wrapped in each other's arms, lost in the tender innocence of this simple, soul-destroying kiss. It's not about sexual gratification, dominance, or submission. It's undiluted, honest love.

"Let's get out of here," I say, interlacing her fingers with mine.

"I need to get this place cleared out."

Turning her to face me, I lift her chin to meet my gaze. "This can wait a few hours. I'm not kicking you out of your office. We can talk about all of it later. Let me take you for lunch, kitten. Take a breath, and just come for a walk with me."

"Is that a request or a command?" she asks with a playful edge to her voice.

"A command. It's my job to look after you."

"Lead the way, Master."

With our hands still intertwined, we walk through the offices, and I can't take my eyes off her. I'm sure everyone is staring at the way the color rises in her cheeks, but they can look all they want. Naddie is here to stay.

As the elevator doors close behind us, she heaves a sign of relief. "Everyone knows now."

"We were holding hands. It's not as if everyone caught me spanking you naked in my office."

"Why, has that never happened before?" She chuckles.

I press her into the corner, my hands braced on either side of her as I lean in for a kiss. "That can definitely be arranged, kitten." She darts her tongue out to wet her lips in anticipation.

"I'll be sure to be extra bratty next time I'm in your office." She pushes up onto her tiptoes, planting a soft kiss on my mouth.

"We can go back up there right now," I say as the elevator doors open onto the lobby, and people swarm to get in. Grabbing Naddie's hand, I make a path through the sea of worker bees, holding tight as we navigate the lobby and emerge on the sidewalk.

I take a deep, steadying breath before slinging my arm around her shoulder like I did every day after school, and we fall into step together, everything else melting away.

"What would you like to eat, Master?"

"*You* when you call me that in public. Fuck me, Naddie, I can't even begin to describe how hard you made my cock when you asked to leave that meeting. It's not even funny."

"Venom for lunch?" She wraps her arms around my waist, taunting me with every step.

"I'm taking you somewhere to eat first. You're going to need your stamina."

"Promises, promises, Master."

"I could get used to this twenty-four-seven-Dom thing. Seriously, that is so fucking hot."

She shoves me, even as she remains tucked under my arm. "You *better* get used to it. I just quit my job for you." There's no malice in her voice, but it sobers me instantly.

"Why, Naddie? I told you I would take care of it. I love that you want this to work between us, but I don't want you to lose every-thing you've worked for."

"And I told you… I can rebuild."

As we lazily walk block after block toward one of my favorite little restaurants on the edge of Central Park, I consider how to word this. "You can still work there and be a partner if you want. Things might seem different in a day or two after you've had time to sit with this."

She halts in the middle of the street, pedestrians bustling past us. "Did you ask Douglas to ignore my resignation?"

"No."

"Dalton." She levels me with her stare—all five foot six of terri-fying indignation.

"I gave him two options, which were dependent on whatever you decide."

"I already decided. That's what resigning is."

I coax her to walk with me, the restaurant in sight. "I know. Either way, we need a signed NDA from him now."

"We offered him a contract."

"No. I offered for us to write a contract to absolve the firm of any repercussions. The fact that you quit means he could call the Bar Association right now and ruin you. Even if he didn't go that far, he could still blackball you with any firm in New York. I need him to sign an NDA stating that he won't breathe a word to anyone about us."

Her shoulders sag as it hits her. "So, you're going to have to pay him off anyway. My career is still a dollar amount at this point."

When we reach the restaurant, I open the door and usher her inside the cozy, warm space. I've always thought of her when I come here, so I love that I finally get to share it with her—original crown molding, bookcases full of musty old books, and quaint tables for intimate dining.

It thrills me to watch her take it all in, a genuine smile spreading across her flawless face. "It's so beautiful."

I kiss the top of her head before leading her over to my usual table. "I've been coming here for ten years, and every time, I thought of you."

Holding the seat out for her, she brushes her fingers down my arm as she sits. "Really? You thought about me?" There's a shyness to the way she says it, and it sparks such a warmth in my chest.

"Is it that hard to believe?" I say as I sit across from her and offer her my hands which she gladly takes. "You've never been far from my mind, Naddie."

The waiter interrupts us for a few moments, and the second she walks away, Naddie's smile turns somber. "What did you offer Douglas?"

"We didn't agree on a sum. I told him he can sign an NDA and continue to have an amazing partner at his firm... if that's something you want… and when he's ready to retire, I will buy him out for a margin above value."

"And the other option?"

"He signs the NDA for a few million, we all go our separate ways, and I agree not to ruin his firm and legacy."

"You wouldn't…"

"In a fucking heartbeat. He hired you for a reason, Naddie, and that shouldn't change because we love each other. I hate that he is judging you for the kind of relationship we choose to have together."

"And that's exactly why I *can't* act like nothing has changed. Tell me you understand. I'm sorry that my actions are going to cost you money to silence Douglas. It wasn't my intention, and I'll pay you back… someday."

"The money doesn't matter. I understand you don't want to feel like I'm paying for you to work with him. I fully support whatever you decide moving forward. But… and this isn't up for debate… the financial agreement I come to with him for his discretion is not for you to worry about or take on the burden."

"But…"

"Kitten, I'm saying this as your Dominant. It is *not* your burden to bear. I couldn't let you go when you told me it could cost you your career. I can't live with the fallout of my selfishness. I don't care about the money. None of it matters without you. I'll handle Douglas. All I need from you is to figure out what you want and how we're going to get it."

"My career is not a *we*…"

"I'm going to stop you there, and you're going to listen to me now. From this day forward, everything is 'we.' We're a team. Your career. My career. Our lives in and out of the bedroom. We agreed to a twenty-four-seven contract."

"And when it runs out in a few weeks?"

I grab a pen from my pocket and the crisp white linen napkin off the table.

"What do you want in a new contract? A month, three months, a year? Forever?"

"I don't know." Not the three words I wanted to hear. Today has not gone to plan, and she just turned her world upside down for me. I want to show her that I'm committed.

"Okay then." I write across the top of the napkin.

A Binding Contract between
Dalton Callaghan and Nadia Sullivan

I sign my name at the bottom, leaving everything else blank. I fold it and hand it to her.

"What's this?"

"Whatever you want it to be. When you're ready."

She opens it up, her brows knitting together, her mouth set in a firm line. "It's blank."

"Exactly. You gave up so much for me today, kitten. Consider this my commitment to you. When you are ready for everything I want to give you in this life, you need only write it down. I'm all in. Now, eat. I wasn't kidding when I said you'll need your stamina tonight."

I watch with delight as she tucks into her meal, and I am so full of love for her.

"Time to tell me all your deep, dark secrets, Master. You know all of mine. I'm here, I'm jobless, and I'm yours," she quips, scrunching her nose as she shoves a forkful of salad in her mouth. She's just taking all of this in her stride, and I haven't even been completely honest with her.

"I'm the luckiest guy in the world, Naddie. I can't wait to see you build your own empire and stand at your side while you do it."

"Sounds like a good plan to me, but first, I think you should take me back to your place and have your wicked way with me."

"Ready for that spanking you mentioned earlier?"

"Yes, Master Callaghan." She says it like butter wouldn't melt, her eyes pinned on me, and it takes all my self-control not to put her across my knee right now and make that curvy little ass of hers red.

"Oh, you want to play. We can do that. Take your panties off, kitten."

"What?" I love it when I catch her off guard.

"Did I stutter? You want to get me riled up in public… take off your panties. You can enjoy the cool afternoon breeze on the walk back to my apartment."

"I'll be back, Master." She moves to get up to go to the restroom, but where's the fun in that?

"You can do it here. No one will notice. The tablecloth is long enough to hide that pretty little pussy of yours." I hold her gaze, a wicked grin tugging at the corners of my mouth. "Take. Them. Off."

Her venomous glare turns sultry as she slips her hands under the table, biting down on her bottom lip as she maneuvers herself. "Where would you like them, Master?"

"Ball them in your hand… then lift it above the table…" Her eyes go wide, the rapid rise and fall of her chest giving her away. She's aroused.

I hold my hand out. "I don't think they're your size, Master," she says like the little brat I know and love.

I take the small ball of lace and slip the panties into my pocket before leaning in, my lips a hair's breadth from her ear. "You're such a good girl, kitten." Her breath hitches as I press a kiss full of promise just below her ear, sending a shiver down her spine. "Now, come with me. I'm taking you home. I owe you a good spanking before I let you ride my face."

Naddie practically jumps out of her seat as I drop some cash on the table and offer her my hand. She almost drags me out of the restaurant, tugging me like a good little brat.

As we step outside, a breeze catches us, and I watch the subtle spike in Naddie's breathing, her eyes closing for just a second, her lips slightly parted as the air kisses beneath her skirt. When a soft moan escapes her, my cock begins to strain against my pants.

"Home. Now."

Chapter 17

NADDIE

I've never walked so fast in my life. Dalton practically chases me down the street as we hurry to the penthouse, unable to wait the length of the elevator ride up to the top floor. His hand slides up my thigh before grabbing my ass, his lips caressing my ear. "I'm going to enjoy turning this red, kitten."

As the elevator doors ping open, I unzip my skirt before letting it fall to the floor, leaving it behind as he messes with his keys. I love that I can make him falter, if only for a few seconds before he throws open the door and drags me inside, ripping at my blouse.

When I'm naked, but for my heels, Dalton lifts me like a feather, carrying me over his shoulder as he strides toward his bedroom, giving my ass one teasing smack.

"You love being a brat, don't you, kitten?"

"If it always results in this, I'll be a brat till the day I die."

Tossing me down on the bed, Dalton shrugs out of his jacket and rolls up the sleeves of his blue, pinstriped shirt.

"I want you leaning over the edge of the bed. Present that sumptuous ass of yours for your Master to see." A thrill courses through me as I scramble to stand up, positioning myself at the end of the bed before leaning forward, my ass ready and waiting for him.

"You're going to count to ten, kitten, and I want you to think about what a naughty girl you've been today."

"Yes, Master C—" My words are cut short with the first smack. So tantalizingly wicked.

"One."

"Good girl." *Slap!*

"Two." My core tightens, my pussy wet for him.

"Three... four... five." His fingertips brush over my aching clit.

"Six." As the sting of his hand takes hold, I relish the bite of pain that jolts straight to my core.

"Tell me how much you like it, kitten."

"I love being punished by you, Master. I want it so bad. Your hand, your cock... *seven!*"

"You're doing so well, kitten. You are such a good girl. Let me hear you." His hand lands once more, the smack so intense I'm on the verge of orgasm.

"Yes... Master. I'll be good. Please, don't stop. *Eight*... nine."

"Come for me, kitten." His final slap is right where I need him, my pussy drenched as his fingers connect.

"*Ten!* Oh God... yes... Master... yes."

Wrapping his arm around my waist, he catches me as my limbs go loose, my orgasm ripping through me in wave after wave of delectable pain and pleasure.

'You're such a good fucking girl, kitten," he says as he unzips his pants and releases his rock-hard erection before taking me in one soul-destroying, earth-shattering thrust.

"Yes..."

Dalton grabs a fistful of my hair, tethering me in place as he hammers into me, chasing his release in a frenzied fuck.

"*My* good girl."

Even though I can't see him, his words wash over me, sating my desire to please my Master.

"Say you're mine, kitten."

"I'm yours, Master Callaghan."

"You are so fucking tight. Made just for me."

"Oh God… yes."

"That's it, kitten. You're so wet." His pace quickens, and he thrusts harder as he forces me to the edge once more.

"Please, Master… I'm going to come." Bracing my hands on the bed, I take every stroke, trying to stem the torrent of pleasure coursing through every muscle in my body.

"Fuck… come for me, Naddie. Fuck. *I love you.*"

His words are my undoing, catapulting me headlong into orgasm, his own following close behind.

"I love you, too, *Dalton.*"

Chapter 18

NADDIE

Dalton smooths cream on my well-spanked ass as I lie naked in his bed, basking in the orgasmic afterglow of an afternoon spent fucking. His hands are so warm and inviting as he rubs gentle circles over my skin.

"This shade looks good on you, kitten," he says with a wry grin."

"Why, thank you, Master. I rather like it myself." Peering over my shoulder, my brain can hardly process the sight of Dalton caring for me as my Dominant.

"I know you enjoyed it. I can still taste your arousal, and it's delicious." His cock twitches to life *again*.

"Do you have to go back to work today? I guess I should go and clear out my office."

"Your office at The Callaghan Group will remain yours. You needn't concern yourself with it. I don't have to go back to the office, but I do have somewhere I need to be."

He shuffles off the bed, resting the sheets over me as he stalks toward his closet. When he returns a minute later in jeans and a plain white T-shirt, looking devastatingly handsome, a pang of concern tugs at my heartstrings.

We never discussed the last time he had some secret place to be that I wasn't privy to.

"What's wrong, kitten? You're supposed to be relaxing, resting that sweet ass of yours."

"Nothing, Master." I can't muster a fake aloofness I don't feel.

He perches on the edge of the bed, his hand resting on my back. "Don't lie to me, kitten. Out with it."

"You punished me the last time I asked where you'd been. So, I'm not going to ask where you're going." I keep my eyes cast down, unwilling to show the hurt that beats at my chest. I want to trust him, but I also want him to trust *me*.

"I was planning to talk to you about this tonight, so we may as well have the conversation now. You're right. I've been keeping something from you, and considering you turned your life upside down for me today, it's only right that you know."

My heart constricts, dread twisting, cutting off my circulation as I wait for him to continue.

"It's my mom. That's where I am when I'm not with you. I go to see my mom."

Relief floods my senses. "Okay. Why wouldn't you tell me that?"

His expression darkens as our eyes meet, pain evident in the tight-knit of his brow.

"She's sick, Naddie." He blows out a steadying breath, tilting his head up to the ceiling.

I reach for his hand, but he pulls away. "She's... dying."

"Oh, Dalton..." I wrap the bed sheet around myself and crawl into his lap, sliding my arms around him. Emotion swirls around him, shadows that threaten to pull him under, and I know what he needs—whatever strength I can give him. "You can talk to me, Master."

And he does.

Dalton starts from the beginning, clinging to me as he explains what he's been dealing with for years—alone—and it breaks my heart. I lightly caress my fingers through his hair as he speaks, letting him know I'm here.

I always loved Dalton's mom. She was as big a part of my childhood as was my own mother, and the thought of her slipping away like this—life can be so unfair to the very best of people.

"I'm sorry I didn't tell you sooner. I selfishly wanted to keep us separate. I didn't know if we'd have much time together. I've been keeping it quiet for so long. She doesn't want people seeing her like this."

"Does anyone else know?"

"Flex. She's been like a mom to him. You know what she's like. Always wanting to look after the waifs and strays." He's fighting back tears. "No one else knows. Not even my father."

I cup his face in my hands, his stubble scratching against my palms as I lean in, capturing his lips with mine, pouring everything into this one kiss.

"Let me help you. I'm here for whatever you need."

"Would you like to come with me? She won't remember you, but I'd really like you to be there with me." There's a childlike insecurity in his voice, betraying the Dominant man I know him to be.

"I'd love to."

As we make our way through his mom's apartment, I grip Dalton's hand, noticing pictures of them throughout the years—the times I missed. Their heartfelt love for each other is evident in every snapshot of precious moments.

Dalton tracks my gaze, a fleeting joy in the glint of his eye. "That one was taken in Paris a year before she got sick."

"You both look so happy."

"We were. She'd always wanted to go, and I promised her after everything that happened with Dad, I would take her one day."

"You're a good man."

"Thanks, kitten. I'm trying." He squeezes my hand. "Are you ready?"

Even now, as we prepare to see Candice, Dalton is thinking of me, making sure *I'm* okay.

"Yes, Master." I lean into the warmth of his body, giving him whatever comfort I can.

As the door to her bedroom opens, I'm torn between a love and nostalgia so deep for the woman shaking involuntarily in the bed across the elegantly decorated room and a sadness so visceral I could cry.

When her eyes meet mine, I swear there's recognition there. *There is!*

"Well, well, well. There's my Naddie bear. I was wondering when you were going to come back."

Dalton scans between us, unsure if this is a memory or the here and now.

"Hey, Mom. You remember Naddie?"

"Of course I do. I practically raised the girl," she says with a sweet smile.

"And me?" He's hesitant, his hand choking the life out of mine as he waits with bated breath, each step toward her stilted.

Her arms and legs jolt with exhausting, involuntary movements.

"What are you talking about, Dally?" My heart lurches into my chest, my pulse spiking as Dalton's entire being radiates sheer delight.

"*Yes!* You recognize me."

"A mother doesn't forget her son's face." Her words slice through him like a knife, the raw emotion written all over his face.

"It's really good to see you, Momma." He goes to her, wrapping his muscled arms around her frail, shuddering body, holding her for a long moment. When he finally sits at her side, he lifts her hand in his, circling his thumb on her paper-thin skin, staring at her with all the love in the world.

"Are you okay, baby boy?"

"Don't worry about me. I'm fine."

"You look tired."

"Work is busy. Nothing I can't handle," he says with a tight smile.

Candice looks to me. "I was wondering when you'd show up."

"It took me a while, but I found my way home." Resting my hand on Dalton's knee, I feel the truth of that statement with every fiber of my being.

"I knew you would someday. You and Dally are soulmates."

If my heart could take flight, it would burst forth from my chest and soar on the wings of her declaration.

"So did I, Mom. I've just been waiting on Naddie to get the memo." His face is alight with honest joy. After everything Dalton told me earlier, having Candice give our relationship such a blessing is a miracle and an honor for me.

"I'm here now. And I'm not going anywhere."

I watch as Candice takes in her surroundings in the bed where she lies as her body continues to tremor. "There's more going on with my health, isn't there? I can see it in your eyes, Dally."

His head drops ever so slightly, and I clasp his hand in mine as he takes a deep, steadying breath.

"The Parkinson's has advanced. You can feel it, I'm sure."

"Yes. But that's not all, is it? Something's not right." The frailty in her voice is devastating. The fear of what her son is about to say.

"You've started to get other symptoms and health issues, but we don't need to talk about that right now. I just want to enjoy our visit."

She levels him with the same stare she did when he was a boy. "Dalton Callaghan, I'm your mother. You tell me what's going on."

He casts his gaze to the floor as tears well in his eyes. "You have advanced dementia, Mom."

Her gasp echoes through the room.

"Oh, my baby boy." She lifts her hand as best she can, reaching to cup his face. "I'm so sorry."

"Don't apologize. You never asked for any of this. Do not say you're sorry." He's fighting back tears, and I ache for them both.

"I know, sweetheart, but you're the one watching it happen. From the expression on your face, I assume I don't recognize you?"

He can't bring himself to say it out loud.

"Sometimes you tell me I remind you of your little boy. Most of the time, I'm just a nice man who comes to visit." It's heartbreaking, having to watch him explain this to her, knowing he has to do it every time she's lucid. Not just for him but for her, seeing how devastated she is by the news.

I get up from my chair, press a kiss to Dalton's cheek, and envelop Candice in a gentle hug. "I'm going to go and let you two enjoy this precious time together."

"You don't have to leave," Dalton interjects.

"I know that… Dally." I caress my hand down his cheek. "But this time is for you. I have some stuff to take care of. Call me later."

"Are you sure?"

"Yes."

I turn to Candice, scared that this is the only time she'll know who I am. "I'll come and see you again soon, Candy. I've missed you."

"And I you. I'm glad Dally has you to take care of him." There's so much weight to her words. A statement. A question. A request for the future.

"Always."

I run my hand down Dalton's cheek, my heart hurting as he leans into my touch. "I love you." With a parting kiss, I leave them to visit. To really *see* each other for the first time in a long while from what Dalton told me earlier this evening.

"I love you, too, kitten."

As I make my way through her apartment, I allow the tears to escape, spilling down my cheeks.

I won't burden Dalton with my problems. I can figure out my career. If I'd known what else he's been dealing with, I wouldn't have blasted his plans with Douglas out of the water. I can work for the firm until Douglas retires if it means less stress for my Master. I'd do anything for him and his mom. I want them to have as much time together as possible, and I know Dalton will dedicate too much to me and my career. He's my Dominant, and sometimes that's going to mean *me* sacrificing for him.

With my mind set, I head back to my office at The Callaghan

Group and start writing the necessary NDA and a contract that pertains to my employment moving forward.

∼

The moment I spot Jenna in the herd of people filtering out of baggage claim, I squeal with joy as she hurries toward me, dropping her bags and pulling me in for a long-overdue hug.

"I've missed you, bestie," she says, squeezing me tight.

"Not as much as I've missed you. I'm so happy to see you, Jen."

"The feeling's mutual." When we finally let go of each other, I help her with the bags and head for the exit. At Dalton's request, his driver is patiently waiting to load Jenna's luggage into the trunk and take us back to my apartment.

"When did you get so fancy? A town car."

"Courtesy of Dalton."

"The elusive boyfriend." She slaps my arm as we settle in the back seat. "Why was he the one to call me? You call me every day. We talk about *everything*. You didn't think to mention a career crisis."

Guilt takes root in the pit of my stomach, its tendrils creeping through my veins as she wraps her arm around me, pulling me close.

"I'm sorry. I haven't been able to find the right words. Besides, I took care of it. Dalton's just worrying for nothing." I thought by me making the deal with Douglas it would be less complicated and would help Dalton, but he's watching me like a hawk. As much as I pretend that I'm happy to have it sorted, every time I look at Douglas, all I see are the dollar signs he sold his soul for.

"Well, we've got a whole weekend for you to tell me whatever has you so wound up that your new beau felt the need to call and fly me down here."

"I can't wait for you to meet him, Jenna. He's so amazing."

"Only you would move to Man-freaking-hattan and find your long-lost high school sweetheart. It makes me want to vomit…" she says with a sly smile, "… and I'm deliriously happy for you."

I wonder if she'll feel the same way when I tell her *everything*. I'm scared, but I told Dalton, after addressing him as Master in front of Mr. Mason, I don't want to hide who I am anymore. If he and I are going to do this and go the distance, I have to be honest with my best friend.

Dalton was hesitant at first, considering what a private person he is, but his best friend is a Dom, and the more we discussed it, he realized what a gift it was that he was able to talk to Flex about us when I showed back up in his life.

I know I'll make friends at Venom, but it's not the same. Jenna is my female soulmate. It's been killing me these last four years, hiding this part of myself from her. Dalton bringing her here now feels like fate. It's not something I've believed in since I was a kid, but then I walked into a conference room in Milan, and my world-view shifted.

When we get back to my apartment, I show Jenna the guest room, but she stares at me like I just grew a second head.

"You know I'm sleeping in your bed, right? I didn't come all this way *not* to have one of our epic movie nights where we both fall asleep together with candy still in our hands and a glass of wine resting precariously between us."

"I love my new comforter. No wine spillage allowed. I'm going to go get freshened up and put on my PJs. Make yourself at home."

"You still wearing the ratty T-shirt your bae gave you back in the day?"

"Maybe…" I say as I head for my room. It's only then that I realize it's at the penthouse. I haven't slept here for weeks. After I forage for an alternative in my drawers, I slip my phone out of my pocket and type a quick message to Dalton.

Me: Jenna's here. Thank you for the ride.

Dalton: You're welcome.

Me: She wants to sleep in my room tonight.

Dalton: You mean in your bed?

Me: Yes.

> Dalton: Are you asking or telling me, kitten?

> Me: I'm asking, Master Callaghan.

He doesn't respond right away, leaving me sick to my stomach. I've never given myself over to a man so completely. It's unsettling because I *want* his permission, and he knows I crave it, yet I trust him not to exploit the faith I'm putting in him.

> Dalton: I'm proud of you for asking, kitten. One night. That's all she gets. Then I'll be warming your bed.

Elation sends a tingle down my spine. Knowing he appreciates me coming to him with a genuine question.

> Me: Thank you, Master. I can't wait to have you in my bed.

> Dalton: Goodnight. Sweet dreams, kitten.

> Me: Night. I love you.

There it is. The words I know will be true until the day I die.

> Dalton: I love you too.

> Dalton: Now, go to bed. I have plans for you tomorrow.

> Me: Yes, Master.

My stomach does somersaults at the thought of what he has in store for me. I can't get enough of him and the way he makes my body sing.

Once I'm in comfy sweats and a hoodie, Jenna and I settle in my bed with snacks and wine, laughing like old times.

"So... are you going to tell me why your boyfriend thought you could use a visit this weekend?"

"Life and work down here are more complicated than I anticipated."

"I get that. You weren't planning on finding Dalton again. It's a lot."

"We told my boss that we're together."

"Shit. How did that go?"

"Not great. But like I said, I took care of it."

"Then what's complicated about it?"

Crap. I don't know if I can tell her everything as a wave of nausea washes over me.

"Nad, what's going on?"

Taking a gulp of wine for courage, I spew forth the secret I've been keeping for four years.

"I'm a submissive."

Her wine sprays my face, dripping from my eyelashes. "What? Shut up! I don't believe you."

I wipe my eyes with the sleeve of her hoodie. "And Dalton is a Dom."

"*Shut the fuck up!* I'd know if you were into the whole *Fifty Shades* thing. We've been best friends for fifteen years."

"*Fifty Shades* is tame compared to me."

"Fuck me."

"Master Callaghan wouldn't like that. I'd definitely be punished."

"You kinky little minx. Tell me everything. Now."

"What do you want to know?"

"When? How? I can't believe you didn't tell me." There's hurt in her voice that's reflected in her eyes as they find mine.

"I'm sorry, Jenna. I was so scared you wouldn't want to be my friend anymore. It's not exactly something I spread around."

"I get that, but I'm not just anyone. I'm... *me*. It's us. There is nothing you could ever do that would get in the way of our friendship." Tears well in my eyes as I release a breath I didn't know I'd been holding for so long. "I want to know everything. Start with Dalton."

"He's a Dom. A gorgeous, perfect, alpha male Adonis Dom." I

stare into my glass, swirling the pale yellow liquid, watching the bubbles explode as they reach the surface.

"Why is that a problem? You want to *submit*. Is that the right word? And he wants to be in charge. Isn't that a good thing?"

"The firm knows that he has specific... tastes. Ergo..."

"They now know you share those same tastes."

"It's unethical to start a relationship with a client. Having a Dom/sub dynamic just adds to their unflattering view of me."

"You're a remarkable lawyer. What you do in your bedroom shouldn't effect that in any way."

"In theory, but people are judged every day for a million different things. Whatever way you look at it, they hired me to be Dalton's lawyer, and I've already crossed the line."

"What does Dalton have to say about all this?" She leans forward and wipes the tears that spill over as I try to hold it together.

"He made my boss sign an NDA and paid him off. I'll continue to work for them until he retires, and then Dalton will buy his share of the company. And... Dalton and I have a contract that is just for our relationship."

"Holy shit. No wonder he thought you needed a weekend with me. That's a lot to take in. How do you feel about him paying them off?"

"I hate it. My gut reaction was to quit, but Dalton already has so much going on, and I don't want to pull his focus right now."

"This is your career we're talking about. The most important thing in your life the whole time I've known you."

"His mom is sick. He's pulled in so many different directions, and I *won't* have him worrying about me right now. I made my bed when I decided to risk starting this with him. I can do this for a few years."

"You said you have a contract. Is that a real thing in your world?"

"It's pretty common when you're a lawyer," I say with a hint of satisfaction.

"Ha-ha. Very funny, chuckles. I mean for a Dom/sub arrangement."

"Yes. We have agreed to a twenty-four-seven contract in and out of the bedroom."

"Oh my God. That sounds hot, but I have no idea what it even means. He tells you what to do? I can totally get on board with that in the bedroom, but I can't imagine applying it to real life."

I know what she means, but there's a note of offense in the pit of my stomach. Judgment.

"This is why we don't tell people."

"What? I'm curious. You're just so in control all the time. I don't understand how you can be two different people."

"I'm not. That's the point. I am the same take-charge, in-control person you've always known. When I'm with a Dom, I am in complete control. With a single word, I can stop anything that's going on. He won't walk away and call me a prick-tease. He won't question my decision. It's a relationship based on trust and transparency. With a career like mine, it feels so good to hand over the reins to someone I know I can depend on."

She tucks up her knees, wrapping her arms around and hugging them to her chest. "So it's your stress relief? I suppose that's not so different from anyone with a healthy sex life."

"It's more than that, Jenna. I'm not explaining myself properly. There's so much more to it. So many... kinks... if that's what you want to call them."

"Okay. Explain. I want to understand."

"Really?" I swallow past the lump in my throat. Although I felt the need to come clean with my best friend, a big part of me expected her to freak out. Instead, she pulls me into her arms, squeezing me so tight I can barely breathe.

"Of course. You're my ride or die, Nad. This doesn't change that. I want to be here for you, and I can't do that if I have no fucking idea what we're talking about."

"Thank you," I whisper as I reciprocate her rib-crushing embrace.

"Okay. So tell me the basics."

"Think of a man whose purpose is to take everything you enjoy and use it to push you to the brink, over and over again, waiting until the anticipation is so overwhelming that he can tell you to come on demand, and it's like a full body explosion." Jenna is staring at me, her jaw almost hitting the floor. "You're drooling, Jen." I giggle.

"I think I just came a little. That sounds…"

"Like it would be the best sex of your life? Yeah, it would."

"*Holy shit.* So, are you even interested in the whole boyfriend-maybe-husband-one-day thing, or is it different when you have a Dom?"

"Can't I have both?"

"I don't know. You tell me."

"I think I can with Dalton, and that's what scares the crap out of me."

"Are you at all worried that he won't satisfy your needs as a submissive? Or are you worried that he's everything you've ever wanted, and you gave up on that dream with him a long time ago?"

"The latter."

"And what does he want?"

"He wants it all. He loves me, and he'll do anything to make me happy. He told me he's not the good boy I once loved. That he might be the bad guy who would do whatever it takes to make me his. This is all so new and yet so familiar, Jenna. It's intense."

"Jesus. My ovaries just exploded. Any guy says that to me *and* can make me come on command, I'm giving up my feminist ways and being his twenty-four-seven naked woman. Get it, girl. I need to meet this guy. I've never seen you like this. He must be something special."

"He is. God, he's amazing, Jenna. Everything about him screams alpha male. His demeanor, his career, his sinfully handsome face, and his voice… low and rumbling when he says my name."

"You've got it bad."

"I know," I say, burying my head in my hands. "It's pathetic."

"So, when do I get to see your sex dungeon?" she says, wiggling her eyebrows suggestively.

"It's not a dungeon... and you can't be serious? You want to go?"

"You can't tell me all this stuff and then not let me see where the magic happens."

"I'll have to ask Dalton. It's an invitation-only members club."

"If you're a member, why can't you invite me?"

"He owns the club, Jenna."

"Oh, this just keeps getting better. I don't care if you have to give him a million blow jobs, you have to convince him. I need to see this place."

Chapter 19

NADDIE

"We don't have to go to the club with Dalton and his friend tonight. If you want to hang out, just the two of us, I can call and cancel. Or we could just go to dinner and forget about going to the club after."

"Are you kidding me? I can't wait!" I still can't believe Dalton agreed to let her go to Venom. I was sure he'd give me a firm no, but when I told him the incentive Jenna suggested, he was surprisingly quick to say yes.

"I just… don't want you to think badly of me if you don't like the club. I know it's not something people outside the lifestyle understand easily. I'm not a bad person, Jenna."

She grabs me by the shoulders, shoving me to arm's length, the stern set of her brow mirrored in the rigid line of her mouth. "Don't ever think that. I would never think you're a bad person. I'm really intrigued to see what it's like. It's not about judging you, I promise. I love you, Nad, and I just want the best for you."

"Dalton *is* what's best for me. All I ask is that you be open-minded when it comes to him." I'm nervous on so many fronts tonight. I want them to get along. Thinking about it now, I should have introduced them to each other *before* telling Jenna about our lifestyle. I worry that it might cloud her perception of him. There's so much more to him than this one little part of our life together.

He offered to come and pick us up in the town car, but I'd rather they not be introduced in the enclosed space of the back seat of a car. The thought of it made me nervous. We hail a cab outside my building and head for Dulip. It's the hottest restaurant in the city, so, of course, Dalton had no problem getting a last-minute reservation. If I remember correctly from reading up on recent contracts, he owns that whole block.

The line outside is crazy as we pull up. People are willing to wait two hours on the sidewalk, in the cold, to get into this place. There's a crackle of excitement in the air, but it's nothing compared to the lightning bolt that hits me when a familiar frame in a perfectly tailored blue pin-striped suit turns to face me with a smile so hot, my knees turn to Jell-O.

Striding toward me with a confidence that's undeniable, Dalton commands the space around him as he slides his fingers into my loose waves, holding me steady as his lips find mine in a slow, sensual kiss.

"I missed you today, kitten."

"Jesus, if this is how tonight is going to go, we may as well leave them now." You can always count on Flex to chime in with something inappropriate. "I'm Flex, the best friend."

Jenna has that doe-eyed look she gets when she thinks a guy is hot.

"I'm good with that. Where do you want to take me… Flex?"

She caresses his name as they shake hands for way longer than necessary.

"Anywhere you want, beautiful."

"It's nice to meet you, Jenna," Dalton steps in. "I've heard so much about you."

"All good, I'm sure," she says with a sly smile. "I've heard… some interesting things about you."

"So I've been told."

Dalton positions his hand at the small of my back, guiding me inside with the easy confidence I love so much. "How was your day, kitten?"

"Better now," I whisper.

"Good answer. You'll be rewarded for that later."

"Promises, promises, Master." His hand snakes around my hip, his fingers gripping me tight.

"You can't say that when I'm trying to make a good first impression on your friend."

I meet his gaze like butter wouldn't melt in my mouth. "But I love the way your eyes darken, and you look at me like…"

"Like I want to fucking eat you," he rumbles under his breath.

"All right, lovebirds," Flex jibes as he slaps Dalton on the shoulder. "It's customary to have a few drinks before going straight to dessert."

My cheeks flush as he flashes me a knowing smile. Having spent a few hours here and there over the past few weeks chatting with Flex at the club, he's a shameless flirt.

"Sometimes dessert is the best appetizer," I reply.

"Shit. Feeling feisty tonight, little sub?" he says with a wink.

Dalton takes my hand before leaning in to whisper in my ear. "Are you going to be a brat tonight, kitten?"

"I wasn't being a brat."

"Any dirty thoughts you may have about this evening are for my ears only. Flirting with another Dom won't win you any points."

My heart lurches up into my throat. "I would never flirt with another Dom." I take exception to the assumption.

"I know, but Flex is a shameless flirt. He'll pull you in, all in good fun. But it's not fun for me. Not when the sub in question is you."

"Understood."

"Good girl." He kisses my temple before weaving us through the crowd, his hand tight in mine all the way to our table—the best in the house.

"Good evening, Mr. Callaghan. Your waiter will be over in a few minutes to take your order."

"Thanks."

I quickly glance behind me to check Jenna has made it through the crowd. I'm not entirely surprised by the sight of her winding through the restaurant, following Flex like an eager, lovesick puppy. I'm going to have to tell Dalton to make sure Flex doesn't try to seduce Jenna. She's not into our lifestyle and has no desire to dip her toe in the water. Wanting to see the club and wanting to be a submissive are two entirely different things.

When we're all seated, Dalton orders drinks as Flex considers me from across the table, his head cocked to one side. "So, Nad, you've known our boy since kindergarten. You must have all kinds of dirt to dish on him." His wicked grin makes me giggle.

"Oh yes, we lived next door all our lives." I look to Dalton, who has a wistful expression, dreamy as he leans in, resting his arm around my shoulder, pulling me a little closer before pressing his lips to my cheek. "You look… fucking edible, kitten," he whispers in my ear. "I'm looking forward to a taste later."

I physically shudder, but I'm quickly pulled back to the here and now by my best friend.

"Down, boy. This is a public place. At least feed her before you eat her." Oh my God. She did not just say that out loud.

"Nadia." My back stiffens, unaccustomed to him using my given name. I know what it means. He knows how much I hate it. I always have, since I was a kid, getting into trouble for sneaking over to his house or being caught playing doctors and nurses in his bedroom.

"Yes… Mr. Callaghan? Dalton."

"Come now. You obviously have no secrets from your best friend. Jenna won't mind you addressing me properly."

"My apologies, Master Callaghan."

Jenna's face is priceless as she watches me submit. I'd go as far as to say she looks turned on, and Dalton is clearly amused.

"Did you carry out my request? My stipulation for attending the club with your… outspoken friend?"

"Yes, Master Callaghan." When I asked if we could take Jenna to see Venom tonight, Dalton decided I would enjoy the evening better without underwear. The fact that he then sent me the dress

I'm wearing, which is rather short, only makes me squirm under his watchful eye.

He unfolds the crisp white napkin in front of him and offers it to me with a wry grin. "I wouldn't want you to spill anything on your new dress. I suggest you rest this on your lap." Heat rises in my cheeks, a delicate blush of pink as I do as I'm told.

"Thank you. For the dress and the napkin. It was very kind of you to send an outfit for me, Master."

The waiter arrives to take our orders and brings drinks from the bar. Small talk is short, and Jenna is going for the jugular the second they're out of earshot.

"So, Dalton, what are your intentions for my submissive friend?"

Dalton traces the edge of his glass, fighting every Dominant urge to put her in her place. "You don't mess around, do you? I normally like that in a woman. I'm happy to answer your questions regarding Naddie, but I don't appreciate discussing what happens in private. It's not your business, and this is not the place for such things." There's enough bite in his tone to let her know he's not kidding around.

"Are you ashamed of what you do behind closed doors?" she says, lifting her glass to her lips.

"No. But I don't think anyone needs to flaunt their sexual preferences. It's between me and my partner. Call me old-fashioned, but it's nobody else's business."

I shift uncomfortably in my seat, my eyes flitting between them.

"I don't think contracts are old-fashioned."

"I disagree. A marriage license is signed by both partners, agreeing to work together for the life they want to share."

"Are you saying you plan to make Nad your wife?" Holy shit. Our appetizers haven't even arrived yet, and she's not holding back or easing into the conversation.

"Stop it," I interject. "That's not your place to ask, Jenna. I agreed to this dinner so you can meet the man I'm involved with. If you're going to conduct the Spanish Inquisition, we're not going to the club."

"I just want to know he's going to look after you, Nad. You kept a box of his stuff and only told me about him recently. Sorry if I'm playing catch-up here, but I don't want to see you getting hurt."

"*There's a box?*" Dalton's eyes light up, and my cheeks heat with embarrassment. "My intentions are to give my all to Naddie. She was always the love of my life, and that didn't stop because I sent her away to live her life without me."

"Why did you, then? If you knew she was the one?"

"Because it would've been selfish to ask her to stay. She knew what she wanted when she was six years old. Who am I to take that away from her?" The memory of that day comes flooding back, and all I want to do is grab Dalton's hand and drag him to the club, close the door, and forget about anything else. I never want to feel that kind of pain ever again.

"And now? You don't think it's selfish to jeopardize her career?"

"I won't let that happen."

"But you can't guarantee it."

"I don't appreciate your tone. When I set my mind to something, I make it happen. I'll ensure Naddie's career remains on the upward trajectory she's worked tirelessly to build."

"I'm glad to hear it."

"I appreciate your candor, but I don't answer to anyone but Naddie."

"Would you sign a contract to that effect?" She's playing around, but I can see Dalton visibly bristled.

"Wow. You really spilled your guts, didn't you, kitten?"

"You said I could tell her about us. I'm sorry."

"You don't have to apologize for confiding in your best friend, Nad," Jenna interjects.

"Do you have any idea what something like this could do to her career if it got out?"

"I would never betray Nad's trust. I'll take it to the grave. I'm not trying to be a bitch. I'm genuinely curious. Why do you want to control her? It's a big red flag to most women."

"Naddie isn't 'most women.' It's not about control. I want to protect and give her what she needs. She's been leading me around by the balls since I was four. If anyone is in control here, it's her."

"I'm not sure I believe you, but for Nad's sake, I'll let you prove me wrong." *I'm going to wring her neck when we get home. I promised a nice dinner and a quick tour of the club. Not the third degree.*

The waiter arrives with our food, and it's a perfect opportunity to lighten the conversation because, if I don't, I'm going to lose my shit. "Flex, you were asking about dirt on Dalton. You know, I used to force him to have tea parties with me when we were in kindergarten. I always wanted to play house and cook dinner for him." The genuine delight on Dalton's face as he recalls the memory makes my heart soar.

"I feel bad for you. She's a terrible cook." Jenna laughs.

"What's the worst meal she's made for you?" Dalton looks at me, a gorgeous smile on his face.

"Lasagna, senior year of college. It was like a brick. We could've used it as a doorstop. That thing was solid. I chipped a tooth trying to take a bite."

"I'll do you one better. When she was seven, she made me spaghetti and meatballs, except we were in her backyard, squirreled away in the little treehouse her dad built for her. She served me worms and globs of mud."

She covers her mouth with her hand, trying not to lose her dinner. "Gross."

"That's not the worst part. I was so madly in love with her, even then, that I ate it." I giggle at the memory, a beaming smile on my face.

"You did not! Nad, how could you let him do that?"

"I told her it was delicious. Then, I went home and puked for three hours straight."

"You never told me that," I chime in, feeling terrible about it after all these years.

"Of course not. I didn't want you to see me as weak. I still don't."

"I've never looked at you that way. You were always so strong and confident. I felt empowered just being around you."

"Okay, lovebirds. I don't know what I'm more grossed out by.

The story of eating worms for love or the way you two are staring at each other like you're about to get naked and do it right here on the table. Can I at least finish my dinner before having to excuse myself?" Flex interjects.

"You wanted the dirt."

"Yeah, not actual dirt that you ate in the name of sickeningly sweet love." Flex stifles a laugh.

"Right!" Jenna agrees with him.

"I don't care what you think, Flex. Sickly sweet will do me just fine." There's the boy I once knew.

"Of course you care. I'm amazing, and I have impeccable taste in submissives."

Jenna's eyes go wide as saucers at the mention. "You're a Dom too? Like Dalton?"

"Fuck, no. I'm not as gentle as Callaghan." I sit back, watching my friend gulp down whatever she was about to say, thinking better of it. "What's wrong, sweetheart? Cat got your tongue?"

"No." Her cheeks flush as we all wait for her to say something. "So, you're not gentle. What? You get off on whips and chains and stuff?"

"And stuff…" He rubs his hand over the scruff of his jaw, his gaze fixed on Jenna, so hot the room might go up in flames.

"I'll never understand it. What's wrong with regular, wild sex?"

"Nothing. It's just a preference like anything else. Why do you go for the type of men you fuck? Tall, short, blond, brunette. It's all about attraction at the end of the day."

"So, you're attracted to doormats? Women who *want* you to hurt them. And you don't see a problem with that?"

My body tightens at her assumption. This was a bad idea. "You don't understand, Jenna. Don't take your frustration with me out on Flex."

Dalton rests his hand on my thigh in a small show of support. He knows I'm uncomfortable.

"Don't worry, Nad. I can take care of myself. I've tamed worse." Flex gives me a playful wink, much to Dalton's distaste.

"Ugh, just listen to yourself. I'm not an animal to be broken in."

"I'm well aware. I don't sleep with women who aren't one hundred percent up for the kind of relationship I'm interested in. Trust me, I've never had any complaints. There's an art to what I do, Jenna. Seeing a woman submit to the pleasure I wring from every fiber of her being is a thing of beauty." He licks his lower lip, making Jenna shift in her chair.

"The sex can't be that much better."

"Whether it's vanilla or kink, sex with me would rock your fucking world." I watch her start to squirm, a slight blush kissing her cheeks.

"Maybe we should just talk about something else."

"Great idea," Dalton exclaims.

"Fine by me. Let's get back to Nad spilling some dirt on you in high school." Flex forces his gaze from my best friend, and she focuses her attention on draining her glass before turning to signal the bartender for another round.

"I'd love to tell you he was a dork with braces and a band uniform, but honestly, he was the coolest guy in school. The cheer-leaders wanted him. The jocks wanted to be him. Everyone hated me for taking him off the market in elementary school."

"I don't believe that for a second."

"It's okay, Flex, you know how shit my life got after high school. Take solace in my years of poverty and struggle while you were living it up at Daddy's Hampton's mansion."

It pains me to think of how Dalton and his mom must have struggled after I left.

"I love that you say it like you weren't a rich kid growing up. I know it sucked for a while there, but you're the richest man on the planet. I ain't crying any tears for you."

With the mood lightened, we enjoy the rest of dinner laughing and joking, regaling each other with funny stories of misspent youth and shameless flirting between Jenna and Flex. But by the time we're ready to go to the club, my nerves resurface and multiply.

Dalton wraps his arm around my shoulder as we journey from the restaurant to Venom in his town car, whispering in my ear. "It'll be fine. Don't worry, kitten. I've got you."

"Promise?"

"Yes, and if you're a good girl for me, I'll make it worth your while." A shiver runs down my spine. The club is my favorite place to be with Dalton. No one bats an eyelid when I call him Master, sitting in the bar area. His friends don't flinch when he tells me I've been a good girl or if I'm being a brat. It's our happy place, and I don't want anything to get in the way of that.

"You ready?" he says as we pull up outside Venom, pressing a kiss to my head.

"As I'll ever be."

Jenna seems a little intimidated as we enter, Flex ushering her to the bar with his hand on the small of her back. She takes it all in—the plush surroundings, the bar, the patrons, and the music.

"What do you think?" I sit on the barstool beside her.

"It's nothing like I thought it would be. It's... stunning."

"What were you picturing? Orgies? Ball gags? People chained up?"

She has the good sense to be embarrassed. "Kinda, yeah."

"I told you, it's not what you think... what most people assume. Everyone in this room is here because they *want* to be. Kink doesn't have to be something sleazy. And when we want intimacy, we have our private room for that. I don't get naked in the bar and let Dalton whip me."

Dalton appears at my side. "I'd kill anyone who even tried to see you naked, kitten. Never going to happen. You're mine."

Jenna winces at his comment. "She's not a piece of property. Don't you think it's a little misogynistic to say something like that? '*You're mine.*' It's archaic." She's not condescending or mean, her tone more inquisitive than it was at dinner.

"Kitten *wants* to be mine. She craves it. I would be a misogynistic asshole if I denied her desires, thinking I know better. You know your friend. She's strong, independent, and capable of knowing her own mind. I won't disrespect her by saying no when she has clearly stated what she wants and needs from me as her Dominant."

"When you say it like that, it doesn't sound so terrible."

"And don't think for a second that it's a one-way street. *I* belong to kitten, and that's the way I like it. It's about mutual respect."

"Then why do you call her kitten? I get cute pet names, but the way you say it... it's different."

"She chose the name she wanted to be called as a submissive. She is truly in control of everything that happens."

"Okay. But, if you ever hurt her, I will hunt you down and cut off your balls."

"Duly noted. Now, I'm going to steal my girl for a dance." Lacing his fingers with mine, he leads me to the center of the bar.

His hands snake around my waist, pulling me flush against his body, swaying to the music. Dalton was always the guy who could lead you around the dance floor like a pro. His mom taught him to dance before junior prom, and as he anticipated, I melted in his arms, the same way I do now. Putting everything else out of my mind, I give myself over to the way his hips grind into mine, his hands caressing my back as he leans in, his lips caressing my ear. A jolt of desire goes straight to my core, knowing how wicked his mouth can—and will—be by the end of the night.

Wrapping my arms over his shoulders, I tilt my neck, giving him unfettered access, loving how my body comes to life at his touch.

We lose ourselves in the music, moving together as one, Dalton's growing arousal thick against my thigh. One. Two. Hell, it could be ten songs later when he slides his hands in my hair as he leans down to talk to me.

"I want to take you into our private room." A thrill courses through me.

I slip my hand between us, rubbing my hand over his erection. It's answer enough. He pushes into my palm before reining himself in and turning my back to his chest. His cock caresses my ass through my dress, making me squirm for more.

"Did I give you permission to touch me, kitten?" I love how his voice drips like the most decadent chocolate, tantalizing my senses.

"No, Master."

"Come with me." Before I take his hand, I scan the room for my best friend.

Jenna and Flex are slow-dancing. "That's a bad idea. I don't want him trying to sleep with her. She's not into BDSM. Maybe we should stay in here."

"Don't worry, kitten, I've already told him she's off-limits."

"Doesn't look like he heard you unless your definition of off-limits involves grinding."

I follow as he walks toward them, pulling Flex aside for a quick word in his ear.

Flex gives me a wink. "Simply passing the time, little sub. I wouldn't underestimate your friend. She knows her own mind, and she thinks I'm a sexual deviant," he says with a wicked grin. I can only imagine how women fall at his feet.

"That's *why* I'm worried."

"Worried about what?" Jenna appears at my side.

"Dalton and I are going to slip into our room for a while. Will you be okay out here?"

Her knowing look makes me blush. "I'll be fine. Go get yours."

"I told them I'll take good care of you." Flex's voice is smooth as silk and full of innuendo.

"You're such a gentleman, for a…" Jenna's words trail off, but Flex is quick to finish her sentence.

"For a manwhore Dom."

"No one said you're a manwhore. Are you?" she says with a wicked grin.

"Does it matter?"

"I guess not."

Dalton rests his hand on the small of my back, his voice a dark rumble. "Get this sweet little ass in our room. I want you in the position *now*. I'll grab us a drink, and when I come in, I expect to see every delectable inch of you, ready and waiting."

"Yes, Master Callaghan." I practically skip down the hallway, so happy that I don't have to hide anymore.

Chapter 20

DALTON

"Are you ready for round three, kitten?"

"Where would you like me, Master?" God, she's beautiful. No matter how much time we spend together here, it's never enough. I always want more with her. More time to please her, love her, make her laugh, and worship her heart and soul.

"Face down on the bed." She does as I ask without question. I pad over to the drawers, selecting a sturdy set of black hogtie ropes, running them through my hands. These will do nicely. The delicious curves of her ass are so enticing.

"Wrists behind your back," I say as I stalk toward the bed and slip the first ties around them, tightening them just enough to bite.

When they're securely in place, I grab her ankles and bend her knees, tethering them to her wrists, the black ropes so perfect against her alabaster skin. When they are good and tight, I stand back to admire my handiwork. Naddie is completely at my mercy.

"How does that feel, kitten?"

"Good, Master."

"If only your friend could see you now. What a dirty girl you are. Do you like being tied up like this? Helpless."

"Yes, Master. I love being your dirty girl." Fuck, her voice is downright sinful.

"And I love seeing you like this, kitten. So trusting and eager to please."

With her unable to move, I walk to the side of the bed before leaning in and pushing her onto her side, her breasts on display and so fucking luscious. I capture her nipple between my lips, flicking my tongue over the tip until it's tightly budded. Then, I bite down just enough to send a jolt of pain through her, and I'm rewarded with a groan of pleasure.

"Mm… you are so fucking sexy, kitten. Where else would you like my mouth?"

"Everywhere, Master." Her breaths are ragged as she whispers the words.

"I'm going to need more specific instructions, kitten." I envelop her other nipple, teasing and kissing her until she's panting. "Tell me what you want."

"I want you to fuck me with your tongue, Master."

I slide a hand down her naked body before slipping a finger deep inside her. "Here? Is this where you *need* me, kitten?"

"Yes…" she gasps, and I thrust harder, adding a second finger.

"Yes, who?"

"Yes, Master Callaghan. I want your tongue on my pussy."

"I can tell. You're soaking wet."

I slowly kiss a trail down her stomach before flipping her onto her stomach and pulling her to the edge of the bed. Dropping to my knees, I whisper against her entrance. "Tell me how much you want it."

"I *need* you, Master. Please, please, kiss me. Fuck me with your mouth, Master."

"Who do you belong to?"

"You, Master Callaghan. I belong to you." I drag my tongue from her clit to her entrance, applying just enough pressure to her thighs that it'll hurt.

"Fucking right. You're mine." I kiss and lick the length of her before pushing my tongue into her entrance just a little.

"Yes... oh God, yes... Master."

"That's it, kitten, be a good girl for me." I kiss her again and again, my cock rock-hard as she begs for more, lost to the pleasure and pain.

The door to my room flies open, a wild-eyed Flex bursting in.

"What the fuck are you doing, Flex?" I cover Naddie with my body, grabbing a sheet to wrap around her. Uncontrolled rage builds in my chest, my adrenaline ready to rip his fucking eyes out for seeing Naddie this way. "Get out!"

His face sobers. "It's your Mom."

"What?" I quickly loosen the hogties at Naddie's wrists and ankles while pulling the comforter over her.

"They've been trying to call you, but it must be on silent. We gotta go. *Now.*"

"Dalton..." I don't hear anything else as I shrug into my pants, grab my shirt, and take off at a sprint.

I slam into Jenna in the hallway, wearing nothing but Flex's suit jacket wrapped tightly around her body. "I'm sorry. Look after Naddie. I have to go." I don't stop to explain. I can't.

I weave through the club, stuffing my arms into my shirt as Viv and the others look on in confusion, Flex hot on my heels. "Dalton! Shoes."

I turn as Flex throws my shoes at me. I shove my feet in them and keep going. The second I reach the exit, I assess the traffic. It's Manhattan on a Saturday night. There's no way the town car is getting me there quicker than I can on foot.

I take off running, my heart ricocheting off my ribcage as I push myself faster, moving swiftly through the crowds of people, their lives moving at a normal pace while mine is crumbling in slow motion.

My lungs ache as I heave in the cold night air, my ears ringing as my feet pound the pavement. Fear courses through my veins as I sprint through the streets of Manhattan. *I have to get to her.*

I don't know if Flex is still behind me, my pulse thumping so hard in my ears it drowns out everything around me. Every block feels like I'm getting farther away rather than closer to my building. Like I'm in an eternal loop, just out of reach.

Digging deep, I force myself to move faster, using every ounce of adrenaline with maximum efficiency. I push down the well of emotion fighting to get out of me as my building comes into sight.

When I reach the front doors, I launch myself into the lobby, almost slamming into the elevator as I hit the button, my breath ragged as I wait impatiently. "Come on, come on, come on."

The rational part of me knows that waiting will still be faster than taking the stairs, but my body is vibrating with nervous energy. Flex comes barreling in the door just as the elevator doors ping open.

"*Hurry.*" He's just as out of breath as he comes flying into the elevator, dropping his hands to his knees.

I hit the button for her floor, my world suddenly so surreal— suspended in this metal cage, soft music playing as we move up the building. Thankfully, it doesn't stop on any other floor. I take the opportunity to button my shirt, having left the club in such a rush that I didn't bother. I don't want to be a mess when Mom sees me.

Flex puts his hand on my shoulder, but we don't speak. We can't. Maybe if we don't say it, it won't happen.

I've known this moment was coming, but I'm not ready.

The second the elevator reaches her floor, I take off running toward her apartment, the handle crashing into the wall as I fling open the door. Everything feels so small. So quiet. My stomach lurches into my throat as I get to the bedroom's entrance.

"I'm so sorry, Dalton," the nurse says with such compassion, and it cracks me wide open.

"No. No."

I push myself forward, dropping down at my mom's side, taking her hand in mine.

"She passed a few minutes ago."

Her fingers are cold and slack, her body no longer plagued by tremors, and her face is soft as if she were simply asleep.

"I'm so sorry, Mom." Everything I've been holding together since the day she was diagnosed shatters inside me. "I failed you.

I'm so sorry. I was supposed to be here with you. You weren't supposed to be alone."

Flex rests his hand on my shoulder, but I shrug it off.

"She wasn't alone. I was with her," the nurse offers tentatively.

"What happened?" I thought I would know when the time came.

"Her breathing became labored about an hour ago. I gave her oxygen and called her doctor. They said to monitor her levels and keep them informed. As per her directive, she has been on palliative hospice for some time now. You know she didn't want any extraordinary measures."

"I was talking to her last night." I squeeze her hand, staring at her chest, willing it to rise and fall, but it's so still. *Devoid* of life.

"I was trying to call you. Then, she started seizing fifteen minutes ago. I called 911, and then I called Felix to see if he could reach you. I did everything I could within her directive. I'm so sorry for your loss."

Then it hits me. I wasn't here because I put my fucking phone on silent. Too busy having sex in my custom-built kink palace to be disturbed by my mother. Fucking. Dying.

"I would've been here if I left my phone on."

Flex sits at my side, a single tear trickling down his cheek. "Don't do that to yourself. There was no way you could've known she was going to have a seizure."

I keep my voice low out of respect for my Mom. *How fucked up is that? Like she cares now.* "She's been sick for years. I knew she was going downhill fast. I should've been here."

"Dalton…" Naddie is here. Her voice is a soothing balm and a stake through my heart.

"I just want to be alone right now."

I turn to see her eyes filled with tears. She loved my mom too. Everyone who met her couldn't help but love her. And now she's gone.

"I can sit with you until the coroner gets here."

"No." I don't want her to see me break. To see the failure I am in this moment.

"I need you to go."

I look to Flex. "Can you please take Naddie and Jenna back to her apartment?"

"I'm not leaving you, Dalton." Her voice is pained, and I don't have the energy to fight her. Comfort her. Or *be* comforted by her.

"Fine. Go up to my apartment. Jenna can sleep in one of the guest rooms. I'll be up later."

Flex gives her a stern nod but makes no move to stand.

"Can you go with them, Flex? I need some time."

"Are you sure? I'll come back down before they move her. Do you want me to take Jenna up and get her situated? Maybe Nad should stay here with you."

I don't recognize the sound of my voice, a feral, hollow, whispering growl. "Get out. Everyone. Get. Out."

Dropping my head in my hands, I wait for them to leave, unable to fucking breathe. When I feel they've gone, the nurse takes a moment before she speaks. "I canceled the ambulance and asked that the coroner be sent out. I'll wait for them in the living room if you need me." Then, she leaves me with Mom.

I sit in the overwhelming silence. I've spent so many nights in this room, sitting in this chair, relieved at times when Mom fell asleep because it hurt to have her talk to me like a stranger.

What kind of man feels like that? *Relief.*

Now, all I want is for her to open her eyes and talk to me one last time. I don't care if she knows it's me or not.

The only sound is my breathing, and the only movement is the rise and fall of *my* chest. There is no relief now. Alone, I let my tears fall and the guilt pull me under until there's nothing left.

It's always been Mom and me against the world. Even when I was young, my dad was too busy out swindling clients and fucking anything that moved. He was a shit husband and an absent father for all intents and purposes. Mom and I only grew closer after he got locked up. I wanted to be everything he wasn't—to give her security and the life she deserved.

I worked my ass off to build a life for us, and now I have all this money, and it doesn't matter worth a shit. When it came down to it,

I couldn't buy her a cure. There was no miracle for her—the sweet-est, most kind-hearted woman I've ever met. She'd give someone the shirt off her back if they needed it. And what did the universe see fit to give her? *Parkinson's in her forties. Dementia in her fifties.*

I can't bear it.

"I came as fast as I could, Mom." I take her ice-cold hand in mine once more, a sob escaping me as I take in the fragility of her frame and every line of her sweet face. "I'm so sorry. I... I couldn't save you. Please, forgive me. I'm sorry."

The silence is an agony I've never felt before.

"I'm sorry."

Time ceases to exist, and I have no idea how long I sit at my mom's bedside, praying I'll wake up from this nightmare when Flex appears at the door.

"The coroner is here when you're ready." His voice is thick with emotion, and as I turn to face him, his grief reflects my own. The second he sees my expression, he strides toward me, and as I stand, he pulls me into a hug, holding together whatever shreds of me are left.

"I'm not ready, Flex."

"I know, brother." I cling to him for the longest time.

"I'll go talk to them. You take a minute with Mom."

"Are you sure?" His eyes well with tears.

"She was your Mom, too, Flex. You know she loved you as if you were her own."

He breaks down, a sob escaping him as he moves toward the bed. I force myself to put one foot in front of the other, the pain growing with every step as I attempt to steel my emotions long enough to deal with what needs to happen next.

When I reach the living room, I call on every ounce of strength in my soul to survive the next hour. Everyone is professional while offering condolences and talking me through procedures—logistics I haven't wanted to contemplate in the months leading up to this moment.

All I hear is that they need to take Mom now, and my body goes numb. I can't think about it because the second they move her, she's really gone. Right now, she's tucked under the covers of her bed. She was breathing in an out last night, asking if I knew when her family was going to visit. I thought I was heartbroken as I assured her they'd be here soon, and she should close her eyes and get some sleep. I promised to wake her when her family arrived.

Except I didn't keep my promise. I never arrived.

When I return to my mom's room, Flex is still holding her hand, saying his final goodbyes, his eyes red as he wipes the tears away.

"They need to take her now, Flex."

He moves aside, letting me walk over to the bed. I gently tuck a loose tendril of hair behind her ear before leaning down and pressing a gentle kiss to her forehead, like I've done a million times before.

That I'll never do again.

"I love you, Momma," I choke past the lump in my throat.

The medical staff suggests it would be best if we don't watch them move her, but as I walk to the doorway, I keep my eyes on her until the last possible moment. When she's out of sight, I can't conceive of a world without her in it.

I pace the living room, my hands in my pockets, clenched into fists so tight it hurts. Flex is on the couch, his head down, trying his best to keep it together. Mom's nurse stays close by, knowing there's nothing more she can do.

We go through the motions as they complete their job, leaving with the woman who brought me into the world. I thank them. They are doing what's necessary. It seems polite to say thank you. I hug Mom's nurse and express my eternal gratitude for everything she did for my mom.

I watch out the window as the coroner's ambulance pulls onto the busy Manhattan streets, the city as it's always been, as if the world didn't just stop turning. I don't fight Flex when he ushers me out of the apartment and up to the penthouse.

Naddie is waiting at the door, her tear-stained cheeks more than I can cope with. She gingerly walks toward me, her arms wrapping around my waist as Flex disappears, taking Jenna with him. To my office down the hall. Maybe to a bedroom. I don't care.

I let Naddie's scent envelop me for just a moment until it's too much. Her concern. The love in her voice as she tries to soothe me. The warmth of her body against mine. I shut it all down. I have to. The pain is too much.

Staring off into the distance—into nothing—I let her lead me to my bedroom and into the bathroom. I smell like whiskey and sex. I reek of debauchery and death. Naddie doesn't talk as she heats the shower and gently removes my clothes. When she guides me under the showerhead, I brace my hands on the tile, letting the water cascade over my face, drowning out the sobs that rack my entire being, washing away my tears, only to be replaced with more.

Naddie washes my hair and body with such tenderness before simply wrapping her arms around me, her head against my back, giving me nothing but love.

When we eventually shut off the water, everything feels wrong. Surreal. I towel myself dry before crawling into bed. It's such a normal, everyday action. Naddie slips on my old T-shirt before getting in next to me, her damp hair fanned out on the pillow as she faces me, her hands clasped under her chin. She's afraid to touch me, probably worried I'll crack.

"Is there anything I can do for you, Dalton?"

I turn her so I can pull her back against my chest, wrapping my arm tight around her waist. It's all I can manage. I'm terrified that if I open my mouth to tell Naddie how I feel, I won't be able to piece myself back together.

Sleep doesn't grace me with her presence tonight. Instead, I replay the moments I was sprinting through the city while my mom took her last breath, hating myself for putting my wants and desires ahead of what she needed.

She needed me to be the man my father never was, and in the end—in her final hours—I was just as selfish as him. I wasn't there, and she died.

My mom died. And nothing will ever be the same again.

Chapter 21

NADDIE

It's been weeks since the funeral, and Dalton is a ghost. He doesn't talk about how he's feeling. He's thrown himself into work and doesn't want to go near the club. I've been trying to give him space to grieve. He's not a man who ever wants to show weakness, but I had hoped he'd open up to me in the days after his mom died. As the days pass, he only drifts farther away.

Dalton is a broken man, and my Master is nowhere to be found.

Chapter 22
DALTON

You'll find salvation in your work. That's what I keep telling myself. Everything that tethered me to the world around me seems so distant. The funeral came and went. Planning it gave me purpose and ways to still honor my mom. But, the next day, everyone went about their daily lives as if nothing happened. So, I figured I would do the same thing—throw myself back into work.

Early mornings and late nights have become my new normal. Audrey has gone on maternity leave, and although she left me with a PA who will suffice in her absence, I've already let my schedule go to hell.

It's a good excuse not to talk. I work late. Naddie works late. We fall into bed at the end of the day. Rinse and repeat. The ride into the office today was deathly quiet, but I didn't know what to say. She deserves more than I have to give right now.

As the town car pulls up outside her office building, she turns to face me, the distance between us palpable. "I love you, Master."

Where my heart once took flight at the term of endearment, now it only fuels my guilt.

"I love you, too, Naddie." All I have to do is reach out and pull her into my arms, but I can't. Her shoulders sag as she leaves me behind. "See you tonight."

As the door shuts, I fight the urge to punch the window that reflects the pitiful man I'm letting myself become.

"Change of plans, Ryan. Take me back to my apartment."

"Yes, Sir."

I'm fucking up. Reaching for my phone, I tap out a quick message.

> Me: You busy today? I'm blowing off work.

> Flex: I can move a few things around. Everything okay?

> Me: No.

> Flex: What do you have in mind?

> Me: Let's take the Bentley to the track. Some high-speed driving sounds pretty good today.

> Flex: Twist my arm, and I'll take it for a spin. What are you going to drive?

> Me: Meet me at the track at ten.

> Flex: Done.

Driving has always been a release for me—a way to blow off steam when life gets to me. Flex is the only one who understands all the plates I'm trying to keep spinning right now, and I know I can vent without judgment.

I make a few calls on the way back to my apartment before changing into something more casual than a three-piece suit, grabbing my keys, and heading for the garage. With my phone set to Do Not Disturb, I slide into the comforting leather seat, letting my hands caress the steering wheel as the scent of leather tantalizes my senses. The engine's roar calms my mind as she purrs to life, and I peel out of the parking garage.

By the time I reach the track, Flex is ready and waiting, steadfast as always.

"Hey, bro. What's got you playing hooky today?" he says as he hands me a helmet with my name emblazoned on the royal blue, glossy carbon fiber.

"Same shit, different day."

His shoulders sag, his smile turning sour. "I'm sorry, man. What's happening? Can I do anything to help?"

"Can you figure out why I can't be the Dom I need to be for Naddie right now?"

"You're grieving. She understands."

"That's what makes it so unbearable. She's being so incredible, giving me the time and space to get my head straightened out."

"You're doing everything you can, bro."

"It's not enough."

"What can I do? Do you want to talk, or would you rather drive?"

"Drive."

"Then, let's do it. We can talk later... with booze."

I clap him on the back. Flex isn't the kind of guy who gives empty platitudes. What you see is what you get, and I've always valued that in my best friend. The fact that he doesn't *need* me to act a certain way is a breath of fresh air. "Thanks, Flex."

"Anytime."

We spend most of the day driving the track in healthy competition to get the fastest lap. History has taught him nothing. I'm always going to win. *I'm me.* With each lap, the tension I've been holding in my shoulders eases. It feels odd to smile. To *feel* anything at all.

When we're done, Flex convinces me to go for a drink at Venom. Once I drop the car back at home, we head out, but the second I set foot inside the bar, an ache forms in the pit of my stomach. I don't want to be here.

With a whiskey sour in hand, Flex asks the one question I'm not sure how to answer.

"How are things with Nad?"

"Don't ask." I take a long sip of my drink and signal the bartender for another round.

"You can't fool me, bro. Why have you been out with me all day instead of spending some time with your submissive?"

"You're my best friend. Is it that crazy I want to spend some time blowing off steam?"

A shit-eating grin spreads across his stupid, chiseled face. "As amazing company as I know myself to be, you've not been in here in weeks."

"I don't want to talk about it, Flex."

"Well, I think you need to. You're pushing her away."

"I'm protecting her."

"From what?"

"*From me!*" I sling back my drink and signal for another.

"She doesn't want your protection. All Nad wants to do is love you. She wants to please you."

"I can't be her Dom right now."

"What? She's the fucking love of your life. What the hell are you even talking about?"

"Just drop it, Flex." My skin bristles as he pushes me.

"Your mom wouldn't want you to stop living your life, Dal."

"Don't fucking mention her. She doesn't want anything anymore. She's dead, Flex."

He's up in my face, and I know what he's trying to do. "Yes, she's gone. It's heartbreaking. And here's the big kicker, Dal. You're. Still. Alive. You're punishing yourself for no reason."

"No reason? *No reason!* You want to talk about punishment? I can't stand being in this club. It makes my fucking skin crawl. Do you know what I was doing while my mom was fighting for her life?" I'm off my chair, growling at him as we stand toe-to-toe. "I had my face buried in Naddie's cunt, taking *what* I wanted *when* I wanted it, and I didn't give a shit about anything else."

"Dalton..." He reaches out a hand to calm me, but I shove it off.

"I should've been there, Flex. And instead, I was fucking a goddamn submissive. *I can't even fucking look at her!*"

He drops his head in his hands as everyone in the room seems to stare at me. Past me. Turning to follow their gaze, I see Naddie at the other end of the bar, tears rolling down her cheeks.

I expect her to run, but she just stands stock still, rooted to the spot.

"Naddie... I didn't..."

Viv strides past me, wrapping her arm around Naddie. "I think you've said enough right now, Dalton. I'm taking Nadia to my room for a few minutes."

"Like hell you are."

"I'm not a toy. I know you didn't mean it, Master Callaghan. I just came to check if you were okay. You are. I'm going home. I'll see you tomorrow."

"Naddie, wait."

Flex grabs my arm. "Let her go, Dal. You need to cool down."

When Naddie doesn't give me so much as a second glance, I head for my private room, away from everyone's prying eyes. Flex starts to follow me, but I stare him down, letting him know in no uncertain terms that I want to be alone.

The familiar click of my keycard and the scent of leather as I step inside make my insides twist. Everything has been put back in its place. Fresh sheets are on the bed. The only item that remains of the night I ran out of here is my cufflinks, set atop the chest of drawers.

I roll them around in my hand for a moment, feeling the weight of the Cartier platinum in my palm before hurling them at the wall.

How could I have said those things in front of Naddie?

I reach for anything that's not nailed down, tossing, throwing, obliterating the sanctuary I built for myself, ruining the room I had remodeled for Naddie. After weeks of trying to contain it, I let all my rage out. The darkness surrounding me takes hold, and I roar as I give in to the most primal part of myself. By the time I'm done, it looks like a tornado swept through the room, taking any comfort I once had with it.

It's only in the aftermath and the eerie silence that befalls the broken room that Carter appears in the doorway. "You done? I hope you feel better now." His arms are crossed over his chest as he leans against the doorjamb, ever the picture of serenity and control.

"Go away, Carter."

"What kind of friend would I be if I walked away right now? I get it. Despair so vast you feel like it's going to drown you."

"How much death have you dealt with? You have the perfect marriage, kids, the whole nine yards. Forgive me if I think you have fuck all to say right now that's going to make me feel better."

He rights one of the upended chairs and sits—cool, calm, and collected as always. "I found out my 'uncle' was abusing my little sister when we were young. I became feral in the moments after. I would've clawed him to shreds if I hadn't been physically restrained."

"I never knew Vittoria had been through that. I'm sorry."

"So, I wouldn't let any woman get close to me until I met Addi. And when I did, I screwed up, time and time again."

"You seem like such a perfect couple."

"Yeah, now that we've weathered the storms. She left me that first year. I didn't know where she was for months. I had zero idea she was pregnant. Then, she almost died in my arms when she hemorrhaged. I thought I'd lost everything, and knowing how close I came to that being my reality… it was hard, fucked up, and totally worth it."

"I don't know what to do, what to say… how to feel."

"That's okay. Just don't stay too long in this place, letting the anger consume you. From what I've seen of Nadia, she's a strong woman. She can handle whatever comes her way, but even the strongest people have a breaking point. Don't push her away."

"How do I come back from everything I said tonight?"

"You apologize. If that's how you feel right now, then that's the truth. You won't feel this way forever."

"This room makes me feel physically sick."

"I did such a great job on the remodel as well," he says with a wry grin. "Leave it with me. When you're ready to come back here with Nadia, it will be a different room. Hell, do you want a new room altogether?"

"No. I can't run away forever. A remodel would be great."

"Leave it with me, but promise you won't trash this one after a few months."

I take a look around at my destruction. "You have my word."

"Well, okay then."

"When did you get so wise, Carter?"

"Years and years of fuckups. If it weren't for Addi, I'd still be fucking my way through Manhattan, miserable and lonely."

"I need to make things right with Naddie."

"Give her a night to process. There's been a lot going on, and everything will seem clearer in the morning."

"Maybe."

"Now, go home. This clearly isn't the best place for you right now. Call me, day or night, if you need anything."

"Thanks, bro."

"Anytime." He leaves me to survey the damage, and I can't help but replay what I said tonight on a loop. The hurt in Naddie's eyes was—I never want to be the cause of such pain ever again.

Maybe Carter is right. I need to give her time to process it before I go to her place, demanding she forgive me.

As I leave the carnage behind and make my way through the club, Viv comes to offer her condolences, even though she did so at my mom's funeral.

"I'm so sorry, Dalton," she says as she wraps her arms around me.

"Thanks, Viv."

"She's wonderful, but I'm sure you already know that."

"Yeah, I do. I'll make it right."

"Good. Go home. You don't need to spend any more time here tonight."

"I'm just leaving."

"It gets easier. I know it doesn't feel like it now, but there will come a time when you get to the end of a day and realize you didn't think about it or you'll smile without that pang of guilt in your chest. Your world will start turning again, and it's okay when that happens."

I hold her tight.

"Thank you. Goodnight, Viv."

"Night, Dalton."

~

It was hard to go home alone. I walked to within a block of Naddie's apartment three times before turning around and continuing to walk the bustling streets of Manhattan. She deserves a Dom who can give her what she needs. She's given up so much for me, and I'm some pale imitation of the man I was a month ago.

My apartment feels so empty without her around. I've gotten so used to her presence, even if it's just in the same room in comfortable silence. So, as soon as I'm up, washed, and ready, I head into the office.

When I open the door, I immediately twist the lock, my heart hammering in my chest at the sight of her.

Naddie is on her knees, fully dressed, but with her eyes cast to the floor and hands clasped behind her back.

"What are you doing here, Naddie?"

"I came only to keep you company, Master Callaghan. I won't interrupt your work. If you'll allow me, I just want to be here in silent support. Please, don't send me away."

My heart grinds to a halt. She would do this for me.

"Okay," is all I can manage.

Sitting at my desk, my heart aches as she continues to stare at the floor, but something inside me can't ask her to meet my gaze, so I do what she asks.

I work for hours, and Naddie is the perfect submissive. She doesn't once move from her position, offering quiet comfort that I didn't know I needed.

After a long morning, I reach out and brush my hand down her cheek, lift her chin, and give her permission to look at me. "Thank you, kitten. You're such a good girl." It warms my heart to see her blush at the praise.

"Thank you, Master."

THE CONTRACT

"Now, go to your office and work. It is a waste of your talent to sit at my feet all day."

Her expression is pained, but she quickly schools her features as she gets to her feet. "As you wish, Master."

She doesn't attempt to kiss me, and I let her walk out the door without another word. I know she wants me to open up and be physically and emotionally present with her, but a part of me can't let myself be happy with her because I know when that happens, I'll lose myself in her. I'll forget all the pain, the grief, and the guilt I carry.

Working long past dinner, I realize my driver hasn't sent word that Naddie got home safely. I make a quick call, only to find out she's still at Mason, Porter & Associates. Against my better judgment, I have Ryan pick me up and take me to her office. I don't like the idea of her in there this late at night.

The place is deserted, offices dark except for Naddie's. I can see her poring over files at her desk, her hair swept up into a messy bun, reading glasses perched on her sweet face. My emotions are all over the place as I watch her work. I was surprised when she changed her mind and said she wanted to remain with the firm and let me buy Douglas out when the time is right, but I respect her decision.

I stand back and watch her for a few moments, loving her from afar. As if she senses my presence, she looks up from her paperwork, but all I get is a curt smile, and she returns to her task. I take my time crossing the open-plan workspace, leaning against the door to her corner office. "Hey."

"Hi."

"I was worried when Ryan said he hadn't taken you home yet."

"I have a lot of work to catch up on, Dalton. I *wasted* my time this morning." She doesn't look up, her words dripping with disdain.

"That's not what I meant."

"You seem to say a lot of things you don't mean lately or a whole lot of nothing."

I tuck my hands in my pockets, unable to look her in the eye. "I'm sorry about what I said at the club."

"Are you? If you meant it, then why apologize?"

223

"Naddie… I know I haven't been very forthcoming since…. I appreciate your patience."

"Listen to yourself. *I appreciate your patience.* You sound like a fucking call center employee. I'm not complaining about my cable bill here."

"Don't curse."

"Or what? What are you going to do? Take me to the club and spank me? Fuck me but not let me come? Fine. Punish me. I don't care. I'll take whatever you've got. What I can't stand is you shutting me out completely."

"I…" The tears welling in her eyes are a dagger to my soul.

"I can wait, Dalton. I've waited more than a decade to be back in your life. I understand that you're grieving, and I'm not demanding your attention, but I need to know if I'm waiting for something that may never happen."

"What are you saying?"

"Did you mean what you said at the club? You barely said a word to me for weeks, and then you announce to the whole club that I'm the reason you weren't with your mom that night. What was it… *you had your face buried in my cunt.* That's the reason we haven't been intimate since that night. You blame me. You can't even look at me."

"I was upset."

"You didn't answer the question."

"Naddie, I blame myself. Not you."

"It's one and the same thing. You were with me. Fucking me. Are you ever going to be able to look at me the way you did before?"

I stalk toward her, my panic rising. "What do you want from me, Naddie?"

She stands from her desk, her heels kicked off already—she's small as she attempts to stand toe-to-toe with me, the rapid rise and fall of my chest betraying the war raging inside me.

"I want *anything.* Talk to me. Hate me. Love me. Use me. Fuck me. Punish me. *Need me.*"

"I don't want to feel anything right now. Don't you get it? I could hurt you, and I'd never forgive myself. The darkness that's consuming me isn't something I ever want you to see."

"*I love you!* That's not going to change because you're grieving. It won't change even if you don't want to be with me. I'm not afraid of you… Master. I know my safeword. I won't let you do anything I can't handle."

I have no words. I can feel myself shutting down, terrified that I can't be in control right now. I've never felt this way before, and it goes against everything I've based my life around. She stalks toward me and, without warning, shoves against my chest. "Feel something, goddammit."

"Stop." She does it again and again before I grab her wrists. "Stop it, Nadia."

"Fucking make me… *Master.*"

"Why are you doing this?"

"Because you need it. You're lost. So stop being a pussy and punish me."

"Don't," I growl.

Tears stream down her cheeks as she fights against my hold. "What? Don't call you a pussy because you won't even look at me? What good am I if you shut me out? You want me to shut up and stop pushing you, then either sit down and talk to me or fuck me. What are you so afraid of? That you'll enjoy punishing me too much?"

"I'm trying to protect you." My pulse is racing, my entire body vibrating with an anger that's been simmering for weeks.

"I don't want your fucking protection!" Her breathing is labored and ragged as she struggles against me.

"Stop swearing at me or so help me God…"

"What? You won't bury your face in my *cunt.* You won't *fuck* my mouth. Is your *dick* even hard right now?"

I snap, and in one swift movement, I turn her around, capture her hands behind her back, and hike up her dress before tearing her lace panties off. "Is this what you want, Nadia?"

"I want *you*, Master."

I quickly unzip my fly and release my cock, positioning myself at her entrance as I bend her over the desk, her ass ripe for the taking. I grab a fistful of her hair with one hand, still holding her wrists with the other as I sink balls deep inside her with one brutal thrust.

Any coherent thought is gone as I pound into her, letting every dark and twisted part of myself run wild as I fuck her so hard she cries out.

"Is my dick hard enough for you, Nadia?"

"Yes, Master Callaghan," she screams.

I make her take every inch of me as I thrust over and over, holding her tight by her hair. "Fucking say it, Nadia."

"Your dick is so hard, Master."

I'm feral as I chase release, hammering into her until her muscles clench around me, milking me for everything I've got. When I can't hold back any longer, I push harder, faster, until I'm roaring, my release pulsing through me, ripping me open, emotion crashing through me as I ride the aftershocks.

When I release Naddie, she's crying, and I know I hurt her.

"Are you okay? I was too rough."

"You think I can't take a hard fuck?" she says as she stands up, moving her dress back into place. "You can physically hurt me as much as you want, and I'll lap that shit up. What I won't do is have you fuck me like some cold, detached asshole. You knew the only thing that would hurt me was calling me *Nadia*." She spits the name at me.

"I… it's your name." She's right. I did it to detach myself.

"Bullshit. You've known since I was a kid that I hate it. I've told you how it makes me feel when you say it. Tell me you didn't do it on purpose."

"I won't lie to you."

"Exactly. We wrote a fucking contract. If you want to be the Dom, you call me kitten. If you want to be the boy I fell in love with, call me Naddie. I gave you time and space, even when it killed me to do so. You pushed me away at every turn, belittling my attempts to comfort you as your girlfriend and as your submissive. Something I hold sacred."

"Naddie…"

"Oh, now it's *Naddie*. Too fucking late. I love you, Master, but calling me *Nadia* with the intention of hurting me, while you're inside me, is a hard fucking limit. Fucking me like I'm nothing to you is a hard fucking limit!"

I fix my pants, completely disgusted by my behavior.

"Just go. I have work to finish."

"I'm sorry."

"So am I. I thought you were better than that."

"Naddie."

"Go."

I leave with no defense of my actions. I knew better than to lose control, and I ended up hurting the one person in the world I wanted to protect from this ugly rage that's taken root inside me. I punished her for my shortcomings, and for that, I will never forgive myself.

Chapter 23
NADDIE

The dark circles under my eyes have become noticeable over the past few weeks since Dalton and I had our fight. I work and lie awake at night, lonely in my own bed. I swung by his office a few days after we fought, but he wasn't there, and I left a message for him to call me back.

I thought I was doing the right thing—provoking a reaction out of Dalton. Clearly, I was wrong. Now, he hasn't spoken to me in weeks. I've sent him a few texts and told him he could find me at the club if he wants to talk.

The only thing that gives me any hope right now is that Ryan appears every day to take me to and from work. I'm really trying to give Dalton the space he needs to grieve. Being at his side wasn't working. Forcing him to react was a major mistake, and now I have no idea how he's doing. Not firsthand, anyway.

I've seen Flex at the club and inquired about Dalton, but he seems to be getting shut out as well. I don't want to put him in an awkward position, but I'm going over there if I don't hear from Dalton soon.

I can't bear the distance between us. It's eating away at me, turning my insides rotten with every passing day. I thought I understood heartbreak when I left Dalton for college, but this is different. It's an ache so deep in my soul, and it threatens to pull me under at any given moment.

Tonight is the same as every other lately. I grab some mail off the desk at work and stuff it in my briefcase before having Ryan drop me at Venom around seven. I'm pleasantly surprised to see Genevieve at the bar, and the second she spies me, she's out of her seat, her elegant heels click-clacking on the wood floors as she makes her way over to me, pulling me into her arms.

"Come have a drink with me. I have some time before my trainee arrives."

"That would be really nice, thanks." Some of the tension releases in her embrace. I didn't realize how much I needed some physical touch.

When we sit at the bar, I can't believe my eyes. There's a new bartender, and he looks familiar.

"Eli?" The guy who gave me his number when I went out with Jenna months ago.

He smiles with heat in his eyes. "The woman who broke my winning streak."

Genevieve turns, her expression enough of a question.

"When I moved to Manhattan, my friend and I went to Viper. Eli asked for my number. I refused, so he gave me his."

"And now I know why she didn't call me," he says with a smirk.

"You work here now?"

"I'm the new weekday manager. Carter knew I was hoping to move up the ranks at Viper, so when this came up, he asked, and here I am."

It's cute how he blushes as he looks between Genevieve and me. "Well, congratulations. I guess we'll be seeing a whole lot more of each other."

"I knew there was an upside to taking this job." And there's the shameless flirt I met at Viper.

Genevieve is quick to put him in his place. "Venom 101. Don't flirt with the submissives. If her Dom catches you, he'll have your guts for garters."

"It's fine. He's just playing around." I rest my hand on her arm, but she is every inch the Domme.

"Do you think that's how Dalton would see it?" She levels me with her stare.

"Honestly, I wouldn't know because he won't return my texts or calls. If he wants to assert his dominance, I'll happily comply, but that doesn't seem high on his list of priorities right now. You heard him the last time he had anything to say in here. Everyone did."

"Is everything okay?" Eli speaks up.

"Stay out of it, pretty boy," Genevieve hisses.

"He was just being kind, Genevieve. He's not your submissive, and neither am I."

"Watch your tone, Nad. Dalton is a dear friend of mine. I know he hurt your feelings, but he's grieving."

I stand from the barstool, downing the last of my drink. "Maybe *you* should watch your tone, Genevieve. My relationship with my Master is none of your business. He's the goddamn love of my life. You think I want to be here night after night without him? He won't talk to me. You think I would cast him aside over something he said in anger?"

She's speechless as I continue.

"I've tried everything short of squatting in his penthouse. He hurt me that night. He's hurt me in the days since, and I still kept reaching out. I don't come here to hang out and enjoy the ambience. I told him when he's ready to talk, he can find me in *our* private room. So, I'm going to talk to whomever I choose in the moments before I enter the room and wait, hoping like hell that he's going to come."

"I'm sorry, Nad. I didn't…"

"Exactly," I interrupt. "You don't know anything about what he and I share. And trust me when I tell you, he'd be a damn sight more annoyed that you tried to treat me like a sub than Eli saying one nice thing to me. Keep your opinions to yourself. Now, if you'll excuse me, I'm going to wait for my Master."

I turn on my heel and march from the bar, fighting like hell not to let the tears welling in my eyes overflow until I'm in the safety of room one. The moment I let the door close behind me, I fall apart, sobs racking my body as I drop onto the bed.

Every time I walk in here, I replay that night in my office on a loop. The look on Dalton's face. The coldness in his voice as he fucked me. I would've taken any amount of pain he had to give or suffered any punishment if it helped him process his grief. The way he fucked me without feeling—anything—that was devastating.

When I stop crying, I fix the comforter, strip out of my clothes, and fold them on the chair, just the way my Master likes. Then, I take my place on the floor, spreading my legs and clasping my hands behind my back, my eyes cast to the floor, awaiting instruction. The same as I did yesterday, the day before, and the week before that. But he doesn't come.

He never comes.

Maybe it's for the best tonight. It's a losing battle to hold back my endless tears. I wait for hours—the same time every night—until eleven o'clock when my phone alarm goes off. My legs ache as I force myself to my feet, get dressed, and head for the door, emotionally exhausted. I don't need to look in the mirror to know my eyes are puffy from crying.

My heart is shattered, my soul broken as I make my way through the bar. Thankfully, Genevieve is nowhere to be seen. I can't deal with a major conversation now. Eli is wiping down the bar as I pass by, his gaze telling me I look as bad as I feel.

"Do you want a drink before you leave?"

"Sure." I slump onto a stool, too tired to fake being okay.

He sets down my dirty martini with cocktail onions, not olives. "On the house."

"My Dom owns the house."

"Even better if he's the one upsetting you."

I manage to crack a smile. "Thanks. I'm sorry about earlier. Genevieve was out of order. You didn't do anything wrong."

"Neither did you. Do you want to talk about it? Bartenders are notoriously great listeners."

"Not really."

"You sure?"

"Not really…" I mess around with the skewer in my glass, stirring it mindlessly as I begin talking. "My Dom isn't speaking to me."

"Did you do something wrong?"

"Yes and no. I pushed him, and it was a bad idea. I ended up pushing him away, and I don't know what else to do. So, I come here every night and wait for him."

"How long has this been going on?"

"Weeks."

He leans his elbows on the bar, searching my gaze for answers. "You seem like an intelligent woman. Why are you letting him treat you this way? If he doesn't see how amazing you are, it's his issue, not yours."

"It's complicated."

"It doesn't have to be. It can be as easy as a cute bartender giving you his number and you letting him take you on a date. No strings. No complications. Just a fun night." He has that glint in his eye that tells me he'd be nothing but trouble in the best possible way.

"Thanks, but…"

"Is Ryan waiting outside to take you home, or do you need a ride?" I turn to find Flex, his arms crossed and his question laced with a warning.

"Ryan should be outside. I don't need another Dom trying to boss me around tonight. You'll have to get in line behind Genevieve."

"Do I need to be concerned?" His gaze flits to Eli.

"You all need to just mind your own business. If Dalton wants to be my Dom, he can come and tell me himself. I don't do *Dom by proxy*."

"He's having a hard time."

"Don't start, Flex. I got an earful from the Domme. You all seem to know what's going on in my relationship. Did Dalton tell you about the last time he fucked me?"

The furrow of his brow deepens as he attempts to stare me down, but I'm too tired of all this shit.

"I didn't think so. Why don't you go talk to him before chastising me like a child? He hit a hard limit, and I won't be fucked like a cheap, dispensable whore."

"I'll talk to him."

I reach into my bag, pulling out the stupid napkin I've been holding onto for weeks and shove it against his chest. "Good luck. When you see him, give him this. It seems it was complete all along. A contract full of absolutely nothing."

As I turn to leave, he tries to stop me. "Wait."

"Go to hell, Felix."

I walk as quickly as I can to the exit, the cold night air even more chilling as my tears come unbidden once more.

Ryan opens the car door, his face solemn as he takes in the sight of me. "Is everything okay, Ms. Sullivan?"

"Just take me home, please."

"Of course."

He doesn't press me further on the drive back to my apartment, and I appreciate it more than words can say. By the time we arrive, I can barely keep my eyes open, the sting of tears painful as I drag myself out.

"Thanks, Ryan."

"I'll see you in the morning. Same time as usual?"

"Yes."

He waits until I'm inside to drive off, and I wonder if he calls or messages Dalton to let him know I'm home. Maybe he doesn't care at this point.

When I crawl into bed, I've never felt more exhausted in my life. Or more alone. Under the comforter, I pull up Dalton's number on my phone and hit call.

Ring. Ring. Ring.

After what feels like forever and for the first time in weeks, he answers, but he doesn't speak.

"Please talk to me."

Silence.

"I miss you so much it hurts."

Nothing.

"Dalton, talk to me. I don't deserve this."

I wait him out, and finally, his voice floods my senses. "You're right. You don't deserve any of this." Fear takes hold, twisting my insides. He sounds completely hollow.

"I've left messages."

"I know."

"That's all you have to say? I've been waiting for you…" I push past the lump in my throat. "Should I stop?"

"I'm not the Dom you need." I can't breathe, my skin on fire as my world stops spinning.

"Don't use me as an excuse. If you don't want me anymore, at least be man enough to own it. Don't bullshit me with what *I need*."

"You really believe I don't want you?" I don't recognize his voice.

"Yes, I do. You announced to the entire club that you can't bear to look at me, then you fucked me like a common whore. I've been at the club every fucking night, waiting for you. I'm right here, blindly wanting you like a fucking idiot, taking abuse from your friends."

"What? Who?"

"If you want to talk… really talk, come and face me like a man. I deserve that much."

"Kitten…"

"Don't call me that unless you're ready to be the Dominant I love. The man I gave up my fucking dignity for."

"I…"

"Goodnight, Dalton. When you're ready to be real with me, you know where to find me." I hang up the call before he can say anything else, my heart beating so hard I feel like I could die. Did he just try to break up with me over the phone? Am I that pathetic?

I cry myself to sleep in the silence that comes with utter desolation. How could he say he's not the Dom I need? All I want is his love. It's all I've ever wanted.

~

I almost called in sick today, but I don't need to give Douglas any more reasons to dislike me. He's kept his distance since signing the NDA, and it suits me just fine. I wish I could say the same for his son, Robert. He's been hanging around like a bad smell, using any excuse to check up on me.

We have a meeting today to discuss Dalton's upcoming contracts, but I don't even know if he's coming. I spend the morning doing anything else to avoid thinking about it. I remember I took my mail home last night, but I was too upset to bother with it, so I grab it from my briefcase and flick through it. One envelope catches my eye, only because there's no address on it, and it says:

For the attention of Dalton Rutherford

My stomach drops. I know that Dalton has gone to extremes to ensure all ties to his dad and his last name are impossible to find. Should I open it? It was in my office, but it's not addressed to me. I pick up my phone and send a quick text.

> Me: We need to talk. I just got an envelope F.A.O. Dalton Rutherford.

He's quick to reply, and it smarts. I've been texting him for weeks with no reply.

> Dalton: What's inside?

> Me: I didn't open it. It's not addressed to me.

> Dalton: Open it.

> Me: Come and get it.

> Dalton: Now is not the time to be a brat. Open it.

If I weren't so concerned about it, I'd tell him where to shove his brat talk, but the manila envelope staring back at me gives me pause.

Dalton: Well?

I slowly rip it open, my pulse quickening as I reach inside and pull out the contents. I gasp as the photographs in my hand fall to the floor.

My phone starts ringing. It's Dalton. My hands are shaking as I answer his call.

"Kitten, what's in the envelope? Tell me, now."

"Someone knows. You need to get over here."

"Knows what?"

"Dalton, don't say another word. We need to talk in private."

"I'm coming over."

I think better of it. "No. I'll come to you. Whoever sent this has been in my office. I'll be there in twenty minutes."

I quickly gather the photographs and stuff them in my purse before heading out to hail a cab. I feel sick to my stomach. All I've wanted for weeks is to be in the same room as Dalton and figure out where we go from here. This was not what I had in mind.

Every cell in my body is itching to be where he is. To help in whatever way I can, and what saddens me most is that I don't know if he'll let me. When the cab pulls up outside The Callaghan Group building, I think I'm going to vomit.

I search my purse for my ID card, but the concierge waves me through. Dalton must have told them I was coming. The elevator seems to take forever, and yet it's too quick when the doors open on his floor.

He's waiting for me, looking disheveled in jeans, a T-shirt, and a worn leather jacket, pacing back and forth, wringing his hands through his hair. His face is a little gaunt with dark circles under his eyes.

Without a word, I follow him to his office, only pulling out the photographs when I hear the door lock behind us.

"What's going on, Naddie?" I can barely catch my breath, overwhelmed at the sight of him. He looks as exhausted as I feel, yet he's still effortlessly handsome as he paces the room.

As I hand him the photographs, I'm visibly trembling, and his fingers brush mine as he takes them from me. "Shit. Where the fuck did these come from?"

He flips through the pictures. His father's mug shot. The old office building where his dad conducted one too many shady deals. The house he grew up in—the place we fell in love all those years ago.

"I don't know. The envelope was sitting on my desk last night."

"I don't want you going back to that office until I know who's doing this."

"Well, that can't happen. I have work to do."

"It was delivered to my lawyers' office. I have no idea how much this person knows about my life. My investigator works through the firm."

"And if they're involved, they can't be trusted."

"Exactly. I have to find someone else to look into this as discreetly as possible."

"I know who can do it."

"Who?"

"Jenna."

"What?"

"She's a computer forensics expert. An unparalleled hacker. A private investigator for hire."

"Call her. I can get her on the first flight down here."

"I'm on it."

He continues to pace, and it breaks my heart to see him like this. He's been through so much already. I take a deep breath, steel my nerves, and then drop to my knees.

"Master, I would like to hug you. Please, let me help you through whatever is going on."

"Naddie, get up."

"I know you think I don't deserve you, but I love you, Master."

He sinks to his knees, cupping my face in his hands, the slight touch making my heart gallop in my chest. "I have never thought you don't deserve me. Not in the way you think. I'm the one who doesn't deserve you."

My eyes find his, searching for the answers I've been craving for weeks. "We had a fight. I thought if I provoked you, you would open up to me. I shouldn't have pushed, but then you disappeared. You shut me out completely."

"Because I hurt you, Naddie. I physically hurt you. And I willingly pushed you away by not addressing you as you requested as my submissive. But I fucking *hurt* you. I was brutal and unfeeling. It wasn't pain for the sake of pleasure. It was just pain, and I can't forgive myself. And you shouldn't want a Dom who is capable of that."

My heart splinters into a million pieces as I stare into the eyes of the boy next door. Lost and afraid of himself. *But, I'm not.*

I tentatively lean in, begging permission before pressing my lips to his in a ghost of a kiss. "I'm not scared of you, Master Callaghan. I love you, and these past few weeks have been torture."

"I know, but…"

"But you made a mistake, and so did I. It doesn't mean we don't belong together."

"I'm afraid I'll hurt you. I feel so angry all the time."

"You're grieving." I kiss him again. "I have a safeword, Master. I promise you that I will use it if necessary. I won't let you drown, but you have to let me help you keep your head above water. I'm yours. I always was, and I always will be."

He rests his forehead against mine, his breaths ragged.

"I've relived that night over and over, hating myself for crossing the line. I pride myself on being a Dominant and always being in control of my life, my business, and my submissive. To have failed *you* makes it all the more unbearable, Naddie. I love you so much, I couldn't eat or sleep. I couldn't even look at myself in the mirror. Can you ever forgive me?"

"I love you, Dalton, but you ripped my beating heart from my chest. The only thing worse than having you fuck me like I was nothing was not being able to comfort or see you these past weeks.

Knowing how grief-stricken you are and you wouldn't let me be there for you, I thought I was going to lose my mind."

"I'm so sorry, Naddie. You have every right not to forgive me, but I'm still going to beg for it. I can't do this without you. Life. Grief. Love. Everything. None of it makes any sense without you. Forgive me, please."

"Of course I forgive you. You are *mine*."

"I've missed you so much. My heart has been broken in two."

"Then never let me go."

"I won't... kitten."

I melt into his arms and soft, lazy kisses as his love spirits me away from the pain I've been carrying around for weeks.

"Call Jenna, then the rest of this can wait until she gets here. Right now, I'm taking you home to my bed. To *our* bed. And I'm going to make love to you until you never want to leave."

"Yes, Master."

It takes all my resolve to pull away from Dalton to get my phone and dial Jenna's number.

"Hey, Nad. How are you doing?"

"Hey, Jenna. I don't want to go into detail on the phone, but we need your investigation skills here in Manhattan."

"What? Who's we?"

"Dalton and me. We have a situation, and we need someone we can trust to handle it."

"Okay, send me whatever info you have, and I'll get started."

"I know it's terrible to ask you to drop everything, but is there any way you could come down here? Dalton says he can get you on the next flight."

"So, he's talking to you now?"

"I'll explain when you get here... if that's a yes?"

"Send me the flight details, and I'll see you tonight."

"Thanks, Jenna. You're a lifesaver."

"I know. I'm amazing. Love you, Nad. I'll see you soon."

"Love you too."

When I hang up the call, Dalton's eyes are on me, dark and full of desire. "I'll have my PA arrange everything. Should I book her a hotel?"

"No, she can stay at my apartment."

"I don't want to be away from you another night, kitten."

"Then I guess *you're* staying at my apartment, too… Master."

Chapter 24
DALTON

"Thanks for coming, Jenna."

We've been poring over all the information we could find that might be useful. Jenna hit the ground running, barely setting her bags down before insisting I brief her on the photographs that were left in Naddie's office.

"When was the last time you were in contact with your father?"

"I haven't seen him since he went to prison. Last I heard, he was coming up for parole soon, but I never followed up with Mom being so ill."

"He's been released." The knowledge doesn't hit me as hard as I thought it would.

"Okay, so we're assuming he's looking for a payout to start his new life?"

"He's on parole. There's no way he's dumb enough to do this alone. I need a list of people who work at your firm, Nad. They should be our starting point."

"Robert Mason. Douglas's son has a chip on his shoulder. I was brought in to take over Dalton's account when Douglas retires. Robert hates me for it." Naddie isn't wrong. Robert has every reason to dislike her at this juncture.

"And what about Douglas?"

"He stands to make good money from the deal we made regarding Naddie's continued employment." I pace the floor, my hands tucked firmly in my pockets. "Besides, he and I were on good terms for a long time. He knows my dad can't be trusted."

"Is there anyone else who might be worth looking at more closely?"

"I don't know. I work with these people, but I haven't exactly gotten to know them," Naddie interjects.

"Okay. Get me the list, and I'll do some basic background work so we can start checking people off, and I'll get moving on a deep dive of Robert Mason."

Naddie pulls up the company directory on her laptop to get Jenna the information she needs while I talk further with her.

"Is there anyone you can think of from your old life, any of your father's former colleagues who might be willing to help him pull something like this off?" Shit. My dad pissed off everyone who ever crossed his path. Surely, none of them would help him.

"I don't think so. He screwed over everyone he ever met. I'll put together a list of those I can remember. My current investigator with the firm has a lot of background on my dealings over the years, but it'll raise a red flag if I go looking through all his files."

"Yeah, stay clear of that. I want both of you to go about your lives as normal. Go to work, be pleasant, but keep your eyes open for anything that's amiss. Nad, you have to act like that envelope never made it into your hands. I'm going to have prints pulled from the photographs to see if they were lazy enough to make a mistake. I'll put some feelers out to see if we can get a location on your dad. I'm already working on hacking the CCTV camera system around Nad's office building. We might get lucky."

"Sounds like a plan. Let's get to work."

For the first time in a month, I feel something close to happy. Naddie's apartment feels like a home. The deafening loneliness of the penthouse has been replaced with the comfortable silence of Naddie's apartment as we work together to figure out who is behind this threat.

We work long into the night, stopping only when I have food delivered, feeling a little more like myself as I demand Naddie keep her strength up. When she can't keep her eyes open any longer, I scoop her into my arms, bid goodnight to Jenna, and carry her down the hall, laying her gently down on the bed.

I deftly remove my clothes before stripping her and crawling in beside her, pulling her tight against my chest. As I breathe her in, I release the tension I've been holding in my body for weeks now. Yes, we have a threat that needs to be taken care of, but we'll face it together.

"You should always fall asleep in my arms, kitten."

"Where do I sign?" she rasps in a sleepy whisper.

I clasp her hand in mine and place it over her heart. "Right here."

"Make love to me, Dalton."

Without another word, I gently move her onto her back, positioning myself between her legs, fighting my inner demons as I claim her in a slow, steady stroke, my lips capturing hers in a song of worship and loving her with the tenderness we both need—our calm in the eye of the storm.

"I love you, Naddie. God, how I love you." Our bodies move in sync with each other, perfectly matched as we make love, soft groans of pleasure as we savor every moment lost in each other. When we eventually fall asleep, we're wrapped in each other's arms, right where we're meant to be.

Tonight, we're celebrating. A rare night off as Jenna, Naddie, and I work to find who sent the photographs of my dad last week. Jenna has found everything there is about my dad's whereabouts, down to what he ate for breakfast yesterday. Unfortunately, we've yet to confirm if he has anything to do with this.

Naddie officially passed the New York Bar today, so Jenna and I decided it was only fitting that we take her out to celebrate. It's been a long time since I've set foot in Venom, but the girls insisted. Jenna swears blindly it's because it's Naddie's favorite place, and the bar is nice, but I suspect it has something to do with her being half naked the last time I saw her there.

I hesitate as we pull up outside the club, a flashback of blind panic and fear slamming into me like a tsunami. Naddie must sense it, lacing her fingers with mine as we head for the lobby.

"It's okay. We'll make some new memories." The scent of her perfume intoxicates my senses with a hint of vanilla.

As we approach the security guard, he signals for my attention with a brown manila envelope in his hand. My stomach drops, but thankfully, Naddie is caught up talking to Jenna.

"Go on in. I need to talk business for a moment."

She smiles up at me so sweetly I can't bear to ruin her evening. "You sure?"

"Yes. Can you order me my usual?"

"Yes, Master." She gives me a peck on the cheek before grabbing Jenna and heading inside.

As I approach the desk, I can see the handwriting on the envelope is the same, but this time it's addressed to *Dalton Callaghan*.

"This arrived about an hour ago."

"Was it a courier?"

"I don't think so. They weren't wearing any kind of uniform." He eyes me warily.

"Can you pull the camera footage before I leave tonight? I want to know who hand-delivered this."

"Of course, Mr. Callaghan."

"Thanks."

I head straight for my private room, bypassing the bar to take a look without Naddie seeing. Just walking into the room again is hard, even though Carter has had it completely remodeled. But I have more pressing matters to deal with. I tear open the envelope to reveal its contents, and I can't contain my anger. "Fucking bastard."

There in black and white are photos of Naddie and me, taken from outside her office the night I—that night. My shame comes flooding back, and I can see exactly why Naddie was hurt by the way I treated her. I've got a tight grip on her hair and hands as

I'm pounding into her, my face devoid of anything close to affection.

This time, there's a Post-it note stuck to the first photo with a phone number. I pull out my phone and dial the number.

You've reached the New York Bar Association. If you know the extension…

I hang up the call, rage boiling inside me. If this fucker thinks I'll let them ruin Naddie's career, they can think again. This has gone far enough. I don't care if people find out about my past. I won't be held to ransom by my father if that's who's behind this. Bringing Naddie into it crosses the line, and I will tear down the fucking world to keep her safe, even if it costs everything I own. Whoever is threatening her career will regret it.

I take the envelope back to the security guard and ask him to have Ryan pick it up, along with a flash drive of the security footage, and personally deliver it to the penthouse. Then, I paint on a happy face and head to the bar.

I was expecting Flex to be here already, flirting with Jenna. I never pulled him up for sleeping with her when I told him explicitly not to. I've been somewhat preoccupied. However, I see I have someone new to warn off. My friend, Pierce, is sitting with Naddie and Jenna, his eyes fixed on her like a predator stalking its prey.

When I reach the table, I lean down, pressing my lips to Naddie's. "Hello, kitten. Do I need to run interference?"

"Thank you, Master, but I've already set the ground rules."

"Good girl."

I turn my attention to Pierce. "Keep it in your pants, or I'll snap it off."

He flashes his attempt at an innocent smile, but I know him too well. "I'm on my best behavior."

"What if I don't want you to be on your best behavior?" Jenna quips, too innocent to know what she's asking, but I'm quick to level her with my stare.

"Trust me. Based on the grilling you've given me, Pierce is not your type."

"I'm sitting right here, bro. A little harmless flirting never hurt anyone."

"Since when have you ever been harmless?"

As I take a seat, Naddie shifts onto my lap. "We're celebrating. Let's not get into a Dom pissing match, please, Master Callaghan." And just like that, I couldn't care less what our friends get up to tonight.

Sliding my hand into Naddie's long, chestnut hair, I pull her lips to mine, fireflies taking flight as her tongue darts out to meet mine. After all these years, she still makes me feel the way I did the night of our first kiss—like I could take on the world as long as she's by my side.

"Dance with me, Master."

"It would be my pleasure, kitten."

We leave Jenna to her shameless flirting, but I keep an eye on her as Flex strides into the bar and straight to their table. The last thing I need is those two fighting over her. She's not even remotely interested in being a submissive, especially not with their tastes.

Naddie rests her head against my chest, wrapping her arms around my waist. "I've missed this."

"I'm so sorry, kitten. It won't ever happen again."

"I know. I just wish we could enjoy it without so many issues."

"Don't worry. I'll take care of whoever sent the pictures of my father. I don't want you worrying about anything tonight. We're here to celebrate your achievement."

We dance for a while as the bar begins to fill, friends congregating at our table. Jenna seems to be the shiny new toy, but thankfully, Viv just emerged from her private room and shoos the men away like naughty dogs, sniffing where they shouldn't be.

The moment Naddie spots her, she pulls back, leaving me bereft. "I need to talk to Genevieve. She and I had words the last time I was here."

"What happened?"

"It doesn't matter. I just want to clear the air." Pushing up onto her tiptoes, she melts me with a soul-crushing kiss.

I can't take my eyes off Naddie as she weaves her way over to

Viv, my friends greeting her with such genuine smiles and hugs. She and Viv can only have exchanged a handful or words when Viv pulls her into her arms in a warm embrace, her eyes finding mine over Naddie's shoulder. A nod of understanding passes between us.

She came to see me while I wallowed in my shame, yelling at me to get off my ass and fix things with Naddie before it was too late. I knew she was right, but it came at just the right time, a few hours before Naddie called me. If it weren't for Viv, I'd have stewed in my squaller a little longer, unable to face the love of my life and admit that she was right.

Looking at her now, happy and laughing, surrounded by the people in my life who truly matter to me, I can't imagine what would have happened if I'd let her get away. If losing my mom has taught me anything, it's that time is precious. She would've kicked my ass up and down Fifth Avenue if I lost Naddie again. She knew so much more than she ever let on.

Being in this club—the place I built as a sanctuary—feels so different tonight. Sharing it with Naddie and enjoying *her* with my friends is so beyond anything I could've hoped for. She senses my eyes on her, finding my gaze with an earth-shattering smile, and for the first time I realize the club is no longer my sanctuary. *Naddie* is my safe place. She's my home. Wherever she is, that's where I want to be.

An idea falls into place, but I bury it for now and ignore the latest threat to our relationship. Tonight, I just want Naddie to have fun and revel in her vast achievements. She did it. The goal she had when she was five, this is it. Twice over. I'm so fucking proud I could burst, and as she stalks toward me, sashaying those sexy hips, an equally sultry smile lights her face.

"What are you so happy about?" she says as she slips her arms around my neck.

"You."

Her gaze becomes quizzical as she considers me. "Have I been a good submissive or a bad submissive?"

"Which would you like it to be?"

"Am I getting punished?"

"Perhaps." I give her a quick peck on the nose.

"Then I've definitely been a naughty sub, Master Callaghan." She gives me a sly wink.

"I bet you have." She looks at me with that wicked grin. "It seems your friend is popular." I nod in Jenna's direction.

"I think Pierce is winning. That silky smooth voice of his has her weak at the knees."

"He tends to have that effect on women, however, I wouldn't let him near Jenna. His tastes are… interesting. Possibly a little dark for a woman with no interest in the lifestyle."

"Does she look disinterested to you?" Naddie gives me a conspiratorial wink.

"It's not a good idea. These guys are not the fun one-night stand she thinks they are."

"So, you've never had a one-night stand with a woman who wasn't a sub?"

"I didn't say that, but my kinks are tame compared to Pierce."

"I'm intrigued." I pull her in close, my lips grazing her ear.

"Think about any other man, and you'll be punished."

"Is that supposed to be a deterrent?"

"Such a brat," I say, darting my tongue into her ear, letting her squirm as I hold her in place.

"Just the way you like it, Master."

"Our room. Now. I'll be in shortly."

"Yes, Master Callaghan," she purrs.

I watch as she sashays across the bar and disappears down the hallway. Before I can go to her, I have to talk to Jenna, and I'm not even a little sorry to interrupt my friends vying for her attention.

"Excuse me, gentlemen, I need to speak with Jenna for a few moments." She reads the furrow of my brow and the fact that Naddie isn't by my side. Following me away from the crowd with promises to be back in a few minutes, Jenna sobers at my expression.

"What's wrong? Where's Naddie?"

"She's fine. In our private room."

"Okay…"

"I received another envelope tonight, here at the club."

Her body stiffens and becomes tense as I continue.

"It contained compromising pictures of Naddie and me in her office. Whoever this is has been watching her. I need to shut this down before anything happens that could be damaging to her career."

"And yours."

"I don't give a fuck about mine, Jenna. Whatever it takes, we have to keep Naddie safe. Can you help?"

"Of course. Do you want to get started now? If you give me the evidence, I'll get to work."

"First thing tomorrow. Tonight, I want Naddie to relax and enjoy celebrating. This achievement has already been marred by what's happened. I'll tell her tomorrow."

"Make sure you do. I don't like knowing something this big about her, and she's in the dark."

"I understand that you don't necessarily agree with the nature of my relationship with Naddie, but I will *always* put her first. She trusts me, and I would never betray that. I just want her to have this one night. She's... amazing. It's been one thing after another since we found each other again, and I'm ashamed of how I've acted at times, but..."

Jenna reaches out and rests her hand on my shoulder, her gaze softening. "You're grieving, Dalton. We all deal with it in different ways. Don't be so hard on yourself. Naddie gets it. And, for the record, I don't disapprove of you and her. I don't understand it, but I don't have to. She loves you, and as long as you have her best interests at heart, we're good."

"Thanks, Jenna. For everything. I know you have a life to get back to, and I appreciate you putting it on hold to help us."

"Don't thank me yet. When I've found the asshole or holes behind this, then you can inflate my ego."

"Come to my office tomorrow morning, and I'll fill you in on everything I know."

"Sounds good. Now, can I get back to flirting with stupidly good-looking men?"

"If I say no, will you listen to me?"

EVA HAINING

She doesn't hesitate. "Nope."

"Then, enjoy flirting. Just remember what guys like them are into."

"Yes, *Sir*," she says playfully.

"Don't address Pierce like that unless you're ready to be dragged into his private room."

Her eyebrows shoot up in surprise, but she quickly tries to recover her composure. "Noted."

The moment she rejoins the group, I quiet my mind and think of the woman waiting for me in our private room. I practically run to the hallway, eager to be with my submissive.

My submissive.

There's nothing more beautiful than that.

As I enter the room, my kitten is ready and waiting for me like the good girl she is, her head down.

"You may look at me."

"Thank you, Master Callaghan." She looks up at me through hooded lashes, and it's all I can do not to ravage her right here on the floor.

"Tell me, kitten, what would you like this evening?"

"Whatever you wish, Master. I am yours to play with." She bites down on her bottom lip as I lower my gaze to between her thighs.

"Are you aroused?"

"I'm wet for you, Master. Would you like to taste me?" My cock hardens, my mouth going dry, desperate for her to quench my thirst.

"I want you to taste yourself, kitten. Slide those pretty little fingers of yours over your pussy and tell me how fucking good it is."

With her eyes locked on me, she does as she's told, and when she sucks her fingers into her mouth, I could shoot my load. She's so fucking beautiful. I've missed this.

"Sweet, like honey."

"Now, thrust your fingers inside and let *me* have a taste." I drop to my knees, greedily awaiting her touch. She brushes her arousal across my lips before I catch them and drag my tongue down their length. Fuck, she tastes good. I savor it, my pulse racing as my cock grows so hard it hurts.

250

"Is it to your liking, Master?"

"You were made for me, kitten. You taste sublime. Now, be a good girl, and tell me. What. You. Want."

"I want to undress you, Master."

"As you wish. Tonight, I am at your disposal. Take the reins, kitten."

Her eyes light up. "Really?"

"Yes, so make good use of me. This is a one-time offer."

"Thank you so much, Master." She leans forward, unbuttoning my shirt with practiced ease, greedily taking in every inch of exposed skin.

"Stand up... Master."

I do as she asks, holding my tongue. I've never given myself over to a submissive before, and I'm a little apprehensive. As I stand before her, she divests me of my shoes and socks before slowly unzipping my fly and unleashing my cock, licking her lips as she slides my pants and boxers down my legs.

There's something different about standing before her, naked—a buzzing in every nerve ending, heavy with anticipation.

"Get on the bed, Master. Hands clasped above your head." I feel exposed as I crawl onto the bed, getting into the position she requests, every dominant bone in my body screaming to stop. But, I want to give her this—a gift—an apology.

She stalks to the chest of drawers, opening each one, leisurely perusing the toys.

"Have you ever done any anal play, Master?" she smirks. *Fuck.*

"No, kitten. I haven't. Is that really the way you want tonight to go?" Damn, I can't switch off the Dom in me.

She pulls a rather large set of anal beads from the drawer, running her fingers lazily down them with a wicked grin. "Not really." I heave a sigh of relief, never realizing how vulnerable she makes herself to me every time we step inside this room.

Naddie takes her sweet time picking what she wants to play with tonight, but as she turns to face me, she's running a set of nipple clamps through her fingers. My cock twitches at the thought. I've never had any toys used on me before, yet I've used virtually every item in that chest of drawers on her since she became my sub.

"Oh, Master, don't look so worried. I promise they feel good." She clips one of her nipples and then the other, looking so fucking hot I can barely stand it. There's no way I'll be able to keep my hands to myself.

"Jesus, kitten. Your breasts are fucking perfect."

"Such a shame you can't touch them. I do love how you knead them with those strong hands of yours and the warmth of your mouth on my nipples."

"I can do that for you, just come here."

"Ah, ah, ah. You're mine tonight. I get to do the touching while you watch."

"You're going to enjoy this, aren't you?"

She crawls onto the bottom of the bed, straddling my legs as she moves up my body, the chain of the clamps swaying from her heavy breasts. When she's hovering over my erection, she stays just out of reach, making me ache even more.

"Do you love me, Master?" she says, leaning forward to suck my nipple into her mouth, unclipping one of her clamps before putting it on me.

"*Holy shit!*" She repeats the process with my other nipple. The metal is cool against my skin, but I'm on fire for her.

"You didn't answer the question."

"Yes, I love you more than life itself, kitten. The clamps... not so much."

How does she find these pleasurable? They fucking hurt.

Kissing my chest, Naddie makes her way up to my ear. "Trust me."

"Always."

Positioning herself over my cock, she lowers herself painfully slow, her eyes fixed on me, dark and sultry, as she takes every hard inch of me until she's seated to the hilt.

"Do you like that, Master? Do you want me to ride your cock?"

"More than my next breath." I move my arms, desperate to

grab her by the hips and fuck her so hard she can't remember her name, but she's quick to swat them away.

"Hands clasped above your head. If you're a bad boy, I won't let you come."

"Duly noted. Never let a brat have control for the evening," I quip as she tightens around me, stilling herself until I comply. Then, she starts to move, circling her hips as she takes the cold chain of the nipple clamps in her hand, giving them a slight tug.

"Tell me how much you need my pussy, Master."

I can barely think with her arousal coating my cock, her muscles tight as she grinds on me. "Fuck, kitten. I... I need every part of you. Every inch of your mind, body, and soul. You feel so fucking good. I'll never get enough. *Ever.* Your pussy is mine."

She tugs on the chain, sending a shiver down my spine as she quickens her pace. "Fucking right it is." Throwing her head back, she moves faster, pumping her hips up and down, leaving me helpless to set the rhythm, but at this moment, I don't care. She's glorious, her breasts bouncing up and down as she moves harder. Faster.

"Holy shit, kitten. If you don't slow down, I'm going to come." She doesn't heed my warning, relishing the power she has over me right now.

"Not until I say so, Master." Her voice is a sultry whisper as she continues to ride my cock, her breaths ragged as she climbs toward release. I have to close my eyes to try and stem the orgasm I feel building deep in my core.

"Jesus, kitten."

"That's it, Master. Let me hear you groan my name." She'd make a good Domme, but I'm so fucking thankful she's a sub. *My submissive.*

"Yes... kitten... you're mine. *Kitten!*"

She continues to ride me harder until a slick sheen of sweat covers both our bodies. My muscles begin to spasm, and I know she's ready, my climax so close I can barely contain it.

"Yes, Master. Come with me." As the words leave her lips, she starts to shudder, milking my cock, and when she feels it coming, she tugs hard on the nipple clamps until they release. Pain and pleasure explode as my orgasm pulses through every fiber of my being.

"Jesus Christ. Fuck. Kitten." My release goes on and on, every wave more delicious than the last as she rides the aftershocks before collapsing on my chest. I immediately wrap my arms around her, starved for her skin beneath my fingertips.

"Was that okay, Master?" And just like that, my submissive is back, and all is right in the world.

"Yes, kitten. You're such a good girl. It didn't escape me that you called me Master throughout."

"Thank you for letting me take the lead. I know it can't have been easy for you."

"That's the understatement of the century. I'd be a terrible sub."

"Yes, you would, but that's what I love about you."

"Did you enjoy it?" There's trepidation in my voice.

"Yes…" I wait with bated breath, "… but I'm your submissive, and I would never want it any other way."

"Thank God for that."

She chuckles against my chest, her hand resting over my heart. "You were a good boy."

I roll her until I'm hovering over her, pinning her in place. "Less of the *boy*," I say as I position myself at her entrance and take her with one hard thrust.

"Take my cock like a good girl."

"Yes, Master Callaghan."

Chapter 25

DALTON

A single tear escapes Naddie's eye before she pulls on her immeasurable inner strength, steeling herself as she stares at the photos of us in her office.

"Have you informed Jenna? This might help her figure out who's doing this."

"She's coming by this morning. I wanted to check with you first. She'll need to have them examined for fingerprints and to find out where these pictures were taken. It looks like the photographer must have been in the building across the street." I watch her cringe. No one wants to have themselves on display this way, especially not to a friend.

"Fine." Her voice is cold. Dejected.

"I know it's hard, kitten. I don't want anyone seeing you this way in our intimate moments."

"It wasn't intimate. I'd have an easier time if the pictures showed the bond we share. These…" she says, tossing them onto my desk, "… are just a reminder of a night I'd like to forget."

My heart aches, knowing I hurt her so deeply.

"I'm so sorry, kitten."

"I know that. I... I never want to feel that way again, Dalton. Like I could've been anyone. Like I didn't matter."

Cupping her face in my hands, I force her to meet my gaze. "Even in my darkest moments, *you* matter. I love you, Naddie, more than anything in the world. Please tell me you know that."

"You didn't come. I was at the club every night for weeks. I waited for you. For my Master to come. I was there, in the position." Her words are a knife to my chest.

"How long did you sit there, kitten?" I don't want to hear the answer because I know it will break my heart, but I owe her this.

"Every night from seven till eleven. I wanted you to know I could be here for you. That I could be strong enough for both of us."

A lump forms at the back of my throat, having someone who loves me this much and for it to be Naddie. I press my lips to hers, begging for forgiveness. "You *are* strong. I could never have gotten through the funeral without you, Naddie. You're everything I hung onto in those moments. It wasn't my intention to shut you out."

"Really?"

"Yes. No. I don't know. Losing Mom has hit me in ways I didn't think possible. I thought I'd prepared myself. I had time to wrap my head around the fact that she was dying. She was suffering so badly, and I knew she didn't want to go on the way things were, but in the end, I wasn't prepared at all."

"I don't think anyone can ever truly be ready for the death of a loved one."

"That pain. It's all-consuming, and the thought of letting you in... it means I have so much more to lose."

"Shutting me out is how you lose me, Dalton. I love you." She wraps her arms around my neck, pushing up onto her tiptoes and kissing me with everything she's got. Electricity courses through me from where our lips meet to my fingertips.

"I can't lose you again, Naddie. Please, just give me some time to get my head straight."

"I'll give you all the time you need, but don't shut me out or treat me like I'm a stranger. I loved your mom, Dalton. So did Flex. He's been hurting too."

I'm the worst friend. Of course, Flex has been grieving. My mom was the closest he had to a real parent. "Fuck. I'm sorry. I've been so wrapped up in myself."

"No one would fault you for that. You're not invincible, and I don't expect you to be a Dom, twenty-four seven."

"That's what we signed up for."

"And do you think that means you can never be vulnerable with me?"

"Yeah."

"How can we build a life together if you can't open up to me? This is a two-way street, Master. I *need* you to be honest with me about how you feel. I *want* to be your anchor, but you have to *let* me."

I've spent so long being there for everyone around me that it never even crossed my mind to let myself be vulnerable.

"The last person I let myself trust fully died. And the one before that betrayed us and got locked up. And he's probably the one extorting money out of me right now. It's not easy for me, Naddie."

Resting her hand on my chest, she entreats me. "I'm here, and I'm not going anywhere. I've been here the whole time, wanting and loving you. I gave up my career because I love you *that* much. Even if I'm mad, I'll still be here. Get that into your thick skull, Master Callaghan."

I'd chastise her for being a brat, but her words are music to my ears and one hundred percent the truth. "Move in with me."

"I already sleep at your apartment almost exclusively... until this latest hiccup." Her eyes flit to the licentious photographs in black and white.

"I don't want 'almost,' I want it all, Naddie. Move in with me. One house. One life. *Together.*"

"Don't you think it's too soon? So much has happened, and we're facing problems as we speak."

"Exactly. Time is precious. My mom taught me that you never

know the day. Everything else, we can face together. I don't think it's too soon because I've been ready to move in with you since high school."

"When should I schedule the movers?" she says with a sweet smile so bright it makes her eyes sparkle.

"What?" Dragonflies take flight in my chest, swarming my senses with a hope I'm scared to want.

"You're right. I sleep with you every night. I don't know if you're aware, but I'm somewhat close to unemployment. If we're a team, then it's probably a good idea to have one place. Headquarters, if you will." She gazes up at me through hooded lashes, holding her breath as if there's any reason to be bashful right now.

"Are you serious? You want to move in with me? Don't play around, kitten."

"I'm not."

"So, I'm a meal ticket of convenience? If you were still with the firm, you'd say no." I'm being playful, but I'm also nervous.

"Are you kidding? I've been trying to play house with you since we were five years old. I'm ready. *You're* my home, Dalton. You always have been. Why do you think I was wearing your ratty old T-shirt when I moved to Manhattan? After all those years, I went to you for comfort when my life was changing all around me. Let's do it. I want to live together."

I'm out of my chair and sweeping her into my arms before she has time to change her mind. "You've just made me the happiest man in the world." I crush my lips to hers, claiming her as mine. "I've wanted you to move in since I showed up at your hotel room in Milan."

"Then, what are we waiting for? Take me home, Master." My heart is about to explode out of my chest, so full of love for this woman that it can barely be contained. It's not until I see the photos mocking us from the desk that I come back to my senses.

"If I could, I would. There's nothing I want more right now, but Jenna will be here soon."

"Then I guess we better be quick… Master." The gleam in her eye is wicked as sin, and I love it. Moving to the wall on the far side of my office, I press Naddie against it, coaxing her to wrap her legs around my waist as my lips crash down on hers, our tongues twisting and tangling, celebrating that we are one in this moment. A team. Friends. Lovers. And so much more.

She reaches between us, making short work of freeing my cock as I pull her lace panties aside, taking her in one harsh thrust, making her moan.

"Who do you belong to, kitten?"

"You, Master Callaghan," she whispers as our kiss deepens into a frenzy of pure desire, trying to claw its way out. "I belong to you." Fisting her hands in my hair, she takes all of me, lost to the sensation as the door to my office opens and Jenna stands, mouth agape.

"I'm not into threesomes, guys. At least lock the door. I don't need to be mentally scarred by Dalton's ass."

I shield Naddie as I slide out of her, adjusting her panties and dress. Then, I quickly tuck my now aching cock and blue balls into my pants.

"Don't you ever knock?" I say, my voice irate.

"Your assistant said it was fine to come in."

"I miss Audrey." Maternity leave can't be over soon enough. I want my right hand back. She'd never let someone come back here without calling me.

"If you're going to rock out with your cock out at work, you've got to live with the consequences." She looks set to continue when she spies the photographs, her jibing forgotten as she sees the damning pictures of her friend.

"We have a problem," Naddie interjects, a little too shy for my girl.

"Oh, Nad. What the fuck is wrong with people? I'm assuming this is what you need help with?"

I snatch the photos from her hands. "We don't need to be casually flipping through these, thank you very much."

"I need to know what I'm dealing with. Where were these pictures taken?"

"In Naddie's office at Mason, Porter & Associates."

"Do you mind if I access the building security cameras?"

"I don't have access to their offices."

A devious smile tugs at the corners of her lips. "I meant, do you mind if I do some illegal hacking? I can access it myself."

"Whatever rules you break are fine with me, and anything I can provide will be at your disposal, Jenna. This needs to be shut down ASAP."

"Understood. Where can I set up base?"

"Naddie has an office here at The Callaghan Group. You can work from there."

"Good. Let's get started. Dalton, I want a list of all your security staff, one of all employees who have access to this building, and the name of your head of I.T. Are your systems bespoke or is there a specific platform you're using?"

I'm impressed by how matter-of-fact she is.

"It's not bespoke. I have a headhunter looking for a specialist to build a system for The Callaghan Group as we speak." I pull up our current system and beckon Jenna to take a look.

She sets to work immediately, and I wonder if my headhunter may be obsolete.

"Can you give me access to this from Naddie's office? Then you can get on with your day, and I'll get to work."

"Yes. I'll have a login created in the next fifteen minutes."

"Thanks. In the meantime, I have a few phone calls to make regarding these photographs."

I slip them back into the envelope and hand them over. "Thanks, Jenna."

"I guess I need to go back to the firm for now," Naddie interjects. I hate the idea of her going back there after this, and I make it known.

"Not today."

"What?" She shoots me that bratty, displeased tone, and I have a good mind to put her over my knee for it.

"Jenna, you can go. My assistant will show you to your new office. I have a few things to discuss with kitten." She doesn't come up with a snarky comment—neither of them do.

When it's just Naddie and me, I twist the lock on my office. I won't be making the same mistake again.

"Dalton, I have to go to work."

"You can address me as Master Callaghan today."

"That doesn't change the fact that it'll look suspicious if I don't show up."

"You're *not* going back there until I know who's trying to tarnish our reputations. It's not up for discussion."

"I signed a contract of employment with Douglas when I returned. I'll be in breech if I just don't go back."

"I don't give a fuck. You should never have gone back there."

"I did it for you!" She stomps her foot at me.

"What? Why would you think I wanted you to go back?"

"I didn't. When I found out how much you were dealing with…" her voice becomes a whisper, "… with your mom, I made the decision not to put more on your plate. You'd have thrown yourself into helping me set up a new firm, and I didn't want to take precious time away from you that you could spend with her."

"Kitten." I push past the lump in my throat. "I had no idea."

"As it should be. It wasn't your burden to bear. I *wanted* to do this for you. Now, I just have to suffer through it until the time comes, and I'll start up my own firm."

"That's not happening. I love you so much for putting me and my mom first, but…" I hesitate. The reality slams into me as if it happened yesterday. "That time has come and gone. My mom isn't here anymore, and I refuse to put you through anything else, especially with these new developments. You're not going back. Contract or not. I'm sorry, kitten, but I can deal with Douglas and whatever he wants for you not showing up at work."

"You mean how much you have to pay him. It's all about money."

"*None of this is about money*. Don't you get it? You're the only thing that matters to me in this world. Do not question my motives. I am your Dom, and I'm telling you, you're not going back there until I deem it safe. Now, take your clothes off, kitten. This isn't about a kink. You need to learn a fucking lesson."

"Master…"

"I won't tell you again. It's not safe for you to go to Mason's office. I'll call and make excuses for having you work here on one of my new ventures and buy us some time. It's the truth. I have contracts I want you to draw up, and you're safer doing it here where I can protect you."

"No one has threatened my physical safety, Master Callaghan."

"And they won't get the chance." I close the distance between us, my fingers unbuttoning her blouse as I explain. "Do you have any idea what it would do to me if any harm came to you, kitten?" I say, scrubbing my hand over the stubble on my jaw. Life wouldn't be worth living if anything happened to Naddie. "I don't think an orange jumpsuit is my look, and I would fucking murder anyone who even threatened to hurt a hair on your head. I protect what's mine. End of discussion." Just the thought of it causes anger to take root deep in the pit of my stomach.

Her shoulders sag as she releases the tension she's been holding since we were interrupted earlier. I divest her of everything except her white lace panties. Enveloping one nipple with my mouth, I tease it till it's tightly budded before repeating the process on the other side. Then, I capture her lips with my own, darting my tongue out to stroke hers, pouring my fear and fierce desire to protect her into every lick.

"Now, you may take a seat, and I'll send you the contract details. You can work in here with me today."

She squirms against me. "Are you kidding?"

"Are you going to question me all day? I'm more than happy to take your panties too. Or maybe you'd like to sit in the position while you work? I'm sure that would focus your mind on addressing me properly without questioning every decision I make. Is that what you want?"

"No, Master Callaghan," she says with a petulant huff.

"Good. Get to work, kitten." When she turns to retrieve her briefcase, I give her a swift slap on the ass just enough to sting. I want her good and wet by the time we leave here.

Once Naddie has settled down with her laptop, I make a call to

Douglas—quick and to the point. He and I are past the jovial point in our relationship since I had to pay him for his silence regarding Naddie.

I make her remain where she is until lunchtime before reluctantly telling her to put her clothes back on. It's an exercise in submission. We are never more vulnerable with another person than when we're naked and on display. Having Naddie comply teaches her to put her trust in me and only me. It is designed as a punishment and a pleasure, building anticipation for both of us, but I've just been in pain for the last three hours, my cock aching to take her.

"Come sit by me, kitten." I pull her down into my lap, happy to have her close while we have a quick bite to eat and continue to work into the afternoon. I love having Naddie with me, knowing she's safe and sound. There's a peace that her presence brings me, unlike anyone else.

It's not until four o'clock that my phone rings, popping our little bubble as I answer.

"Hello. Is this Dalton Callaghan?"

"Who's asking?"

"James Stanley. I'm a reporter with *The New York Times*, and I've recently come into some information regarding you and your... personal life. Would you care to comment?"

Fucking bastard.

"Are you looking for an interview or informing me of the story you *think* you're about to drop?"

"This information either fell into my lap or it has been sent to multiple reporters. I want an exclusive."

"Have you run this by your editor? He's a good friend of mine, and I doubt he'd approve of your rather foolish decision to come at me with a cold call."

"Aren't you even a little curious about the evidence I have?"

"I already know what it is. I'd bet my business on the fact that you received the same bullshit I did. If you value your career, I suggest you hold off until you hear from me."

"You have five days."

"Don't threaten me, boy. *I* will decide when, where, and what information you share. I'll be in touch."

"You need my…"

"No, I don't. You have no idea who you're dealing with." I slam the phone down before grabbing it, tearing the cable out, and throwing it across the room. It takes everything I have to contain myself, but I don't want to alarm Naddie more than I already have. Reaching for my cell, I dial my friend and patron at Venom, Ford, the editor in chief of *The New York Times*.

"Dalton. To what do I owe the pleasure?"

"You need to rein in one of your reporters. I just got a call from James Stanley. He thinks he's about to run an exclusive story on me, and I need you to shut it down. Now."

"Done."

"You might be able to help me, Ford. Discreetly."

"Always. What do you need?" I go on to explain my current predicament, and he's only too happy to do some quiet research on my behalf. We've been friends for six years now, and as a man in the lifestyle, I know I can count on him for absolute discretion. I've helped him on a few occasions, and he understands the damage I could wreak on his livelihood if he were to cross me. I trust him, and I can't say that about many people in my life.

"Thanks, brother."

"Anytime. I'll be in touch when I've done some research."

As I finish the call, Naddie unlocks the door to my office, and Jenna struts in like the cat that got the cream.

My pulse races as Jenna hands me a bundle of papers. "I think we have our culprit."

I can't believe my eyes. "Are you sure?"

"Yes. I'll get you everything I can dig up, but you can see the recent transactions and communications. The odds of coincidence are impossible."

"Send me everything as soon as you can." I stride toward Naddie, cupping her face in my hands. "I need you to go back to the penthouse and wait for me."

"What's going on?"

"I'm defending what's mine, kitten."

"Don't go, Master Callaghan. I don't want you putting yourself in harm's way."

Rage unfurls in my gut, reaching out, its darkness spreading through every fiber of my being as I let it take over. Every ounce of pain, grief, and worry unleashed, ready to shred anything and anyone who gets in my way.

"It's not me you need to worry about, kitten."

Chapter 26
NADDIE

"What's he talking about, Jenna? The papers you gave him… who has been trying to blackmail us?" My heart is hammering so hard in my chest I'm worried I might drop dead of a heart attack.

Her face is white as a sheet, her breathing shallow as she meets my gaze. "It's your boss."

She's confused. I should've made sure she knew who she was digging into.

"You mean Robert. He's the son."

"No…" There's sympathy in her eyes. "It's Douglas Mason."

What.

It can't be.

We paid for his silence.

I went back to work for that weasel.

"There must be a mistake. He signed an NDA. We had an agreement. I've been busting my ass for that firm."

"It's not a mistake, Nad. There are transactions between him and Dalton's father, starting…"

"What? Spit it out."

"Starting when he headhunted you." My world comes crashing down around me. All of it has been a lie. A plot to get to Dalton.

Not a single moment of my life has been real since I moved to Manhattan. I'm just a pawn in some old man's plan to double-cross Dalton.

The realization sends a shock of ice down my spine, and anger blooms like a twisted rose bush—beautiful but riddled with thorns. Using me to get to Dalton is one thing, but extorting *my Dominant* is something I will not stand for. He is mine, and *I* will also protect what's mine.

I quickly dial Flex.

"Hey, Nad. How's my favorite kitty cat?"

"Dalton is about to do something dumb."

"Tell me everything." His voice sobers. I explain what I know as I grab my coat and purse, heading for the door.

"I'm going to need backup. He's ready to rip them to pieces, Flex. I'm scared of what he's capable of."

"He won't want you there, Nad. Let me go alone."

"Just because I'm a submissive, it doesn't make me weak. *He's mine.* I'm going whether either of you like it or not."

"Fine, but when he messes up my pretty face for letting you come, you're going to feel bad about it."

"I'll take the risk."

"I'll be there in fifteen minutes."

"Thank you."

Jenna follows close on my heels. "Should I come with you?"

"No. Stay here and find as much as you can. I'm going to put them both behind bars for this."

I leave Jenna to gather information as the elevator doors close behind me, and I'm on my way to confront Douglas. How dare he use me against Dalton.

The cool air assaults my senses as I rush out of the building and hail a cab.

"Seventy-fifth and Amsterdam."

Traffic is like any other day—gridlock. I'd be faster walking if I weren't in ludicrously high heels today. I sit impatiently in the back seat, willing us to move as we edge slowly through the streets of Manhattan. Any other day, I'd sit back and enjoy the delights of people-watching in this beautiful city, but right now, every fiber of my being is screaming to be where Dalton is.

My knee bounces with nervous energy as I attempt to channel the adrenaline coursing through my veins. I've never seen Dalton as angry as he was before he left, and I don't blame him. His father has caused enough heartache to last a lifetime, yet the moment he's free, he can't help his selfish greed, dragging Dalton into his affairs once more.

Each block takes me closer to him, but he feels a million miles away. I can only hope that Flex was closer than me and has already arrived to ensure Dalton doesn't do something he'll regret.

"Are you okay, miss?" The driver asks, glancing in the rearview mirror.

"I'm fine. I just have to get there as fast as possible."

"The traffic never seems to let up in this city."

I appreciate that he's trying to make small talk, but I don't have it in me, the gnawing dread in the pit of my stomach taking over.

By the time we pull up outside my office building, I throw a fifty at the driver and run into the lobby as fast as I can in these heels. Suddenly, everything seems to be in slow motion. The elevator takes a lifetime to arrive, people getting off on every damn floor before reaching mine. Just the sight of the company title emblazoned behind the reception desk makes me sick to my stomach.

Mason, Porter & Associates

It should be *Liars, Cheats & Corruption*. The gravity of the information Jenna exposed before I left settles over me in a dark cloud. My name was never going to be added to the firm. I came here thinking I'd earned a new high in my career. That everything I gave up to pursue law was worth it, only to find out that it had nothing to do with me.

∼

My heart beats wildly in my chest, my pulse thrumming in my ears as I make my way through the eerily quiet offices. It seems they have been cleared of all unnecessary staff, judging by the silence. As I walk the familiar halls of Mason, Porter & Associates, a hand grabs me, dragging me into the closest office.

"Let me go," I protest.

"Keep your voice down."

"Robert, let me go, or so help me, you'll regret it."

"I'm on your side, Nadia. I had no idea what my father was doing."

"Bullshit. You've been watching me for weeks."

"Yes, because I had to be certain before bringing such sensitive information to light. Please, take a seat and let me explain." My pulse is racing, adrenaline coursing through my veins as I search his body language for any sign that he wants to harm me. When he takes a seat across the desk, I shift a chair close to the door and take a seat.

"Before you say anything, where's Douglas?"

"He's in his office with your boyfriend and another man who just turned up."

Flex. I heave a sigh of relief.

"Say what you're going to say, Robert. You have two minutes." I channel the strength of my Dom as I speak with cold determination and conviction.

"How much do you know about Dalton's father?" I've never been a person to harbor hate in my heart, but the mere mention of him sparks a dark disgust I can't contain. His actions took Dalton from me once, and I'll be damned if I let it happen again.

"I was there when his misdeeds ruined Dalton and his mother's lives fifteen years ago. I know more than I'd like. He's been conspiring with Douglas?"

He drops his gaze, his body sagging as if he holds the weight of the world on his shoulders. "Yes. I need you to know I wasn't involved in any of this, Nadia. I would never try to extort a client. I've been sick to my stomach for weeks, trying to quietly gather information. I knew something was off the day I was sent away from The Callaghan Group."

The day I went off the rails and quit, only to contact Douglas later that week and grovel for my job. It makes sense that Robert was made aware of my resignation.

"You may not think it, but I've grown to respect you in your time at the firm. At first, I thought my father was looking to replace me. He's never been my biggest supporter. Apparently, I'm not enough of a shark."

"There's more to law than baying for blood," I offer by way of consolation.

"I know. Over time, I realized that you were a great pick to take over Mr. Callaghan's account. When you quit, and then came back a few days later, I knew my father must have something on you. He's been a little off-kilter lately, but I put it down to old age. I started doing some investigating of his recent comings and goings. Together with his treatment of you and sudden distaste for his decision to hire you, I began to put the pieces together."

"I have to know *why*. Why would your father betray Dalton this way?"

"I'm as surprised as you. Why does any wealthy man double-cross someone? For more money. Millions can always be tens of millions. Tens of millions become hundreds of millions. Greed, plain and simple, and boringly basic."

"But… Dalton's father? Really? Why would he make a deal with a convicted felon?"

"Mr. Callaghan is not the only man with the means to change his past. Our fathers were friends once upon a time, back in their college days. My dad aided in many of the shady deals that put Mr. Rutherford behind bars, but paid him handsomely to keep his name out of it, and in return, my father was able to walk away with his pristine reputation intact."

"Why jeopardize it by taking Dalton on as a client?"

"Keep your friends close and your enemies closer, Nadia. It's the first rule of business. Besides, The Callaghan Group is now the most sought-after account in the country. It wasn't that way in the beginning. I think initially, my father had a small kernel of conscience. Mr. Callaghan and his mother were left destitute, while my mother and I still lived in the lap of luxury. Rutherford's silence was our good fortune."

Hearing it now, my heart aches for the many years of deception that Dalton has suffered. Unwittingly putting his trust in a man who, at any moment, could out him as the son of Craig F. Rutherford.

"If he had this much power, why use me? How did he know I was a weakness in Dalton's armor? We hadn't seen each other in fifteen years. It doesn't make sense."

"Well, I guess you left an impression on him. Mr. Rutherford was convinced that his son would still do anything for you, and the gamble paid off."

My heart sinks. "I was brought here simply to use Dalton for his father's financial gain. It had nothing to do with my career or hard work."

"I speak from experience. Do not let my father or anyone else make you question your validity. You are an amazing lawyer, and the firm was lucky to get you. I wish it were under better circumstances and that my father wasn't as much of a disappointment to you as he has become to me over the years."

"What do you plan to do with the information you've uncovered?" I'm scared of what Dalton is willing to do for my safety, but I don't want to tell Robert that.

"I've toiled with this decision for weeks now, but in my heart, I have to do the right thing. The man who raised me… I'd like to tell you that I'm surprised and shocked by his behavior, but I know he's capable of such narcissism and single-minded cruelty. I've been trying to wait it out in hopes that he'll retire and I can run a firm based on truth and justice. Maybe I'm naïve. I'm not a duplicitous man, Nadia. Every time I looked at you recently, I wanted to tell you everything, but I had to be sure. This will tear my family apart, and the firm probably won't withstand losing Mr. Callaghan as a client."

"I don't think you're naïve. I believe we all went into law with these ideals. Somewhere along the way your father lost his moral compass, just as Dalton's dad did. All we can do is what we see fit."

"I have to turn them over to the authorities." He hesitates, the silence filling the air between us. "Does that make me a terrible son?"

"No. It makes you a man of moral fiber. A brave man. It is much easier to stand up to our adversaries than it is to those we love."

"Thank you, Nadia. I hope you will consider staying with the firm after my father is removed."

"I appreciate the offer, but I can't stay. Too much has happened." Tears well in my eyes, but I push them back as I straighten in my seat. "I need to find my place in New York. In law. On my own merits. Not because I love the man I do and not as a pawn in someone else's game."

"I understand. I assume you have your own intelligence regarding Dalton's father and his scheme with mine."

"Yes. We've had a private investigator looking into it since I received a set of pictures featuring Mr. Rutherford's mugshot and rap sheet."

"If we pool our resources, it will be an open and shut case. I have access to all the financial transactions my father has made recently, including numerous payments to Mr. Rutherford."

He hands me a flash drive.

"Everything you need is on there. I have a copy that I'll submit to the police department today."

"Thank you."

"Tell Mr. Callaghan I'm sorry. I am ashamed on behalf of my family and extend my sincerest apologies."

"You can tell him yourself once the dust settles. Of anyone, he understands not wanting to be judged by the sins of your father. I'm sorry, Robert, but I really have to find Dalton. Thank you for being willing to set things right." As I head for the door, he stops me.

"Nadia... I can see why Dalton would do whatever it takes to protect you. He's a lucky man."

With a sympathetic smile, I leave him to his thoughts. I have to find Dalton before he does something stupid.

I make my way to the old man's office, unfamiliar voices echoing down the hall. My heart is racing as I quicken my pace, my heels clacking against the polished floors. With each step, it's as if I'm getting farther away, and no matter how fast I walk, the hallway keeps getting longer. A lump forms in the back of my throat, my lungs tight as I finally reach the oversized mahogany doors, my hand wrapping around the cool metal handles before throwing them open. I'm not prepared for the sight that meets me as I step into Douglas's office.

The cops are already here, handcuffs at the ready. I'm dumb-struck as Flex gives me a curt nod, his lips fixed in a grim line.

Shit.

Chapter 27
DALTON

"Did you really think you could fuck with what's mine, old man?"

"You know better than anyone that your father has a way with words, Dalton. What should I have done? Let him throw me under the bus after all I've done for him over the years?"

"You could've come to me. Told me he was bribing you. Anything other than what you've done. Using Nadia to get to me was a step too far. What did he tell you about her?"

"I don't owe you anything."

I slam my fists down on the table. "You owe me *everything*, you ungrateful piece of shit. I put you on the map. Sure, you had some sway in Manhattan, but I made you the titan you became."

"He was going to tell them everything. I either paid up or went down for ten years."

"What did he tell you about Nadia? I won't ask again."

"As he approached parole this year, he reached out. Told me I had to find twenty million dollars, or he'd talk. You were the quickest means. Fortune smiled on me when he gave me your lady's name. The woman you never got over. The fact that she happened to be a great lawyer just made it so much easier."

"He never showed any interest in my life."

"Craig is a man who sees everything. The best con men can read anyone and find their weaknesses. When you thought he wasn't looking, he saw what Nadia meant to you. He guaranteed me that you would put your fortune on the line for her." I want to slap the grin right off his face. He's not wrong, but rage tightens every muscle in my body.

"And you were only too happy to oblige."

"It's not like you would miss a few million."

"You think this is about the money! I couldn't give a flying fuck about the pocket change. The second you brought Nadia into this, you made your bed. She's *mine*. I protect what's mine, Douglas. You should know better than to mess with someone I love."

"Love! What do you know of love? She's a pet to stroke your ego. A groveling, glorified whore."

Flex has to physically restrain me. "He's not worth it, Dal. Let the cops deal with this. He's going down, and you being up on assault charges is the last thing you need."

"She's not a fucking whore. She's the goddamn love of my life. Something you will never understand."

When Flex is sure I won't lunge for the old man, he releases me to pace the room, adrenaline pumping in my veins like a freight train. I wring my hands through my hair when I spy Naddie in my peripheral vision, immediately striding toward her. Taking up a protective stance at her side as the cops scrutinize her with their stares.

"You shouldn't have come, kitten." I tangle my fingers in her hair, pulling her into a kiss.

"I was worried, thinking you might hurt him and end up in trouble. I didn't want to cause any more problems for you than I already have."

"Is that what you think, kitten? That you are a problem to be solved."

"Douglas Mason, you are under arrest for extortion." That's only the beginning of his newfound rap sheet. The cops cuff him, reading him his Miranda rights before leading him away, telling us to come to the police station for interviews.

"I'll have my investigator send you everything we have so far. We'll be there in a couple of hours."

"Very good, Mr. Callaghan."

After they're gone, I cup Naddie's face in my hands. "Do you really believe you're a problem to be solved, kitten?"

"I…" She dips her head, unable to meet my gaze, but I don't let her away with it, forcing her to look at me.

"You what?"

"It wasn't fate that brought us back together. It wasn't skill that got me partner. They *used* me to hurt you. To bribe and extort money from you. How can I stay now?"

"What are you saying?" There's a dark menace in my voice I don't recognize—a challenge.

"I don't know." Tears fall from her eyes, blurring her vision as my lips crash down on hers.

"*I* know."

"I'm just going to make like a tree," Flex interjects from across the room. "You're about to have a moment, and…"

"And you're ruining it," I say with amusement.

"Exactly. I'll meet you guys at the club later."

The moment he walks out, I lock the door and begin pacing the room again, anger radiating off me in waves coursing *through* me.

"How dare he! I'm going to hunt that motherfucker down and kill him. My *father*. That's a joke if I ever heard one. He's brought nothing but misery, and somehow that asshole is still walking the earth while Mom is…" I can't bring myself to say it out loud.

"I know," Naddie reaches out, resting her hand on my chest. "Life isn't fair, and you don't deserve any of this. You're such a good man, Dalton. You were a wonderful son, you're an ethical business-man, and you're the most amazing Dom I could ever hope for." Looking up at me through hooded lashes, everything else falls away, leaving only us, in this moment, with the possibility of a real future together.

My instincts take over, and my need to claim her is so visceral I can't control it. Sweeping her up into my arms, I find the nearest wall to back her up against and coax her legs around my waist.

Every kiss is urgent—a frenzied fuck as I reach up her skirt, tearing her panties off before claiming her mouth once more. "I don't give a fuck how you got here, kitten. You're mine."

I grab her blouse and rip it open, the delicate buttons scattering on the floor as I palm her breasts with my hands, my tongue ravishing her mouth. "Fate doesn't define us. We are simply righting a wrong from many years ago. You've always been mine, kitten. Tell me you feel it."

"I feel it, Master." Her words are a red rag to a bull. I hike her skirt up around her waist before unleashing my heavy cock and positioning myself at her entrance. "Oh God, yes!"

I take her in one primal, almighty thrust, slamming into her until I'm seated to the hilt.

"No one takes what's *mine*." Trailing my tongue down her neck, I set a punishing rhythm while caressing my thumb over her clit, sending her spiraling.

"No, Master. I'm yours. Forever." That's all I've ever wanted.

We lose ourselves in each other as I rail her against the wall, rocking into her again and again, pushing her toward the explosion I know is imminent. This is not the time for lazy lovemaking. I need her more than my next breath. To claim her as mine.

"*Forever*," I growl, and it's all the encouragement she needs. Naddie detonates around me, pulling me under with her as I shout her name. "Naddie... fuck... yes, kitten."

We almost collapse, but I brace my hands on the wall to keep from falling before coming back to earth with a bang, realizing where we are and what needs to be done.

"We should go." Naddie's blouse is ruined and useless without its buttons.

"We need to go down to the police station. They want to see us quickly, but it might be an idea for you to go home and get changed first."

I escort Naddie to her office to retrieve her belongings, her time here at Mason, Porter & Associates is officially at an end. "They only brought me here to hurt you. Robert confirmed it." Her voice is soft. Hesitant.

"And what of his part in all of this? Where is he?"

"In his office. He has been gathering information to give to the authorities." She relays everything Robert told her. How his father had been an accomplice to my father's illegal activities fifteen years ago, leading up to what Douglas told me.

One thing is certain—I'm going to track my father down and make him pay for bringing Naddie into his dirty schemes. I'm so fucking angry I can barely stand it, and yet I can't help but be grateful that it brought her back into my life. I'm thankful that I get another chance to build a life with Naddie, and knowing my father had a hand in it is a kick in the teeth.

"Let's go. The quicker we get these interviews over and done with, the sooner we can go home and start living our life together."

"He can report me to the bar association now. He doesn't have anything to lose."

"I won't let that happen, kitten. He'd be in breach of the NDA and knows I'd sue his ass for every penny he's ever made. Trust me."

"I do." Her smile is tight, her body tense as she slips her hand in mine, and we leave this place behind.

With Douglas safe in a jail cell and a mountain of evidence against both him and my father, it didn't take long for the cops to trace my father's whereabouts and pull him into custody. Freedom is short-lived when your only desire is money. I'll deal with him another day. He's not going anywhere anytime soon, and that gives me a great deal of satisfaction.

Today, I just want to be with Naddie. To make her feel safe and loved. We haven't even had time to enjoy moving in together, so I'm making her a special dinner at the penthouse. We moved the rest of her stuff a few days ago, and it turns out she has a subletter for her apartment.

Jenna.

It takes a lot for someone to impress me in business, but Jenna has skills that far surpass any investigator or computer expert I've ever encountered. I offered her a position at The Callaghan Group, which she promptly refused, but made Naddie and me a counteroffer. She'll work freelance for me, building a new bespoke software to meet all the business's needs, and she'll also work freelance for Naddie at her new firm as a private investigator. Everybody wins.

When I say I'm making Naddie dinner tonight, I mean I've had her favorite Chinese food delivered, just like we did in high school.

"Kitten, would you like some more noodles? You look like you haven't been eating well enough recently."

"Yes to the noodles. There's just so much to get done. I'm starting a new company. You know what that involves." I pad over to the couch with our plates, then open some beers as we cuddle up together like old times.

"It would be a hell of a lot easier for you if you'd just take on my account already."

She stuffs chopsticks full of noodles into her mouth before talking around them. "I already said no. I want to do this myself, and not just because I'm your girlfriend."

"I see I haven't quite tamed the brat in you yet."

She eyes me with that butter-wouldn't-melt expression of hers, and I know I'd give up everything I own just to see her smile. "Would you really want me to be a truly domesticated kitten?"

"Hell no. Where's the fun in that?"

"Exactly."

We eat, drink, and laugh long into the night, watching old movies and reminiscing about days gone by. I never thought I'd have this again with anyone, especially not Naddie. And yet, there has always been a part of me that hoped we'd find our way back to each other.

With her silky-smooth legs draped over my lap, I sit back in awe as she watches the television. I don't even have to look at the screen to know what's happening. The happy, sad, funny, and tense moments play out on her face—that beautiful face.

"I have something for you, kitten. Actually, I have two, but you get one tonight and one tomorrow."

"Why?"

"Did you think I wouldn't remember your birthday? Consider tonight's gift a little pre-birthday surprise."

"I should have known you'd never forget."

"Not after your sweet sixteen. If I recall, the sweetness didn't last long," I say with a wry smile.

"A girl doesn't forget the night she loses her virginity." Her cheeks flush at the memory.

"That was the night you ruined me for any other woman, Naddie Sullivan. No one could ever live up to the submissive next door."

Naddie stands from the couch, only to turn around and rest her head in my lap instead of her feet, gazing up at me with those emerald-green eyes sparkling with visions of the people we once were. "Is it crazy that we never realized what we were back then?"

"I always knew you were my soulmate, kitten. I spent the last eight years convincing myself that I was okay going through life as half a man."

"Eight?" The furrow of her brow is too cute, so I lean down and press a gentle kiss to her forehead. "Have you forgotten the math? It was fifteen years."

"It might have been fifteen years since you saw me, kitten, but the last time I saw you before Milan was eight years ago."

She pushes up onto her knees, her breathing labored. "What are you talking about, Dalton?"

"When you graduated Harvard Law."

Tears well in her eyes. "You came?" Her hand shoots up to cover her mouth.

"Of course I did, kitten. It was everything you ever dreamed of. I couldn't stay away."

"Oh, Master." She wipes at her eyes, the tears flowing freely as I continue.

"I spent seven years trying to become a man worthy of you, Naddie. I had your graduation date on my calendar for years to spur me on to succeed. I came to tell you I still loved you and wanted to build a life with you."

"Why didn't you speak to me?" She fists her hands in my hair, searching my gaze for the answer.

"I felt unworthy. It was the proudest day of my life to watch you walk across that stage, kitten. I thought my heart was going to burst out of my chest. You looked so fucking happy, and as I watched you in the crowd after the ceremony, I realized you had a whole new life. One that didn't include me anymore. I had been living in the past, and I couldn't bring myself to come crashing into your present and risk you hating me for it."

"I could never hate you, Dalton. I remember that day like it was yesterday. The ceremony. The afterparty with family and friends. Everyone thought I was the happiest woman alive. What they didn't see was me crawling into bed that night, clothed in only your Rolling Stones T-shirt, crying my heart out because the price of my achievement felt too high. It wasn't an even trade. It never could be. Losing you was too high a cost."

"I'm so sorry, kitten. I was too afraid of losing you again. I'm still afraid. I couldn't fucking take it."

"You'll never lose me, Master." Her lips crash down on mine in a declaration of love, which I gladly reciprocate.

"I love you, Naddie. I love you." My voice is barely above a whisper as I deepen our kiss. "I love you."

"I love you, too, Master. Always." She breaks our kiss, getting to her feet, leaving me bereft as she stands before me.

I watch in awe as she slips her hoodie up over her head, revealing my old T-shirt, before shrugging out of her sweatpants, her pussy ready to be fucked. She grabs the hem of my T-shirt.

"Leave it on, kitten. You look so fucking hot in it. Your curves are divine." She leans her hands on my legs, spreading them just enough for her to kneel between them before reaching for my gray sweats, unleashing my growing erection.

I'm mesmerized by the sight of her as she licks her lips, her eyes finding mine. "May I taste you, Master." Jesus, I'm going to come just looking at her, and she hasn't even touched me yet.

"Yes, kitten."

"Thank you." With her eyes fixed on me, she flicks her tongue over the crest of my cock before wrapping her lips around the shaft and taking as much of me as she can.

I let my head drop back on the couch, trying to calm myself to last a while. I want to savor every minute with Naddie, but I also don't want to shoot my load in three seconds flat.

"Holy fuck, kitten. You're taking my cock like a good little girl."

"Mm." She hums her pleasure, sending a delicious vibration down the length of me, making me so hard it hurts.

I wrap her long, chestnut hair around my fist, forcing her to take me deeper. "Such a good fucking girl, aren't you, kitten?"

She's stunning with that perfect pout of hers wrapped around my cock, letting me set the pace like the perfect submissive that she is.

Staring up at me through hooded lashes, she's a sight to behold. My entire world at my feet, greedy for my pleasure. *Fuck...* your mouth was made to take my cock, kitten. Your mouth, your pussy, your ass. It's all mine."

I tighten my fist, setting the rhythm as I climb closer to climax, pulling back when I'm on the cusp. The only place I want to come tonight is inside my submissive. When I reach the limit of what I can handle, I tug her head back, watching as she wipes her lips, her gaze still fixed on mine.

"Get up." She does as I ask without question. "Straddle me, kitten, and ease that wet pussy onto my cock."

"Yes, Master."

"Jesus," I cry out as she lowers herself onto me. "You feel so fucking good. My perfect girl."

She wraps her arms around my neck, circling her hips until she's seated to the hilt.

Capturing her mouth with mine, I tease her lips with my tongue, beseeching her to open for me, loving her response as she moans—a slow, sensual fuck. Naddie rides me with wild abandon, chasing our joint release as we buck and thrust, push, pull, love, and fuck as one.

"Can I come, Master? I... please..." I will never tire of being her Dom, hearing her address me while I spill myself inside her. She's everything I'll ever need.

"Good girl. Come for me, kitten."

"Yes... Master... oh God... *Yes!*" Naddie cascades headlong into an orgasm, pulling me with her as her name falls from my lips in a litany of worship.

"Naddie... fuck... yes. Naddie... you're mine."

"Always, Master."

We make love long into the night until Naddie falls asleep in my arms, right where she's always meant to be. I'll never let her go. She's the air I breathe, and she always will be.

"I'm not sure I want to do this, Naddie." I feel sick to my stomach as I stand outside Queensboro Correctional Facility.

Pushing herself up onto her tiptoes, she presses a tender kiss to my lips. "You can. You are Master Callaghan. You're more of a man than he ever was or will be. It's time to close this chapter and move on with our lives."

Cupping my face in her hands, she forces me to meet her gaze, entreating me to take strength in her presence.

"Have I told you lately that I'm madly in love with you?"

"Once or twice, Master," she says, scrunching her nose as she moves her hands to rest over my heart. "I'll be right here when you're done."

"What did I do to deserve you, kitten?"

"You must have been pretty damn amazing in a former life."

"I'm sure you were there with me if I was." Tears well in her eyes.

"Go before I start crying. I'll be standing here when you come out."

"Thanks, kitten."

I have to physically force myself to relinquish her touch, putting one step in front of the other as I walk into the prison, trying to calm the storm raging inside me.

The last time I saw my father, he was being escorted from the courtroom after his trial, my mom sobbing in my arms. The memory bristles as I steel myself to face the man who robbed our family of so much and broke my mom's heart. I can't linger on the time he deprived me of with Naddie, or I wouldn't be able to face him.

Once I get through security, they usher me to the visitation area, where I'm told to sit and await my father's arrival. Some winged beasts take flight in my stomach, and not the fireflies that excite you, giddy with anticipation of something wonderful. Instead, they are more akin to bats, fleeing the dank, dark depths of an ancient cave, flocking out into the night sky, scavenging for anything to sate their base urges.

I want to run, to leave this place like the boy I was when I didn't know how to stand up to him and couldn't protect my mom from all that he would bring down on our family. When I'm two seconds away from walking out, a man who resembles my father appears. The sharp business suit and clean shave have been replaced by an unkempt beard and the most basic prison-issue uniform. Not orange as I pictured but a simple pair of jeans and a white T-shirt. How odd that this is the first time I've seen my father wearing denim.

There were never ball games or playing together at the local park. Even when I was captain and MVP of the high school soccer team, my father was never there to cheer me on in the stands. He always had an excuse. Business. Meetings. A work dinner. Code for —he'd rather have been anywhere but at home with my mom and me. She was his greatest achievement, and he couldn't even see it. I will never do that to Naddie. She'll always be my number one priority and will know how much I love and adore her every day of her life.

"Hello, son," the stranger says as he stands before me. I rise to meet him, knowing how I tower above him, the strongest I've ever been in his presence. I'm *not* a boy anymore, helpless and seeking his approval. I'm a man, a titan of industry, and a good man who will treat the woman I love with the reverence she deserves, something he could never understand.

"Hello, Craig," I say, my voice devoid of emotion. I won't give him the satisfaction. I take a seat only after he does, his hands clasped together on the table, still in handcuffs.

"Why are you here, Dalton? To gloat?"

"I sure as hell didn't come for you. I came to put all of this shit in my rearview mirror. I knew you were a lowlife, but I didn't think you would stoop to trying to ruin and extort your own son."

"Desperate times…"

"Did you ever care about us? Me and Mom."

"I loved your mom dearly. How is she?" My heart drops into my stomach. Sadness and downright anger explode in my belly.

"She's dead. You loved her so much that you didn't bother to check if she was dead or alive upon your release? Forgive me if I consider your declaration of love to be somewhat lacking."

"What happened?"

"None of your fucking business. I didn't come here to answer your questions, Craig. I came for my own selfish reasons to put the boogeyman to bed once and for all. You ruined us and left us with nothing. *I* built a life for Mom and me. I took care of her and loved her with all my heart." I struggle past the lump forming in the back of my throat.

"How dare you come along and think you're entitled to anything I've worked so damn hard for. And to use Naddie… you're unbelievable."

"You should be thanking me. Douglas told me you and Nadia are a vision of love's young dream. I knew you'd find a way back to her someday. I just sped up the process and gave fate a little nudge."

"How selfless of you. Except wait. You did it so that you could bribe me for your silence. You did it so you could do none of the work and walk away scot-free with millions of *my* hard-earned dollars. Would you even have reached out to me if you'd got the money?"

"Probably not." I want to smack the sneer off his gaunt, unfeeling face. "You were always such a simpering momma's boy."

"Rather that than be like you. You broke her heart and soul for money." I stand from the table, unwilling to give this man another minute of my time. "Goodbye, Craig. I'd say it's been pleasant, but you're as big a disappointment as ever. You weren't worthy of my mom, and you sure as shit aren't worthy of any more of my time. Rot in hell."

Without another word, I stride to the exit and don't look back. My heart is pounding as adrenaline courses through my veins, my pace quickening with every door that gets me closer to freedom. Closer to Naddie.

By the time I make it outside, I'm gasping as I draw in a lungful of fresh air. Naddie runs into my arms, knowing exactly what I need before I can give voice to it. "I'm so proud of you, Master. You did it."

I drink her in—the soft and inviting scent of her perfume, the way her curves fit so perfectly against me, and the sparkle in her eyes as she stares up at me with adoration. And I know in this moment that I'll never need anything else. The money. The accolades. Even being a Dominant. *None* of it matters without Naddie.

"Say you'll always be mine, Naddie." I cup her face in my hands, "Say it."

"I'll always be yours, Master."

"No. Say my name. I need you. I love you more than anything else in this world, Naddie. Nothing makes sense without you. You're all I'll ever need. I can face anything the world throws my way as long as I have you by my side."

"I am and always will be yours, Dalton." My lips crash down on hers, our declarations sealed with a kiss. She's all I'll ever need in this life, and I'm going to make damn sure she always feels loved, protected, and cherished by her Dominant. My submissive. My love. My best friend. And the one who almost got away. She will forever be *my kitten.*

Epilogue
NADDIE

The club is buzzing tonight. It's the opening of Venom's new expansion, and all the VIPs are here. It's the first floor of five they will be adding, and I'm excited to share in the revelry with Dalton and our friends.

"You look stunning tonight, kitten."

"Why thank you, Master Callaghan. You look pretty amazing yourself." I'm a sucker for Dalton in a three-piece suit. It's a surefire way to get me wet with anticipation. Not that I'll need it tonight. This is going to be an opening night to remember. I can feel it. Dalton spared no expense, and all the usual suspects are here.

Flex is beaming with pride. This was his brainchild, and I have to say, he really pulled it off. Floor two now houses a communal area and a viewing gallery of rooms. I'm not even sure if this floor has any private rooms.

Genevieve is already working the crowd, introducing herself to possible new members and showing regulars the new facilities. The rest of my newfound friends are just enjoying the show. Dalton brought in Carter's friend, Logan, to do a Shibari demonstration tonight, but sadly for him, Logan's sub and model for the evening is Carter's sister, Vittoria. I can only imagine how that conversation went down. It makes sense now why Carter spends such little time at Venom. I know he's not into the lifestyle, but I see the way he looks at his wife, Addi. There's no way they're strictly vanilla. He's way too hot for that.

Logan's rope work is second to none, and although his sub isn't naked, no man wants to see his sister being tied up. Carter excused himself to the bar downstairs for the duration.

Logan is a man after my Dominant's own heart. No one is seeing what's his. He has Vittoria in a sexy but tasteful basque and panties to maintain her modesty. I doubt Dalton would let me wear so little in this setting. Heck, I'm surprised he let me come up to this floor tonight. I don't think it will be somewhere we frequent.

The customers are loving it, watching in awe as he creates the most stunning ropework I've ever seen.

"She's beautiful," I say wistfully as I lean my head against Dalton's chest, his arms wrapped tight around me.

He nips at my neck, whispering against the shell of my ear. *"You're beautiful."*

I move my head to the side, opening my neck to him, which he gladly peppers with kisses, his hands wandering my curves. "Are you trying to seduce me in the communal area, Master Callaghan?"

"The fuck I am. You're mine, kitten. No one gets to see you in the throes of passion but me."

I love how possessive he is. I reach between us, rubbing my hand over his growing erection. "Then take me to your room downstairs and seduce me there." My voice is barely recognizable, like velvet caressing my senses.

"Not tonight, kitten. I have a surprise for you."

I turn in his arms, giddy at the prospect. "I love surprises."

"You've been such a good girl, kitten. Starting your own firm, building a kickass client base, and here… at the club… you've been such a naughty girl in all the right ways. I think my little brat deserves something special."

"I have been a good girl. Will I get to be a bad girl tonight?"

"You can be anything you want with me, kitten. I love every

facet of your personality. The brat, the lawyer, the girl I grew up with, and the strong, powerful woman you've become. Follow me."

As Dalton weaves through the crowd, guiding me with his hand at the small of my back, Genevieve gives me a knowing grin. That's one thing about being at a kink club—everyone knows how your night is going to end.

A thrill courses through me as we navigate away from the communal area, past the viewing gallery hallway, and find ourselves outside an ornately carved door. Dalton pulls a blindfold from his jacket pocket. "Close your eyes, kitten."

The rise and fall of my chest quicken with anticipation, butterflies taking flight in the pit of my stomach. "Yes, Master Callaghan."

He plunges me into darkness before unlocking the door with a keycard of some sort by the sound of it. Taking my hands, he presses his lips to mine, quick and sweet. Then, he guides me into the space. I don't know if it's a room. It could be a broom closet, for all I know.

When he has me where he wants me, he leaves me standing alone with the rustling of different things I can't quite place. I don't hear drawers for toys or restraints of any kind. In utter blackness, I can't even sense where he is in the room at this moment.

A few minutes later, I start getting antsy. "Master Callaghan, are you still here?"

"I'm here, kitten. You can remove the blindfold now."

Nerves overtake me as I reach with trembling hands to untie the knot and slip the blindfold off.

I'm lost for words.

Dalton is at my feet, in the submissive position, fully clothed in his mouthwatering three-piece suit. He stares up at me with those ocean-blue eyes, and tears begin to well in mine.

The room around us is stunning. Soft twinkle lights are draped over every surface and hang in a canopy above our heads. It's so ethereal it takes my breath away.

"I have three questions to ask you tonight, Naddie."

My heart is hammering in my chest as he holds open a box with a delicate necklace—some kind of collar.

"Will you be my submissive? My one and only. As long as we both shall live." I fight back tears until I see the charm hanging from the platinum collar. It's the key. The one he kept in his wallet when we were kids when he gave me the heart locket that remains in my keepsake box in *our* home.

"I can't believe you kept it." Tears stream down my face as he pulls his wallet from his pocket and holds it up for me to see the imprint of the key.

"I've carried it with me all these years, kitten, hoping you would come back to me. You've always had my heart, and you always will."

I drop to my knees. "Will you put it on for me?" There's a shyness in my request. Another first for me. I've never been collared.

"Of course." Lifting the dainty collar, he secures it around my neck, the clasp requiring a tiny Allan key to secure it. When he's done, he slips it in his pocket. "It can only come off if I choose to do so. Are you okay with that, kitten? Being mine, twenty-four seven?"

"Yes, Master Callaghan. It's an honor."

He pulls a second box from his inside pocket.

"Naddie..." he says, opening the ring box, "... as much as I want you to be my submissive, it's not enough. I want to be tied to you forever. To have all the things we wanted as kids. I want to give you it all and enjoy every step and phase of life with you by my side. I've loved you since we were five years old. I've loved you through every stage of your life thus far, even when it was from a distance. I want to be the man you grow old with, be the father of your children, and be a man worthy of your love. Naddie, will you marry me?"

I don't even hesitate to look at the ring, throwing myself into his arms. "*Yes!* Of course, I'll marry you. I want to be yours in every way possible. I love you so much, Dalton. The answer will always be yes when it comes to us."

His lips crash down on mine, claiming me as his once and for all, and I know that in this moment, nothing will ever separate us again. No matter how hard life may get, we will face it together.

"I have one last thing to give you, Naddie."

"You've already given me everything I've ever wanted."

"It wouldn't be us without a contract." He hands me a manila envelope, my heart skipping a beat.

I'm not prepared for the contract I hold in my hands as I gently remove it from the envelope, letting it drop to the floor. "How did you find this? Did you get it from my box?"

"What?"

"My Dalton box."

"There's a Dalton box? I need to see that immediately," he says with a wry grin. "And no. Did you keep your copy?"

Realization dawns, and I gasp at the sight before me. It looks exactly the same, yet knowing he kept his copy of our first contract all these years makes my heart overflow with joy, pride, and undying love.

"I have mine. I can't believe you kept this, Master."

"I couldn't bring myself to let you go, Naddie. Never. Not for a moment. Sign it anew. I want to make every single one of these promises to you now, as the man I've become, and hold them close to my heart until my dying breath. Be mine, Naddie. Always."

He hands me a pen, and as I reread the vows we made to each other all those years ago, I can't contain my love for this man. I quickly sign and date just above where I did as a teenager, meaning every word and then some.

He does the same before pulling me into his arms and kissing me with every ounce of love we feel for each other, setting my body alight. I match his ferocity, reclaiming the boy in this contract, the man I love today, and the second chance fate saw fit to grant me with the Dom next door.

THE END
FREE DOWNLOAD DALTON AND NADDIE'S HIGH SCHOOL CONTRACT
https://dl.bookfunnel.com/xxrbr6411d
PREORDER THE MASQUERADE

sign up for EVA'S NEWSLETTER to be notified of new releases!
Follow on AMAZON

Join my reader group

buy romantic comedy FUMBLE
buy A VERY FUMBLING MERRY CHRISTMAS
buy romantic comedy INTERCEPTION
buy romantic comedy SCREWBALL
Buy STRIKE ZONE

buy the complete MANHATTAN KNIGHTS SERIES

buy MUSTANG RANCH SERIES BOX SET
buy MUSTANG CHRISTMAS
buy MUSTANG BELLE
buy MUSTANG PLAYER

buy WILD RUGGED DADDY
buy A CHRISTMAS TO REMEMBER

Acknowledgments

As always, my amazing husband has been such a strong supporter of this project—willing to be my sounding board, and my plaything when I needed to do some 'research.' I feel beyond blessed to share this life with you, Sir. All my love.

Ria – Every project is special when we work together. Thank you for helping me find Dalton and Naddie's story and bring them to life. Love you more.

Nicki – Thank you for helping me elevate my work to provide readers with the best experience.

To my readers I want to say a huge thank you. Without your support I wouldn't get to wake up every morning and do my dream job. I knew I wanted to fly on the pages of the written word, but you gave me wings.

About the Author

I'm happiest when wandering through the uncharted territory of my imagination. You'll find me curled up with my laptop, browsing the books at the local library or enjoying the smell of a new book, taking great delight in cracking the spine and writing in the margins!

I'm a native Scot but live in Texas with my husband, two kids, and a whizzy little fur baby with the most ridiculous ears. I first fell in love with British literature while majoring in Linguistics, 17th Century Poetry, and Shakespeare at University. I'm an avid reader and life-long notebook hoarder. In 2014, I finally put my extensive collection to good use and started writing my first novel. Previously tradition-ally published under a pen name, I decided to branch out on my own and lend my name to my full back catalogue!

I write contemporary romance with all the feels, sports rom-coms and paranormal romance, and I am currently working on some other exciting new projects.

Social Media

http://www.evahaining.com/newsletter
www.instagram.com/evahainingauthor
www.facebook.com/evahainingauthor
www.twitter.com/evahaining
www.amazon.com/author/evahaining
www.bookbub.com/profile/eva-haining
https://www.goodreads.com/author/show/20271110.Eva_Haining
https://tiktok.com/@evahainingauthor
http://www.evahaining.com/newsletter
www.evahaining.com

Made in the USA
Coppell, TX
16 August 2024

36096379R00176